THE WOMAN ON THE BRIDGE

By the same author:

Try Not to Breathe
Don't Close Your Eyes
Love Will Tear Us Apart
The Hit List

THE WOMAN ON THE BRIDGE

Holly Seddon

ORION

First published in Great Britain in 2022 by Orion Fiction,
an imprint of The Orion Publishing Group Ltd
Carmelite House, 50 Victoria Embankment
London EC4Y 0DZ

An Hachette UK Company

1 3 5 7 9 10 8 6 4 2

A CIP catalogue record for this book is
available from the British Library.

ISBN (Mass Market Paperback) 978 1 4091 9552 8
ISBN (eBook) 978 1 4091 9553 5
ISBN (Audio) 978 1 3987 0720 7

Typeset by Born Group
Printed and bound in Great Britain by Clays Ltd, Elcograf S.p.A.

www.orionbooks.co.uk

For Carole.

What are little girls made of?
What are little girls made of?
Sugar and spice
And all things nice
That's what little girls are made of.

Charlotte

Now – Friday Night

Charlotte screams into the emptiness. All around, the world has dissolved from grey to inky blue to deepest black. Now it has no colour; it is just nothingness. Even the stars that had hung above her car like beautiful threats have disappeared, blinked clean out of existence like dead matches.

On this black night, whipping along these dead roads, Charlotte could be anywhere. She presses the accelerator with her boot but, no matter how fast she goes, she outruns nothing that matters. The anger still sits in the car with her, panting like a beast. She presses on anyway, driving as fast as she dares, then faster still. Hurling her car around corners, hoping, for just a moment, to slam into something.

Her knuckles turn white on the wheel, adrenaline boiling her from the inside as she scores a deep groove along this empty map. Her headlights bounce along, picking up startled animal eyes and sudden silhouettes at the side of the roads. Their glow briefly sketching gates and the swinging signs of small farms. Tyre tracks leading off towards unknowable lives.

She goes faster still, trying to outrun her panic. Swinging around bends and adding ten, twenty to the speed limit. Why not? Thirty miles an hour over. Fuck it. What difference does it make when you're alone on the road? *You know very well what difference it makes.*

Charlotte curses her electric car, inherited from her mother, nearly new. Right now, she needs gears to crunch, an engine to roar. Instead, she whispers along like a ghost. To the outside world, to these bright-eyed animal witnesses, she must seem calm.

Where is she anyway? Wales, she knows that because she surged over the Severn ages ago. But which bit of Wales, and how far from the border; those details are mush. She looks at her screen, but the map just shows the varicose veins of unnamed roads and the threat of a river up ahead. She could be anywhere.

No one will hear me coming, she thinks, *if they step out into the road*. She eases off the accelerator but then she thinks of Anne. And then she hopes, by some mix-up of time and space, that her oldest friend might somehow stumble in front of her without warning. That she can't stop herself from ploughing into her soft body, grinding her into this country dirt and whispering away again.

She presses the pedal harder.

Earlier Today

If you'd asked Charlotte just seconds before it happened, she would have said everything was fine. And yet. When Anne came back from the toilet and tripped just slightly on the price tag of a Persian Lilihan rug, something shifted below the surface. Anne was always poised, never clumsy. Even as an eleven-year-old, Anne's long straight back and keen eyes had aligned her more with the teachers than the other kids. Until you knew her properly, and few did. But today, something was off.

Charlotte had offered Anne a cup of tea, and, as Anne had looked up from her screen opposite, the briefest shadow had passed over her face. Wasn't it obvious then? Didn't Charlotte suspect, in the pit of her belly, that the world had shifted a tiny degree off its axis? That the argument they'd had the day before had torn something deeper than she'd realised?

★

Yesterday she'd been due to meet Rob for lunch but he'd cancelled while she was en route, something to do with his dodgy cousin Cole. With nowhere else to go, she'd swung around and headed back, only stopping to grab a sandwich from the supermarket on the way. Anne's Mercedes had been outside Wilderwood Antiques, and a big sleek BMW was next to it. Most trade came by appointment but people did drop in to browse from time to time so it hadn't struck her as odd. She'd only hoped Anne, with no formal training, wasn't out of her depth.

She'd been surprised to find the door locked. She'd rattled it a couple of times and then pulled out her key, but Anne had suddenly opened the door. 'Charlotte,' she'd said. 'I thought you were meeting Rob?'

'What's going on?' Charlotte had replied, frowning as she'd stepped inside to see a slick and suited man, dark-haired and expensive-looking, seated at the Rosewood dining table they'd been hoping to shift by now. 'Is he interested in the table?' she'd whispered, then smiled in his direction.

'Are you going to introduce us, Miss Wilkins?' the man had asked, standing to full height as Charlotte had walked towards him, hand cautiously outstretched. Anne had taken a quick breath and then, as Charlotte's skin had connected with his in a firm handshake, she'd told Charlotte he was a potential investor. In response, he'd held out a business card. Charlotte's mouth had puckered into what her mum used to call her vinegar face but she'd managed to hold her outrage in until the man had left, asking Anne to call him later with her answer.

'I know it was an overstep,' Anne had said, hands up in surrender. 'I just wanted to hear him out.'

'We don't need investors,' Charlotte had argued. 'We just need to carry on sorting the website and clearing this old stock to make way for some fresh stuff.'

Anne had nodded, blushing.

★

3

But despite these tiny paper cuts, these atomic-level ripples, when Anne had asked to speak to Charlotte in private earlier today, after their assistant Dorian had gone home, she would have said, hand on heart, that she hadn't seen it coming.

Anne locked the door and closed the shutters, plunging them into soupy gloom until the lights flicked on. They both blinked as the grey outlines of bureaux and armchairs, mirrors and vases were coloured in by the electric bulb. It was a harsh light, highlighting both of them as faded facsimiles of the girls they once were. Crinkled at the eyes, a dusting of grey at the roots.

'What's this about?' Charlotte said. She was still sitting at her desk in the back of the room and Anne stalked towards her.

Wilderwood Antiques is Charlotte's family business, her late father's first love, and should be her domain, but she sat cowed and confused while she waited for an explanation. 'Is this about yesterday?' she said. 'That investor?' But Anne shook her head.

As Anne opened a small folder of papers, Charlotte noticed her shellaced fingers were trembling. And as her old friend lay the pages out carefully like Tarot cards on the rich surface of the mahogany, Charlotte noticed Anne bite her lip just for a moment. An echo of the Anne she used to be, all those years ago.

'I've noticed some irregularities,' today's Anne said, her glossy hair falling in front of her face like a curtain. 'And I think you need to leave.'

Now

She should turn back but instead Charlotte scores through the countryside like a knife. She doesn't feel entirely safe here, imagining urban myths gathering force in the dark. A silent

4

army of mad men and black-eyed children and killer clowns. The stories she and Anne used to tell each other, faces lit by torches, heads close under a shared blanket.

She doesn't dare squint into the dark to make out the shapes. The man at the side of the road, ready to leap onto her car with a head on his spike. The tap tap tap that will soon come from above. Maybe a Victorian child floating, forlorn, just a few centimetres from the ground.

Heart thumping, she looks behind her just once. No mad men there. No one at all. Not in the backseat. Nor on the passenger seat, no one waiting at home, no one warming the bed or calling her phone. No one.

But anything out there is less risk to her than inside the car where her anger sits still panting like a beast, willing her to surge faster, to fling her car around corners, to do some damage.

The lane ahead is lit up silver by the moon and she grits her teeth and presses harder, faster, the speed reading fifty, sixty, seventy . . . why not? Her hands grip the leather like claws, shoulders locked. Maybe she should just slam into one of these trees and be done with it. How would you like that, Anne? Fuck you all, mic drop.

A viscous rain is pelting her car. What was a thin-lipped dribble a few minutes ago has become a great mouth, spitting salty gobs down from all angles. The wheels shudder sideways as she turns sharply again. And then a town slides onto the map up ahead: Usk.

She can just make out the lights on the horizon, softening the night back from black to navy blue. A velvet sky. As she surges closer, distant buildings come into view. She can make out the industrial fringe now, warehouses and factories, grey shapes scattered like abandoned cardboard boxes along the horizon.

She whips through a knotty chicane of gravelly Tarmac and shouts again, animal and incoherent, into the grey of the night. She dares herself to speed up – there's no one out here but her – using up the last little bit of control she has. Fuck it. She presses her foot down and curses the silent Tesla. This should sound like a roar.

A bridge suddenly looms into view, looking obscene and dangerous. With huge balustrades like military shoulders, the great metal monster squats over the swollen river. She makes out its sharp edges, the solid steel arcing twenty, thirty metres above the water. If she were to rattle off the road and drive straight for one of those legs, what instant and total damage would it do? How would Anne feel when she got the news? And so begins a silent negotiation. Charlotte is both hostage and hostage taker. She dares herself, taunts herself.

Just drive.

Just point the nose, shut your eyes and drive.

Hard.

She takes a long blink, a trial run, but as her lids flick back up with their doll-eye reflex, Charlotte suddenly sees the figure. Up there on the bridge, white dress dancing in the wind, is a woman. And she's about to fall.

Charlotte

Now

The car stops dead. An ancient bit of brain controlling Charlotte's foot before she can think about it. Now she's staring at the bridge, the engine whooshing politely as it waits.

In the background, the lights of Usk twinkle knowingly, but between that life and her car, there is this: an empty road, a big old bridge over a furious black river and a woman standing on the handrail. What looks like a wedding gown clings to her. In her hand, a small bouquet hangs tattered and wet. She is motionless and tiny, like the ballerina in a closed music box.

6

Charlotte's heart drums faster, her headlights barely illuminating the scene. Most of the light comes from the moon, which has slunk out from behind a cloud as if summoned by a finger click.

The woman in white hasn't noticed the car, which is still some fifty metres from the bridge. She remains fixated by the water below her, her arms hanging limply by her side and her neck bent. She could almost be a child, but she's a scaled-down woman. Maybe five foot nothing, a wisp. Charlotte feels a pull in her chest; the woman is so little, so defenceless against the wind. The handrail is thick but surely slippery from the rain, and one giant gust – or one small leap – could send her small body tumbling down to its death. *Unless she's already dead.*

Charlotte feels cold sweat pouring down her back, her temples throb and her pulse rushes so fast the individual beats blend into chaos. She can't stay here watching, she has to do something or her heart will explode. Charlotte rolls forward a metre, another half metre, then stops again. The woman does not look over. She remains deathly still.

Maybe she can't see me because she's not really there.

Charlotte could still reverse as silently as a snake, slither back around the corner and forget what she has seen. Unless that's what this woman wants. Unless this is the start of some kind of folk tale where an idiot from the city reverses back around the corner and into the arms of . . .

For fuck's sake, stop; you're thirty-five, not fifteen.

Charlotte drives at a creeping pace to the bridge then pulls over next to the woman, wrestling out of her seatbelt and stumbling into the driving rain.

'What the hell are you doing?' she says, treading slowly closer now, as if approaching a stray dog, aggression levels unknown. The wind swallows Charlotte's words and for a moment she thinks the woman hasn't heard, but then she looks, just briefly, over her shoulder. She is definitely wearing a wedding gown. Its train dances behind her, the beading catches what little light the moon has to spare and the bodice, its structure as rigid as this metal bridge, makes this little woman princess-shaped.

7

'I said—'

'I heard what you said,' the woman replies without taking her eyes off the black river rushing below. She has a look of someone, or maybe of some *time*, that Charlotte can't quite place. An anachronism, and incredibly alone. Like the Little Match Girl.

The rain coats Charlotte's face, blurring her vision. Her cardigan is already so soaked with rain that it feels like a concrete overcoat.

'Aren't you cold?' Charlotte says, cautiously taking a step closer, hands still outstretched. She feels an urge to wrap the woman up, to warm her. The woman shrugs and keeps her eyes on the water. Through the balustrades, Charlotte can see that the black water is fringed with moonlit foam, the currents taking no rest for the night.

'Please,' Charlotte says, taking a careful step closer. 'Let me help you down.'

'No, thank you.' The woman's voice is barely audible. Her hair is filthy with rain but, when the moon catches it, a glimmer of red shines through. She is young, mid-twenties at the most.

'Please,' Charlotte insists. 'You could fall.'

The woman laughs just briefly, the sound stolen by the roar of the river. Her shoulders shake a moment longer as raindrops slide down them and soak into the beaded bodice of her dress. The joke, Charlotte realises, is that she wants to fall. Charlotte sighs, wrings some of the rain from her black curls and shrugs too. 'Fuck it. If you're not getting down, I'm coming up.'

Earlier Today

'But this is bullshit and you know it,' Charlotte said, her voice more shrill than intended. 'Anne, this is *me* you're talking about.' She thumped her chest. '*Me!*'

8

Anne looked down, cheeks pink. 'Charlotte, I know that business admin isn't your strong suit and you're not—'

'What?'

'Look, I know you're out of your depth, but this isn't just one or two mistakes, this is months of . . . this is really bad, Charlotte. It's really bad.'

'What are you saying? You're going to, what, *tell on me*? For mistakes that I've not even made!' Charlotte waved at the paper in front of her. *Where did all this come from?*

Anne stared at her, her eyes soft and sad. 'It's for the best if you go; your dad's company is at stake here.'

'Yes, *my* dad's company,' Charlotte snapped back. 'My family business that I brought you into in good faith and now you're trying to take it from me! How could you? I gave you a chance! A fresh start!'

'A fresh start?' Anne laughed. A sudden squawk, like skin on a balloon.

The penny dropped. 'Oh, OK,' Charlotte said, nodding. 'I get it now. This guy's offered money to buy a stake and you think you can just push me out and cash in but that's not the way it works. It's my family name over the door and I'm damned if you're going to—'

'Charlotte, you're playing with fire if you stay. I only realised how bad it was when I looked back through old stuff to . . .' Anne looked down for a moment and cleared her throat, as if to compose herself. 'When I looked at this stuff to prepare for my meeting with them. And it's bad, Charlotte. There's cash unaccounted for, fake invoices, customers that don't exist, missing products. Your family name is going to land you in prison if you don't—'

'But I haven't done anything!'

Anne swallowed. The mechanism in her long thin throat sliding up and down like an elevator.

'Look,' Anne said, holding Charlotte's eye and then looking down at the papers fanned out on the table as if someone else had laid them there, 'you can still draw a salary. I'll keep you

9

on the books as a part-timer but I'll take you off at Companies House. I'll be sole director and then you're insulated, you're—'

'What the fuck?'

'But you need to sign it over to me and step down as director and then we can try to save things. I'm a new broom, I won't get the blame, and hopefully we can tidy things up enough and keep everything intact. But if not, I can't protect you.' That sleek hair, that straight back. 'And I won't protect you.'

Charlotte gripped the chair tightly, knuckles pressing into the Regency rosewood chair that the investor had sat in yesterday. Then she shoved it towards the wall so hard Anne jumped, her poise finally shattered.

'You'll have to prise it from my cold dead hands!'

Now

'What are you doing?' the woman in the dress says, wobbling precariously as she shuffles away from Charlotte and grips on to one of the tall posts, her hands squeaking as they slip around on the wet metal.

Charlotte swallows, looking down momentarily at the furious river below. Then she clambers up onto the space next to the woman, feet sliding. Panic tugging her gut and groin. Holding her arms out for balance, she reaches for the next post along and holds it with her left hand, offering her right to the woman.

'You're nuts,' the woman says, her eyes wide and panda-ringed with make-up.

'You started it,' Charlotte says, shrugging her shivering shoulders. 'And I've got nothing to lose so I'm staying up here with you until you get down.' She looks at the water. 'Whichever way we get down.'

For a moment, the woman says nothing. Then she looks over her shoulder at the Tesla waiting obediently nearby. 'You don't look like you've got nothing to lose,' she says quietly.

Charlotte follows her gaze.

'That car? That car was my mum's. My mum and dad died six months ago and I inherited it. Compared to having my parents still alive, that car really is nothing.'

'I'm sorry about your parents,' the woman says.

'It's not your fault.'

'How did they die?' the woman asks, still ignoring Charlotte's outstretched hand. It's funny how few people actually ask this when it's obvious that everyone wants to know.

'They died in a car crash.'

The woman frowns and looks at the Tesla again. 'They crashed in my dad's car,' Charlotte clarifies, her voice flat. 'They were on their way to the airport for their first holiday in forever and . . . they say he probably fell asleep at the wheel. It was the early hours of the morning, he was tired from—' she laughs then, despite herself. 'Tired from never taking a holiday. They both died straight away. So the police told me anyway.'

The morning that everything changed, that's how Charlotte would come to think of it. Pushing a thumbtack into the map of her life, before and after, all of it pivoting on one tiny point.

She remembers apologising to the police for the state of her as she'd opened the door to her London flat. She'd only been asleep a few hours and was probably still a bit drunk from going to the pub with her new team. She'd joined the museum just that week, finally landing a job she relished.

The officers had stood like solemn sentries in the communal hall as she'd yanked at the ties of the dressing gown she'd just chucked on.

'But I only spoke to my dad the other night,' she'd said, as if this negated everything the police had just said. As if that meant that they had actually made it to Jamaica as planned and were now sitting in the sun, bickering.

'You're wrong,' she'd said. The officers had stood patiently, having, no doubt, seen this reaction many times.

'My name's Charlotte, what about you?'

'Maggie,' the woman says, through chattering teeth, hands gripping the post and dress flapping wildly.

'So why are *you* up here, Maggie?' Charlotte says, lowering her free hand in semi-defeat. 'Your new husband or fiancé must be . . . I mean you're wearing a—'

'I don't have a husband or a fiancé any more. I don't have anything,' the woman says, her gaze back on the freezing water below. 'Look, you've done your Good Samaritan thing but now you need to get back in your car and drive away.' For all her bravado, when the woman looks at Charlotte, her eyes are soft and pleading. 'Please,' she adds. 'Just go. With my blessing.'

'I really can't do that,' Charlotte says. 'You're soaked through, you must be freezing.' She pauses. 'And if you wanted to jump, you'd have jumped. So now you're just getting cold for no reason.'

Maggie scowls but doesn't disagree.

'I'm not letting you go but *I'm* freezing,' Charlotte says. 'So why don't we just sit in the car for a bit so we can both warm up and you can dry your dress out?'

Maggie looks down at her dress as if surprised to see it. She's silent for a long time as if listening for an answer in the wind.

'OK,' she says finally. 'Just for a minute or two.' Charlotte offers her hand again and this time Maggie takes it, looking nervously around as if coming back to consciousness after a dream. Charlotte swallows; if she can just get this girl off the bridge and into the car, then she can decide what to do next.

Charlotte is still holding the post with her left hand when Maggie lets go of her own post and crouches down carefully. Charlotte starts to lower herself too when a sudden noise comes from below the bridge. A snap of something, a loud crack that rings out through the wet air. Maggie gasps and loses her footing, her little white ballet pumps sliding along the metal handrail.

Charlotte

Now

Charlotte's arm is yanked hard by the movement and Maggie's hand breaks free. Now they're both swaying and scrabbling separately. Maggie's left foot slips completely from the handrail and she collapses backwards towards the water. She is hanging from the railing by her knees, the rest of her is upside down with layers of the dress falling over her face. She isn't screaming, or crying; it's more of a desperate whimper.

'Hang on,' Charlotte pants, trying to keep herself steady. She's holding a support post with her left hand, facing the water. Trying to ignore the drop below, she squats slowly, reaching down with her right arm. 'Grab my hand!'

Maggie's face is obscured by the white flapping fabric of her dress and her arms flail uselessly. 'I can't hold on,' she sobs. 'Please help me.'

'Fuck.' There's no other way. Charlotte climbs carefully over the railings so she's river side. Now there's nothing to stop her falling but she ignores the water and the tremor in her legs, and inches closer to Maggie. Holding tightly to the wet handrail with one hand, she reaches for the woman's arm with the other. She pulls as hard as she can, managing to swing Maggie's body back up until she can grab the rail by herself. Maggie teeters on top of it for a moment, chest heaving up and down, and then she slumps down to the safety of the Tarmac where she sits, looking dazed.

'Please help me down,' Charlotte says, climbing back over the railing with trembling limbs and hands that can barely grip now. 'I can't stop shaking.'

Maggie scrabbles to her feet, which Charlotte notices have lost their shoes to the current below. Charlotte shuffles carefully along on her backside and Maggie reaches both her hands up, the way a parent offers reassurance to a newly toddling child.

Charlotte seizes them quickly and then half-jumps, half-tumbles onto her. They both sit on the road, backs against the railings and cling to each other like match-end boxers. 'Oh my god,' Maggie finally says into Charlotte's hair, and then she starts to cry. 'You saved my life.'

'Your dress,' Charlotte says gently, as she disentangles from Maggie, who wipes under her eyes self-consciously. 'It's ripped. And your shoes . . . they've—'

Maggie's toes curl into the gritty Tarmac. 'My feet are killing me,' she admits.

'We need to get you cleaned up.' Charlotte looks around but there's nothing nearby. 'Do you live far away?'

Maggie is shaking her head, frantic. 'I don't live anywhere any more,' she says. 'I was living with Mike but—' she looks down at her dress '—that's not possible any more.'

Mike. Charlotte makes a mental note to ask who he is but not yet. They're still in the triage stage.

'I could take you to a hotel or . . .' Charlotte rubs her hand over her face, top to bottom, a gesture she knows she got from her dad and seeks comfort from. 'Look, this is going to sound weird but after what just happened and, honestly, after the day I've had, I don't want to be alone. Do you?'

Maggie shakes her head just slightly.

'Why don't you come back to mine?' Charlotte says softly, clearing her throat. 'It's really late and I'm sure you have a lot to think about but you obviously need somewhere safe and warm to rest for a bit.'

'Oh, I don't know, I—'

'No pressure but I've got a spare room made up already and you can have a shower and borrow some comfies.'

'Comfies?' Maggie laughs and it surprises them both. 'Do you mean like joggers?'

'Joggers, PJs, cardies . . .' Charlotte smiles back. 'I've got the lot. Shoes too,' she says, nodding at Maggie's feet. 'And more importantly, you can have a stiff drink and a good sleep. What do you reckon?'

They both stare at the bridge for a moment longer. The rain is slowing but the wind is still wild, chucking grit and loose twigs onto the car, bending the nearest trees into menacing shapes.

'I'm not a weirdo,' she adds.

'That's exactly what a weirdo would say,' Maggie says and smiles, just briefly.

Charlotte probably shouldn't invite random people to stay at her house, that's stranger danger 101. But after facing down death together, Maggie doesn't feel like a stranger. Nor does she feel like a friend. Friend-adjacent. Linked by experience, by fear. By the blood that was nearly spilled.

Charlotte remembers when she and Anne were eleven and, on a count of three, they'd nicked their arms with razorblades, wincing at the pain, and then pressed the red blots together so they'd stung as one. 'Blood sisters forever.' Maybe she and Maggie are bridge sisters. And besides, maybe strangers are more trustworthy than the people we think we know. Anne proved that earlier.

Maggie is squinting into the darkness as if looking for an answer. 'OK,' she says, finally. 'Thank you. Yeah.'

Maggie

How can she feel colder now she's sitting inside this warm car than when she was out there, on that slippery bridge? Maybe she's already died a little. The nerve endings in her skin snuffed out by the cold. Her blood turning slowly blue like someone had dipped their paint brush in it and swirled it lazily around.

Maggie shivers and her jaw rattles; her back is still aching from slamming upside down into metal but this heated seat is helping a bit.

Maggie looks at Charlotte's hands as she fiddles with the controls on the swanky flat screen. Hands that just a few minutes ago were the last line of defence between Maggie and that freezing river. Hands that, there's no other way to put it, just saved her life.

Charlotte looks normal enough, just an ordinary slightly plump, fairly short, middle-class thirty-something. But up there on the bridge she was a lioness. And Maggie really didn't deserve it and would never have predicted that kind of display of fearsome bravery. After her brief bout of uncontrolled tears back there, Maggie has now parcelled up those feelings and got herself back under control. She straightens up and tries to think of something to say.

'My dress is ruined,' is the best she can manage. This latest bout of dirty drizzle has finally turned its skirt grey and painted the beading with droplets of sludgy brown. The train is fringed with green from the discoloured iron, and even her feet are coated with slime. She tries not to wipe them on the carpets of this car. Although these aren't particularly clean, people get protective about things like that, and she doesn't fancy getting booted out into the cold again just yet. 'How long were you up there?' Charlotte asks.

Her throat is scratchy from the chilled night air and Maggie sounds wheezy when she asks what time it is now.

'Just gone ten,' Charlotte replies quietly, as if breaking difficult news.

'It's later than I realised,' she says flatly. 'I guess I was there for an hour then, maybe more.' How long *has* it been? Nearer two hours, on and off.

Maggie feels ridiculous, like some sugar plum fairy down on her luck. The dress she once loved is taking up the whole passenger seat and footwell, and its damp train has spilled across the middle where a gear stick would normally be. She pulls it back and tucks it down the side of her legs, trying not to wipe its disgusting edges onto her skin.

'This car is like something out of a film,' she says, with more wonder than intended. 'I've never been in an electric car before.'

Charlotte swivels to face her; the thighs of her grey jeans are black with rain, and she has make-up streaked all down her face, gathering in black lumps along her jaw. Maggie swallows down a ragged knot of guilt.

'You don't have to tell me but . . . what the fuck happened today?'

Maggie rubs her hands together then presses them to her chest to try to warm her lungs, to loosen the story from where it sits, thorny in her chest. 'I don't know where to start, 'cos today was just the latest part of it.'

'Latest part of what?'

'A total nightmare.'

'THE DAVID SITUATION'

She'd met him at work on her first day at the bookies. No one wanted her to take the job. Her mum thought gambling was immoral and her fiancé Mike thought it was beneath her. But she was cautiously optimistic.

She liked watching the horses thunder along on the tiny suspended screens. She liked the feel of the little pens bucketed along the counter. And she wanted to witness the wins. To see people's lives changing right in front of her.

She'd crashed out of school with only a GCSE in drama; the opportunities weren't exactly lining up and they had a wedding to pay for. That showstopping white dress that had caught her eye, that was a whole pay cheque as it was and she'd already put down a deposit. She didn't have the luxury of making a fuss.

'Who gives a shit?' her new colleague David said to every mistake she made. 'None of this matters.' Then he showed her how to make a tiny hat out of a betting slip and whispered funny anecdotes about the regulars.

Whenever she mentioned David to Mike, he didn't see the burgeoning friendship as a good thing. He didn't recognise that you took your silver linings where you could when you found yourself behind the counter of a small-town betting shop at the age of twenty-five, when you'd rather hoped life would have more in store for you. Mike just heard another man's name. So she stopped mentioning David at all. But Mike was right to wave a red flag.

What Maggie thought of as a companionable friendship, David had mistaken for foreplay. And when her 'friend' tried to kiss her one evening after closing up, when he'd argued that she knew what she wanted, that she'd been building up to this for months, it was the sudden lack of friendship that hit her hardest. She'd apologised for any misunderstanding because that's what good girls are taught to do. But an apology was not what he wanted.

'I need to go,' she said. 'Mike's outside waiting for me.'

But he wasn't, and David knew that.

'Call me sentimental,' David said, pressing her against the wall of the staffroom and ignoring the old paint that crumbled to the floor, 'but a deal is a deal.'

'We don't . . . what deal?'

His heavy breath mingled with hers when she opened her mouth. She could taste the crisps she'd shared with him and her stomach flipped.

'I've helped you out,' he said, moving her trembling hand down his own body. 'Now you help me out.'

Eyes screwed shut, brain slipping backwards. She didn't notice he still had his phone in his hand.

She ran home afterwards, sat in a scolding bath and tried to reorganise it in her head, clean it, file it away. She didn't fight him, not in the staffroom or now. It never crossed her mind to go to the police. And she didn't breathe a word to Mike.

Funny how the way you think you'll behave is relegated to the way other people get to behave. Fusses are not for you.

She didn't go to work the next day or the day after. Claiming first a migraine and then the flu. Asking Mike to call in for her and tuning out his recriminations. 'We have a wedding to pay for.'

When she finally returned, she was called into Pete, the manager's, office. David was sitting on Pete's side of the desk as she was dismissed. She was still in her probation period, and she'd proven to be a flake.

'Do you have anything to say?' Pete asked. She had many things to say. She said none of them. Instead, she held her breath so she shared no more of David's, and then she ran all the way home.

Dazed, she let herself in and went up to the bed where Mike was still sleeping off a night shift.

'What do you expect when you keep bunking off?' he asked, his voice still thick from sleep.

Then the phone calls started. Breathy nothings from a with-held number. She went to the police then, Mike reluctantly at her side. 'Can you trace them?' she'd asked the police officer taking her statement. 'We're not MI5, love, and it's just a phone call.'

She opened her mouth to tell them that it wasn't just a phone call. But it'd been three weeks, and in that time she had worked harder than ever to seem normal. She'd laughed some-times. She and Mike had had sex. How could she explain that?

Next, the unwanted taxis started arriving, late at night and early in the morning. Mostly when Mike was on the night shift, and she'd dug out money from his cash pot to send them away. A condolence card came next. Blank inside, address printed, untraceable. 'I think it's a threat,' she told the same police officer, who slipped it into her file, offering no guar-antees. Then came the taps at the door at night when Mike wasn't home. She felt someone watching her whenever she dared go out. Eventually she just stayed inside.

All she had left was the wedding and every ounce of energy went into it. And today, it finally came. The good news story she'd been waiting for, a season finale of her own personal soap opera. She'd stood at the altar, Mike's hand in hers and her mother at her side with something like relief on her face. The same note of relief that had run through the announcement in the local paper, which she'd wished her mum hadn't placed.

The vicar warmed the crowd up like a pier-end pro and finally reached his show stopper. 'If anyone can show just cause why this couple cannot lawfully be joined together in matrimony, let them speak now or forever hold their peace.'

She gazed up lovingly at Mike, gripping his hand to pull both of them over the finish line. And then David spoke from the back of the church, his voice as loud as a town crier.

'Me. I can.'

Every head in the church turned to stare at the stranger as he marched towards the altar like a crusader. 'I'm here to stop this sham of a wedding,' he shouted. 'She's in love with me. And I have proof!'

Mouths gasped and heads fell into hands. David waved a wedge of photos around, some of them slithering to the floor, their subjects staring up at the wedding party. Silly shots from when they were still workmates, wearing their tiny betting slip hats. Arms around each other behind the counter when a punter won. But others too. A photograph of her hand on his body, her engagement ring sparkling. A blurred close-up of their faces: his lips against hers, her eyes closed. And then there was a photograph of her, in her nightdress, asleep.

'These aren't what you think!' she cried as Mike dropped her hand to snatch up the pictures. 'He forced me! I didn't know he'd taken pictures but I didn't want this, this isn't what it looked like. These aren't real!'

Everybody watched in silence as Mike flipped angrily through the pile, then stared at her with a venom she'd never seen before, not even from David. 'But that's our bed,' he said, his voice so sharpened by anger it could have sliced a piece of her heart clean off.

'He must have broken in,' she pleaded.

'So you're saying they *are* real?' Mike said, so quietly she had to lean in.

'That one is and those ones in the shop with the hats, they were just . . . just mucking around. Those others,' she'd panted, 'you have to believe me, I didn't want to. I hated it.

20

He forced me. But I don't know how he got a photo of me sleeping, Mike, I really don't.'

'If it was just that, Maggie,' Mike said, his eyes filling, 'I could . . . maybe I could understand but—' he'd pulled out the worst photo and held it up to her face so she shrank away '—I can see your hand on his dick.'

At that, her mother had collapsed into a nearby pew, fanning her face.

'Perhaps we could take a brief pause and collect our thoughts,' the vicar said, gesturing towards the vestry with a shaking hand. Mike didn't move. 'You've humiliated me in front of everyone,' he said, shaking with shock, tears falling onto his suit and the blue buttonhole flower she'd carefully made for him. 'I just . . . I can't do this.'

'But they're not . . . this is what he wants,' she cried. 'He's winning!' And then she turned to her mum, she still doesn't know why, and said, 'Mum, please tell him. Please tell Mike I'd never hurt him like this.'

Her mother turned away.

David stood in the middle of the aisle, grinning like a joker in a mismatched suit. 'Come on,' he said, offering her his hand grandly, dipping at the knee, 'you're out of this mess now.' She stared at him. Looked him in the eye for the first time since that evening in the staffroom. Searching the face of someone she'd once liked, looking for reasons he might want to light a bomb under her life. Finding only a dented ego, and a warped idea of women.

And then she ran. She ran as fast as she could in her strait jacket of taffeta and satin, in her white ballet pumps that she'd found on eBay for an absolute song.

When she turned just briefly at the church door, her mum was comforting Mike, a circle of well-wishers huddled around them. David was the only one looking her way, smiling with all of his teeth.

Charlotte

'You're saying . . .' she grinds to a halt. Where to start? She doesn't want to retraumatise this woman and found the matter-of-fact way she told her terrible story troubling. As if her nerve endings were singed by it all.

'I'm so sorry you weren't believed,' she says slowly, carefully. 'I believe you.' Her hand hovers near Maggie's arm, the human need to touch, to emphasise without words at odds with the need not to frighten or violate. She drops her hand and Maggie looks out of the window. Her eyes are wet but not leaking, a feat of control playing itself out in the visible fluttering pulse of her thin neck.

'And you just fled, wearing that?' Charlotte says, relieved to be back in the present, on easier ground, if only barely, than a man grooming, attacking and then destroying a woman's life.

'I didn't know what else to do,' Maggie says, tugging her dress up a little over her narrow chest, the straps slipping from her shoulders. 'It's not like I could go home, not to Mike's flat. I mean, I thought about going to the hotel we'd booked but the thought of that was just—'

'Your friends or parents?'

'Most of my circle were just Mike's friends' girlfriends or his sisters,' she says quietly. 'I've never been good at making friends.'

'Me neither,' Charlotte says. Until Rob had paid her attention in the later years of school, and her social capital had slightly risen, she'd been known as 'Beg-a-mate'. She'd hovered eagerly on the edges of friendship groups but was never invited in, having to stick with Anne instead.

'And my mum has finally given up on me,' Maggie says.

'You don't know that. She must have been shocked but, surely, knowing what David did to you—'

'She's always had a pretty low opinion of me. Today is confirmation that she was right all along.'

Charlotte wants to argue this, to reassure her but Maggie's expression tells her to stop.

'How did you end up all the way out here?' she asks instead, turning the heat up another degree as she notices Maggie's hands are still trembling.

'I don't know, I just walked. I didn't know where I was going. I didn't even care if David followed me. It was then that I realised I didn't care if David killed me; in fact, he'd be doing me a favour. And, god, the relief I felt at the idea of leaving all of this behind. Every mistake and disappointment.'

She closes her eyes and a tiny tear shimmers as it falls to her cheek.

'This humiliation, it's like . . . it's like it's burning me from the inside out. So when I saw the bridge, I just decided right then to . . . y'know. But it's not that simple when you're up there.'

Maggie stares at the bridge through the windscreen, brushing long damp hairs from her face. Charlotte passes her a hairband from the hidden compartment in the centre of the dash. She takes it wordlessly and twists her hair into a bun, securing it deftly.

'Now you,' Maggie says, turning to Charlotte.

'Now me?'

'You climbed up on that bridge pretty damn fast for someone without a story. Tell me.' Maggie's voice is softer now, but insistent. 'Tell me why someone like you has "nothing to lose".'

Charlotte pauses, unsure where to drop the needle. The start of the record, when the police knocked on her door on that dreadful morning? There aren't enough hours in the day and this bride doesn't look very patient. Charlotte exhales. She tries to scrunch it all into a neat compact story, sloughing off some of the rougher edges as Maggie listens, eyes widening.

'So let me get this straight, you lost your mum and dad in an accident, inherited your dad's business and gave your oldest friend a job when she needed one.'

'Pretty much.'

'And then she turned around and said you had to sign over your business to her?'

'Yep. That's about the size of it.'

'But she can't do that, right?'

'Well . . .' Charlotte closes her eyes and breathes out so long she imagines the sides of her lungs sticking together. 'She might be able to.' How much to say? *Oh fuck it.* 'Basically, it looks like there are some irregularities. From before, I mean.' She can't bring herself to say 'from my dad's time'.

'And there was a lot of money sitting in the account when I took it over so the business is doing fine, but it doesn't look good to have all this mess.' She exhales. It feels . . . not good exactly, but a bittersweet relief to say this stuff to someone. Especially someone with no horse in the race.

'I think she might have stitched me up, Maggie. Faked the accounts and made it look like there was illegal goings-on but, honestly, I'm not so sure that I can risk going to the police, 'cos if I'm wrong, I'm fucked.'

Outside, the rain keeps up its relentless pestering but, inside, the only sound is the whoosh of the engine and the swish of the windscreen wipers. Neither woman speaks for a while.

'OK, your story checks out,' Maggie says finally, smiling bitterly. 'So we both have nothing to lose.' Then she wrestles her sprawling bun back onto the top of her head and leans back against the car seat, eyes closing.

'Hey, are you OK?'

'I'm knackered.'

'Let's get you back to mine. It's a bit of a drive but you can rest and I'll shut up.'

Maggie falls asleep while they're still on Welsh soil, her fists balled in her lap like a toddler. When they pass under the tall yellow lights of the Severn Bridge, her pale skin shines luminous.

Tonight is a tale of two bridges. The former, a dirty old metal beast, offering no protection from the churning river

24

beneath. And now this elegant creation. Suspended high above the water as if strung between two stars, one keeping watch over England and the other over Wales.

They don't look alike – Maggie is milk-skinned with dirty-red hair and green eyes, narrow boned; Charlotte is dark-haired, olive-skinned and solid – but she feels something like the sisterly duty of care she once yearned for. For as long as she can remember, she'd pestered her parents for a baby sister. Right up until the car ride when she was nine. She'd been out for the day somewhere with her mum – her dad had been away at an auction – and she'd been playing with a doll in the backseat. 'I could help change my baby sister,' she'd said and her mum had screeched to a halt, slapped the wheel with her hands and said, 'Get this through your thick skull, Charlotte: I don't want another child with him.'

She'd never mentioned it again.

Charlotte pulls off the motorway and swings through Bampton-upon-Avon, the A road skimming her old haunts. The stop where she caught the school bus home, the fish and chip place she and Rob would sneak to in year eleven, the pub that asked no questions in sixth form.

And then her headlights bounce across the front gates of Bampton Grammar. The place where she had first met Anne, all those years ago.

1996

'Charlotte Wilderwood, you sit there. Anne Wilkins, you sit next to her . . .'

Bound, by alphabetical luck, into a friendship on day one of year seven. Both girls relieved to have it taken out of their hands. Charlotte had never really understood why, but, for all her eagerness, friends were always hard to come by.

She pulled out her pencil case and opened it up like a jewellery box. She noticed with delight that her new desk mate – a tall, skinny girl in mismatched uniform – was gazing at the contents with something like yearning. She slid the pencil case towards her like a cigarette pack.

'Would you like a pen?'

'Oh, yes please. I left my pencil case at home.'

'I've got more pens than I need,' Charlotte said, smiling awkwardly at how stuffed the case was. 'You'd be doing me a favour if you took some of these things.'

They spent their lunch break amongst the trees on the front lawn of the school, unwrapping sandwiches from home and, in Charlotte's case, also a Trio bar, a banana and a pouch of Sunny D.

'Ugh,' she said, playing for laughs really. 'Cheese and pickle. Mum knows I don't like that. What've you got?'

'Marmite,' Anne said, shrugging.

'Even worse!' Charlotte said, inspecting the paper bag in Anne's lap. 'Did your mum not give you anything with it?'

Anne chewed slowly, swallowed and looked at Charlotte like she was doing a sum, some difficult equation like they'd been shown in second period.

'I make my own sandwiches,' she said finally.

Charlotte went home that night and informed her mum, inaccurately as it turned out, that she'd be making her own lunch from now on because she wasn't a baby any more. 'OK, Lotty,' her mum said, scepticism barely hidden.

'My new friend Anne makes all her own food. And also can I get a perm soon? Anne's getting a perm when she turns twelve because it's kind of a tradition in her family. Why are you laughing?'

'You've already got curly hair, Lotty.'

'But it's the wrong kind of curly hair. And also, by the way, me and Anne are going to be best friends for the rest of our lives. No matter what.'

Charlotte

She slows as she enters Little Wickton, Rob's village. She'd not long moved from her rented London flat and into her inherited family cottage when she'd come to this village to post a letter and had walked straight into Rob.

They had stared at each other, eyes wide. She'd wanted to say, 'is it really you?' but her tongue had jammed. His mouth had fallen open just slightly, breathing fast, his chest filling in front of her like it might explode.

Rob. Three tiny letters, carved into the tree trunk of her life. The first boy she ever kissed. Whose expressions could turn her teenage self into a useless soup. A country bad boy, who would have been eaten whole by an actual delinquent, but was the closest thing their school had to a rebel without a cause. A caution for shoplifting here, a fist fight there . . . Whose body and heart she'd allowed to entwine with hers, only to find it tattered and broken when he'd dumped her out of the blue, after everything they'd overcome, just after she got her A-level results. The scab that had grown over those sores still brittle and ugly.

Rob. Whose appearance in front of her, like an apparition, had melted her like butter.

'Charlie,' he'd said, finally. His voice was lower than before, which had made her feel somehow cheated. Not by him but by time. Fifteen years apart after every day together. And he had not been set in amber. He had grown, changed and broadened, all behind her back.

Breathless and still unable to speak, she had pulled him to her. They'd hugged awkwardly at first, which was pain itself. Their softer, rounder bodies had no longer fitted together as precisely as they used to, but that same familiar warmth had spread through her nonetheless. Across her chest, down her thighs. She'd pressed harder into the hug and so had he.

How long had they stood there, saying nothing with their mouths? A minute, an hour, a lifetime? Meshing together, tracing the parts of each other's landscapes that had been missing from the other's map. Until all there was left to do was walk back to her cottage in silence and tell each other everything through sex. It had been out of their hands.

Rob was secrets made flesh. He was the memories she still drew on sometimes, when in bed with someone lacklustre and disappointing. He was the secret benchmark against which all other men – many men, who gave a shit how many – were judged. She told herself, told women at work, told anyone who would listen, that monogamy was for losers. Men were to be picked up and dropped, played at their own game. Reduced to a series of eggplant emojis in WhatsApp groups.

But that day, bathed in Somerset sunshine and pickled in grief, she couldn't deny what still lay at her core. Not a thing or a concept, but a person. Rob. The one around whom she had moulded herself when she was still pliable, and hardened that way.

And everything was the same as it always had been. The way that he kissed. The snap of the condom. The way they moved instinctively together, waves curling onto a beach, controlled by some larger force. Even the sounds he made were the same, sounds she could not have described and didn't know she remembered until she heard them again and it was suddenly all she could remember about anything.

'I can't believe you're here,' she'd said afterwards, running her hands carefully along his skin, half-expecting him to dissolve back into a memory.

'I've always been here,' he'd said. 'And I always hoped you'd come back.'

'Yeah?'

'I'm so sorry,' he'd said then. 'About your parents and about . . . I shouldn't have . . . I regretted it immediately.'

'Breaking up with me?'

He'd nodded.

28

'Oh Jesus, Rob, you were eighteen,' she'd said gently. 'You're supposed to break up with people when you're eighteen. It's OK. It's not done me any harm.' And then she'd tugged his discarded T-shirt over her body like she always had and went to make tea so he wouldn't see how obviously she was lying.

A vague sense of misdemeanour had run up and down her bare arms as she'd brought the mugs up and saw him there in the bed, suntanned skin from working outside, hair messed up from her hands. It had been the middle of the day. Her parents had never trusted Rob but her parents were dead and, besides, she was allowed to have sex.

They were proper adults. Him more than her. No longer a tough teen tearaway, he was a respectable member of the community, divorced with a child and a gardening business of his own, one he'd started just after she'd left. Him becoming his own boss while she'd slid into three years of sleeping in, sleeping around and sleepwalking through lectures to collect a degree in the history of decorative arts, hoping it might prove to her dad she could be useful to the business.

'I haven't been in this room for years,' he'd said, sitting up and flattening down his hair, revealing more scalp than used to be on show. 'Where are all the posters?'

'Imagine if you'd come here, both of us in our thirties, and my bedroom was still the same as it was when I was eighteen,' she'd said, and it was the first time she'd laughed since the police had knocked.

'I would have escaped out of the window, Charlie.'

He'd got dressed soon after, gesturing shyly for his T-shirt. 'You can't stick around?' she'd asked, pulling it back over her head and hiding her breasts under the duvet.

'Well, I'd love to, but I was on my way to do a quote and wasn't actually intending to . . .'

'Oh, of course,' she'd cringed. 'You weren't expecting to bump into your old girlfriend.'

'Exactly.'

He'd patted himself down, looking for his phone amongst the covers and sliding it into his back pocket. 'But how about dinner tomorrow night? My place or, like, out somewhere, whatever you fancy really.'

She'd smiled and nodded, tried to stop her eyes filling. Exhaustion and grief, yes, but also relief. Maybe she wasn't fully alone, out here in this little village she'd made such a song and dance about leaving in the first place. And maybe she wasn't mad to have kept this Rob-shaped hole for him all these years. Maybe he would fill all her missing pieces.

'Dinner would be lovely. At your place, if that's OK? I don't really . . . I'm not quite ready for . . .' she'd trailed off, waving her arm towards the window. To the outside world and all its eyes and opinions.

Had they ever had dinner together, just the two of them? They'd definitely had dinner made for them at their respective family homes before he was no longer welcome. They'd smashed burgers and kebabs into their faces on nights out with his mates and made toasties in his Breville machine after school but not dinner. Not grown-up dinner.

'Are you actually going to cook?' she'd asked and he'd snorted through his nose but smiled widely. 'Yes, I have evolved just a little bit since school, you know.' She'd smiled. At least one of them had.

'Oh, Anne's back, by the way. Have you seen her?' he'd added, fussing his hair in the mirror she'd first applied make-up in.

'Anne? Wow, I haven't seen her in years. God, we used to be inseparable.' A tugging feeling that had disappeared almost immediately.

'You should look her up. She'd love to see you. It was her who told me about your folks. She was really cut up actually.'

By the time they pull up to Charlotte's cottage in the next village, Maggie's rigid sleep has softened in on itself and she is slumped, chin lolling over seatbelt, arms limp as spaghetti. Charlotte wakes her gently and she murmurs and then snaps to, startled.

'Hey, it's OK,' Charlotte soothes. 'We're here.'

Maggie stretches as much as she can in the limited space, twirling each wrist until they click. 'Is this your place?' Maggie asks, voice damp with sleep, as she unbuckles and squints at the cottage through the windscreen. Charlotte watches as she takes in the front door, the frou-frou wreath and the antique fox door knocker.

'Yeah, it is now.'

Maggie doesn't respond; she's looking back down the lane they'd just driven up, as if trying to get her bearings. She stares out into the squirming black of the country night and then turns back to stare at the cottage.

'It's beautiful.'

It is beautiful. The kind of cottage you'd stick on a Christmas card or a box of biscuits. Charlotte didn't think so when she grew up here. Yearned for the neat edges and right angles of her classmates' modern homes. The gas bar heater of Anne's front room that didn't spit out tiny jewels of fire or involve blowing on kindling to get it going.

But now she gets it. What this cottage meant to her parents, how pivotal it was to the life they worked to give her. The cottage is what's left of her mum, and the business is what's left of her dad. She feels her eyes prickle. She can't lose it. Can't lose *him*.

Fox Cottage is double-fronted and made from Bath stone, which looks almost silver in the moonlight. Two bay windows sit like big dark eyes either side of the heavy oak front door.

The porch light comes on automatically as they get closer and Maggie lifts her dress to climb the two steps to the door, revealing two mud-splattered feet. 'Shall I carry you over the threshold?' Charlotte jokes and Maggie blinks. 'Sorry, I was just, I make bad jokes when I'm . . .' but Maggie has started to laugh now and Charlotte joins in with relief.

'You're so kind to let me stay,' Maggie says as she steps into the hallway. 'Oh wow.' Charlotte sees it as if through Maggie's eyes. The antique umbrella stand, the White Company diffuser, the staircase carefully painted with Farrow & Ball's 'Elephant's Breath' during her mum's last redecoration initiative.

'You're so kind, and *so rich,*' Maggie says, and then they laugh again.

It's gone one in the morning. Charlotte is still wired from the night drive, from the adrenaline spike of a near miss.

Maggie is sitting in the opposite corner of the sofa to Charlotte, bare legs tucked under her and loosely draped in a pair of borrowed shorts and a T-shirt. Charlotte steals several jealous glances at her smooth legs. They're un-mottled by age, unlike Charlotte's thighs, which are hidden inside thick flannel pyjamas. She wonders pointlessly when her last good leg day was, and if she even realised.

Maggie's freshly washed hair has wound its way out of the towel and lies drying on her shoulders, vibrant red against her pale skin. Her green eyes dance with fire, reflected from the wood burner that Charlotte hastily lit while Maggie showered. Surprisingly, she doesn't have a Welsh accent, but she looks like a miniature Celtic warrior nonetheless.

Once upon a time she and Anne would stay awake until they were crazy with tiredness, sharing ghost stories and gossip. But since they met again as adults, there was always a sheet of glass between them, something invisible stopping them from truly connecting. She doesn't have that same sense with Maggie. How could there be any barriers up when they'd seen each other on the brink of death?

Maggie stares at the fire, her jaw jutting and eyes glassy. She is picturesque. No doubt photogenic. What Charlotte's mother would have called 'striking', which meant something different to pretty. In this setting, Maggie could be a model in a Toast catalogue. Or perhaps in a Cox & Cox catalogue, there to highlight the beauty of the room, her skinny prettiness reflecting in the trinkets. And it is a lovely room, the antique Chesterfield scuffed and creased in all the right places, a black and brass 1920s travelling trunk, a garland along the fireplace that cost a lot to look handmade, and a clutch of Tom Dixon candles. All of it was here when she moved back in. She'd brought boxes of her own stuff from her London flat, but everything she had was a cheaper, flimsier version. She threw most of it away and the rest was donated or shunted into the garage.

'Something's been puzzling me,' Charlotte says, cautiously. It's a question that's rolled in and out of her mind since the car. 'I just keep wondering . . . How *could* your stalker have photos of you asleep?'

'David?' Maggie looks rattled but answers softly. 'I don't know. I mean, they were definitely taken in Mike's flat.' She shivers then, her skin puckering into goose pimples.

Charlotte passes her a blanket, one from a pile her mother must have bought.

'I guess he crept in while Mike was working nights but, I don't know, I didn't realise he was capable of that. The thought of him in there with me, alone . . . he could have done anything.'

She looks quickly at Charlotte, her pupils huge in the soft light. 'He could have done anything, *again*.'

'I'm so sorry. I just can't believe . . . no, it's not that I can't believe he got away with it, because they do, don't they? I just *hate* that he got away with it.'

Maggie says nothing.

'Do you think he'll stop now? Now he thinks he's broken you and Mike up?'

'He *has* broken us up. Mike didn't even consider my side of the story, didn't even flinch when I said that David had attacked me, *forced* me. He just saw me as a cheat. After everything. Honestly, he can just sod off.'

33

'Damn right.' Charlotte raises her glass and Maggie takes a deep sniff of the blanket. 'But as for David . . . sodding off is not in his nature. I honestly don't think he'll stop until I'm . . . until I'm dead or, I don't know, married to him instead. I have to get him off my back, Charlotte.'

Charlotte watches the flames dance behind the ornate iron grate until her eyes start to water. 'I need to get Anne off my back too,' she says. 'For good.' She takes a sip; the wine has warmed over time. 'But I don't know how.'

This moment carries an echo of the time Rob had looked up into her eyes, his arm around her in his teenage bed, and said, 'but how could I get hold of the tools to start the business? I don't have any money.' The start of a chain of bad decisions. But tonight, there's silence from the other sofa. She looks over and Maggie is already asleep, phone in hand. Charlotte creeps over and lays another blanket over her. Maggie's mouth is slack and her forehead has a slight sheen. For a moment, Charlotte thinks about kissing her goodnight, the way she might have done with a sibling. She stops herself just in time.

Maggie

Saturday Morning

Maggie wakes with a jolt. Her body is tangled in an unfamiliar blanket and she's twisted awkwardly, her neck and shoulders aching. She dreamed of her imaginary father for the first time in a long time. A guessed face. A hand outstretched to her, their fingers never reaching. As a child, she always used to imagine him finally turning up on the day of her wedding, a heroic stranger, just in time to walk her down the aisle. As if. He's probably as dead as Charlotte's dad.

As she comes to, she remembers everything that happened yesterday in a sickening rush and lets her hand fall.

Somewhere nearby, a radiator is clicking into action but the fire has long burned itself out. Her dry mouth tastes like wine and charcoal. She's suddenly desperate for a drink of water but what is the etiquette here? This is a whole new situation and she's out of her depth. She didn't expect to end up here last night and she sure as hell didn't expect to still be here this morning.

The heavy curtains are closed but, even without the view, she knows she's in the middle of nowhere. No hum of traffic, no kids' laughter, not even the screech of a bird. Alone in a house with a stranger, wrapped in silence. She regrets falling asleep on the drive here; she only meant to pretend so she could avoid talking for a bit. Now she's entirely without bearings and still doesn't know if she made the right decision.

Maggie looks around at the expensive details, the trinkets and *objets d'art*, the antique bureau, the stack of mohair blankets and the matching cushions. She tries to price it all up and fast runs out of numbers.

Her toes creak and complain as she steps gingerly onto them. She did them no favours standing on that cold bridge in those stupid ruined shoes for so long. Her back is aching and tender from the fall. She shivers at the memory. So close.

She stretches her legs, bending carefully at the waist and letting the blood fill her head, bringing her back to life. She slips behind the sofa and gingerly peels back one of the curtains. The sun isn't too punishing. A pale light that has already lost itself in a lacework of distant tree branches by the time it reaches the house. She stares out, straining to see down a lane that's been pinched out of view by blocky green fields dotted with sheep.

Is he out there, watching?

In the corner of the room, her filthy wedding dress hangs from an upholstered satin hanger, hooked over the picture rail that runs the length of the room. *Shit*. She treads quickly, lightly, and unhooks it. It's dank, smelling of river slime and

35

armpit sweat. A couple of small twigs have snagged on the train, there are rips in the skirt and it's in desperate need of a wash.

As she grapples to lift it down, it tumbles onto her. So many slippery layers, slithering through her arms onto the floor. She scoops it up and reaches into the panel behind the bust, fumbling around. It's gone.

'Looking for this?'

Charlotte is standing in the doorway, dressing gown and pyjamas on. Her dark-brown hair is scraped into a ponytail that billows at the back of her head like a cloud and she has a dusting of freckles on her nose that weren't visible last night. Her hand is outstretched and lying on her palm is a mobile phone.

'Yes,' Maggie says, nervously. She can hardly lie.

For a moment Charlotte says nothing but then she smiles. She looks younger without make-up, her brown eyes less intense without the kohl and her smile softer. 'It fell out when I hung your dress up. You're lucky my mum used to have one of these so I had a charger. I plugged it in before I went to bed.'

'Oh, thank you,' she breathes out in relief. 'It was dead before I even left the church.'

Charlotte frowns just briefly and then hands it over. She tries not to snatch it, to slow her panic into calm, steadied movements.

'You don't have to pretend with me,' Charlotte says. 'I'd want to see if he's texted too.'

'Who?'

'Mike. Isn't that his name? Your fiancé.'

She nods, fumbling to switch it on and wishing she could do this in private.

'I bet he has messaged and he's full of apologies,' Charlotte says kindly. But then a shadow falls across her face as she realises. 'Oh god, I'm sorry. You're worried about messages from David, aren't you? I wasn't thinking.'

'It's fine.' The screen is taking ages to light up and she dare not imagine what's waiting for her.

'God, I hope that mental bastard *hasn't* messaged you. Do you want me to look for you?'

She freezes then shakes her head. 'It's OK. I . . . do you mind if I make a drink while this wakes up? I'm really thirsty.'

'Let me. You just sit down and catch your breath. If you change your mind and want me to look at the phone for you, just come into the kitchen. Tea or coffee?'

'Um, tea, please. White, no sugar.' She realises that was discourteous; she's 'acting bratty', as he would say. Her mum too. 'I mean, that would be so lovely, thank you.'

'It's really no trouble,' Charlotte says softly, as she backs out of the room.

As she hears a fierce rush of water filling the kettle in the kitchen, she takes a deep breath and clicks to see the unread messages.

'I followed you,' the first one says. 'Like I said I would.'

Charlotte

'You look white as a sheet,' Charlotte says, sliding the heavy Le Creuset mug across the cherry wood farmhouse-style kitchen table.

'It's beautiful in here,' Maggie says, sipping at her drink in little pecks, like a bird.

A cream-coloured Aga, pale-wood kitchen cupboards, a wine fridge, for goodness' sake. And this pristine family table, the eighteenth-century Japanese Arita Imari bowl in the centre, by rights too pretty to be used for storing over-ripe fruit. It's so very much her mum's style and so far from her own that Charlotte still feels like she's living in someone else's Pinterest board.

'Thank you. It was my parents' house; my mum was a decor addict and my dad was her dealer, antiques dealer that is, so it was never finished.'

She tries to keep it clean, puts far more effort in now than she ever did when she lived here before, leaving trails of milk-shake powder and toast crumbs, rolling her eyes at the tutting tongue when her mum found her mess. It feels like living in a museum, but when didn't it? And her brief time working in the furniture museum in London was one of her happiest, so perhaps this is the way it should be.

She looks at the cutlery drawer. Should she have hidden the knives and locked the paracetamol away? But that's not how it works, is it? And looking at the expression on Maggie's face now, reading her eyes, Charlotte knows that the moment on the bridge is locked in the past, just like her own death-wish driving has been relegated to the shuttered part of her brain.

'Was it weird moving back?'

'Yeah, it was. I'd given up on . . .'

Maggie raises her eyebrows. 'On what?'

Charlotte puffs out her cheeks; how to explain? 'I'd given up on getting back here. Well, I mean not *here* here − I never imagined I'd be living in this house again in my thirties − but the business.' Her voice cracks and she coughs it back together. 'I was always desperate to work with my dad. When I was little I used to ask him if we could call it 'Wilderwood and Daughter Antiques'. He, er, well, he used to laugh it off but when I got older, and got more serious, I'd hoped . . .' She shakes her head; these are dangerous memories. The kind of memories that sour her feelings, and you're not really allowed sour feelings for the dead.

'Why didn't your dad want you involved? Did you not get on?'

'We got on brilliantly, he was my absolute favourite person in the world. That's why I can't let Anne get away with this. This was my chance to prove to . . . well, him, even though he's gone, but I guess me . . . that I did deserve a place at the table.' Charlotte runs her palms over the surface in front of her, brushes away a crumb. 'And that I could keep his legacy going and build on it, bring it into the modern world a bit.'

'You still can,' Maggie says gently.

'Not if Anne gets her way.' Charlotte's voice hardens.

'Well,' says Maggie, putting her mug down with a clonk and then rubbing the table in apology, 'we'll have to stop her then.'

Charlotte smiles despite the pit in her stomach. 'I've been churning it over in my head all night and I just don't know a way out of this. Anne has had access to everything, I completely trusted her. To be honest, I was so caught up in reorganising the showroom and trying to get a new website up that I let her get on with the money side. There was plenty of cash in the account, that's all I knew.'

Maggie frowns but says nothing.

'And she had this folder with these invoices, duplicates, she said. Showing that the same things has been sold numerous times and stuff like that. And things were missing, antiques we'd bought to sell that weren't anywhere in the showroom. I don't even know if I'd seen any of it before, but some of the invoices were dated *before* I took her on but *after* my dad died so . . . I mean, I'm in the frame.'

'But does anyone else actually know that?'

'Know what?'

'That this magical folder exists. That there are extra invoices and missing products and stuff?'

Charlotte breathes out. 'I don't think so, I mean, I don't know who she'd tell. And the reason she wants me gone is – *apparently* – so she can clean it all up and insulate the business from any investigation so—'

'Does anyone else work there?'

'Just Dorian,' Charlotte says, and then catches Maggie's expression and can't help but laugh. 'Oh no, Dorian is nothing to do with this. She's nearly seventy and she's been my dad's Girl Friday for as long as I can remember. It was in the will that she had a job for as long as she wanted but she only comes in part-time and does a bit of tidying, sending out catalogues, that kind of thing. No,' Charlotte says, 'this is nothing to do with her, this is all Anne. Anyway, forget her. Were there any messages from . . . anyone?'

'None from Mike,' Maggie says, her voice flat. 'But loads from David. He genuinely thinks he's saved me and that I owe him.'

Charlotte frowns. 'Owe him?'

'Owe him my life,' Maggie says, staring at her half-empty mug.

'Jesus. That's next level, Maggie. He attacked you and now he's threatening you. We should go back to the police.'

Maggie puts her hands on her cheeks and slumps forward. It's a childlike move. The way a school kid might act when they're bored in class or lonely at lunchtime. Not petulant so much as defeated. 'The police can't do anything. It'll be "he said, she said" and I'm not going through that.'

'It's different now, though,' Charlotte says gently. 'He turned up at your *wedding*, there are witnesses.'

'It's not a crime to stop a wedding. I mean, that's literally what that bit in the ceremony is for. And anyway, what about you? Why don't you go to the police about Anne? What she's doing is blackmail, right?'

'Yeah, it is but . . .' Charlotte sighs. In for a penny, in for a pound. 'I can't be totally sure that my dad *did* run everything above board; maybe he made a few mistakes. If I go to the police and they start probing around, it may work out worse for me. For the business too. Fraud is serious, Maggie, I could go to prison.'

'Prison? For a few fake invoices? But David is never going to be punished for what he's done.' Maggie stands abruptly, the chair squeaking on the tiled floor that cost Charlotte's parents more per square metre than a week's rent on her former flat. She paces to the sink and pours the rest of her tea away. 'Sorry,' she says, 'but it wasn't very nice. Can I make another cup?'

Charlotte laughs in shock. 'OK.' *So that's it, conversation over?*

'Do you want one?'

'A cup of tea? Um, yes please. I put too much milk in this one. The teabags are there, and—'

'Milk's in the fridge, of course.' Maggie smiles as she flicks the kettle back on, standing at the sink with one foot on top of the other like a flamingo. 'So where is this folder now?'

'Oh.' The lurching in topics is dizzying but she feels a flutter of gratitude that Maggie's still trying to come up with a way to help. It's more than that too: that intoxicating scent of a potential new friendship, the thrill that maybe this will be The One.

She'd had it with Anne all those years ago, but whenever she thought she'd had it with anyone else, it had puttered out. 'You're an acquired taste,' her dad used to say, 'like an olive.'

'Charlotte?' Maggie's looking at her expectantly. 'Where's the folder of evidence now?'

'I don't know, maybe at the showroom still.'

'Is anyone there today?'

'No, we only open by appointment at weekends and there weren't any. Are you thinking we should—'

'Forget the tea,' Maggie says, her young face newly excitable. 'We need to get dressed.'

Maggie

It's important to be thorough, she thinks. She's always been thorough, to the chagrin of her mum. Late for school as a kid because she had to get her socks lined up just so, erupting in screaming fits as she was pulled into the car with uneven hems. Or staying in the classroom to finish her work at lunchtime, a pile of discarded paper at her feet from where she'd coloured over the lines and started again. Then getting to the lunch hall too late to eat any food.

'The school nurse called to say you have an eating disorder,' her mother had said briskly one day when she was in year five. 'And don't deny it because *adults* have seen you skipping meals.'

'How can someone see me not do something?' she'd asked, mystified.

'Don't be smart. I'm paying for those school lunches and you'll bloody well eat them.'

So this trip to an antiques shop wasn't exactly part of the idea. Nor was it in the step-by-step plan she'd gone over again and again in her head this morning, pulling at it from all angles to make sure it would work before trying to suggest it. But despite what everyone says, she knows she's capable of coming up with good ideas. And this is one of them.

For now, she's sitting back in the heated passenger seat that brought her to the cottage last night. In the daylight, she can see how muddy it was, splashes and splodges along the doors like starburst. Inside, entrails of countryside dot the floor, a slick leaf, more mud, some grit dotted around. The dash is a little dusty and she wonders when Charlotte last cleaned it, and why she is content to leave it like this. This is not the kind of thing to ask though, she knows that.

She watches the sunlit countryside whip by as Charlotte drives them along the edge of Bath. 'The company moved into this place when I was about three,' Charlotte's saying. 'So I don't really remember a time before he worked here.'

'You're sure no one will be there now?'

Charlotte shakes her head.

'But if someone does appear,' she says carefully, as Charlotte indicates onto a small trading estate with a faded sign, 'I'll wait in the car.'

'Don't be silly, you look fine.'

She looks down in surprise. It hadn't crossed her mind that she might look odd, but of course she does, regardless of what Charlotte says. She's several inches shorter and probably two stone lighter, so Charlotte's mustard-coloured jumper is baggy in the chest and its sleeves are too long, the jeans she's borrowed billow around the belt and have had to be rolled a couple of times at the ankle. 'I'd just rather.' It comes out more wobbly than intended and Charlotte looks at her with sympathy. It feels raw to receive, like a graze being licked, and Maggie looks away.

But there are no other cars here anyway, and Charlotte

pulls right up to the door. The sign over it says 'Wilderwood Antiques' in eighties typography. The nearby units house panel beaters and furniture makers, a company that make pet crates and another that she can't make out. 'They make plastic things like the bits that go along the top of shopping trolleys,' Charlotte shrugs, as if this is some poor reflection on her.

'That's interesting,' she lies and then catches Charlotte's eye and they both laugh in surprise. 'No it's not,' Charlotte snorts. 'Come on, I'll open up.'

'Aren't antiques shops usually in towns?'

'Sometimes, but we can have a much bigger place out here for the same money and people don't mind a drive out. If they're on foot in a town, they're more likely just browsing. Here they come to buy. We sell a lot to trade too, people looking to decorate hotels and stuff.'

Charlotte opens up and they step inside. It's an Aladdin's cave of furniture and decorative items. Big brass lamps loom over them like giraffes and a clutch of mirrors fracture their image into pieces. It's not quite what Maggie had in mind. She'd imagined something more . . . posh. Diamond jewellery and Ming vases, not that she'd recognise one, but this is more like a jumble sale. She looks around, trying not to show her disappointment, and heads towards the back of the room.

'Is that Anne's desk?'

'How did you know?' Charlotte asks, raising her eyebrows.

'It's practically empty. The other two have photos on or flowers or mugs, this just has a cable for a computer and an empty paper tray. It's temporary.'

'I just thought she was neat,' Charlotte says. 'But it's obvious now you've said it.'

'Maybe she always planned to take yours.'

She knows which desk is Charlotte's; it's full of giveaways, but she keeps that to herself. There's a point where being observant becomes creepy. But it's all clear to a practised reader of circumstance – the big wooden desk is clearly one that Charlotte's father bought and she has since taken over.

It's bulky and masculine, but sentimental too. On top of it sits a tower of papers, a vase full of slightly wilting white flowers and a Le Creuset mug like the ones at the cottage.

They make their way to Anne's soulless desk instead.

'It's locked.' Charlotte is tugging on the filing cabinet underneath. A slim old Bisley with six slim drawers and no names on any of them, tougher than they look.

'Maybe the keys are in the desk drawer.'

Charlotte pulls both drawers out, rummages around and then smiles as she pulls out a small key. She slides it in, twists it and then pulls open each drawer in turn, smile fading.

'They're all empty.' Charlotte says, shoving them closed again. 'Completely empty.'

'I think I have another idea but can I use the loo first?' she asks, and Charlotte waves in the direction of the tiny toilet. Inside, the strong stench of cheap air freshener clogs the windowless room and she coughs and pulls on the ceiling fan before sitting down on the lid and pulling out her phone.

When she gets back, Charlotte is scrabbling under the desk to look in the waste-paper bin as if someone as strategic as Anne would have just binned an essential part of her scam. And this clearly is a scam; it's not even subtle.

'Charlotte,' she says softly as the other woman scrambles back out, knocking over the desk chair and wincing as she stands again, knees clicking, 'I think we should go.'

Charlotte

The text comes through from Rob as they get back to the cottage. 'One sec,' she murmurs to Maggie as she pulls the phone from the charging pad.

Fancy doing something today? X

She closes the message and lets the phone fall to her lap.

'Your boyfriend?' Maggie asks and Charlotte nods. 'I'll get back to him in a bit.'

Rob has no idea what's been happening and the thought of bringing him up to speed is exhausting. And he's friends with Anne too, he trusts her. What if he takes Anne's side? Given his past indiscretions and brushes with the law, he's keen on giving second chances. He will always choose to see the best in people. Even his cousin Cole, who was always a waste of space and has grown up to be a black hole.

'How long have you been together?'

'Either twenty years or six months, depending on how you want to slice it.'

Maggie frowns so Charlotte explains. 'We started going out when we were teenagers but we broke up before I went to uni. I was devastated.'

'He was your first love?'

'Yeah,' she says. 'Sad as that sounds.'

'It sounds lovely,' Maggie says with no trace of sarcasm. 'I've only ever had one boyfriend too.'

'Oh,' Charlotte laughs. 'I've been with plenty more men than Rob. But he was the first, and that's . . . it leaves an imprint.'

'Will you think I'm silly if I admit I still want to be with my first love?'

'After not taking your side, do you mean?'

Maggie nods and then shakes her head. 'Not just that, and I'm still not sure I have forgiven him yet. Though I miss him a lot.' She looks wistfully towards the window. 'But to stay with the first person who . . . I mean from fifteen to twenty-five, ten years with . . .'

Charlotte shakes her head. 'I'm not sure I used those ten years any better.'

She opens the fridge and passes out eggs, bacon and sausages to Maggie who ferries them to the Aga wordlessly. Charlotte washes two field mushrooms thoughtfully and sits them on the griddle next to the sausages. From her side eye, she catches sight of Maggie's narrow fragile body and wonders how often she relives what David did to her. Rage rises and she grinds her teeth but says nothing.

'You don't have to ignore your boyfriend on my account,' Maggie says, her frown intense with childlike concentration as she starts to cut the beef tomatoes in perfect halves along the middle.

'I know,' Charlotte says, pushing the attack to the back of her mind. 'But Rob asked to meet up and I'm really not in the mood. I'd have to tell him what's been happening and—'

'Maybe we can still fix it before you have to tell him anything.'

The griddle is spitting, the sticky liquid from the sausages and bacon caramelising under the mushrooms. God, she's hungry. Hollow and empty in all ways.

'Maybe.' She shrugs, not believing that for a second.

'Wasn't it Rob that suggested Anne join the company?' Maggie asks.

Charlotte adds the tomatoes to the griddle. There's a satisfying pop as their skins split but she's too rattled to enjoy it. 'Yes, why?'

'You don't think he could be involved in what she's trying to do, do you?'

Maggie

'Rob?'

Two perfect slices pop up from the expensive polished toaster. They both jump.

Charlotte stands up straighter, for just a moment, then shakes her head, reaching for the golden toast. 'No. Why would he be involved?'

'Did Anne and Rob see each other much before you came back?'

Charlotte pauses just briefly. 'A bit. They're old friends.'

She opens her mouth to say more. To point out that sometimes the people who seem the most straightforward can be the most cunning. *The widest eyes tell the biggest lies*, as her mum used to say whenever she refuted an accusation. Charlotte won't want to hear that just because she knew Rob inside out twenty years ago, it doesn't mean she knows him that well now. And if she pushes the point and gets kicked out, where will she be then?

So instead they work in quiet tandem, taking their time. As if this meal they're making is the most important thing in this moment. As if food and company is worth something. When did she last cook a meal like this? A proper hot meal with fresh ingredients rather than grabbing a sandwich on the go or eating noodles straight from the pan while the man she loves listed all her faults.

She watches as Charlotte squats down slowly to get sauces from the fridge. Can't help but stare as her belly folds like freshly made meringue before it's baked. Everything about Charlotte looks soft. The flesh of her arms sways gently as she scythes off a curl of butter, then another, and spreads it on the toast until it glistens. She has to stop herself asking for a hug. She might not let go.

She looks down at her own body. It's small and bony in comparison. 'Like cuddling a stick insect,' he sometimes says as he rolls away after sex. But she knows other men like it; she's seen them looking. The little sonar system pinging to life inside her, warning her of mal-intent.

'Have you heard from Mike today?' Charlotte asks as she gives the eggs a final stir to stop them furring up. There's a sharpness to the question, a pointed changing of the subject away from Rob.

'No.'

A gentler voice: 'Any more messages from David?'

She pauses. 'Yes, but I deleted them.'

The wooden spoon in Charlotte's hand stops momentarily. 'I know you won't want to, but you probably should keep hold of them. As evidence, I mean.'

'You're right,' she says, though she has no intention of keeping any messages. 'Maybe there won't be any more.'

Charlotte gets two matching plates out of a compartment of the Aga where they've been warming. So many little doors, like an advent calendar.

'How about I keep your phone for you, so you don't have to deal with it?' Charlotte says, moving a saucepan of beans off the heat.

'No way.' It comes out sharper than she meant it to.

Charlotte freezes for a moment, then dishes the food onto the plates in silence.

'Sorry, I didn't mean to snap,' Maggie says, as they sit down at the table. Charlotte has laid out two silver bowls with hinged lids and little spoons. 'Salt and pepper,' Charlotte explains. 'And don't apologise, I was being big sisterly and overstepping.'

'I always wanted a big sister,' Maggie blurts out before she can stop herself. Luckily Charlotte just smiles.

Charlotte eats quietly, thoughtfully, and she finds it unbearable. Her mother used to insist upon silence at the table and the absence of noise would grow over her head like a rain cloud. It was a challenge, to see if she'd crack and speak first, and she always did. Her mother would smile wryly and then launch into an airing of her grievances. Or, if she was slightly luckier, a lecture about trust, or about boys, or about wasting opportunities.

She can't bear this quiet. 'It's just, I'd rather keep my phone because if Mike does send a reply, I want to see it immediately.'

Charlotte looks up from her plate. 'So you've sent Mike some messages then?'

'Yes,' she lies.

Charlotte

Could Rob be involved? He's not exactly flushed. He said the other day that maintenance to his ex-wife was quite a lot and his business isn't doing so well. Didn't he say something about the rent going up on his house too? Her fork freezes in mid-air.

But this is Rob we're talking about. He's an adult now, a father. He's a good person. He always *was* a good person, she corrects; he was just easily led when he was younger. A friend suggesting they nick sweets from the Spar. His cousin Nigel flogging sunglasses that 'fell off a lorry', sending Rob into school with some swag to offload. Or the worst one, the time in sixth form when his cousin Cole said he'd got hold of some 'bric-a-brac' from a house clearance. Eager to show her dad that she could spot an opportunity, she'd carefully examined it all and identified some pieces that she thought had potential. If they could sell them to her dad for a good price, Cole would split the profits with him and Rob could get the tools he needed to set up as a gardener. It was perfect.

Rob had brought the stuff round in a box on the front seat of his mum's Fiesta. Her stomach drops at the memory. Her dad's big hands, gently turning the vases and figurines over, Rob's eager face, blushing as he always did around her parents. The way her dad had stood up sharply and asked Charlotte to leave the room so he could talk to 'Robert.'

'No,' she'd said, oscillating between protectiveness towards Rob and total embarrassment.

'This is all nicked,' her dad had said. 'So how come you've got it in your grubby little paws?'

The stuff had been stolen in a burglary, the pictures had been sent around all the dealers in case someone came in trying to sell it. 'I'm supposed to have reported it,' he'd told her after.

'So he's lucky I'm a soft touch but he's not welcome here any more, and if you've got a brain in your head, you'll get shot of him.' Cole was famously light-fingered, and Rob must have suspected if not outright known, but he'd gone along with the plan because Charlotte had told him to. He was only young.

But then . . . being easily led was apparently one of the reasons his wife Debbie had divorced him, and that was only a few years ago. He'd painted it less of a failing and more of a misunderstood attribute. He would always make himself available to his brothers, his cousins. But he could never see Cole's schemes for what they were. And he could never say no to a mate looking for a drinking buddy. Could never say no full stop. Did Anne lead him into something?

Rob always called Charlotte brainy and himself stupid but that's not true either. He was below average for grammar school, always in the bottom sets and limping to pass his GCSEs, but that's nothing like the same as being stupid. 'I'd never put her through that,' he'd once said, when Charlotte asked if his daughter would be taking the eleven plus exams.

'It's like a private education for free though,' she'd said, astonished.

'For you maybe,' he'd replied. And she vaguely remembered the way he'd colour red when picked to answer a question in class. But it was no wonder he always planned to leave education at eighteen and start his own company. She didn't understand it at the time, had tried to get him to apply for the same universities as her, not accepting that he couldn't and wouldn't get in. When she'd finally accepted that he wasn't coming with her, she'd planned to turn down the university place she'd been offered at Manchester to find another course locally and live with him. He'd broken up with her before she could make her bold gesture.

But someone stupid couldn't have raised the funds to start his own company while he was still a teenager, let alone make a success of it, regardless of any bumps in the road. No, Rob is not stupid but he's not sneaky either, he's straightforward. Isn't he?

'You OK?' Maggie asks and Charlotte unfreezes, slides her fork into her mouth and nods. But then she shakes her head. *I need to see him.*

She swallows slowly, giving herself time to think. This girl is a stranger, she doesn't have to explain herself, and yet, in these intense few hours, they've become somehow entwined. Maggie is so young and damaged but so keen to be friends and to help. And, if Charlotte's honest, it's so nice to have someone here who seems to want to be with her. To spend time together, to talk intensely about everything. She doesn't want Maggie to feel abandoned. And it's not like she can chuck her out knowing she could be back up on that bridge, or some other bridge, soon after. But she can hardly take her to see Rob.

And the more she thinks about it, the more she needs to see Rob, to set her mind at rest. She needs to see his eyes when she tells him about Anne and the business. Needs to see his apple cheeks and whether they slowly blossom red just like they did when he was a teenager. And when she sees that he isn't involved, which she'll surely see, she really needs a hug.

'Actually, would you mind if I went to see Rob this afternoon?'

Maggie says nothing.

'You can stay here, you don't need to leave or anything. But—' As she's saying it, her mind is wandering through the rooms of her parents' house, the antiques they collected, her mother's jewellery, the various iPads, laptops, her passport, handbags . . . *This girl is a stranger, even if, somehow, she doesn't feel like one.*

'But what?'

'But, um . . . nothing. You can stay here. I just don't know how long I'll be, is all, so if you wanted to go somewhere, I mean I could take you wherever you want to go.'

Maggie smiles a thin, lonely smile that churns Charlotte's insides. She has a look of Anne, back when she was young and desperate, before she built herself into a very different animal.

'I don't have anywhere to go,' she says quietly. 'So I'd like to stay here if that's OK?'

Charlotte nods. She can hardly rescind the offer. Discomfort is probably written on her face but she's stuck now. 'I'll text him back.'

Maggie

Belly still straining in surprise at the big lunch, Maggie rinses plates and passes them to Charlotte to load into the dishwasher.

'I was thinking . . . about while you're at Rob's.'

'Oh?' Charlotte is trying her damnedest but she clearly doesn't want to leave her unoccupied in the house. In every room there is pocketable stuff and it's bound to be worth plenty, given her family business. That's before thinking about identity fraud, bigger-scale stuff. All these letters lying around, probably some old bank cards too. No one really cuts them up and returns them. And she's a total stranger, even if Maggie feels a pull to Charlotte that's so strong it's shocked her. Perhaps she misread the same feeling in Charlotte.

People don't want total strangers picking through their things and trying their life on for size. Even when those strangers have stupidly let themselves fall in love with the house, have felt settled and welcome. Want to stay here forever.

'Well, I had an idea. You know how we didn't find Anne's file of *evidence* at the office.' She's looking across at Charlotte but she doesn't reply.

She tries to keep her voice light, as if she hasn't been building to this one way or another since they were at the showroom, hasn't been trying to find an angle. 'Do you think she took it home with her?'

'Probably,' Charlotte shrugs.

'I could always . . . I mean, you know where she lives, right?'

Charlotte puts the saucepan in the dishwasher and then stands up. 'Of course,' she says cautiously.

'Does she have a house or a flat?'

Charlotte pushes the dishwasher tablet into place, shoves the door shut and presses a button so everything inside rattles and clangs.

'A house, why?' Charlotte wears three antique rings on her fingers, a diamond and two wedding bands, one thick and one thin. She wonders if they belonged to her parents. And how much they're worth. Whether someone who loves their parents would ever part with such artefacts.

'I'm just thinking,' she says, aiming for spontaneous, 'it's Saturday afternoon and most people are out doing stuff.'

'Well, some people might be,' Charlotte says, frowning. She's reminded, briefly, of her own mum. 'But we're not.'

'No, but you will be later and, well, if Anne went out, I could pop in and have a look for the file.'

'Pop in? You mean break into her house?!'

'I guess that's one way to put it but I'm not talking about burgling her!' She can feel her cheeks glowing red. She hates this, but she's bolted onto these tracks now.

'I don't like where this is going,' Charlotte says, her deep brown eyes crinkling as she tries to laugh. 'This is insane, Maggie.'

'I'm just talking about retrieving a bit of paper. It's kind of your property anyway really, when you think about it. It's from your business. And who would know?'

'Anne would know when she goes to get the file on Monday so she can carry on bloody blackmailing me. And if it was taken, she'd know full well that I took it and she'd definitely call the police!'

'But you wouldn't have taken it, would you? I would. And you'd have an alibi 'cos you'd be with Rob. And you could make sure plenty of people saw you go to his house too, go to a shop nearby or something . . .'

'Maggie, this is crazy. Alibis and breaking and entering and—'

'As it stands, you could lose your business if you don't do something. Your *dad's* business. She's obviously very determined.'

Charlotte says nothing.

'And maybe I can't get in or it's not there anyway and you're in the same position but at least you've tried something or—'

Charlotte's eyes take on a haze. Somewhere behind them, she's thinking about it. She's actually considering it.

'Can you access Anne's back garden from the street?'

'I think so but this is ridiculous,' Charlotte says, but her tone is slightly more engaged, slightly less dismissive.

'And does she have a home office or a safe or—'

Charlotte is shaking her head. 'No, this is bonkers. We don't even know if she'll go out today. She doesn't have a lot of other friends and the guy she was seeing broke up with her just before I got back. She could easily be at home.'

'Well, if she is home and I can't get in, so be it. Nothing changes. But if she's out . . .'

'Pretend for a second that I'm up for this plan. And that Anne is out of her house, and that all the planets align . . . How would you sneak into her house without being seen?'

'I don't know without looking. I need to see the road and the neighbours' houses and stuff. What's her address? Let me look at it on Google Maps.'

'This isn't going to happen,' Charlotte says, attempting a light laugh that sounds anything but.

This is it. This moment, this pivot point; god, it's electric. The moment when things change, even before it's happened. She waits, breathing in slowly, calming herself. The eye of the storm.

'Just humour me.'

As Charlotte reads the address from her own phone, she taps it into a draft text for safe keeping. 'Actually, Maps is being really slow on my phone. Can I look at it on yours?'

Charlotte pauses and then hands it over. Maggie looks at the layout of the neighbourhood, the trees lining the road and all the little hiding places. And then she smiles.

Charlotte

Surely she can't even consider this? She looks at Maggie who stares back, child-eyed, awaiting approval of her idea. Was this how Rob felt when Charlotte suggested selling that stuff to her dad? Oscillating between the sure-fire knowledge that it couldn't work, and the exhilarating flicker of possibility that it might.

If Maggie tried to get into Anne's house and it went wrong, that failure could take almost infinite forms. The possibilities refracting like a hall of mirrors: arrests, embarrassment, humiliation, prison. But if it went right, it could only really go right in one way. Maggie would retrieve the paperwork, Charlotte would be able to destroy it, and Anne would have no more cards to play. There'd be nothing to link Maggie to Charlotte, in Anne's mind anyway. Anne could prove nothing and Charlotte could draw a line under it, sack Anne and get the business straight. *Cover everything up.*

'What if you got caught though?' Charlotte asks. 'What would you say?'

'Nothing about you, don't worry. I'd just say . . . I don't know. I'd think of something. It would depend on the circumstances.' She looked up at Charlotte. 'Look at me, even if the worst thing happened and Anne came home and found me inside her house, she's not going to think I'm some hardened criminal. She's more likely to let me run back out like a stray cat than anything else.'

'She'd call the police, anyone would.'

'She's not going to grab me and detain me! I'd just leave.'

'And what about the police?'

'Unless she's got police permanently parked on her driveway, I'd be long gone by the time they arrived.'

Charlotte sighs. They're getting into ludicrous hypotheticals about a situation she surely can't countenance.

'You're thinking of the worst-case scenarios when there's no reason to suppose it wouldn't work out,' Maggie says. 'And you'd be miles away anyway; it's really, in a way, nothing to do with you. In fact—'

Maggie is smiling now, one of her little feet back on the other in that flamingo stance she seems to do when she's thinking. Charlotte thinks again of the little sister she always imagined. How nice it is to be helped by a keen, sweet girl. '—how about this. You've told me the address now, and you've mentioned the paperwork. You don't need to give me permission, you don't need to make this decision at all. If you can just do me a favour and give me a lift to Bath, what I do while I'm there is my business, yeah?'

'Um, I guess.'

'Can I have a lift to Bath please, Charlotte?' Maggie's eyes twinkle.

'And you're not going to tell me what you're doing while you're there?'

'Exactly.'

Charlotte breathes out slowly. There is only one good outcome, and so many bad, but that one . . . it would change everything.

'OK,' she says, knowing she shouldn't but unable to resist the sliver of hope. 'I'll give you a lift to Bath.'

'Oh god, this is mental,' Charlotte mutters, indicating to turn onto the road parallel to Anne's.

'Remember, you're just giving me a lift, nothing more,' Maggie says.

When Charlotte looks back on this scene in the car, it will

be grainy and historical. A reel of footage watched a million hopeful times over, the finale of which never changes.

She will reanimate it carefully, colouring it in with a delicate hand. Flecking Maggie's eyes with a cat's green, painting her hair the colour of fresh blood and her skin as pale as the foam on last night's river. And when she has edited it, when she has tied it in a firm knot along with all the scenes that followed, this moment will be epic. The start of something cataclysmic. Something diabolical.

But right now, living this for the first time, she is driving up and down looking for a space, with a stranger who feels like a sister. *Maggie wants to do it, so let her try.*

They lock eyes and, for a brief moment, there is nothing but that. An instant understanding that this is crossing a line but they're going to do it anyway. Then the silence dissolves and the whoosh of the engine comes back to the fore, along with the chatter of birds and the low rumble of nearby traffic.

'It's pretty fancy around here,' Maggie says, breaking the spell. 'She must have a fair bit of money.'

'Yeah, but I'm not sure how,' Charlotte says. 'She certainly wasn't well off at school.'

Elegant Georgian houses sit a respectable distance from each other, their manicured hedges and freshly painted gates like silent sentries. Shiny 4x4s and low-slung saloons are tucked demurely on driveways, but the road is still lined with parked cars.

'Stop there,' Maggie says, pointing to a narrow space. 'There's an alleyway just up here that cuts through to the next road.'

'How do you know that?'

'I memorised the map,' Maggie says and then smiles. 'I've got a good memory for details.'

Charlotte pulls over and shuffles her way between two big saloon cars. She stops the engine but keeps her hands on the wheel, turning in her seat to face Maggie who is still carefully scanning the pavement. There's no one on the street and no one watching from the nearby windows, so shiny they look like mirrors.

'What if Anne doesn't leave her house this afternoon?' Charlotte says, the holes in the plan growing bigger the more she picks at them.

'Ssh. You're just giving me a lift,' Maggie says, her bottom lip jutting out just briefly.

'Why don't we just go back to mine and have a rethink? Or just watch a film or something, go for a walk or—'

'Stop panicking,' Maggie says, her eyes shining. 'And besides, you've agreed to see Rob.'

Charlotte stares through the windscreen. She should drive away right now. She should abort this stupid plan. But Maggie is so keen to help, so shiny with optimism compared to the flat, devastated girl she plucked off the bridge last night. No one has ever done something so bold, so brave, for Charlotte before. She swallows down a lump. They swap numbers, the first new number Charlotte has added to her phone in a long time.

'You'd better get going,' Maggie says, unbuckling her seatbelt and meeting Charlotte's eyes. 'And just let me do this for you, OK?'

'This is a lot to do for a stranger.'

'You're not a stranger any more,' Maggie says. 'And consider it payback for saving my life.'

Charlotte doesn't say anything; she scans the street but it's still filmset empty. For a moment, she imagines a lighting rig overhead, a boom just out of shot. None of this feels real.

'I'll call when I need collecting,' Maggie says, opening the door. 'And have a nice time with Rob.' She smiles but Charlotte catches her thin wrist as she climbs out.

'Are you really sure about this?'

Maggie nods and leans back in quickly and kisses Charlotte's cheek. 'You saved my life. And besides, you're just giving me a lift,' she says, squeezing Charlotte's arm. And then she's out of the car and slipping into the alleyway that leads to Anne's road. As she watches her go, Charlotte has no idea what she's just started.

★

It takes half an hour to boomerang back to Rob's place, just a few miles' drive from her own. He still lives in Little Wickton, where he grew up which is no surprise, because – unlike Charlotte and Anne – he was in no rush to leave. It's a working village: pretty but not touristy. Unlike Charlotte's village, which has an Instagrammable tea shop and tiny boutique, Rob's village is made up of farms and small businesses, a no-frills pub and a bike repair shop that operates out of a living room. Most of the companies are owned by Rob's relatives.

The Parsons are a family of sprawl. Of brother-cousins and step-aunties and houses passed around numerous branches of the family. As a result, half the village seems to have variations of the same face, and, at any one time, another member of the family could let themselves in to any of the others' houses. They're not exactly village royalty – some have fallen foul of the law a few too many times for that – but there's a rogue-ish nobility to the determined spread of the genes.

On paper, Charlotte loves the intimacy of a big family, that sense of familial community that only children of single-child parents can imagine. Had at one time pestered for. In reality, she finds it annoying to never know who she'll bump into in the night on the way to the loo. A cousin that's let themselves in after a row with their wife or a mishap on the way home from the pub. Cole, hiding from someone or other.

Rob takes his family at face value, will take anyone he loves at face value, in fact, and will calmly and resolutely refuse to think badly of them. That has to be a good thing.

Today, though, as she pulls up outside the two-bedroom cottage that he rents from an uncle and tucks her Tesla behind his work truck, there's not a soul about. She thinks about Maggie right now, skulking like an adolescent, waiting for an opportunity to steal into Anne's house and save Charlotte's skin.

And you could make sure plenty of people saw you . . . go to a shop nearby or something . . .

Charlotte doesn't knock on Rob's door yet, instead walks down the main street and into the post office slash village stores. She takes some cash out at the little ATM in the wall, the one that was TSB when she first lived around here, and then she goes into the shop.

'Alright, maid?' One of Rob's cousins, or maybe second cousins, has looked up from the magazine she was reading behind the till. Charlotte can't remember her name, knew her as a child from family barbecues and village fetes.

'Hi there,' she says, glad to have been seen. 'I didn't know you worked here?'

'For my sins.' The young woman smiles, then looks back at her weekly. Charlotte grabs a nearby box of Cherry Bakewells.

Rob opens up the same way he always does: slowly, with a slight smile. She pushes the box of tarts towards him and he looks at them with amusement. 'OK,' he laughs and then leans down to kiss her. He smells, somehow, like he always has. Although when they first met he used Lynx body spray and now he uses an aftershave bought for him by his ex, via his daughter, for Father's Day. But his core smell, a peppery undertone that is all his, has never changed.

She follows him inside, leans against the kitchen counter as he fills the electric kettle. His hands look huge on the handle and she feels a pang of something like pity, even though he's the most easily pleased person she knows. He has everything he ever said he wanted: a home in his childhood village, a gardening business, a daughter. *And* – she dares herself to think – *me*.

Charlotte should be content too, albeit it while tinged with grief, because she has the two things she always thought she wanted: her whole life she tried to get in on her family business, to prove that she had the chops; and to have Rob back, when she thought she'd lost him forever. Isn't that special? Rob was the one who got away. The one to whom she would always compare other men, sometimes using him less as a benchmark and more as a guillotine.

Of course, Rob was oblivious to this for all those years. While she was sizing up other guys and placing an imaginary Polaroid next to them, its picture showing a photofit of how she imagined Rob to be at that time, he was getting married, having a baby, getting divorced. But doesn't she, just slightly, compare real Rob to the Rob she'd turned him into over time?

But if he's not the man in the Polaroid then maybe she'd made stupid mistakes, maybe let other good men go, for what? So he must be the man in the Polaroid. This must be her happy ever after.

Rob plucks two mismatched mugs from a mug tree she vaguely remembers from his mum's house and then smiles. The kind of uncomplicated smile that always felt like coming home, both as a teenager whose own brain always seemed such a desperate knot and then as a grieving, listless adult. But is this contentment an act? Does he want more? Or has he got himself in trouble somehow?

The window is open slightly and a breeze flaps the childish drawings Blu-Tacked to the fridge. A gallery in which he takes great pride.

'I know every parent says this, but I really think she's got talent,' he says and Charlotte nods, not having a clue what is and isn't normal for a nine-year-old to produce. And besides, her parents' default setting was never to boast that she had talent. Her mother had talent once, she was aware of that. Pamela had gone to an impressive art college and got featured in culture magazines with her graduation show, but that was the only talent acknowledged. And it was always past tense.

Charlotte walks through to the little living room and sits down heavily on the sofa. It's all too much, this pretence of normality when the last twenty-four hours have been anything but normal.

This sofa has had years of use and dips comfortingly. Her own sofa is far older, but it's an antique Chesterfield worth over five grand. Hardly the same.

In the kitchen, the kettle spits and rattles on its base, a thin crack running down the edge that worries her every time she uses it. Rob drops teabags in the mugs and then turns to her, arms outstretched and gesturing for her to come back to the kitchen and hug him. 'What are you doing all the way over there?' he says. 'Give me some sugar.'

She walks over, thinks about lifting the mismatched sugar pot and making a joke, but she can't muster a smile let alone a stupid gag. She just can't act like everything is OK. Can't keep cool. Can't ask nicely. Can't hug him. Can't, can't, can't.

'Did you know that Anne was planning to blackmail me?' she says.

The kettle clicks off like the tut of a tongue.

Maggie

This is the second rich woman's orbit she's entered in the last forty-eight hours, and both of them have been cavalier about their personal safety. First Charlotte picking up strangers from the roadside and now this Anne with her single-lock front door and slide-up sash windows.

If she was so minded, Maggie could probably slip through a side window right now and steal the key fob for that two-seater Mercedes parked invitingly on the weedless driveway. But that's not her style.

A thick tree hides her from Anne's side of the road but she'll have to be careful that she doesn't look dodgy to the houses on this side either. People who live in houses like this are probably too riveted by their own interiors to look out much, but, if they do, they'll immediately see that she doesn't belong.

The house nearest to her is called Avondale Villa. She thinks of her mother's house growing up. How she gave it a name even though it officially had a number. Never happy with her own reality.

She fiddles with her phone, keeping her face turned down towards the screen but looking up through her lashes, checking for movement from Anne's place or a twitch of an enquiring neighbourhood curtain. Those bridge hours were good practise for this. The kind of zen acceptance of boredom that can come from standing in the freezing cold, reflecting on your life and how you messed it up.

In the distance, she sees a small red Fiesta turning slowly into the road. It crawls along, zigzagging slightly, as if the driver is looking for a parking space. Anyone can see that it isn't owned by a resident. Part of one door has been replaced with a dull grey panel, and, as it coughs closer, puffs of grey smoke growl from its exhaust. Her heart beats faster.

The car chugs past her tree and she curls herself tight into the bark, squinting to see the face of the driver, to check his expression. He reaches the other end of the road and swings around fast. Then the car rolls back almost sarcastically slow as it approaches her. As it pulls in behind a Lexus, engine snapping off like the end of an argument, she moves.

The gate of Anne's house swings open easily and she runs towards the front door. It's fringed in wisteria like a miniature manor house. She looks for a bell but instead finds a door knocker in the shape of a ballerina. She pulls a bent knee of the delicate dancer, hitting the door with it over and again until it swings open sharply.

'Hello?'

The woman speaks with a faint American accent, like a Hollywood actress playing a British person. Her bobbed hair is so shiny it looks wet, her perfectly made-up face like something from a YouTube video. She's tall, model tall.

So this is Anne.

Maggie looks up, feeling every bit a child compared to this elegant, tall woman, and making the most of that. She softens her voice, raises the pitch to pre-pubescent. 'Please help me.'

Anne stares down at her. 'Help you? What's going on?'

'Please, there's a man following me, he—'

'Do you know him?' Anne asks suspiciously, craning her neck to look out onto the road.

'Kind of. He's been stalking me, he's hurt me before and—'

'Oh god, I'm not getting involved in this. Just call the police.'

Maggie wedges her foot into the door frame and opens her eyes as wide as they'll go. 'Please, *please!* My phone is out of charge and I don't have any friends in Bath. I just need to get off the street until he's gone. Please, you can call the police for me if you like but—'

She has the stature of a child, a practised look of innocence and vulnerability. There is no way that Anne sees her as a threat. The pause comes from irritation, not fear. In the background, she hears another front door open. Neighbours?

'OK, alright, stop pleading.' Anne looks around, embarrassed. Whoever opened a neighbouring door hasn't appeared yet. 'You can come in for a minute, just come in quickly.'

'You're an angel.' She sees Anne's eyes soften as she holds the door wider.

Charlotte

'Anne's planning to *what*?'

Rob actually laughs. A sharp shock of sound. But his neck creeps red and he frowns as he turns to Charlotte, kettle abandoned.

'Anne's trying to blackmail me.' The ridiculous words squeak out of her, like someone's trodden on a dog toy. He pulls her into him, still looking utterly confused. As he hugs her tight, she feels his heart booming along. It's not racing guiltily like he's been caught out, nothing about him suggests

64

guilt, it's just a fierce steady rhythm. She sinks into him more, lets a few hot tears leak out.

'She's trying to take my dad's business from under me,' she says, her voice muffled by the fabric of his T-shirt and his thick meaty body beneath it.

They sit at his small kitchen table, its scattering of Lego pieces and colouring pencils a reminder of this other world Rob inhabits. She tells the story, the parts he needs to know anyway, watching as his placid face grows angrier and angrier. He doesn't doubt her, not once. Even though Anne is his friend too. She is dizzy with gratitude for that, and guilty for doubting him.

'She's a duplicitous bitch, in other words,' Charlotte says, by way of finale.

He winces and she remembers how he used to hate it when she swore. Some old-fashioned notion inherited from his dad, alongside his blue eyes and the shape of his nose. Something he would deny when asked, but then mention in relation to other people. 'She's not very ladylike,' he'd mutter about a 'ladette' on TV, and Charlotte would sit there in her school uniform agog, taking the piss. 'Alright, Grandad!'

Clearly the aversion has outlasted the Lynx spray and posters of Carmen Electra. His prudishness is not something she'd focused on when she was remembering him fondly all those years. It didn't make it onto the Polaroid.

'So, what are you going to do?' he says. He didn't ask if she's sure, if maybe she misunderstood. A thought, almost out of view, darkens her vision. Did he suspect Anne was capable of this? Does he know something after all? She blinks it away.

'Charlie,' he says again, 'what are you going to do now?' She shrugs and looks away. She can hardly tell him about Maggie, about her batshit plan to steal back the evidence and then . . . what?

'I'm not giving in to her, that's all I know,' she says.

He's pacing now, thinking, his big hands tugging at his hair. 'Can't you just sack her?'

She shakes her head. 'No. I can't just sack her for no reason, she could take me to a tribunal or something—'

'But she's made false documents and stuff, she's trying to blackmail you!'

Charlotte pauses. 'My dad never let me near the business, you know that. So I can't be a hundred per cent sure that he didn't . . .' she feels a pang; can she expose his memory like this? 'I don't know how good an idea it is to get the police crawling all over the company. And I shouldn't have to go to the police about my friend!'

At that he stands up angrily. It's so rare for him to lose his temper that she shrinks in her chair. 'No, this isn't happening,' he says, nostrils flaring. 'She needs to drop this, this . . .' he gropes desperately for the word. 'This campaign! That's what it is, she's trying to take your business off you and it's not bloody on.'

'And why me?' Charlotte asks, more to herself than him. 'Why my business? Anne reckons she's been successful, made some money; why doesn't she start her own company? Why is she so fixed on getting my dad's?'

Rob opens his mouth but closes it again, turns away and starts refilling the kettle. His cheeks are pink.

'What is it?' she says, unease swilling in her gut.

He shakes his head. 'Nothing. Do you want another tea?'

'No, no thank you. What's going on?'

He turns to face her, opens his mouth again but avoids her eye. 'It's nothing. Just . . . nothing.' He looks up then, gestures to the ceiling, the way they always did as teens – embarrassed to use the words but not to do the act – then reaches for her hand.

'I should go,' she says half an hour later, her voice muffled by the duvet, the smell of them all around.

'Can't you stay?' Rob murmurs. 'We could have dinner and you could sleep over? We could come up with a plan together.'

It's tempting to just pull the covers over her head and hide here. To pretend that nothing was happening in Bath. That her oldest friend wasn't now her enemy. That she didn't have a new and immediately adored friend doing unspeakable things for her.

But she can't.

She kisses the soft warm skin on his side, the same soft skin she first touched twenty years ago.

Charlotte slides out from the covers into the muted orange of the room, curtains pulled haphazardly in a rush. She pulls her clothes back on, feeling his gaze on her and trying not to rush, not to cover herself with her hands in a panic. Both their bodies have changed, it's OK.

'I should never have suggested she work with you,' he says.

'It's not your fault,' she says. Glad to find that she really means it.

'I should have thought it through properly. It's just like Deb always complained, that I take people at their word. But that's normally the best way. Especially when I've known them half my life.'

She stops buttoning up her jeans. 'What do you mean?'

He sits up so that the duvet slips down over his chest. A barrel where there used to be a xylophone of ribs.

'It wasn't my idea, not really. Anne was asking how it was going for you and I said it wasn't going that well—'

'You did?'

'I mean, you found it hard by yourself, didn't you? There was a lot you wanted to get on with. And she said that you needed someone with more business experience to do the heavy lifting.' He breathes out and closes his eyes. 'And she said that she'd like to help but that you'd probably be too proud if she asked directly.'

'What?'

'I'm sorry if it was the wrong thing but, honestly, I didn't think she had bad intentions. If anything, I thought she just wanted to be close to—'

'You're sorry if *what* was the wrong thing, Rob?'

'It wasn't my idea to suggest she work for your company, it was hers. She told me exactly what to say. Word for word.'

67

He swallows, looking every inch the embarrassed teenager with a box of stolen tat. 'I thought I was doing the right thing.'

Maggie

The door closes after them and she's swallowed by the chic hallway. She's asked to take off her shoes and bends to slip them off at the heel without undoing the laces. It's a habit that drove her mother to distraction, and one which she's pointedly stuck to ever since she left home. But Charlotte's borrowed trainers are too large so her feet swim about in them, making her gait a bit seasick. It'll be a relief to take them off but she wobbles on the spot, yanking at them. Anne looks on, unimpressed.

She's ushered into what she assumes is a formal living room. Two small green sofas face each other in the centre of the room. A spray of magazines lie on a glass table. There's no TV. Through the thick white shutters, she watches as he prowls along the street, getting closer.

'Could I trouble you for some water?' she asks, her voice as childlike as she dares to make it. Another leftover habit. With most women, this seems to tap into a latent pool of motherly instinct, or at least a drummed-in obligation to care. It's what got her in the door, it's what's got her through many doors – literal and figurative – but Anne's nose wrinkles; she's maybe overdone it this time. 'OK, I'll get you a drink in a minute but I'd like to know what's really going on first. Who is that guy outside my house?'

She starts to tell the story. About David and the betting shop, the attack and the photos and the wedding. But a few beats in, Anne holds up a palm and shakes her head so firmly her hair shimmers. 'Forget it, this is sounding more and more like a soap opera.' Anne smiles, as if she's joking, but her grey eyes don't look amused. 'I'll get you that glass of water.'

As soon as the door swings softly closed, Maggie starts to search the room. A filing cabinet wouldn't belong in a room like this but some kind of fancy basket or a document portfolio is possible. She squats down to check one alcove cupboard after another. They're all empty. Completely empty, not even troubled with dust. It's like a shell, a show home, and she creeps back to the window with a sense of unease just as Anne comes back.

'Here you go.' It's a tall tumbler, no doubt one from an expensive set, but it contains cloudy tap water. She takes the glass gratefully nonetheless and drains it fast, taking care not to burp. 'Thank you so much,' she says, wiping her chin.

'Is that guy still out there?' Anne peeks through the slats with obvious cynicism but then she clocks his heft and the way he's loitering purposelessly on the pavement. Her stance thaws and she even reaches out a hand but lets it fall before it connects. 'Would you like to use my phone to call the police?' Anne asks, more softly now.

'It will make it worse.'

'You've tried before?' Anne's tone hints at an understanding.

'Yeah, they said it was his word against mine.'

'Really?'

'Yeah. Really.' She pauses and lifts her tone. 'Your house is beautiful, by the way. Did you decorate it yourself?'

Anne looks around as if appraising it for the first time then gives her hair another bob-shimmering shake. 'God no. I wouldn't have chosen any of this bougie junk.' Her accent is more pronounced when she's showing off. 'It's just a rental.'

'Oh, are you new to the area?'

Anne frowns and looks at her, then looks out of the window carefully. 'What did you say your name was?'

'Oh, I don't think I did. It's Jane.'

'Jane, a little pro tip. When you worm your way into someone's house in the middle of the day asking for salvation, don't start grilling your saviour, OK?'

'Oh god, I'm sorry. I ramble when I'm nervous.'

Anne stares a moment longer then her shoulders fall and she sits carefully on one of the sofas and indicates for Maggie to sit on the other.

'Sorry,' Anne says, 'I'm just a bit . . . stressed. Work stuff, you know.' She smiles apologetically. 'I'm not new to the area, no, but I was working away for a while and I stupidly came back for a man.' She rolls her eyes. 'What a cliché.'

'This is his place?' This is news to her. Charlotte gave no indication that someone else could show up. She pats her phone in her pocket, wondering if she could send a text but remembering that she told Anne her phone battery was dead.

'No.' Anne makes the word longer, sadder, than usual. 'No, this was just going to be where I stayed until he got his . . .' she trails off.

'Ducks in a row?'

'Shit together.'

Maggie laughs then. She hadn't meant to. Didn't want to like Anne, but no one is ever just one thing and she isn't just a blackmailer.

'So what happened?'

'He . . .' Anne seems distracted. She leans across the little table. 'It just didn't work out. Hey, where did you get that necklace from?'

Maggie's hand slides to cover it defensively; she thought it was hidden. 'It was my mum's.'

Anne moves closer and gently cups the pendant in her hand. 'It's my job you see, antiques.'

'Oh?' Maggie says, trying to calm her heartbeat and failing.

'Yeah,' Anne says, staring intently at the ruby that Maggie now strongly regrets stealing from one of the bedrooms while Charlotte was in the shower. Regretting even more pulling it out of her pocket and slipping it on – for luck – when Charlotte's car drove away.

'It's an expensive piece, I think.'

Maggie shrugs. 'It's got sentimental value, that's all that matters to me.' Anne stares at it a moment longer and then lets it sit back down against Maggie's borrowed jumper.

'I'm not an expert, but my . . .' she trails off. 'Anyway, what about you?' Anne asks, her eyes still on Maggie's neckline. 'What line of work are you in?'

'I'm an actress. Well, I mean I did work in a betting shop like I said but I'd like to be an actress. One day.'

'I see. Well, good luck with that.' Anne smiles and Maggie knows she's being humoured but she doesn't care, she's acting the hell out of this scene no matter what anyone thinks. She's nailing it.

Don't get cocky, she hears a familiar voice say. *That's when mistakes happen.*

She swallows and looks at the empty glass. 'I shouldn't have drunk all that,' she says, with a self-deprecating laugh. 'I'm busting for the loo now.'

Anne doesn't say anything, she's looking at Maggie's neck again, her head slightly cocked to one side and her mouth twisting in thought.

'Can I please use your toilet?'

'Yeah, sure,' Anne says distractedly. 'Use the one upstairs as I need to change the towels in there anyway.'

'Thank you.'

'Top of the stairs, on the right.'

As she leaves, she imagines Anne's eyes beating on her back like noonday sun. When she turns quickly in the doorway though, Anne is looking out of the window. One finger hooked through the slats, looking for him.

Upstairs, the house feels cold. Even in Charlotte's borrowed socks, her footsteps on the wooden floor echo in the emptiness.

Through an open door she sees a perfectly made bed with matching white linen, standing adrift in the middle of a master suite.

71

She pokes her head further into the room. It's almost empty. A wardrobe, a chest of drawers with a framed photo on it, and the tail of a phone charger lying on the carpet. Nothing else. Certainly no folder of papers. She glances again at the framed photo as she leaves, wondering if that was the man Anne mentioned. The man who never got his shit together. He's not what she was expecting. Anne seemed more likely to go for a slick male model type than this.

She reaches the bathroom, then pauses to listen. No one is coming so she pads past to check the next room. Finally, somewhere promising. There's a small desk in here, presumably a 'bougie' one that came with the house. Three cardboard box files are stacked on it haphazardly and a pile of unopened mail threatens to slide on to the floor. She listens out then steps inside and opens the first file. Inside, there are bank statements and bills and she flips through, but finds nothing about Charlotte or her company. She places it down as carefully as she can.

The next file seems to relate to this house, and she's surprised to see a familiar name on the contract as a guarantor. C. Wilderwood. She thought Charlotte moved back after Anne already lived here. Maybe Anne faked it? That would fit with the long con, wouldn't it?

She thinks about taking photos on her phone but time is a factor and she's already pushing it. She lowers the file and picks up the next.

This looks more like it, although it's hard to be sure. There are bank statements in the name of Wilderwood Antiques. Bank statements with surprisingly high numbers. And invoices too, some with red pen on them, question marks and circles.

She closes the file and then lowers it gingerly, as if it might be booby trapped, her jumper sleeves pulled down over her fingertips.

Downstairs, she thinks she hears the squeak of a door. She freezes. Perhaps Anne is taking the rubbish out. But then just outside the office, she hears cautious footsteps approaching. She lowers the file and ducks down behind the desk, which barely covers her. Anne steps inside, her voice uneasy.

'Jane?'

Charlotte

How long has Anne been planning this? From the moment Rob mentioned the business to her or before? Is this why Anne looked Rob up, as a potential route to Charlotte?

'How long was Anne back before I came home?' she asks him. His cheeks are flushed and he looks more like his younger self than ever. She can picture him sweating and begging her dad not to call the police.

'I don't know, not long,' he says. 'A few months? I don't know exactly when you got back.'

'And you immediately started hanging out with her? Talking about me?' She can't help it, she sounds shrill, judgemental.

'I . . . well, I mean, we'd seen each other a few times over the years. We're old school friends, aren't we? Surely you saw her too?'

'I never even saw you, Rob. When would I have seen Anne? We . . . we fell out just before you and I broke up, remember? Anyway, I didn't see her until I moved back and you suggested it. I didn't think you got on with Anne at school; she certainly didn't like you very much.'

'Charlie, I think you're reading too much into this and now you're getting nasty. I didn't see Anne a lot or anything, but she used to come back to see her parents sometimes over the years and we'd occasionally hang out.'

'Hang out?'

'Never like that. God, Charlie!'

'Sorry, I just . . . there's this whole relationship I didn't know was happening.'

'It wasn't a relationship. She was . . . an acquaintance, a mate. Nothing more. I was married for most of that time and she met Deb. She came to see Ruby as a baby!'

Charlotte raises her eyebrows, trying to stop her eyes filling with tears.

2010

Charlotte hadn't had the money for the train back to Somerset, but she'd put it on her credit card. Several years of experience had taught her that even a maxed-out Mastercard will normally go through on one of the portable ticket machines the conductors carry. It had been touch and go, the machine chugging and whirring and, for a moment, she thought she'd have to get off at the next station, talk her way out of a fine. But eventually the tickets were spat out, folded up and handed over.

Charlotte tried not to think about the extra fee for going over her credit limit, focused instead on seeing this trip as an investment. It was harder and harder to plead for a bit of cash over the phone, but her dad wouldn't be able to say no in person. He never could. It was just a loan though, she was emphatic about that. One day she'd pay him back.

It cost a fortune to live in London on a starter salary; before you'd even got up in the morning your rent had wiped out half your pay. It turned out that there wasn't a huge demand for people with a history of decorative arts degree and no real world experience. Her dad didn't believe you could learn good business from books, so a business degree wouldn't have impressed him. But she'd wanted to prove that she should be a part of the company and thought knowing all about eras and styles would help. Then she'd graduated and there was still no job for her at Wilderwood Antiques. She'd huffed off to London, hurt, and slid into a series of by-the-hour temp jobs.

And by now she was having to pay the whole rent by herself since her flatmate had left her in the lurch. They'd seemed to be fast friends, getting on famously in the first few weeks, setting up washing rotas and taking it in turns to cook. But Charlotte had been too intense, she'd realised too late. And the more that Susie, a PA working in EC1, had backed away, the more Charlotte had pressed on the bruise. 'Beg-a-mate' was always there, just below the surface.

She rested her cheek against the window, the steady motion of the train rattling her cheekbones. As the train finally pulled into Bath Spa, she spotted that it was her mum rather than her dad standing on the platform, arms crossed.

'I wanted to pick you up,' her mum said, as they drove back to the cottage.

'Why?'

There was a pause that, if it was anyone else, Charlotte might have interpreted as sad. Hurt. But this was her mum. She didn't do hurt; she did spiky.

'There's something I wanted to tell you, and Dad's not . . . this isn't Dad's area of expertise.'

Charlotte slid around in her seat to face her mum. Her dark hair had a more definite line of grey along the roots, her brown eyes were set deeper, fresh wrinkles surrounding them.

'Are you ill?' she asked quietly, and then a worse thought gripped her. 'Is Dad ill?'

'No.' Her mum half-smiled, an accidental display of relief. 'No, it's nothing like that, but I bumped into Robert Parsons' mum recently.'

Charlotte shifted in her seat, faced the road again. 'Oh?'

'I just thought you should know that Robert's getting married.'

She swallowed. 'Why would you tell me that?' Then she burst into tears while her mother drove in silence.

She got the requested money from her dad but even her mum would have given it to her this time. Anything to stop her haunting the house with her tears and her silence. It was only as she was packing her bag to head back to London on the Sunday night that she finally acted. She hid her red eyes as best she could with make-up, pulled on her most flattering jeans, held in her belly as she turned this way and that in the mirror, then borrowed her mum's Volvo without asking, and drove to Rob's village.

She couldn't just . . . not. She couldn't just go back to London without even trying. Without even telling him that she missed him like a limb. That no one else fit. That her heart still beat for his, and she would still give up anyone and everything for him. She was not thinking about this girl he'd said he'd marry. Not thinking about the seven years they'd been apart, and how much he could have changed even if she hadn't. She wasn't thinking about the realities of trying to mesh together two totally separate lives. All she was thinking was that Charlotte Wilderwood and Rob Parsons belonged together and that was just fucking final.

She parked by the duck pond and popped open the door. She knew he'd moved into his cousin Nigel's old place – her dad had let that slip – and she headed up Church Street to look for it. As she walked, she remembered to stand upright, hoiked her bra straps up and tried to suck her gut into place.

She got closer and just knowing his body was nearby started the electricity building in her own like a kind of madness. She found the right door, the same place they'd come to a couple of times as teenagers to smoke weed with Nigel and Cole, which she'd never enjoyed. Rob did it because Nigel and Cole did it and Charlotte did it because Rob did it. She'd thrown up in the garden she was now standing in more than once.

The front door was right there but Charlotte paused. This was it. This was what she should have done years ago, but it's never too late. She checked her armpits quickly, did a breath test into her cupped hand, and then started towards the door.

It opened before she reached it. The woman in the doorway cocking her head to one side. 'Can I help you?'

Charlotte swallowed and looks down at the small bump on the woman's stomach and the way her hand went to it protectively, even though Charlotte was clearly not dangerous.

'Oh,' Charlotte managed. 'Um. I was looking for Nigel.'

The woman smiled in relief, pulling the door closed behind her as she stepped out fully. 'He moved out. Me and his cousin live here now. Nigel's up on Temple Street, do you know it?'

'Yeah,' Charlotte managed. 'Thanks.'

She cried all the way back to London.

Now

Could Maggie be in Anne's house right now? Breaking and entering, stealing documents. Would anyone believe Charlotte had just dropped her off, that she didn't 'sanction' the plan? Her stomach flips. *Am I an accessory to theft? A conspirator?* Her mouth fills with saliva and nausea sweeps up her body.

What am I doing?

'Are you angry?' Rob asks, misreading her expression.

'About you doing Anne's bidding?' she says, swallowing the nausea away.

He looks away, hurt.

'No,' she says. She's not angry with him. She feels sick about it all but she's not angry. If anything, she's relieved about what he's told her. Rob wasn't in cahoots with Anne, he was just her stooge. He has always been too trusting and he probably always will be. A slight warning bell rings in the back of her head; *do you really want to have to do all his thinking for him?* But that's a thought for another day.

She climbs up the bed again on her knees until she's straddling him, feeling faintly ridiculous to be fully dressed compared to his nudity. 'I really am going to go,' she says, kissing him again. 'And I'm not angry. I'll call you later, yeah?'

'I thought you had plans?'

'I do, but I can make time for a call.'

'Don't worry,' he says. 'Let's speak tomorrow. Or do you fancy a roast? Lunch in the pub? My treat?'

'That would be lovely. But halves at least,' she says, mindful that his money is always tight. Another warning bell, ignored.

Maggie

Her legs almost give way as she scrambles for the door, crunching into the desk on her way out. She glances back at Anne, just quickly, her fingers gripping the folder.

'I'm so sorry,' she whispers. 'I didn't mean for this to happen . . .' It's meaningless, trite, and it dies in her throat.

She is trapped. She can hear him in the house, making his way around it as if he owns the place, whistling. It's a horrendous, familiar tune that she will hear in her sleep. She listens hard and then closes her eyes, calculates where to go, what to do. Now all the theoreticals she's been playing with lie in tatters like children's toys.

What were you thinking, leading him here, she thinks. *You were never one step ahead of anything*.

He's in the nearby bathroom now, pissing into Anne's glossy toilet. Maggie should run but her legs are trembling so fast she struggles to control them. She hears a tap, gushing lustily, no effort to be quiet. It's like he's toying with her. Any second and he'll be back out in the hallway, heading right this way. She casts one more look at Anne, her face now permanently frozen in horror. No longer a threat to Charlotte. No longer anything to anyone.

'What have I done?'

Then she runs.

Charlotte

Charlotte takes the A roads, unable to face the cut and thrust of motorway traffic. It's four o'clock now so it's been a couple of hours since she dropped Maggie at the side of the leafy road. 'You're just giving me a lift,' Maggie had reminded her. It makes sense that she's not messaged with updates, not if they're maintaining this farce. But Charlotte still would have expected a call asking to be picked up by now.

Maybe her phone is out of battery. She was certainly tapping away on it a lot earlier. 'Mindless scrolling.' Maggie had shrugged and flipped the phone screen away when she'd seen Charlotte looking. 'A bad habit.' Though what she'd been scrolling through was anyone's guess as she'd said she's not on social media. 'Not even Facebook?' Charlotte had asked and Maggie had laughed, making Charlotte feel horrendously old. She thinks bitterly of how she'd hovered over Anne's name on there for years, never connecting. She should have left it that way.

Charlotte watches her speed; there's no rush but her adrenaline is coursing nonetheless. Thinking about Maggie and Anne, rerunning the conversation with Rob and feeling a cautious relief that he was just a pawn in Anne's plan but a cold fear about the business. What is Anne's actual end game here? Charlotte has called it blackmail, but has Anne already shown her full hand or does she have something else tucked up her sleeve? Is getting Charlotte out of the way and taking the reins, 'cleaning up' enough for her? How long would the promise of Charlotte's salary remain in place? How the hell would that even work? Could this whole mess be just the beginning?

Her phone vibrates as she slows to enter the village of Wick. It's a withheld number but when she answers on speakerphone, Maggie's desperate voice cries out.

'Charlotte? Is that you?'

'Yes, it's me, are you OK?'

Maggie says nothing but her ragged breathing seems to swirl from the speakers and all around the car.

'What's going on? You're scaring me.'

'Please come and get me.'

'What's happened?'

'Please, I need you.' Her voice is strangled, the words forcing their way through sobs. The same voice Maggie used as they clung together on that bridge, seconds after cheating death.

'I'm coming,' she says, heart beating faster. 'Are you still outside the house?'

'I'm a few streets away, I'm . . . I don't know exactly, I can't see straight, I can't—'

'OK, take a deep breath. Don't worry, OK? Right, do you remember that park we passed on the way, Alice Park?'

'Um.' It's more breath than word.

'Maggie, please, you need to focus. It's the big park about ten minutes from where I dropped you, if you follow the main road. Alice Park, OK? Just use your phone map.'

'I'll find it,' Maggie pants. 'But please hurry, I'm really scared.'

'Scared? Oh god,' Charlotte lowers her voice. 'Why are you scared? Did she see you?'

The call shuts off.

Maggie

She walks slowly, willing her legs to work. Every curtain seems to twitch, everyone who walks past stares at her as if she has something foul written across her face. She tries to shrink, to stay close to the parked cars and slip into the shadows.

In a carrier bag taken from Anne's kitchen, the file and photo frame bash into her leg. Her fingers tremble so violently that she drops the bag, scrambling quickly to make sure nothing falls out.

She's desperate to see Charlotte now, desperate to be back in the safety of her cottage. And trying desperately to make sense of what just happened.

She's rolled the right cuff of the mustard jumper several times. She rolls the other cuff up, knowing it's important not to stand out more than she already does. Anything, any tiny detail like mismatched cuffs, could be enough to plant a picture of her in someone's mind. Someone who could be standing behind one of these big picture windows right now or sitting in their expensive car ready to drive away, wondering about that terrified girl who has no right to be here.

It's taking every bit of blood in her body to keep her legs moving in the right direction; there's barely any left to power her brain. These calculations she's having to make are exhausting. Shameful.

What have we done?

She manages to find her way to the main road, remembering snatches of the journey that brought her here, then finally catching sight of a couple of signposts to Alice Park, reassuring her she was heading in the right direction. The thought of Charlotte heading to her gives her a brief swell of warmth, but there's something she needs to do first.

Maggie stops and tucks off the road and down an empty footpath. She checks she's not being watched and pulls out the photo frame. It takes several attempts to unclip it, her hands shaking so much that she slices her finger against the glass and has to suck the blood away, eyes stinging with pain.

She's done this many times with old frames picked up to sell, but this is opposite to those times. Instead of pulling out old photos and chucking them away, this time she teases the photo out carefully and then pushes the frame into the nearby rubbish bin, under some bags of dog shit.

She rolls the photo up carefully and slides it into her waistband, unsure when or if to show it to Charlotte. She wants to check it first, to work out if it is who she thinks it is. Another calculation she doesn't have the blood to make.

The last leg of the walk is made more uncomfortable by the face in her waist, but she welcomes the distraction, trying to focus purely on the way her belly is getting scratched, the way her bleeding finger stings. Her own blood.

When she finally reaches the park, she pulls the file out and places it on the bench in front of her, checking through it. All of that for this. She hopes to god she got the right ones. Pages full of numbers, glistening with red marks, like some kind of horrific modern art.

Charlotte

Later, Charlotte will look back and wonder how she drove under the speed limit for fifteen, twenty minutes. How she remembered to indicate or check her mirrors. How she was able to find her way to Alice Park, the sedate and gentle place to which her parents used to bring her and their old dog on Sundays.

Fear stirred after Maggie's call but, given everything that had just happened, she still managed to remember details about those old family picnics, of being hoisted on to her dad's shoulders. How did she even manage to smile at the memories as she tucked her car into the corner of the wood-chipped car park? But it was easy, because Charlotte didn't know yet.

She sees Maggie a little way ahead on a bench. Her knees are tucked together and she's clasping a carrier bag to her chest like a comfort blanket. Her long red hair has been pulled back into a ponytail, making her look haunted, like a ghostly child in a faded photograph. Much like she looked last night on the bridge, when Charlotte's headlights first picked her out in the dark.

She waves and Maggie stands unsteadily and walks slowly towards the car, still clutching the Waitrose bag. She doesn't smile and her face looks drawn and pale.

When she gets into the car, Charlotte realises that Maggie's whole body is trembling. Her thin fingers claw uselessly at the seatbelt until Charlotte reaches across and tugs it into place for her, like a child, something liquid stirring in Charlotte as she does so.

Maggie's smell is so acute that Charlotte pulls away. She's only smelt that distinctive sour odour once in her life, from her own skin. The morning she opened the door to the police. It's the smell of pure animal fear.

'What on earth happened?' Charlotte asks and Maggie gestures to the bag in the footwell, the familiar folder poking from the top.

'I think I got what you need,' she says, her voice hoarse, choking back tears.

'Are you OK?' Charlotte asks but Maggie doesn't answer. Instead, she turns to face Charlotte, her green eyes wide and ringed with blueish skin as if she'd never slept a night in her life. She looks furtively around the near empty car park, then pulls some papers from the folder. Her fingers shake and the papers fan out and flop about.

'I can't believe you managed to . . .' Charlotte starts to say then trails off, noticing the red dots and smears. They aren't the same red marks that Anne's pen had briskly made; this looks like something else entirely. She looks up at Maggie, hoping she's misunderstood. But Maggie swallows, opens her mouth but can't seem to find the words.

Charlotte tries, although her own voice seems to have collapsed in on itself. 'Is that . . . blood?' She throws the papers onto Maggie's lap in disgust, where they slide to the floor.

Maggie nods, swallowing so sharply that her jaw seems to judder. 'Charlotte, it went . . .' Tears slide down her face now. 'It went really wrong.' She hiccups and pushes the door open just in time to throw up on the bark floor of the car park. Charlotte instinctively reaches over to rub her back and Maggie splutters, 'I'm so sorry.'

'But what . . . what actually happened?'

Maggie closes the door and faces her, her skin so pale she's see-through, lips wet with saliva and eyes bright red. And Charlotte knows. Somehow she just knows.

'Oh god.' Charlotte puts her head in her hands and covers her ears, trying to crawl away from what she fears Maggie is about to say. Crushing the sound out and replacing it with the roar from her own veins.

'No,' she says, as firmly as she can manage, shaking her head. 'No, I don't want to know actually, I don't want to know.'

But it doesn't matter what she does, it doesn't matter what she says or how much she regrets any of this. It doesn't matter what she intended, or that she'd thought about calling it off. It doesn't matter that she 'just gave Maggie a lift'. It doesn't matter what Anne did, or whether she was good or bad. None of it matters now.

Through the flesh of her hands, over the rush of her blood, she still hears Maggie's words as loud as a tolling bell.

'Anne is dead.'

Maggie

Charlotte is coiled in the seat, chest pressing against the steering wheel, grabbing her own head as if she's trying to rip it clean off her neck. Her curly dark hair is loose around her shoulders, her hands tangled in it, tugging it so hard Maggie can see the slivers of scalp. She is top-to-toe monochrome, as she always seems to be – even her pyjamas are black gingham. Today it's black jeans, black jumper, black boots with a vicious point. Maggie looks down at the bright, borrowed jumper drowning her and can't imagine that Charlotte has ever worn it.

Maggie's stomach swoops over itself again and she closes her eyes to settle the nausea but that just makes it worse. There's no escaping the sickness, just like there's no escaping the memory of what just happened. Her arms sting with pain and she's scratched great chunks from her forearms before she realises what she's doing. Sleeves pushed back, nails digging.

There is blood snaking down her arms, but she's not sure if the strong iron smell comes from the blood she's just unearthed or the blood she is trying to forget. She feels her stomach contract fast and manages to push the door open in time but there's nothing left and she just dry heaves until her throat hurts.

When she finally shuts the door and sits back up, eyes streaming, Charlotte has turned to face her. Her skin is ashy and dull, her eyes that were so warm earlier now look like pools of black, deadly water.

'Tell me exactly what happened,' she says, as if each word is painful.

Maggie opens her mouth but she has no words. Her throat burns from the crying and the vomiting but Charlotte's eyes stay fixed on her.

'He was following me,' she says, finally. And it doesn't sound real from her mouth.

'Who was?' Charlotte snaps.

'David.'

Charlotte closes her eyes as if to say *of course*.

'I saw him coming up the road and there was nowhere to go. It's not like I could get back to you without him seeing me and I was sure you'd already driven away anyway.'

'You could have called me, I'd have come straight back.' Charlotte's voice is urgent, strangled. Hurt. More than anything, Charlotte sounds hurt. Maggie wants to placate her, to soothe her, to take it all away again. To lie. She feels her stomach churn again and puts a hand on it.

'It was too late, I had to get away from him quicker than that so . . . I improvised.'

That was her strength at school, improvising. Thinking on her feet and pivoting to stay one step ahead. And, yes, she could remember her lines like a machine, and that was important.

But anyone could learn lines; not everyone could live and breathe a scene so completely, so unconsciously, that they could take the audience wherever they wanted to take them. To not just act it but to truly *believe* it, to a molecular level. It was the only time any of her peers or teachers even noticed her; she was usually too small both figuratively and literally. But on stage, she was too involved in the moment to care. The only person who didn't believe her act was her mother.

Charlotte swallows and nods slowly. 'You improvised.'

In the distance, across the wet grass of this country park, a family are battling the wind and rain in matching coats, a berserk spaniel bounding next to them.

'What do you mean you improvised?'

'I knocked on Anne's door,' she says, looking down at her feet through her tears, borrowed trainers tucked into the footwell, surrounded by paper she didn't want to touch.

'What?!'

'I'm sorry, please don't shout at me, I—'

'But why the hell did you knock on her door? That was never the idea!'

'I figured if she didn't answer the door then it meant she was out and I could just slip in, and then, by the time I'd finished, he'd be gone.' Her voice is hysterical, the story unspooling now whether she likes it or not. 'And if she did answer then I could just make something up and ask to come in.'

'And she answered?' Charlotte prompts and still Maggie stares at her own feet, the toes swimming in the outsized shoes. She nods.

'What did you tell her?'

Another rush of words. 'I told her David was following me and he was my stalker and that I needed to hide.'

'So you told her the truth.' It's not a question. 'And she just let you in?'

'I must have looked terrified, I mean I *was* terrified, and I guess she took pity on me.'

'OK, so then what happened?' The words from Charlotte's mouth are normal, reasonable words. But the effort it's taking her to cough them up is painful to watch.

How much detail does Charlotte really need to know? 'Well, once I was inside, I asked to use the loo and I took a gamble.'

'A gamble?'

Please don't be angry with me, Charlotte.

'I saw her home office while I was upstairs and decided it was worth the risk. For you, I mean, to help you. So I went inside and I found this folder, these papers. They looked like they might be the right ones.' She smiles limply but Charlotte doesn't return it. 'Anyway, I was about to leave when . . .' she trails off, the memory swallowing her. 'Anne found me in there.'

'Oh my god. Oh my god. But you didn't have to—'

'She recognised something, Charlotte.'

'Recognised what?'

The frames of the memory stack up on top of each other like playing cards. She rubs her face, faltering. She can barely remember exactly what did happen, let alone what she's supposed to say. Anne recognised the stolen necklace, long gone now, but she can't admit that. She feels sick again but swallows it down, grimacing.

'Maggie?'

'She recognised your jumper, Charlotte.'

'My jumper? Oh Jesus, I didn't think. I've only worn it to work once but Anne said she liked it. Shit.'

'She was about to call the police, she was going to tell them that you'd sent me, she was going to ruin everything and I —' she stops. Charlotte has reached across and put a hand on top of hers.

'Slow down, I can't . . . I can't follow what you're saying.'

Maggie sucks in a breath and tries to let it out slowly. 'I tried to stop her. I just wanted to get the phone out of her hand, to buy myself time to think something up but when she dropped her phone, she picked up a letter opener from the desk.'

'A letter opener?'

'It was sharp, it was like practically a knife and she was waving it at me, threatening me with it. She's so much taller than me and she was—' The words are tripping over themselves.

'Slow down, slow down, *please*. She was *threatening* you?'

Maggie nods. 'I don't know exactly how it happened but I was just trying to stop her hurting me and at the same time trying to plead with her that it was a misunderstanding so she wouldn't call the police and somehow, I don't know exactly but . . . the letter opener went into her chest.'

'Oh my god. Her chest?'

Maggie nods. 'I didn't mean for it to happen, I just wanted to stop her.'

'So it was self-defence? It was self-defence, I think that helps. I think that's—'

'I wasn't defending myself though, Charlotte. I was defending *you*. She knew you'd sent me there.'

Charlotte snatches her hand back. 'But I hadn't sent you there! This whole thing was your idea, I didn't even want you to go!'

'Please don't shout at me,' Maggie squeaks. 'I was doing my best.'

'They'll think it was me! I told Rob we'd fallen out and that she was blackmailing me! What if he thinks . . . Oh god, what if someone saw my car near her house and thinks *I* did it?'

'No one will suspect you, you were with Rob,' she says then sucks in a breath and scratches her arms again. 'But there is something even worse you need to know.'

Charlotte looks up, her hand on her chest like she's trying to hold her heart in. 'How could this possibly get any worse?'

Charlotte

'David was there.'

'I know, you said, that's why you—'

'No, I mean *there*, he came into the house.'

'He was inside Anne's house?!'

Maggie nods, her eyes wide as moons.

'But you were hiding from David, that was the whole reason you went in there!'

'I *did* go in there to hide,' Maggie splutters. 'And I didn't realise he'd seen me go in until it was too late.' She coughs, her chest heaving up and down like a piston engine.

Charlotte tries to soften her voice but she wants to slap Maggie senseless, to shake the truth out of her and then bury it in the soft mud of the park. To bury *herself* under the park. Anything, *anything* but deal with this.

'It's OK,' she manages. 'Just tell me what happened.'

'He let himself in the back, I heard the door when I was upstairs but then I had Anne to . . . to deal with.' She wipes her eyes on the cuffs of that bloody distinctive jumper.

'Did he see what . . . what you did?'

Maggie pauses but then shakes her head.

'He didn't see it happen, but he was heading towards the office so he's bound to have found her. I heard him whistling, a song he used to whistle at work, and then I heard him go into the bathroom and I just ran out.'

'Whistling? So you didn't actually see that it was him?'

'No, it was definitely him. I saw him in the bathroom as I ran past. And even before I saw him, I knew. I'd know that song, I'd know that *feeling* anywhere.'

'But you can't know for sure that he saw her . . .' Charlotte grinds to a halt and finishes in a whisper, 'her body.'

'No,' Maggie says, 'but I'm pretty sure he must have.'

Charlotte rubs her hand over her face, trying to make sense of this. She's had some fucked-up conversations over the last twenty-four hours but this is the worst yet. This is worse than anything she could have imagined.

'Even if he didn't see her, which is really unlikely . . .' Maggie is saying, seemingly groping for the words, her voice still croaky '. . . when it's all over the news, he'll put two and two together and realise he was in the house when it happened. He'll know it was me.'

'How did he know you were there in the first place?!'

A creak of thunder rolls through the sky. As a tendril of lightning zips down, the parents and the spaniel run for the car park, kids trailing, paying Charlotte and Maggie no attention.

'He knew I was there because—' she closes her eyes, grimacing '—he followed us from your house.'

'What? He knows where I live? But how could he know that?'

Maggie says nothing but puts her hand to her pocket and pulls out her phone, holding it carefully like a grenade. 'He told me so,' she whispers.

'He *what*?'

'He texted me last night but I didn't see it until this morning because my phone was dead. I mean, I told you that he'd texted, didn't I? I didn't lie—'

Charlotte's voice hardens like granite, her jaw crunching in anger. 'Maggie, what did he say?'

'He just said, "I followed you".'

'And you didn't think to tell me that?!' She puts her head in her hands, scrunching her eyes as tightly closed as they'll go, trying to fold herself away. When she looks up again, she catches sight of herself in the rear-view mirror. Smeared mascara and eyeliner, a fancy dress Alice Cooper.

'It was like ten hours later or something when I saw the message.' Maggie is pleading now, her voice rising higher and higher. She's so childlike, Charlotte thinks, just a stupid little baby and yet she has just done something so violent, it's unthinkable. Her spindly child's arm, stabbing through Anne's skin. She can't make these two sides fit together but they're both threatening to pull her life to pieces.

'I looked out of the window this morning but I couldn't see him anywhere. I thought he was just bluffing.'

'Bluffing?' Charlotte's eyes fly open in shock. 'This is the guy who . . . who attacked you!'

Maggie cries out, covering her face.

'He ruined your *wedding*! He took photos of you while you slept and got you sacked! Why would you ever think he was bluffing?'

Maggie whimpers, her voice now so high it could cut glass. 'But to be at your house he would have had to follow me all the way from the church to the bridge and then hide without me seeing him for *hours*. It just seemed so unlikely and I didn't want to scare you and I didn't want you to throw me out. I felt so safe with you and I just wanted to stay because,' she whispers, 'I like being with you.'

'You didn't want me to throw you out,' Charlotte repeats. It's not a question. 'And that was more important to you than keeping both of us safe.'

Maggie says nothing and Charlotte doesn't dare fill the silence, doesn't dare move, in case the anger that's boiling in her gut spews out and covers everything. It won't help, the logical part of her knows that, but the rage is filling her vision anyway. Coating her mind like an ink spill.

The family and their matching coats drive away in their estate car, dog bouncing around in the back. That was her, back in the day, her big Labrador Bingo in the back of her mum's Volvo, Charlotte strapped safely into her seat. Listening to her parents having their adult conversations – her mum's clipped voice and her dad's low rumble, his market stall patter – while trying to divert their attention back to her. When she was a little older, Anne would sometimes come with them. Anne who just this morning Charlotte hated so vehemently.

The Anne of this morning was adult Anne, jealous, duplicitous, scheming, investor-schmoozing Anne. But we're never just our present day and the Anne that died was every Anne that had ever lived. The tired, ignored little girl of her childhood. The hard-working, bookish girl of secondary school. Charlotte's only real friend as a teenager. All the Annes, compressed together like a folded paper doll.

She misses all those other Annes so suddenly, so acutely, it's as if someone has scooped out her insides and thrown them at a wall.

How can Anne be dead? She closes her eyes and fades to black, but when she opens them again, Maggie's face is confirmation. Charlotte's tears come faster than they did with her parents. Back then she'd staggered, mute, around her flat while a uniformed police officer made her a strong tea with her own teabags. But now, they're falling so fast it's like they're coming from somewhere outside of her. A leak sprung, a rain shower.

Anne is dead. Because of an argument with her. And yes, Anne was trying to do something despicable, but it was just words. Maybe she wouldn't have gone through with it. Now she can't go through with anything.

'Oh god.'

She feels Maggie's hand, light and unsure, on her arm. *These hands*. She shakes her off.

'I'm so sorry,' she hears, but it's at the end of a long tunnel.

'What the hell are we going to do?' Charlotte cries. More to herself than to Maggie. 'He could be telling the police right now!'

'He won't tell the police,' Maggie says, her voice brittle.

'How can you be so sure?'

'Because he'd have to admit he broke into her house.'

'He could tell them that he saw you go inside.'

'But she let me inside, that's not a crime.'

Charlotte closes her eyes, sucks in a breath and tries to let it out slowly. What would her dad do, if he were here? Her dad who more than tolerated Anne, who humoured her even when he could surely have done without her shadow. Who knew she just needed guidance and that with the right help she could outgrow her upbringing. Her dad who allowed Anne to work at the business part-time while telling Charlotte she couldn't, that he didn't want her distracted from school work. A black mark against both their names that now seems petty and spiteful. What *would* her dad say?

He always taught Charlotte to ask for help but who the hell can help her now? And her dad had also told her to always keep her wits about her, to put herself first and not let anyone lead her down a slippery slope. Is that where she is now, at the top of a landslide? If she were to call the police, to tell them everything, would they understand? Or would that be the start of her fall?

No, Charlotte already started to slide down the slope the moment she let this girl into her car. Now she's careering towards the bottom and it's far too late to appeal for understanding. Instead, she needs to stop taking Maggie's lead, grab her own ropes and hold on for dear life.

The sky is near black now, inky swirls blotting out every inch of blue until they can barely see the park in front of them. They are alone, just as Charlotte thought they were alone on that bridge, just like she thought they were alone last night and this morning. She wipes her eyes onto her jumper, where the black mess melts into the sleeve. There but unseen, just like David was last night and today. Could he be planning to return? He knows where she lives, what could he find out about her by creeping inside? Charlotte closes her eyes and tries to think about what to do. She thinks of Fox Cottage empty and vulnerable, of the memories of her dad that remain there, comforting more than helpful. God, she wishes he was here.

'We should go back to mine and make a plan,' she says firmly.

'OK,' Maggie says quietly. She looks cold, her pointed teeth chattering, but that could be shock.

'We'll need to keep watch for David,' Charlotte adds. 'He could be heading there now.'

Maggie shakes her head. 'He wouldn't,' she says.

'You can't be sure,' Charlotte says as she turns up the heat. She can't bring herself to do any more for Maggie, not now.

She starts the car and reverses slowly, her lights coming on automatically in the gloom. As she rolls the car forward, the swoosh of the engine is meditative, almost calming. She tries to set aside the terror of what's happened to Anne, just for now while she runs through the loose ends. Trying desperately to focus on the minute details and not the big picture, the great big noose around her neck.

Her dad is not here to save her. Her mum isn't here to judge her. They clearly never trusted that she was capable of full adult life, certainly not taking a role in the company, but now she's got to navigate running that company and so much more besides. How clichéd it is to be angry with one's parents, how pedestrian, but Jesus Christ if they'd only let her make her own mistakes young and learn from them, she might be better equipped now.

She sits up straight, tries to ignore the pounding headache flashing between her temples like lightning. *Take control of the situation, starting right now.*

'Maggie, where is the letter opener?'

'It's still in the office. It's—'

Charlotte brakes sharply as she approaches the road. 'It's where?'

'It's in Anne's . . .' she breaks off, claps a hand over her mouth.

'In her what? Her desk?'

Maggie swallows and lowers her hand but doesn't make eye contact. 'It's in her body.'

'Oh my god . . . But your fingerprints?'

Maggie shakes her head. 'Your jumper was baggy, I had my cuffs over my hands.'

'I don't know what to say. I really don't know what to say to any of this.'

They drive in anxious silence. The turning for Chew Valley Lake appears in front of them after a few minutes. 'That's where my dad used to go fishing,' Charlotte says, more to herself than Maggie. 'If he'd lost out at an auction or my mum was pecking his head, he'd drive out here.' What would her dad do if he was here now? Fixing this was far beyond even him.

As she passes the turning, her head throbs with images. Anne, that face she'd so recently grown to hate, contorted in pain and fear. The pool of blood, the letter opener surrounded by raw flesh. Charlotte imagines someone stumbling upon the body, a friend, a cleaner, a worried neighbour, Anne's poor mother, Janine. That vision will be life-changing.

'Maybe we should go back and move her?'

'We can't risk going back,' Maggie says frantically. 'If we're seen, we've blown it. And someone might have already found her! How would we explain being there?' She sounds hysterical. Except hysteria suggests an overreaction, and there is no reaction big enough for what she's done.

What we've done, Charlotte corrects herself. Because she wasn't there but her hand might just as well have been on that letter opener driven into Anne's heart.

Maggie

They shivered the whole way home, despite the heated seats. There was no sign of David, no car or tyre tracks. Now they're sweating in front of the barbecue, despite the weather. Of course, it's not so much a barbecue as an outside oven. A 'Big Green Egg' with dials like a spaceship.

'It's lucky you don't have neighbours,' she says, from under the hood of a big borrowed raincoat, probably Rob's. Charlotte looks at her quickly.

'They'd wonder why we're barbecuing in the rain, I mean.' She lowers her voice.

'I'm not in the mood for jokes.'

'I wasn't joking,' she says, hurt, but Charlotte has turned away again. There's a small pile of charcoal already inside the barbecue, now Charlotte places the papers carefully, almost reverently, on top. Then Charlotte reaches in with some kind of special long lighter and flicks it. In her mind's eye, she dares to imagine a future garden, a future barbecue of her own, a whole adult life where things work out.

'I hope these were the right papers, I can't make head nor tail of them,' Charlotte says quietly, closing the lid.

'It doesn't matter now. Anne's not going to take your business any more, is she? Not now she's—'

'No,' Charlotte says quickly, but doesn't sound happy about it. It would be nice if she was a shade more grateful, Maggie thinks, watching the flames dance across the surface of the paper through the little hole on the top of the lid.

Charlotte turns away and looks at her own cottage as if seeing it for the first time. The sky has turned slate grey, receding into the darkness, the windows glowing like a mirage. 'You should probably stay again tonight,' Charlotte says. 'While we work out what to do next.'

'OK,' she says, trying not to sound happy about it. The thought of curling up in the warm for another night, waking up to a warm drink in another Le Creuset mug. Pausing real life, delaying the inevitable. But maybe it's a mistake. Perhaps she should cut and run. No way to get answers now, she's on her own. This is her moment to navigate. With Charlotte's back still turned, she eases the lid quickly, pinches the last remaining fragment of paper with her sleeves over her fingers and pulls it away from the charred remains. It has a streak of blood on it, almost invisible, but there. She pushes it quietly into her pocket.

Charlotte

Charlotte's nearest neighbour lives two hundred metres back down the lane. Joan is eighty-five years old, half-deaf and wholly unsociable. Charlotte's parents seemed to love the solitude here, even as they got older, but she'd only come to appreciate it after coming back from London where she financially contorted herself every month to live cheek by jowl with strangers.

She'd wrung as much as possible out of her salary. When she finally got a graduate job and stopped temping, she worked as a marketing assistant at a skint little museum in Brockwell held together by donations, school trips and Blu-Tac. But she'd loved being around the artefacts, loved listening to the historians and watching the experts bringing in a new item and setting it up. It hasn't paid her rent though. She'd had to ask her parents for help more times than she'd have liked, and sometimes worked a few evenings in a pub to hold it all together. She'd finally got a job at her dream museum, special-ising in mid-century life, when her parents died. Finally just about able to pay the rent with relative comfort.

Then she'd come home and found herself with all this space and ample money; the peace and quiet was part of the package. But now she's out here, alone, in the dark empty countryside. With a murderer. The expression sounds absurd in her mind, but there's no other word for her.

For all Charlotte's fears as she drove those dark Welsh roads last night, all her worries about mad men and killers on the loose, it didn't stop her popping her car door open and letting an actual murderer slide into her passenger seat.

And no matter how placid she looks, no matter that she's small and skinny, Maggie has ten years on Charlotte. And she's strong and wily enough to wrestle a weapon from Anne and then plunge it into her body.

I wasn't defending myself though, Charlotte. I was defending you.

She should be scared, but she looks at Maggie now, the way she holds herself, upright and eager to please, draped in an old coat. The way her jaw juts out purposefully, and she smooths and resmooths her hair when she doesn't think Charlotte is looking. Nothing about her suggests she's capable of hurting anyone. She looks like an overgrown four-year-old on her first day of school.

This time last night she was on that bridge, willing herself to jump. And that was before all this.

'Maggie?' she says softly. 'Are you . . . you've had an enormous amount to deal with and yesterday you were at a crunch point. I just—'

'I've seen death now,' Maggie says, her voice barely above a whisper. 'And I know more than ever that I couldn't have . . . I wouldn't really . . .'

I've seen death.

Charlotte exhales. 'Let's go inside,' she says to Maggie, gesturing to the back of the house, the route lit by little solar lanterns. And then a brief chill runs up her back. 'After you.'

Charlotte's phone buzzes in her pocket as they walk in silence and it slips from her hands as she fumbles to get it out. Could it be the police already? Oh fuck, could Anne have called them when she realised Maggie was snooping around? Could they have arrived too late and found . . . She plucks

the phone up from where she's dropped it onto the damp
grass. It's just Rob. Oh thank god.

I hope you're OK. I can't stop thinking about what Anne's
been up to. I'm gutted I sent her your way. I'm so sorry. x

They troop back into the kitchen and Charlotte puts the kettle
on. 'I think we need sweet tea,' she says and Maggie smiles
gratefully. 'Could you get the milk?'

Charlotte pulls down the mugs from the shelves, drops a
teabag and sugar cube in each and then slides open the cutlery
drawer. All those knives. Was it really only this morning that
she thought she should hide them so Maggie didn't hurt herself?
Now she wonders if she should hide them for other reasons.

She feels breath on her neck and spins around startled,
slamming the drawer.

'The milk,' she says quietly, stepping back in alarm.

'Thanks.'

She drains her tea before it's really cool enough, burning her
mouth and throat. Maggie holds her mug with two hands and
blows on it before taking a long gulp.

Charlotte stares at Maggie's hands, those same pale fingers
that must have hooked the jumper cuffs carefully over themselves before picking up the weapon and driving it into Anne's
body. That takes more calculation than purely acting in self-
defence, surely? It takes more calculation than Maggie described
when she told the story.

And those same fingers managed to call Charlotte rather
than an ambulance. Then they let themselves carefully out of
the back door as if nothing had happened, grabbing paperwork
along the way.

Both their phones are on the table in front of them and
when Maggie's starts to vibrate with a call, they both jump.

'Oh god,' she says, looking up from the screen. 'I think
it's David.'

Maggie

'David?' Charlotte stares at the phone, vibrating its way across the table. They stare at each other, then back at the phone. A number, not a name.

'Hang on, why haven't you blocked him?'

Her head spins. 'I did block him at first but he kept changing his phone number. In the end I gave up. I recognise this one though, it's the one he texted me from yesterday.'

'God, he's determined,' Charlotte says, as if the very notion of determination is disgusting. And still the phone buzzes.

'Just ignore it,' Charlotte says and then rubs her face with hands. 'Or will that wind him up and make things worse? Fuck!'

'I don't know, probably,' Maggie says, her voice small. 'But I don't want to talk to him! I can't!'

Charlotte squeezes her hand. 'He can't hurt you, I promise.' She rubs her hand over her face. 'Just put it on speaker, we'll deal with this together.'

Maggie swallows and nods as Charlotte adds quickly, 'He might have left without seeing her, so don't give anything away.'

'David,' she says quietly as the loudspeaker kicks in, 'what do you want?'

His laugh fills the warm kitchen like smoke. 'Oh Mags,' he says. 'Are you fucking serious, babe? You're going to play the innocent with me?'

The two women look at each other and say nothing. For a moment, all they hear is breathing and then softly, quietly, the whistling starts. 'I was there, mate,' he says. 'And you've been a very naughty girl.'

'What are you going to do?' Maggie asks breathlessly and flicks her eyes at Charlotte who is leaning towards the phone as if she wants to interject.

'Me?' He laughs again. 'I'm not going to do anything.' He pauses. 'Not if you ask me nicely.'

'Please don't do anything,' Maggie says but he's already laughing again. A throaty, smoky laugh that sounds like it's spilling out of a bar. It sounds like trouble.

'Yeah, it'll take a bit more than that.'

'What do you want?' Maggie says and as Charlotte looks at her, she hugs her arms around her body and shakes her head. Charlotte closes her eyes as if imagining the worst. The worst for Maggie, anyway.

'Ten K,' he says, all trace of laughter gone.

'Ten K? You mean ten thousand pounds?' Maggie looks at Charlotte, her mouth hanging open. Charlotte still has her eyes closed, her forehead wrinkled in concentration.

'Ten thousand pounds for what? I mean, I've not done anything,' Maggie says but Charlotte's eyes have sprung open and she's shaking her head. She whispers, '*Don't push him.*'

'If you keep this up, it'll be fifteen,' David snaps. 'So stop fucking around.'

'I don't have any money,' it comes out more whiny than Maggie intended.

'You better get some off your posh mate then,' he says, the laughter back in his voice. 'You bring it to the bridge outside Usk, you know the one.'

'How did you—'

His laughter cuts her off. 'Nine o'clock tonight. Don't do anything stupid and neither will I. But you try to play me, girl, and I'll be down that police station singing my heart out. Got it?'

Maggie nods her head.

'Got it?' he repeats with a growl.

'Got it,' she says, as Charlotte leans over and ends the call.

For a moment they sit in silence. 'We have to pay,' Charlotte says.

Charlotte is scrabbling around looking for bank cards and chequebooks, shaking her head as she looks at banking apps on her phone. Maggie trails uselessly after her, unable to help. 'Can you raise ten thousand pounds before tonight?' she asks, tugging on her sleeves.

'I have to, don't I? If he goes to the police, we're both fucked. I'm sure I'm on all sorts of traffic cameras driving you to Bath and—' she pulls on her hair again, twisting it so viciously Maggie winces. 'Where the fuck is it?'

Maggie doesn't ask, she just ducks out of the way. Charlotte looks up from her rummaging. 'I've got a savings account but the branch won't be open now. The only thing I can do is take it from the safe at work.'

'Will you get in trouble?'

Charlotte looks up at her then as if staring at a child. 'You need to get out of those things and we need to get rid of them. Go and have a shower and wash yourself really thoroughly. I'll find you something clean to wear,' Charlotte says. 'And we should probably burn all of these as well.' She gestures to the clothes she'd laid out so kindly just this morning.

All this waste and destruction. Maggie knows it's essential, but it still feels wrong. She thinks again, surprised by the frequency of this memory, of her mum making her clothes. Of the hours she spent adjusting charity shop buys, or of carefully cutting out patterns. It takes a lot to create something but Charlotte doesn't seem to know or care.

All of her clothes have been new, from birth to now, that much is clear. She's talked a few times about being skint, of how hard it was to live well in London, but Maggie bets that Charlotte could always come back here. Bets that she bought something new to wear every payday. Skint is relative.

They walk into the hall and Maggie is about to climb the stairs when Charlotte stops suddenly and stares at the front door. 'Didn't I lock that when I came in?' she says, more to herself than Maggie.

'I'm not sure, I think so.'

Charlotte is fingering the Yale lock, frowning. She secures it and then pulls a bolt across too, then she turns to Maggie. 'What if David comes back here?'

'He wouldn't do that.'

'Why wouldn't he? Maybe he was right outside when he called! Maybe he was watching us.'

'But how—'

'He obviously followed you to the bridge last night and we know he followed you back here. He's been following you all day, why would he stop now? Maybe he wants to make sure we actually go to the bridge later.'

Then she lowers her voice to a whisper. 'He could be inside right now.'

Maggie shudders at the thought, even though she's certain no one is here.

'You check upstairs, I'll check down,' Charlotte says.

They check methodically, Maggie lowering herself to look under each bed even though it's unnecessary, pulling open every cupboard. Of course he's not here.

Charlotte isn't reassured when Maggie goes back downstairs. 'He could be outside, we need to check if his car's here.'

'OK.'

They walk into the living room and Maggie pulls back the curtain slowly, dreading seeing his face there, unexpected. They both breathe deeply at the sight of Charlotte's car and nothing more. Then Charlotte points towards the lane. 'There's a light down there.'

'Where?' Maggie squints but can't see anything. When she turns back, Charlotte is heading for the front door. 'Where are you going? Please, it could be dangerous.' She catches up with Charlotte and tugs at her arm to stop her twisting the lock.

'Can't we see the road from the upstairs window?' Maggie pleads. 'Let's try that first!'

They thunder up the stairs and head for the window of Charlotte's room. The curtains are still open and Charlotte points, gasping. Maggie follows her gaze and can just make out the fading tail lights of a car before it's too far to follow any more.

'He was out there,' Charlotte says.

'There's no way to know it was him.'

'You're kidding, right?' Charlotte says, sitting heavily on the bed.

'I just don't want it to be true, Charlotte,' she says, and a shiver runs up her arms and back. 'I can't bear the thought of him being that close to me again, of him—' she starts to cry so she doesn't have to finish the sentence.

Charlotte puts an arm around her and Maggie leans into it. She can smell Charlotte's skin, her fear, and the guilt scratches at her.

'Don't worry, you don't need to deal with him alone, OK? We're in this together,' Charlotte says, her voice hoarse and strangled. 'Just . . . he's gone for now so you go and have a shower and I'm going to make sure all the doors and windows are locked. Then we'll work out how to handle David.'

Was it him? She thinks as she locks the now familiar bathroom, trying to picture the red car out there, picture his eyes watching. Why would he have been there? She reaches for her phone, nervously expecting to find a message, but she's left it downstairs.

Maggie starts to peel off her clothes, tries to think but she's so damn tired. She'd love to just get in this roll-top bath and soak herself to sleep. A trace of glitter around the plug that tells the story of Charlotte's last bath, a basket of expensive sparkly bath bombs sits nearby, just outside the splash zone.

She thinks of her mum's bathroom, the Pears soap and Vosene shampoo she swore by, the avocado bathtub. There was no shower, and her mum was careful with how often the boiler went on. There was never quite enough hot water; you had to switch it off just in time or both taps would start spitting out cold and you'd ruin what you had. Her knees and shoulders poking out above the surface were always cold. She'd soak water into the flannel and drape it on her exposed skin, which only worked so well.

She turns on the shower, stands with her hand in the endless stream until its hot enough then washes her hair twice. Dizzy from the heat, she scrubs her face roughly with something minty until her skin hurts. Then she washes her body with something that smells like apples. After slooshing off the bubbles, she can still smell the bitter smell that accompanied her out of Anne's house so she lathers up another glug of apple.

She turns the heat up higher yet, lets the water turn her pale skin red. As the heat lashes down on her head, she looks at her hands and imagines them holding a weapon, covered in blood. Imagines her wrists in handcuffs.

Hold it together. That won't happen.

In the spare bedroom, she finds a neat pile of clothes – right down to socks and knickers – lying on the bed. She pulls them on while her skin's still slightly damp, tugging the jogging bottoms up her legs roughly. They have some paint splatters but fit better than the jeans and she wonders who they belong to; they're too small for Charlotte. Her mother? She tugs the scrap of paper from the jeans pocket and tucks it in her borrowed sports bra.

The photograph that has been ferried around next to her stomach since Bath has creased, the face and its lover's smile is rubbed away in spots. She smooths it out gently and takes a long look, trying to commit all the details to memory, then folds the photo carefully and pushes it deeply into the pocket of the joggers.

Charlotte

They burn everything, even the canvas trainers that Maggie had worn to Bath, and wait, watching through the grate until there's almost nothing but ash, the remaining melted soles stuffed in her neighbour's wheelie bin. All the time, Charlotte listens out for evidence that David is here somewhere, watching. Could he have been outside the house when he made his call last time? Could he have been close enough to watch their reactions without them seeing him? Could he have been inside?!

She thinks about what he's done to Maggie, the lengths he's gone to. Can they really trust him to keep quiet? She shakes her head, feeling at once dizzy and heavy. *What choice do they have?*

Charlotte fumbles with the lock and pushes the back door open. The kitchen is still brightly lit, neither of them keen to turn any lights off. It's nearly six o'clock, already dark. They need to get the money from the safe and get over to Wales in three hours.

Charlotte carries her boots out into the hallway and Maggie trails behind her. 'Did you move my letters?' Charlotte asks, spinning round to look at Maggie who looks nonplussed.

'What letters?

Charlotte's face has drained of all colour. 'There was a stack there,' she says, pointing to a little table next to the front door.

Maggie frowns; she remembers seeing the diffuser there, which is still in situ. 'I don't remember seeing any letters. Did you move them when you were looking for your chequebook?'

'No, I didn't. Shit,' Charlotte says, dropping her boots and checking under the table. 'They were here, I'm sure they were. I'm certain I didn't move them.' She feels suddenly cold, despite still wearing her heavy coat. What was in the pile? Some bills, a couple of bank statements from the company and her personal accounts. Did David take them to see what money she had available? She looks at the time. 'We have to go,' she says, and Maggie nods, her face drained of all colour.

It's fully dark again, the same inky blackness she'd plunged into last night. Jesus, was it only last night? It seems like it was another person entirely who took off into the back of beyond, trying to outrun her feelings. If Charlotte had gone in any other direction, out to Devizes and Chippenham, or down across the Mendips instead of steaming over the Severn Bridge, none of this would have happened. She looks across at Maggie, who shrinks into the seat.

How many seemingly random decisions has she blithely made throughout life that have saved her from something terrible happening rather than brought it on? If only she could have made a right turn once more.

Perhaps if she'd tried to talk to Rob sooner all those years ago, got to him before he fell for Deb, her life would be wildly different. Perhaps she would have a nine-year-old daughter now. She'd gone home that day, after seeing Deb and her bump, and decided not to tell her parents that she'd tried to find Rob and confess her feelings. Their own feelings for Rob were still complicated, and there must have been a part of her mother that felt relief, maybe even glee, as she told Charlotte about Rob's wedding. He was officially off the table. Instead, on the way to the station that day, she'd asked her dad if he ever saw Anne around.

'Last time I heard of her she was in America.'

'America?'

Her dad was a lousy driver and she already felt sick. She'd held on to the coat hook with the tip of her fingers. 'How did you hear that?' she'd asked.

'From her mum.'

Even with his slapdash driving, she'd give anything to be sitting next to her dad now, unburdening herself while he listened patiently.

Maggie is silent next to her now. Her own hands are in her lap; Charlotte is a smooth driver like her mum. The one thing she never wanted to inherit from her father was his driving style. Charlotte catches sight of herself in the mirror; her brown eyes look heavier set than before. She looks like her mother. Especially with this new spray of greys in her roots that she'd not spotted before. Does stress work *that* fast?

They pull into the empty showroom car park and Maggie waits in the car while Charlotte slips inside. The small safe is in the back in the kitchen area, mugs are stacked on top of it. She opens it up, the same combination her dad has used for as long as she can remember. His birthday. 3-1-0-7-6-0.

Inside is just over ten thousand, stored for use at jumble sales and cash events, for handing out to sellers who, for various reasons, don't want to involve banks. She looks behind her as she counts out the stacks and slides them into an envelope. There's no one there, of course, and no need for David to sneak up on her here when he's going to be given it anyway. But she still feels watched. Perhaps, she realises, she will always feel watched now. Like Jacob Marley hovering over Scrooge, will Anne haunt her for the rest of her life? She slaps herself hard across the face. This is no time for imagination, she needs to stay sharp. Her eyes water but she shuts the safe again and rushes back out to the car.

'Charlotte,' Maggie says, as they start off again, the car whooshing joyfully into the silence.

'Yeah?'

'I can't do this.'

'What? What do you mean?' *What now? What now?!*

'I'm sorry,' Maggie says quietly, and when Charlotte looks quickly she sees that tears are sliding down her small face. 'I can't see him, I can't face him, I can't—' she pulls her knees up under her chin and Charlotte notices she's taken her borrowed shoes off. Her little socked feet look so pathetic, so innocent that the thought of her in that staffroom, pressed against by David and forced into . . .

'OK,' Charlotte says firmly. 'You don't have to see him. I'll do it.'

'You will?'

'Yeah,' she says. And maybe this is wise anyway. Less reliant on Maggie holding it together. God knows how much more she can take before she breaks and takes them both down. How much *can* one person take?

'Oh my god,' Maggie says, her voice high and childlike. 'Thank you. Oh god, thank you. I'm so . . . oh god, relieved, I guess, but obviously not fully relieved, but—'

'Where does your mum live?' Charlotte asks, ever more sure that trusting Maggie to carry out the exchange would not have gone well. She's a mess. And understandably so.

'Um. Well, she lives on the edge of Newport,' she says. 'Why?'

'That's not far from where we're going, is it?'

'About twenty minutes or so, yeah.'

'I'll feel better knowing you're safe with family too. I know you don't get on with your mum but you need someone looking after you, Maggie, you've had to handle more than anyone should these last few days.'

They surge over the Severn Bridge at just gone seven but, after numerous false starts, Maggie proves too jittery to guide them to her mum's house. Trying to use her calmest voice, Charlotte gets Maggie to search for the address on the Tesla flat screen. It seems to take her an age, but then they follow the instructions in silence.

Charlotte's hands are shaking so much they're tapping a rhythm on the leather steering wheel. Her teeth are rattling, her tongue somehow too big for her mouth and in the way. Her eyes sting, with tiredness and fear. In the pocket of her door, an envelope of cash sits, waiting to be handed over to a witness. A witness who has previously attacked Maggie. But what choice do they have? If they call his bluff and he does go to the police, there's no hope for them. She prays that his imagination is limited to this one payment, but she doesn't have the luxury of worrying about that.

They finally pull up outside the address Maggie typed in. It's a neat house with freshly painted white windowsills and a shiny red door. Window boxes sit on all four visible ledges, and when it's flower season, they must be full of colour. Maggie seems almost surprised to see it, and Charlotte wonders when she was last here. How on earth the relationship worked in the run up to the wedding.

A shiny blue car sits in the car port attached to the house and a figure stands in the top floor window, watching. Maggie seems to flinch at the sight.

'Charlotte,' she says as she climbs out, 'thank you so much for doing this for me.'

'I'm doing this for both of us. I'll come back here afterwards, OK? Keep an eye out.'

Charlotte watches as Maggie hesitates for a moment on the pavement. She looks up but the figure is no longer there. Charlotte drives away, fiddling with the satnav to find the bridge in her list of locations from last night.

She puts the cruise control on, making sure she doesn't go a hair over the speed limit no matter how open the road. If she was pulled over by police, she doesn't trust herself not to vomit or tell them everything.

A filthy once-white van pulls around her aggressively but she stays level. But then a motorbike roars past and she taps the brake in shock. *Hold it together.* According to the display, she will arrive just before the rendezvous with enough time to park down the lane from the bridge and wait for David to arrive. Will he leave when he sees it's not the object of his obsession waiting for him? Or does he just want the money?

She feels sick. A nausea that is raging from her toes to her scalp. Is there any way out of this? She must be missing something, some solution. *What would Dad have done?* Her dad, she realises, would have got her out of it, which is why she has no idea how to get her damn self out of this now he's dead.

Eight minutes until arrival, according to the Tesla screen. A small red car with a grey panel pulls sharply round her and then zooms off, smoke billowing from its back like it's not passed an MOT since the nineties.

She's only two minutes away now, but it all looks different tonight. Charlotte was driving in the opposite direction last night so when she turns the corner and the bridge looms into view, she jumps. She drives over it slowly then turns round carefully to pull in to the same muddy patch she paused at last night as she tried to make out the shape on the bridge.

Not even twenty-four hours ago and everything has changed. And nothing can possibly be the same again.

She cuts the engine, turns off the lights and waits.

Maggie

Charlotte should be getting to the bridge any moment, she thinks with a shiver. Charlotte, the only one who willingly stopped last night. Who opened up her home, trusted Maggie to share her life, just for a while. Charlotte whose problems were so abstract in comparison to her own story, but were real and true and life-changing nonetheless.

She pictures Charlotte alone in her car, clutching her envelope of cash.

She won't exhale fully until she sees Charlotte again later, knows she's OK. Maggie promised Charlotte that she would ask her mum if she could stay there, just until she got back on her feet. The idea being so laughable, so grotesque, that she couldn't begin to explain why and just agreed. But that's not Charlotte's problem any more. Charlotte has bigger worries.

Please don't hurt her.

She tugs the sleeves of yet another borrowed jumper as she lets herself come back to reality, becoming aware of the rants she's been tuning out. Trying to let the words wash over her, just another list of her errors. She's heard enough of those over the years.

As she nods and apologises, she chews the end of her hair. Then she closes her eyes, smelling just the faintest whiff of apple shower gel rising from her skin.

We're almost there, Charlotte. Don't let us down.

Charlotte

Her heating is on full blast but Charlotte's teeth are still clattering noisily in her mouth and her bones feel achy and frozen.

It's just gone nine o'clock and she's waiting in her car but there's no sign of David yet. Perhaps he never intended to show, just wanted to toy with Maggie.

Oh shit, perhaps he was still following them all along and now he knows Charlotte is out of the way and Maggie is a sitting duck at her mum's house? He could be cornering her, hurting her, hurting her mum too, right now.

The thought makes Charlotte shiver even more. Perhaps she should text her, some kind of coded message to check she's OK?

As if Maggie has heard her, the phone starts to ring on its charging mat. The jangly ringtone sounds absurd in the silent tension of the night. But it's not Maggie calling, it's Rob. As much as she'd love the comfort of his voice right now, she rejects the call. What would she say if he asked what she was doing? 'Just paying off a witness, how 'bout you?'

She wouldn't sound normal, and he'd know something was up. The last thing she can deal with right now is Rob's small-town complacency or, worse, him trying to be a hero.

As she puts the phone back down on its charger, she notices a man approaching the bridge from the other direction. He's on foot, torchlight bobbing as he saunters quite happily down the middle of the road, as if he's invincible.

He pauses on the bridge, rests his torch on the handrail and tries to light a cigarette, shaking his lighter a couple of times in frustration and cupping his hands. Eventually it takes and he leans back against the handrail and glances over at her car.

David.

He's not as tall as she expected, somewhere between five foot seven and five foot nine probably, but solid. He has close shaved hair, broad shoulders and the kind of turtle's shell belly that once-muscly men grow. He seems in no rush.

Still looking over, he holds one hand up to his eyes like a visor, as if he's trying to see through her windscreen from up there on the bridge. Obviously having no luck, he picks the torch up and shines it towards her.

I could drive away now, she thinks. But then the last chance to snip off these loose ends before Anne is found would be gone.

Before Anne is found. How can she think these things? She'd never really understood survival instinct before. It always seemed heroic, somehow. Super-human feats of strength and stamina. But in reality it's corrosive and parasitic. Destroying the host and taking over.

She takes a deep breath, snatches up the envelope and climbs out of the car, her mind seeming to slip outside of her body and follow her from above in disbelief.

'Evenin',' he says, as she approaches. In between puffs of smoke, he starts to whistle. Blood roars in her ears and she can feel the tussle between fight and flight taking place on the surface of her skin, body crackling with adrenaline.

'David?' she says, slowing to a stop a few feet from him. She, for some reason, is using her mum's telephone voice, the one her dad called Hyacinth Bucket behind her back. One of the many ways her mum kept undesirables at arm's-length. And David is definitely an undesirable.

He says nothing, running his torchlight up her body, as if pricing up her clothes and then looking over her shoulder at the Tesla.

'She sent you to do her bidding, eh?' He smirks. He doesn't seem surprised to see her. He must recognise her from when he was following Maggie. And of course he's seen Charlotte's car before, and her face, even her house. This is her only chance to find out how far he's wormed into her life.

'Did you break into my house today?' she asks, trying to hold her voice steady, hearing her mum's clipped and haughty tones instead. He frowns, raising his eyebrows and pecking at the cigarette with thin, wet lips. 'What?'

'Did you let yourself in and go through my things?'

He laughs to himself but says nothing.

She carefully treads closer and can see that he's younger than her. Late twenties, maybe early thirties at a pinch. She can picture him pulling the same shit-eating grin outside local

Spar shops as a teenager not so long ago. Shoving people with his shoulder or spitting by their feet to wind them up. Just one of life's dickheads.

'You got the money or not?' he says, smile dropping. And she remembers yet again that he is not just a dickhead, and he didn't just wind Maggie up. He ruined her life.

'I need your word that you'll leave Maggie alone,' she says, trying to sound firm as her knees shake.

'You two scissor sisters now then?' He grins, flicking his cigarette stub so it sails over the bridge and slips silently beneath the water. She doesn't react so he mimes crudely with his fingers. She keeps her face as neutral as possible, tries not to let him see how scared she is.

'Always pick your ladies up at the side of the road, do you?' he says, sniffing hard and spitting it on the floor before heaving himself up to sit on the handrail, legs spread, one knee casually jiggling.

Charlotte walks closer still, in direct opposition to her instinct.

'I'm not giving you this money unless you leave Maggie alone. If you touch her again—'

'You ain't paying me to leave Maggie alone,' he spits. 'You're paying me to keep quiet about what you two *did*.'

Her body feels like it's been put together wrong. Her knees jammed in the wrong sockets so they rattle and ache, her heart surely incapable of pumping all this panic around her veins. She feels at once tiny and huge, as if all questions of life and death are oscillating within her but broken into minuscule moments and decisions. The decision to take another breath. To make eye contact with this rotten man. To take another step closer. And another.

He opens his knees wider still, the vulnerability of his crotch exposed, leaning back a little as if to receive her. The kind of bloke who will encroach into your space on the Tube, or stand too close at the bar. Making a weapon of himself and daring people to have a problem with that. And the rest. Forcing himself on innocent women whose only mistake is trusting him.

And now I have to trust him.

The river rushes black and busy underneath.

'Was that posh bird in Bath another one of your lesbo lovers?' He winks and Charlotte flinches. *Was.*

'You need to leave Maggie alone,' she says, pulling the envelope from her coat pocket but holding it by her side.

'I don't need to do anything,' he says, shrugging. 'In fact, I've changed my mind. You want me to stay quiet, it'll cost you double. And if you want me to leave Maggie alone—' he mimics Charlotte's voice then smirks again '—that'll cost you far more.'

Something squawks from the riverbank below, some bird or animal disturbed by the argument. He turns to look, slow and unafraid, lifting one arm to rearrange his position. He wobbles then. A leaf on the breeze, a boat on choppy waters. He doesn't seem frightened as he rights himself but overcorrects and wobbles some more. Then he smiles. 'So you give me that to get started, and then we can fix a time for the next payment.'

She had desperately tried to ignore this possibility, but now he's actually said it. This is never going to stop. He has no intention of staying quiet. He's not going to leave Maggie alone and now he's not going to leave Charlotte alone either. This is never going to be over, ever.

Unless . . . She steps closer.

Unless I end it now.

It takes nothing, barely a moment, just a quick push with her fingertips against the meat of his chest. It's done before she can stop herself, before she can think it through any more.

The sneer drops suddenly from his face, replaced with wide eyes as his body tumbles back. He becomes a tangle of limbs and a rush of noise as he plummets, his journey helped by the throne he'd claimed on top of the handrail.

The scream as he hits the water is high-pitched and short, almost childlike. The river is slashed suddenly by his weight, a disruption so acute that a great spike of water surges up and hits her face and chest with a shock of sudden cold.

Then there is silence.

Absolute silence.

That bird's beak snapped shut, the wind holding its breath, the river back to a rumble.

She stares at the surface for two, three seconds. He has not come back up.

Charlotte finally snaps to attention, running back to her car, heart pounding and lungs screaming. She slides into the seat, slams the door and reverses clumsily, then drives away, throwing the envelope of money onto the passenger seat and skidding down the road.

Maggie

She's been looking out for Charlotte's car for what feels like ages. She jumps down from the wall where she's been sat softly, like a cat, and then paces up and down the quiet street, checking behind her for twitching curtains. But no one cares.

Nine thirty-five. Her stomach starts to flip, gently at first, like motion sickness, before tumbling into an aching churn. Charlotte should have made it back here easily by now. It's only a twenty-minute drive. What's keeping her? God, has Charlotte lost her nerve and gone to the police? What should she do if so? Run? Hide? She goes through it in her head, trying to shuffle the cards into the right order but panic is scattering them all over the floor of her brain.

The cars around here are lovingly washed and carefully maintained but they are working cars, the pride and joy of ordinary people. The type of ordinary people who could never afford a Tesla. When Charlotte's car finally appears, rolling slowly like a silent black Orca, the acute sense of relief is followed by a ripple of resentment. She thinks of her mum's car. And the one she herself has lovingly washed many times.

Finally the car stops next to her, its silent engine obliviously mocking all these other cars, and she opens the door and climbs in.

'How did it go?' Maggie says, her voice quivering more than she intended.

Charlotte's hands grip the wheel and her body is shaking so violently it's like she's having a fit. The skin on her face seems to hang from her bones in a death mask.

'David is dead,' she says.

'What?!'

Charlotte turns to face her; her skin shines grey-green under the street light and she seems to have aged ten years since this morning. Her eyes are black and shadowed, her mouth twisted up like she's tasting pure vinegar.

'I don't understand,' Maggie says. 'What do you mean he's dead?'

She stares as Charlotte folds over on to herself, her apple tummy collapsing onto her lap, her arms slumping over the wheel. Her heart is still racing from earlier; now it feels like it could explode.

'I, I pushed him off the bridge,' Charlotte says, her voice desperate. 'He was never going to leave us alone.'

'Are you . . . are you sure he's dead?'

Charlotte nods. 'He couldn't have survived that fall.'

Maybe she should act happy. Or relieved. Or curious. Or worried. But she sits rooted to the seat, unsure what to say. Mute, like she's looking out from the back of her brain, half a world away.

'I'm so sorry,' Maggie says finally, looking away. 'I'm sorry you stopped for me last night, I'm sorry I dragged you into this. David's like a weed, he just gets under everything and pulls it to pieces.'

'He *was* like a weed,' Charlotte quietly corrects her, tears slipping down her face. 'Now he's just another dead body, maybe with loved ones somewhere who'll miss him.'

'I don't know what to say.'

'Tell me we won't go to prison for murder.'

'Oh god, Charlotte, no. No, we won't. No. We'll make sure that doesn't happen, OK?'

Charlotte pulls at her face with her hands, dragging the skin down and away from her eyes like a ghoul. 'How?'

'By staying calm,' she says, sounding anything but. 'There's nothing to link you to David and nothing to link me to Anne.'

'Except each other,' Charlotte says then, looking up.

Charlotte

She looks behind her towards the little house where Maggie's mum lives. Imagines a different end to this story, a different fork in the road taken last night. Imagines instead that the police had arrived here last night to say that Maggie was dead.

Maggie says now that she wouldn't have jumped. But she can't know that for sure. And she could so easily have slipped. She *did* slip . . . She really could have died if Charlotte had driven a different way yesterday. The way David smashed against the water . . . that would have been Maggie. If she hadn't coaxed her to get into the passenger seat she occupies now, her drowned body could have ended up tangled in that wedding dress that is now hanging from Charlotte's picture rail.

'I feel completely out of control, Maggie. I don't feel like I can string a proper sentence together. What if someone finds Anne tonight and the police want to talk to me? I'm a mess.'

'I know, I feel crazy too. I feel like anyone will look in my eyes and know but . . . they won't, will they. 'Cos there's no reason for anyone to think anything.' She closes her eyes and frowns. 'They probably will want to talk to you, I guess. You work together so they'll need to notify you.'

'But I'm so freaked out, they'll take one look at me and know.'

'Anyone would be freaked out if the police turned up and said their colleague and friend had been . . . wasn't alive any more. It would be weird if you *weren't* freaked out. OK?'

'OK.'

'Just whatever you do, don't tell them you'd fallen out. Don't tell them anything except that you're old friends and colleagues and that you're devastated.'

'And if they ask where I was when it happened?'

'Tell them the truth, that's the whole point, isn't it? Just tell them the truth. You were with Rob this afternoon at his place. And you went into that shop too, didn't you, which is really good. And that's it, that's all you need to say.'

'That's it,' Charlotte repeats, unable to think for herself. 'I wish you could come back with me,' she says. 'But our . . . our friendship is the evidence against us.'

Maggie nods, her eyes suddenly glassy. 'I wish you weren't right,' she says quietly. 'Because in twenty-four hours you've become the best friend I've ever had.'

Maggie

'Maybe we . . . I don't know, maybe in time, if this all goes away, we could . . .' Charlotte says.

'Meet up?' Maggie says, unable to hide her smile at the thought. 'Like, um, like as if it's the first time. We could bump into each other and get chatting and—'

'Become friends. Normal friends with other things in common besides—' Charlotte's face falls.

'Yeah, besides *that*.'

They both sit in silence.

'We need to be really careful for now though,' Charlotte says. 'No texts or calls or anything, nothing to link us. At least until we know it's safe.'

'How will we know it's safe if we don't talk though?'

Charlotte wipes her eyes and sighs. 'I don't know.'

They stare out onto the street together; no one in the little houses is paying them any attention. And why would they? There's nothing remarkable about two women sitting together in a car, having a chat.

'We're strangers, right?' Maggie says, forming a thought. 'So . . . I mean, we can be in the same place, as strangers among other strangers and just—'

'Check we're both OK?'

'Yeah, and pass on anything we need to know. Just in case.'

'Just in case.' Charlotte agrees. 'Do you ever come out to Bath or Bristol? Some reason that you're there anyway and I could—'

'Shopping. I've come up to Bristol to go shopping before. Cribbs Causeway, I think it's called. It was a long time ago now when I lived . . .' She stops. No need to get into all that.

'Cribbs Causeway. That's perfect,' Charlotte says. 'We could easily just be two women in the same shop, randomly. No one would know.'

'OK,' Maggie says. 'H&M?'

'H&M, yeah. Next Friday?' Charlotte's eyes seem to light up just for a moment.

'Yeah, next Friday. One o'clock.' The thought wraps around her like a hug.

'What will you do now?' Charlotte asks and for a moment she's struck dumb. What will she do now? What *is* the plan again?

'I'll go back to my mum's house and stay the night in my old bedroom,' she says carefully. 'I'll swallow my pride and call Mike and I'll do whatever it takes to fix things.'

'Are you scared?' Charlotte says. 'I'm really fucking scared.'

'Of course I'm scared, I'm scared about what I'll remember when I'm trying to fall asleep and scared that I'll never forget what I saw.' She swallows, her voice hoarse. 'But I'm not scared of *him* any more. And that's down to you. You changed my life.'

She notices the time and her heart feels heavy. Charlotte reaches her hand across the car and Maggie takes it. They interlace their fingers for a moment.

'No one else in the world knows what we did,' Charlotte says. 'You know me like nobody else.'

Maggie feels a hot tear sliding down her face. 'It's a privilege to share a secret with you,' she says quietly. Charlotte's hand is soft and warm. The first friendly, female skin she has touched in so long. She closes her eyes and tries to make an imprint of this feeling, takes a mental picture and files it away just for her.

'I need to go,' she says finally, reluctantly. 'And you should get home.'

Charlotte nods and lets go of her hand. Its loss is acute and Maggie draws her hand away and presses it between her own knees. Charlotte reaches for her handbag from the back seat, pulls out a purse, then hands Maggie a small folded pile of notes. 'It's three hundred pounds, I couldn't draw any more out in one go but—'

'You got this for me?'

'I got it out on the way to Rob's. I meant to give it to you already. It's not much but I know you don't want to stay with your mum any longer than you have to, and I thought it might help get your new life started.'

She can't let herself speak. Can't say what she's thinking. How she'd love it if Charlotte took her back to the cottage and let her sleep in that cosy spare room just once, but ideally more, ideally a lot more. How she would scrub herself clean in that roll-top bath, take off that grimy layer skin that has covered her for so long. She would be reborn. Cared for. Safe. If she could stay there, hunkering down, for the rest of her life, she'd do it.

Charlotte gestures to the envelope in the space between them. 'I'd give you more but I need to put this back in the safe, it belongs to the business and I don't want any more irregularities if anyone does start looking.'

Maggie stares at the money in Charlotte's hand, knowing she has to take it but wishing she could be the kind of person who would refuse.

'Thank you so much,' she says finally, sliding it into her pocket and pressing the button to open the door. Before she thrusts it open, she turns and reaches across to hug Charlotte. Charlotte pulls her in and clings to her. She can smell the same shampoo that she herself used just hours earlier, can feel Charlotte's soft flesh yield under hers. What a simple pleasure a platonic hug is, what a revelation. She chokes back a sob and pulls away.

She pushes the door open. The cold air hits her like a slap in the face and the pavement feels dangerous, so brittle after the soft warmth of the car seat.

'Until Friday,' she says.

'Until Friday,' Charlotte replies.

She shuts the door and walks away on unsteady legs. She can't look back. She can't bear to see Charlotte's face, the door handle that she could so easily open, or the seat she could so easily collapse back into. She hears the hiss of the engine and crumples just a little.

It's only as she walks away, the Tesla already rolling out of sight, that she realises the photograph from Anne's house is no longer in her pocket.

Charlotte

Charlotte drives back in a daze, switching into auto drive and letting the car take charge like a parent. With every light that whips past, the same line rushes through her head.

I killed a man.

When she pulls off the motorway, leaving behind the neon scribbles of headlights, the black silence is almost too much. Will she ever get over this?

She nearly passes the turning for her village and swerves for it. The is the same road her mum used to use daily, ferrying her between dance classes in Bristol or swimming in Bath. Her brief dallies with tennis club, trampolining, guitar lessons. The artillery route like a seam through her childhood. This was the route her school bus took, collecting Anne along the way. Charlotte would save the space next to her with her bag, even though no one was champing at the bit to sit there. Then she'd smile with relief when Anne climbed up the stairs, slide her rucksack out of the way so her friend could sit down. That same person who was now covered in blood, frozen in the horror of her last moments.

She makes it to her own driveway like she's limping over a finish line and sits, almost panting in the driver's seat.

It's two hours since David died. Died. Such a restrained word. He was killed. *I killed him.* But still she finds it impossible to see him as a victim, not fully. He was a sexual predator. A blackmailer. A nasty piece of work. But someone must love him and someone will miss him.

It's pitch black overhead and all around. But she doesn't feel scared of what's out there. There are no bogeymen squirming in the night. No heads on sticks. The only killer here is her, strapped into her car seat, hands still on the wheel.

I killed someone tonight, she thinks. How the hell can there be words for that? How can the same benign letters that make up an infinite number of other sentences – words and phrases and expressions that other innocent mouths form – be shuffled around and made to say this?

I killed someone tonight.

And that's not all. That's not even the most of it. She is one face of the Gemini, one piece of the puzzle. Two women met, then two people died. And none of these words should be put together. What the hell have they done?

She has a sudden anachronistic desire to call a local radio station or go to see a priest. She's not religious, wasn't raised to believe, doesn't even remember which religion does that stuff. Is it just the Catholics? To confess might be the only thing that offers relief but then, she wouldn't be confessing just for herself, she'd take Maggie down with her. A whole life, a whole future, wiped out by one terrible mistake.

The only person to whom she ever used to confess was her dad. He would absolve her anything, any misstep, any debt. Those she dragged in with her were not so lucky. He never once blamed her for Rob trying to sell him stolen goods.

'It was all his idea, wasn't it?' was all her dad said and she'd nodded, a lie, throwing Rob under the bus to save her own skin.

No one really changes.

And really, if she's honest – no matter the black velvet grip around her throat, no matter the guilt that is stamping on her gut and pressing her bones to the seat – if she's honest, really truly honest, she does not want to get caught for this either.

She does not want every hope she has for her future to be snuffed out. She doesn't want to be shoved into a cell and locked away. What Charlotte wants, more than anything else right now, is to get away with murder.

Outside, the matte night has dissolved all around into individual shapes, near and far, the lights of the village, the trees. She looks around her car as if seeing this dashboard for the first time. The big screen with its map lit up with a constellation of places she shouldn't have been.

And her phone, alive with notifications that she's been ignoring. She can't possibly read gossipy messages in WhatsApp groups that she no longer participates in but lurks in to feast on the drama. She doesn't deserve to have any nice messages from Rob but she has several missed calls from him.

She needs to go inside, boil-wash herself, burn her clothes, hide in her bed and practise her lines for when the police call, and they will call.

The phone lights up again but it's just her voicemail pestering her.

She gives in and lets it play over the loudspeaker while she bites her nails off one by one, the taste of river water underneath them.

'One voicemail from Rob.' She sits up straighter when his voice kicks in, strangled and staccato.

'Charlie, call me back. Please.'

There's a pause so long she thinks the recording has finished but then he speaks again, in a terrified, distorted voice that she's never heard him use before. 'It's about Anne.'

She calls him back, palms slick with sweat as she taps his number on her favourites list, heartbeat thrumming in her temples. Does he know? Does he know Anne's dead? But how could he know?

'Charlie,' he says, and then he starts to cry. In over twenty years, she's never heard him cry before. Not when he thought he'd be sent to prison because of her stupid idea. Nor when he was breaking up with her and she pleaded with him, said she'd rather be dead than live without him. When her own tears jammed all her circuits and she hiccupped and belched and turned herself inside out. He went rigid and pale, but he still didn't cry.

He weeps now. And any uncertainty she had is replaced with cold dread.

She asks, knowing she has to, even though it is the start of a slow march to ruin.

'Rob, what's wrong?' If her tone sounds as fake to him as to her, he either doesn't let on or doesn't care. She closes her eyes and waits for him to tell her.

'I went to see Anne,' he says, his voice hoarse.

'What? Why?'

'I wanted to talk to her. I was so angry about what you told me, I thought maybe I could appeal to her to, y'know, change her mind or whatever. It doesn't matter now.'

'Oh, Rob.' Of course he did. She can see it all. Rob driving over to have his say, to defend Charlotte with his old-fashioned, unrequested chivalry.

'She wasn't answering the door, Charlie, and I was getting more and more angry. I thought she'd realised why I wanted to speak to her and she was trying to dodge me. I thought maybe she'd gone out. But her car was there and I could see her handbag hanging on the stairs through the door. I don't know, it was just a bit weird.'

'What did you do?'

'I went round the back and the door was wide open. I knew she must be in so I went inside and called out to her but she didn't reply.'

'And then what happened?'

His reply is a whisper. 'I found her body.'

Charlotte

She can't breathe. Or think. Instead, Charlotte has collapsed into this single moment, like a black hole, eating itself.

There is nothing. She doesn't hear the whisper of blood through the curls of her ear canal, nor the metronomic pulse in her wrists. She doesn't even notice the wild wind outside, rocking the car like a cradle. Nothing exists.

She shakes herself back to the present, tries to imagine that she doesn't already know the horrible facts. Thinks about what a normal, innocent person would ask.

'How did she . . . I mean she seemed fine when I saw her, she wasn't ill or . . .'

'She wasn't ill,' he says quietly.

'Did she hurt herself?' Charlotte manages to croak, her voice sounding weirdly hopeful.

There's a pause. 'Someone hurt her, Charlie. She didn't . . . she didn't do this to herself.'

And even though she knows the truth, knows the culprit,

is an accessory, for fuck's sake, it's still so shocking to hear these words swirling around on the loudspeaker of her car that she's struck dumb.

'I need to go,' Rob's voice says, bringing her back to the surface with a gulp. 'I can't think straight, I'm sorry. She was your friend and—'

'Come to mine,' she says reflexively. 'You don't have to be alone.'

He says nothing. She thinks of Maggie, remembers that hug and how desperately they had clung to each other. Wishes she could be here now, the only person who would truly understand. Into Rob's silence, she adds, 'And I don't want to be by myself either.'

'I can't,' he says, as if the very effort of making a decision has exhausted him. 'I can't string a sentence together or walk in a straight line. I just need to go to bed. I've been talking to the police for hours and I'm just . . . I'm wrung out. I'm sorry.'

'Don't be sorry. I'll call you in the morning.'

'OK.'

'But if you need me,' she says, 'I'm here. OK?'

'I'm so sorry for your loss,' he says, and then cuts off before she can say anything.

Your loss. Has ever a phrase been less deserved?

The security light springs on as she approaches her front door. The tiny click accompanying it seems sharper tonight, like the tut of a tongue. The fancy wreath and the fox knocker look like props in a murder mystery. She imagines a TV detective shining a UV ray over them, finding her and Maggie's fingerprints lit up like fireworks.

She shuts the door quickly and locks and bolts it, even though there's no more chance of David breaking in. There will be traces of him here, his scent, hairs and tiny flakes of skin. Skin that someone, at some time, will have stroked in consolation, will have helped bathe as a little boy. Everyone becomes innocent in death, she realises, and that is what's choking her the most.

She's struck by the smells in the house. The expensive diffuser no match for the damp teabags, lying in little pats on the sink. Nor the meat tang of sausages and bacon. As they'd eaten earlier, she noticed how fine and pointed Maggie's incisors were and then looked away embarrassed. Was that really just today?

The strongest smells are rising up from her own body though. The smell of fear. She imagines she can see it rising from her skin, her clothes, sketched onto the air like cartoon stink waves.

Has she always had such a keen nose or such a brutal imagination? Maybe this is her origin story. Her spider bite. Activating her senses and turning her from victim to vigilante. She shakes her head at the wishful thinking. She isn't even a supervillain let alone a superhero. She's just a coward with an over-active imagination.

But the images won't stop, even as she peels off her clothes right there in the hall. Avoiding the mirror.

Even though it is dry, she imagines her hair strung with pond weed. Imagines her own eyes bulging like a gargoyle beneath the surface of the river. Are David's eyes still open under there? What did he hear as he gasped for breath and filled his lungs with deadly water? And what was the last thing he smelled? Is algae coating his mouth?

Naked, she bundles her clothes up and shoves them into a binbag in the kitchen. The raw solidity of her body catches her eye in the black shine of the uncovered window. As she tugs the blind down, she wonders if she'll ever stop thinking of David. Or Anne.

Or Maggie.

The thought of seeing her again on Friday helps her find the strength to climb the stairs, to carry on.

She showers vigorously, the water as hot as she can handle. She shampoos twice, scrubbing her scalp hard and then conditions her hair even though it feels perverse to think about bounce and lustre given what she's trying to wash away.

Next she lathers every crease and fold of her body, then shaves herself entirely with the blunt razor that she's been meaning to replace for a week. Tiny red dots appear on soft skin she's never troubled before. It feels over the top, but she doesn't know where and how a body holds onto evidence. And it's not like she can google it, she can't risk laying those breadcrumbs. She'd rather skin herself than leave clues laced into the fine hairs on her arms, inner thighs and toes.

For a moment she considers shaving *all* her hair off. Her huge mane of curls that catch every crumb of her careless eating. Should she pluck her eyebrows to nothing, the 'slugs' she hated so much growing up and that are now one of her favourite features? Pencil them in instead? But the police will surely want to speak to her soon, and finding a wild-eyed bald woman will hardly point them in other directions. And then there's Rob. What would he make of monstrous transformation? What questions might he ask?

She cycles back through her thoughts, filing them into order. The police will need to speak to her. The actual police, investigating an actual murder. And not even the murder that she herself . . . oh god. The thought surges up from her gut, the vomit arriving with a wet slap on the floor of the shower. Will she ever keep anything inside her body again? Food? Drink? Secrets?

As a knock comes on the front door, another mouthful of bile rises.

Charlotte

She thought she would at least have tonight to get her story straight. To *recover*.

She rushes to the bedroom, tugging her dressing gown over her overly smooth, red raw body. She knows she should go downstairs and open the door but she also knows, from being notified of her parents' deaths, that it's OK to take your time. That the police don't hold that against you if you take a while, not if they think you're innocent.

Her fingers tremble and catch on each other as she fumbles at the curtain. It's OK to peek out, surely? It's late at night and she's alone. That doesn't suggest guilt, does it? No, she realises with a lurch, that doesn't suggest guilt but the binbag of clothes in the hallway does, each item inside bearing witness to the splash of a stalker's body into a dirty river.

Perhaps they will assume she's asleep and leave her alone for tonight. Perhaps. She peers out as carefully as she can, keeping the light off to avoid their attention. But when she looks down, it is not two solemn police officers standing on the door mat.

It's Rob.

'Sorry,' he says. 'I should have called back but—'

She doesn't say anything, just pulls him towards her and wraps her dressing gown sleeves around him.

'It must have been a terrible shock,' she says, as he heaves tears into her shoulder. He nods wordlessly, the bones of his head grinding into her so she winces with pain but says nothing. Somewhere in Wales, she thinks, someone else will need to be comforted like this soon.

'Can we sit down?' he says, pulling away and reaching for the living room door behind which hangs Maggie's dirty wedding dress and the binbag of clothes Charlotte just kicked in there.

'Come upstairs,' she says quickly. 'Let's just . . . let's just try to sleep.'

Will she ever admit that they did not sleep? Will she tell the police the truth when they finally work out what happened and she can't outrun her lies? Will she admit that she, a newly minted murderer, took this traumatised man upstairs to bed? And that instead of talking, or consoling, they disrobed like snakes shedding their skins. He had flinched slightly at the blanket of red dots across her body, but said nothing. For the second time that day, they were still the teenagers that first discovered sex, and not the thirty-somethings that had done it to death. Better that than talk. Better that than think.

Yet another secret. Another discovery about what and who she really is when all the rules are crossed out.

'It's when you're under pressure that you find out what you're made of,' her dad had told her when he'd found her sobbing on the floor, surrounded by revision notes for her GCSEs. Anne had been over earlier that day, bringing her own books in a heavy rucksack on the back of her bike. She couldn't get peace and quiet at home, couldn't focus. Instead of revising, Charlotte had convinced her to sneak out across the fields to Rob's village and meet him and his cousin Cole who were working for an uncle, baling hay. They'd spent the afternoon flirting while Anne had looked bored and Cole had made annoying comments to her. Anne had eventually stormed home after Cole had told her he knew her dad because they'd been in the same nick once.

Charlotte had spent the evening crying about their fallout and belatedly worrying about her exam. And what had she done under pressure? Written tiny notes on her arms and inside her fingers on the morning of each exam.

Her dad had been right. Pressure revealed your core self. And the findings so far didn't look good.

Maggie

Maggie walks carefully along the road and turns into the cemetery. It seemed as good a place as any when she chose it to walk to, but now it seems beyond macabre. Like she's laughing at what they've done, but she doesn't find it funny at all. It's dark already but there are little lamps dotted along the path and the moon casts a watery light. She shivers, wishing she'd asked for a coat. Or better yet, wishing she was asleep on a heated seat on her way back over the Severn.

Six days, that's all. Six days and then she'll see Charlotte again. She pictures her now. Those Elizabeth Taylor eyebrows furrowed as she concentrates on the road, her soft jumper sliding up and down her arms as she turns the wheel. She thinks of their hug goodbye and wraps herself in its memory. Thinks too of the invisible bomb, ticking away in the folds of Charlotte's life. What will be left of her, when it goes off?

Charlotte

Sunday Morning

Charlotte feels more dead than alive. Lying all night in that slippery place just next to sleep, but never falling in. She lost the dark hours poking and prodding at her memories, both near and far. Now it's getting light and hopeless. She can't lie here like this any more, her body heavy against every crease of the bedding.

Her gut swills as she stands up, still nauseous with guilt and fear. She's glad of it. She *should* feel sick, it means she's not entirely lost her humanity.

A flash across her mind of that dead drop into the water, the fear in his eyes, the high-pitched shriek.

She scrunches her eyes shut and shakes her head until it goes again.

On the bed, Rob's eyes twitch as he sleeps. Is he reliving his discovery?

She wants to ask more about what happened when he found her. Did the police take his statement there or at the station?

He found her in the early evening, before she and Maggie had even headed for Wales, and he didn't call until late. Was he traumatised, under arrest or both? Was he helping police with their enquiries? All these TV words.

They must have asked about his whereabouts before he found Anne, surely? So how long does it take before the police know the time of death? If TV is in any way accurate, they would know almost instantly. But that can't be true. They've not asked her to confirm he was with her when Anne died.

If Rob's worried about being a suspect, he hasn't said. He's barely said anything, muttering into her hair how sorry he is, how awful he feels for her, for Anne, for her parents. No thought for his own vulnerability. Has she shoved her own boyfriend into the cross hairs by using him as an alibi, a shield? And would he, ever trusting, just let her?

She wants to get away with this, but not at *that* cost.

She pulls on joggers and a T-shirt as quietly as she can and heads downstairs. As the kettle boils, she turns her phone over and over in her hand. Any other question she has, at any time, she googles. She doesn't even think about it, is tapping out the stupid flippant questions before she even forms them fully in her mind. But not these.

How long until rigor mortis sets in?
Is the person who finds a body always a suspect?
When do police charge someone with murder?
What's the prison sentence for murder?
Do police look at the google searches of suspects?

No, she really can't.

Rob plods downstairs just after six. After a working life of early starts, coupled with the monstrosity of his discovery, it's not a surprise to see him awake now. His hair is a mess and he looks decades older than he did yesterday afternoon. She realises with a start that he looks just like his own dad did when she first met the family. All these years, she'd carried eighteen-year-old Rob in her mind, now he's fading and being replaced by the reality. A slightly podgy, greying dad.

'How are you doing?' she asks, sliding the mug of tea towards him that she started making at the first floorboard creak from above.

'Thanks,' he says, his voice thick and uncleared. 'I'm . . . I don't know.'

They sit in silence. The kind of scene she used to yearn for as a teenager: the two of them as adults, in a lovely kitchen, by themselves, companionable and solid. No longer strapped into the rollercoaster of hormones and drama and huge feelings. But she'd give anything for the purity of teenage angst now. The certainty of that longing.

'She was—' he starts.

Charlotte wants to know. *Needs* to know. And doesn't want to hear it.

'It's OK,' she says. 'You don't have to tell me.'

'It was just awful. I knew she was . . . gone . . . even before I got close. She was like a, a, I don't know. A waxwork. Not human. Not—' He stops. He's not crying, it's worse than that. Almost a catatonic state.

'Did you call an ambulance?'

'Of course I did,' he says, frowning. 'I called 999 and described what I'd found and they sent police and an ambulance. They came so fast that I was still on the phone.'

'That's good,' she says, uselessly.

'Is it?'

'I don't know, I don't know what to say, Rob. Did the police . . .?' What is she trying to ask? *Do the police suspect some random woman called Maggie did it? Do the police think I'm an accomplice? Do they know I killed their main witness?*

'Were they suspicious of you, do you think?'

He looks up then, his eyes hostile, but the expression softens and his shoulders fall.

'God, I hope not. They were really nice to me. I mean

134

they asked about what time I got there and where I was before and stuff like that. But that's normal, right?'

'I don't know.' None of this is normal. But Rob will have given her name and details to the police as he was with her, so she'll be on their radar now. It's only a matter of time before they come.

'Did you give a statement there or at the station?'

'At the station. They videoed it too. I mean, the house was, *is*, a crime scene, I guess,' he says, his eyes glazed over as if he's going back there, to what he saw.

'I'm so sorry,' she says and she is. She really fucking is.

'I'm sorry too,' he says, his voice barely above a whisper as he places his heavy hand on hers.

'Why?'

'She was your friend. I know you'd fallen out but you had a lot of history.'

'Did you tell the police that?'

He pulls his hand away, rubs his hair and frowns. 'That you'd fallen out?'

She nods, her heart cranking up again, thudding away at the thought.

'Why would I?'

'I don't know,' she says hurriedly, snatching his hand back and lacing her fingers into his, remembering momentarily the way she had done this with Maggie before they parted. 'I'm not thinking straight. Rob, this is . . . I know it's worse for you, finding her, but . . . it's something. It's *something* to me.'

'I'm sorry, Charlie. Of course it is. Of course.' He stands quickly from his chair and snakes his arm around her shoulders, pulling her into him. The morning musk of him envelops her and she lets herself cry and oh god the relief of that. Even if she doesn't deserve to spill a single tear, it bleeds out of her like poison.

Charlotte

'Am I alright to have a shower?' Rob asks and she nods.

'Treat this place like your own,' she calls after him and hears a pause of his footsteps on the stairs, before he carries on wearily to the bathroom.

It's just gone seven now. They've been slumped at the breakfast table for an hour, pouring caffeine onto their private fears and memories, barely speaking.

She hears the roll of careful tyres up the uneven lane and knows immediately that it must be the police this time. No one else would visit her early on a Sunday morning besides Rob, and he's already here. She pushes the living room door open to get a better look, legs feeling heavy as lead. As she opens up, she sees the damp dirty wedding dress hanging like a criminal from an executioner's pole, and beneath it the bag of clothes she wore last night.

'Fuck!'

She shoves the binbag behind the sofa, crushing it against the wall. Then she grabs the dress and bundles it into as manageable a pile as possible, dashing back into the hall with it. Overhead, she hears the shower judder to a halt and outside the front of the house she hears the twang of a handbrake.

Besides the police, what would Rob think if he saw her with a random wedding dress? It's like something out of a farce. She spins, still holding the big pile of fabric in her arms, unable to make a decision. A car door opens. She knows already the expressions that will be fixed on their faces, can picture them so precisely she may as well have flung the door open already.

Upstairs, she can hear Rob make his way from the bathroom to her bedroom and she knows, just as clearly as she can picture the expressions of the police, that he has used the hand towel from the sink on his hair instead of one from the fresh pile. He will be rubbing at his head furiously, never holding truck with a hairdryer, and then rearranging the larger towel around his waist where it will have slipped. Everyone else is so predictable, but, after yesterday, she's unable to predict her own movements let alone decide upon them. *Think!*

She rushes into the kitchen and opens the back door, opening up the small shed that's filled with fishing rods and tools arranged by size by her father. She pulls back the tarpaulin covering the old petrol mower and lays the dress on top of it, tugs the cover back into place and goes back into the kitchen, washing her hands.

The knock comes, likely the second one already. But it's Sunday, she tells herself, that's OK. The stairs creak overhead and, as she gets into the hall, feeling exposed suddenly with her heavy breasts loose under her old T-shirt, Rob opens the front door. He's dressed in the clothes he arrived in yesterday and smells musty despite his shower.

'Mr Parsons,' one of them says and Rob instinctively puts out his hand to shake both of the officers'. She feels instinctively protective. Why is his name so readily on the tongue?

'We're looking for Charlotte Wilderwood,' the other officer starts and Charlotte steps forward, one arm slung awkwardly across her vulnerable chest.

'That's me,' she says, as Rob steps aside to make way for her. When Charlotte's parents died, the police had come to notify her but also to support her, to offer comfort. It's clear from the stony faces in front of her that these two are here about the crime that's been committed. Not to offer comfort. At least, not yet.

'I'm sure you already know about your—'

'Friend,' she interrupts and Rob puts his arm around her. 'Anne was my friend,' she adds quietly. 'Since we were eleven.'

'I'm very sorry for your loss,' one says, showing his badge. 'I'm DCI Kashani, and this is my colleague DCI Hall.' Kashani is two inches taller than Hall, several degrees more handsome, and she wonders if he's proud of that. If Hall resents him.

'We just need to ask you a few questions to help with our enquiries,' adds Hall.

'We'll try not to take too long,' Kashani adds, softening his expression into something that's almost a smile. He has a trim black beard and alert brown eyes that she avoids. Hall is sandy-haired, dumpy, and looks unimpressed.

'Of course,' she says, opening the door and pointing for them to go into the lounge. Her vision wobbles as her heart rate spikes again. *Fuck. Hold it together.*

'Do you mind if I just—' she gestures to her pyjama bottoms, desperate to buy some time and catch her breath. 'I won't be long.'

'No problem.'

'Can I get you a tea or coffee?' Rob says, pitching the right tone of amiable and concerned. *He'd get away with murder, no problem,* she thinks then jogs up the stairs, appalled at herself. When she gets to her bedroom, she presses her back against the door and lets herself properly breathe. Her face is burning and she wonders if the police noticed. If they already know she's responsible in some way and her shining cheeks have just confirmed it.

Charlotte

'And what time did you leave Mr Parsons' house?' Hall says, his voice brisk.

'I don't know,' she says. *What time should she say?* 'It must have been about four?' It comes out as a question, but no one answers. Instead, DCI Hall makes a note in his pad, a firm little strike. Rob is in the kitchen making another cup of tea at DCI Kashani's suggestion and she wonders how wrong-footed they were by him being here. Are there other questions they want to ask that they'll have to come back for? Is she giving the right answers?

'Is he . . .' she starts but swallows it down. The policemen look back at her, waiting. Their knees are both at forty-five degree angles, their backs upright. The platonic ideal of 'the boys in blue', almost unreal.

She lowers her voice, wipes a tear that's welling on the brink of her lower lid, and just says it.

'Is he a suspect? My boyfriend, I mean?'

'Is there something we should know?' Hall asks quietly, looking towards the door.

She swallows. 'About Rob? No, not at all, not like that. I guess I've watched too much TV but I just . . . I was worried he was, you know, wrong place, wrong time and it would look bad for him.'

Kashani sits forward, his low voice soft and careful. 'We've collected a detailed timeline from Mr Parsons and we've been corroborating it; that's partly why we're here now.' He pauses and looks at Hall just briefly. 'Miss Wilderwood, do you feel unsafe in anyway?'

'Oh god no,' she says, too loudly. 'No, it's not that at all. He wouldn't hurt a fly. He really wouldn't.'

'So far, we've got CCTV evidence that appears to verify Mr Parsons's account and we work very hard to get to the truth. Don't let the TV fool you,' Hall says, his voice slightly salted. 'We only arrest someone if there's very good reason to think they're involved.'

'I'm sorry, I didn't mean . . . this is incredibly hard,' she says.

'We understand.'

'What kind of person would do this?' Charlotte adds, as Rob comes back in, awkwardly carrying four mugs that slop from their rims.

Just what kind of person *would* do this?

It's a question asked more to herself than her visitors but Hall answers anyway, with a candour that reassures her they don't suspect Rob. Or herself. At least, not yet.

'We don't know,' he says.

'Sometimes, these things are random,' Kashani adds, almost apologetically. 'But it's very often someone known to the victim. A boyfriend or ex-partner . . . which is why it's important you tell us anything you think of that might be relevant, however small it might be.'

Charlotte tries to keep her voice level. 'We didn't really discuss our love lives and she certainly never mentioned anyone special.'

'So you've known Miss Wilkins since you were eleven, and in that time you've not discussed boyfriends?' Hall says, one eyebrow raising a fraction.

Charlotte takes a deep breath. 'We . . . we drifted apart after school and only recently became friends again. She's quite . . .' she looks at Rob but he's staring down at his mug. 'She *was* quite guarded about her personal life. I think she was seeing someone before I moved back here but she never really told me about him.'

Rob's head shoots up. 'No, it's . . . that was nothing.'

'Nothing?' Kashani looks at Rob.

'You said it ended abruptly, didn't you?' Charlotte says, groping for a way to send them in the wrong direction but Rob's shaking his head. 'I really don't know,' he says.

Kashani looks back at her. 'And when did you last see Miss Wilkins?'

She takes a sharp breath through her nose. 'Friday,' she says. 'At work.'

'And you worked together at your firm, Wilderwood Antiques?'

She nods. They already know so much about this case. If Charlotte was a victim of a crime rather than a perpetrator, she'd be relieved.

'And no one ever came to pick her up from work or called her there?'

She shakes her head.

'And no office romances of any kind?'

Charlotte snorts in surprise. 'No, there's only me and Dorian.'

'Dorian?' Hall's pen hovers over his pad.

'Dorian Cook. She's worked at the company far longer than me.'

'What's her role?'

Charlotte shrugs. 'A bit of everything. Cleaning, filing, answering the phones. She's only part-time, usually Monday, Wednesday and Friday mornings.'

'We'll come in to see her tomorrow then,' Hall says.

'OK,' she says, hoping to hide her dismay that they'll be back in her world so soon.

With the practised synergy of dance partners, Kashani and Hall place their barely touched tea back down on Charlotte's mother's Royal Delft coasters and stand up.

'We won't take up any more of your time. But if you think of anything . . .' Hall slides a card from his pocket and offers it to Charlotte. Her fingers tremble as she takes it and she hopes he doesn't notice. 'Don't hesitate to call us.'

'I won't,' she says, swallowing so sharply the back of her mouth hurts.

'I'll see you out,' says Rob.

Charlotte

Monday

Rob gets up at just gone six, planning to call into his place to shower and change before work. It was another feverish night. Maybe they'll all be like that from now on. Both of them lying in silence, fully awake while the countryside sighs peacefully around them.

She'd reached across to him at one point, her fingers touching his chest and flinching, thinking about David.

After Rob leaves, kissing her briefly with dry lips and absent eyes, Charlotte peels herself from the bedding. She tries to shower herself sensible but the lack of sleep has punched holes in her brain and she just stands under the stream, staring at the water sliding down the cubicle glass.

How many showers did her dad have in this spot, at this hour, before heading to the showroom to which she will soon head? Hundreds? Thousands?

I'm sorry, Dad.

She needs to get there before Dorian, break the news about Anne before the police arrive armed with questions. And what might they ask her anyway? There's nothing she could know but even being asked is likely to get her worked up.

Dorian has been with the company since Charlotte was tiny. Before that, she was one of the regular visitors to the bric-a-brac stall that preceded Wilderwood Antiques. She can't have been much been older than Charlotte is now, she realises with a start, early forties if that.

That market stall in Bristol was part of family mythology, started before her parents even met. Her dad had set up at the crack of dawn every day with a cash belt he'd hand sewn and worked until the market closed, no matter if it was lashing down or snowing. No matter if no one showed up.

'Dogged,' that's how Charlotte's mum described her dad's courting style, and that's how he approached everything, including business. Perhaps, she allows herself to think, it was his haste and determination that made him overlook his own mistakes and get the paperwork in a muddle. That's something else she'll have to tackle soon enough but the thought of unpicking it all exhausts her and it's not like Anne is going to tell anyone about the inaccuracies now. Charlotte cuts off the water and shivers her way to the towel rail.

There are very few neighbouring businesses open when she pulls up at the showroom. The whole trading estate looks eerily out of time, with its old-fashioned signage and decaying buildings.

She opens up and flicks the bank of switches so the lights spring on. Was it really only Saturday that Maggie was here with her, rooting around like a pair of bloody Nancy Drews, as if this was all a game? The key is still in the lock of Anne's empty filing cabinet and she snatches it out and places it back in the drawer.

This is not a crime scene, not in the eyes of the police, but it is. Everywhere Charlotte goes is now a crime scene because she's a criminal. So this is it, she thinks, the other side of the coin. What would her parents think?

She checks the clock; it's only just gone eight but Dorian is a wild card and has been known to arrive anywhere from half past eight to ten o'clock. Charlotte locks the door just in case and then grabs the cleaning stuff from the storeroom.

As she snaps on the rubber gloves and starts spraying every surface she and Maggie touched on Saturday, she imagines forensic experts in white boiler suits dusting for prints.

If she can make it through today, she can make it through tomorrow. And then it's only a couple of days until she goes to Cribbs Causeway to see Maggie. Her stomach flutters at the thought, the thought of being able to be totally honest with someone is intoxicating. She'll tell her about the police, about Rob, as other shoppers bustle around oblivious of the little bubble the two of them are in. But for now, cleaning.

Charlotte's just finished the kitchen area when the door rattles. She's cleaned the area around the desks and was hoping to do the rest of the showroom but it's too late now. She bundles the caddy of sprays and accessories back into the cupboard, the unused Henry vacuum cleaner clattering after her. She rushes to the front door to unlock it, realising just at the last moment that her hands are still thrust into a pair of Marigolds.

'Where's Queen Anne then?' Dorian asks, hanging her woollen coat up on the brass stand in the office. It's not malicious, Dorian likes – liked – to rib Anne on her newfound fancy ways. 'Are you OK?' she adds, frowning.

Charlotte shakes her head. Her eyes feel gritty from lack of sleep, her mouth feels detached from her brain. The speech she'd practised on the way over has dissolved to nothing and when she opens her mouth to speak, nothing comes.

She hadn't had to do this when her parents died. Someone else, maybe the police, had told Dorian long before Charlotte saw her again at the funeral. Whatever Dorian's initial reaction about her long-time boss and friend's death was, it had dulled to pure sympathy by then.

Who will tell David's family that he's dead? He's not . . . he wasn't old. Might he have a mum who loves him? Who still sees the best in him? Will they have to identify him? Oh god, what the hell does drowning in freezing water even do to a body? A wave of nausea sweeps over her and Dorian watches with concern. *Stay focused.*

'I have some bad news,' Charlotte says. 'I'm afraid that—' she swallows. Each word seems to be glued into her mouth. She extracts them like rotten teeth. 'Over the weekend, I learned that—'

'You look shaken up.' Dorian frowns, rising to her feet and heading to the little kettle, coffee machine and fridge area they grandly call 'the kitchen'. 'Let me make you a tea.' She plucks a mug from the top of the safe, where Charlotte has slid back the stack of money.

'Anne's dead,' Charlotte blurts out to the older woman's back and Dorian stops. When she turns, her face is slashed with a confused smile, as if waiting for the rest of the joke.

'It's true,' Charlotte says, her eyes filling.

'What? Did she have an accident?'

Charlotte shakes her head. 'It happened over the weekend. The police came to see me yesterday and—'

'Someone hurt her?' The colour has drained from Dorian's lined face and she's now the colour of stone.

Charlotte nods then feels her knees buckle. She reaches behind for the nearest desk – Anne's desk – and then pulls her hand away as if it's contaminated. Suddenly Dorian is there, her arms around Charlotte. Dorian is stout and solid; her cream jumper is soft against Charlotte's cheek as she's pulled into a hug that she doesn't deserve.

'This isn't right though,' Dorian is saying, over and over like a mantra. 'This can't be right.'

'What do you mean?'

Dorian hesitates and for a moment Charlotte thinks she knows somehow. 'It's just not the way things are supposed to be,' she says, her voice muffled by Charlotte's hair. 'She was so young.'

Maggie

Sunday Evening

She's back in the flat, as if she never left. Except that it's not just the two of them here. His fury sits next to them on the sofa, slides between them in bed. When she thinks it's died down, it rises up again, burning brightly. Going over and over what happened on Friday, when she fled still wearing her wedding dress and left him, not knowing what to do, red-faced.

Then that he got so close to getting what he wanted, what he *deserved*, and it was ruined. 'All that money down the drain,' he says, and all she can do is nod.

Instead she trails after his silence, over-talking. About the weather being grim and the bread being a bit stale, and does the water taste funny to him and what should they have for tea because she wants to cook something nice for once.

He grunts his answers. He's trying not to punish her, she can tell, but he has his limits. Those limits are like bad teeth, you prod them with your tongue just to check they still hurt. And they always hurt.

He plans to work tonight, so don't worry about dinner for him, he says. He'll get something from a garage afterwards. Or maybe chips. He can't eat before work, he gets too nervous. His temperature rises in front of her, colouring his sallow skin red. And she knows he can't eat before work so why is she asking about bloody dinner anyway? He tosses his half-filled mug into the washing up bowl so it splashes dirty water all over the stuff she's just cleaned. The sudden spike of sludgy water makes her jump.

'Sorry,' she says, and folds a damp tea towel like floppy origami, over and again while he works his jaw. When he turns away, she'll carefully slide all of the plates and mugs from the draining board back into the bowl, rinse them and start again.

She thinks of the Aga at Charlotte's, the little compartments, all the matching plates. Her mother took that stuff seriously too and Maggie rejected it her whole life but sometimes mothers are right.

She'll bleach the bathroom in a bit. She has nothing else to do. She'll clean until her eyes sting. Then she'll do a wash. And she'd like to change the bedding too. She never got to sleep in Charlotte's spare bed. The pile of cushions there just for the sake of it, all matching. It probably would have been the best sleep of her life. For a brief moment she thinks about Friday, about asking to go home with Charlotte when they meet up. But she knows she can't, even if it frays the edges of her heart that she'll never see the inside of that cottage again.

She'd really like to open the windows and air this place out but the exhaust fumes roll along the road like sea mist, and the smell from the nearby burger place gets in your throat. She has to settle for Febreze and a Magic Tree car freshener twirling in the draft as it hangs from the kitchen window.

'I'm going out,' he says quietly. 'You're doing my head in.'

She watches TV for a bit, her knees tucked under her, the duvet dragged through from the bedroom like a security blanket. For some minutes, her thumb hovers over Charlotte's number. But they've agreed no phone calls, no texts, and that's how it needs to be. 'Until Friday,' she whispers. But the thought makes her as sad as it does excited.

*

She's been in bed for hours now in an unsleeping semi-stupor, staring up at a patch of damp on the ceiling and imaging she could reach up and touch it, write her name in it like steam. The curly M, the way her mother used to do it. *Best not think of her.*

At around three, his work bag rattles as it hits the kitchen lino. The sound rings out like church bells in the still night air. When he comes into the room, she lies still and pretends to be asleep. If asked, she wouldn't be able to explain why but she does it every time. A hangover from years ago when she was so shy she had to lie motionless like a corpse while he did it. And then she makes to stir, murmurs lightly as she opens her eyes.

In the moonlit room, she can see sweat glistening on his temples and his nostrils flaring like a bull. A smile curls his lip and his chest heaves. He's always happier when a shift goes well. She smiles with relief, throws back the covers and waits for him to charge.

Charlotte

'So you found out yesterday?' Dorian says, as they sit at the Rosewood table with their mugs on careful coasters. Charlotte nods and then shakes her head. 'No, I found out before that.' She tries to get the timeline right in her head. 'Rob found her, y'see.' Dorian looks up sharply from the mug. 'He went round there on Saturday night and . . .' What's the right word for it? 'She'd been attacked.'

'Why was Rob going round there?'

'They were friends,' Charlotte says quickly, and Dorian asks no more.

Charlotte often wondered about Dorian and her dad. Certainly there was no affair, Dorian is kind and loyal but she couldn't hold a candle to Charlotte's glamorous mum. But it's unusual to work in the same part-time job for decades, pottering along each week and never progressing. She's paid surprisingly well, so maybe that's why.

Charlotte can remember seeing Dorian here years ago, when she'd cycle over to say hi during her summer holiday, hanging around and hoping her dad would let her stay. Sometimes Dorian would come to the cottage with her late husband and their sons, big lumpy teenage boys who would snort and snigger every time Charlotte looked at them.

A car pulls up outside and Hall and Kashani appear at the door moments later, peering through the glass. Charlotte feels her breathing quicken.

Now they're sitting at the Rosewood table, fresh mugs of tea made by Dorian. She imagines her and Maggie's fingerprints everywhere again and has to swallow down the panic. She wishes she'd had time to clean everywhere.

Dorian is sitting up straighter than usual, her usually soft eyes alert, slightly red-ringed from an earlier bout of tears.

'We'd like to understand more about Miss Wilkins' activities and behaviour on the days leading up to the attack,' Hall says.

'Her behaviour?' Dorian asks, bristling a little. Charlotte looks across at her, seeing that famous loyalty in action.

'Not in the negative sense,' Kashani adds. 'We mean, did she meet anybody? Did she mention an argument or getting hassle from somebody.'

Dorian is shaking her head.

'A boyfriend maybe, or an ex-boyfriend?'

'No,' Dorian says emphatically. 'Not while I was here and not that she mentioned to me.'

'And you were here from what time?'

'I got here about nine, and left again at lunchtime.'

'And in that time, did anyone come into the shop?' Dorian shakes her head.

'Or hang around outside, anything like that?'

'No.' Dorian is clipped.

'You had no customers?'

'We often don't.'

'How do you make money?' Hall asks, looking at Charlotte.

'We sell a lot to trade,' Charlotte says, uneasily. *Please don't ask to look at the paperwork.* 'And we're starting to sell more online.'

Hall turns back to Dorian. 'Any strange phone calls or anything out of the ordinary on Friday?'

'Or over the last week,' Kashani adds.

Dorian shakes her head again but Charlotte interrupts. 'There was something,' she says, and the other three turn to look at her.

'I got back from lunch early on Wednesday and there was a guy in here with Anne.'

'Customer?' Hall asks.

'No.' How much to tell? Charlotte can't let on that she fell out with Anne about this, but if the police waste some time ruling out some smarmy suit, it keeps them away from the truth. 'He said he was an investor. But we don't need investors, we're just a little antiques company.'

Charlotte warms to her theme and Dorian looks uncomfortable.

'Anne looked a bit worried by him,' Charlotte said. 'She brushed it off and said he was just a chancer, but maybe he was giving her grief about something?'

'What was his name?' Hall barks, pen posed on his pad.

Charlotte shrugs. 'I don't know, I'm sorry. I don't think he said. He left soon after I got back.'

'Did you meet this man too?' Kashani asks Dorian.

Charlotte frowns, realising with a start that she'd not considered whether Dorian might have been here and heard the man and Anne's conversation, might realise Anne had been planning something. Luckily she's already shaking her head.

'It must have been after I left.' Dorian's cheeks flush and Charlotte thinks back, realising that something isn't right. Now's not the time though. Turning back to the police officers, she tries to dredge up everything she can to get them looking for this guy. 'He wore a nice suit, looked quite . . . moneyed.' Hall is scribbling notes as she talks and she closes her eyes to remember more. 'He was probably in his forties, tall and dark-haired, white with a tan, quite broad.' She opens her eyes again. 'And he drove a black BMW, yes, I remember now. It was in the car park when I got back.'

'What time was this?'

'Not long after twelve. He left soon after.'

'What model of beamer was it?' Hall asks.

Charlotte shakes her head. 'I'm not really a car person. It was big though, definitely one of the more expensive models, I could tell that.'

'OK,' Kashani says, nodding to Hall, who rises. 'If you remember anything else, especially his name, you've got my card.'

When they hear the car doors close, Charlotte sits back down next to Dorian. 'Why did you lie about being here when that man came?'

Dorian gathers up the mugs and shakes her head. 'I didn't lie,' she says, holding the four handles awkwardly, a drip of tea soaking and spreading through the wool of her jumper.

'I saw you waiting for the bus when I drove back,' Charlotte says. 'You must have only just left.'

Dorian dumps the mugs in the sink and twists the hot tap sharply so boiling water splutters from the small boiler. 'It was unrelated to what happened to Anne, anyway,' she says, her back still turned.

'How do you know?'

'He's been here before.'

'All the more reason—'

'No, he came when your dad was still here.' Dorian turns to look at Charlotte but doesn't make eye contact, not quite.

'Why didn't you say anything?'

'Because it's not relevant.' She turns back and squeezes too much washing-up liquid into the bowl then starts to scrub the mugs. There is foam everywhere.

'What do you mean? How can you—'

'I don't think your dad would have wanted the police to know all about his private business . . .'

'But he wasn't interested in investors, so I doubt he'd care,' Charlotte says, trying to grasp this new information. Her dad's reluctance to take on outside investment doesn't stop this being a good red herring to chuck to the police. 'He always wanted full autonomy, he didn't even let me in!' She laughs more shrilly than intended.

'I wanted to honour his wishes,' Dorian says, her eyes filling again. She walks over to the brass stand and pulls down her coat. 'And I didn't want to send the police off in that direction. I don't see how it would help Anne.'

'How is it not honouring his wishes to tell—'

'I really think you should leave it alone, Charlotte. Look, I'm sorry, love, but I have to go home. I'm too upset to work. First your parents and now Anne.'

'*You're* upset?'

'You should take some time off too,' Dorian says. 'I'm sure no one would mind.'

'There's no one left to mind,' Charlotte says quietly.

Dorian hugs her, a lightning flash of affection, then she's out the door, her solid square heels clacking across the car park, her arm reaching into her bag and pulling out her phone. Probably calling one of her devoted sons to come and collect her.

Charlotte locks the door again and drags the vacuum back out. When did Dorian last do the showroom? There are dustballs everywhere. She does around the edges of the room carefully. As she pulls out the dining chairs from the Rosewood table to do underneath, Charlotte spots a card on the floor. It's the one held out by the investor, last week, the one she'd refused to take. She stoops to pick it up, knees clicking in complaint. It's elegant and empty. Just a name, Harry Sedgemoor, and a mobile number. She flips it over, but the back is blank.

Harry Sedgemoor. No company name, no job title, no email. She turns the name over in her mind and tries to remember if she's heard it before. She doesn't think so.

She taps it lightly against her lip. She could call Kashani now, but then they'd speak to this Harry Sedgemoor, clear it all up in no time, and be back to hunting the real killer. She slides the card into her handbag until she needs to give them another distraction.

Charlotte

Tuesday

The British capacity for silence is astonishing. Yesterday, Rob had managed to pick his daughter Ruby up from school, give her tea and a bath and put her to bed at his house, all without letting on what had happened. How Rob's life had changed in one afternoon in Bath.

But then, she's also been able to drink tea, clean the office and make eye contact with the police, all while the memory of that push . . . that splash . . . plays in her head. How many people has she passed on the street who've done terrible things and are still walking and talking as if they're normal human beings? How many people have walked past *her* since Saturday night and not realised they've brushed shoulders with a killer?

Rob called Charlotte last night when the little girl was in bed, and they'd said a whole lot of nothing for half an hour. They didn't talk about Anne. She considered telling him about the police visiting, about the business card. But she stopped herself. This man, Harry Sedgemoor, is just an innocent guy who visited a small business. And yeah, the police will find that out soon enough but it won't be nice to be questioned. Worse, maybe Rob will recognise the name and have questions, opinions. Maybe he'd go haring off to tackle him himself. Or tell her to call the police immediately.

Instead, they made plans for Rob to come over for dinner tonight.

But when Charlotte wakes up – late, skull filled with a pulsing headache – the last thing she wants to do is see Rob. The newness of their adult relationship means they have developed different coping strategies in each other's absence, different approaches to other people's worries. Charlotte likes to chew them over in silence, Rob likes to take charge and try to fix things. And he certainly can't fix this.

How could she begin to explain to Rob what she sees when she closes her eyes? That rushing river, the splash of that man's body. The way David leaned back, almost goading her to push. Or is that wishful thinking? The smell of those clothes burning in the barbecue. The state of Maggie when Charlotte picked her up. Never mind her own part in what happened to Anne. All of it one wild, toxic jumble. Although a determined person could certainly work at the threads, follow the breadcrumbs from Charlotte to Maggie and Maggie to Charlotte. There is evidence all around. The wedding dress, for one thing.

Still in pyjamas and slippers, Charlotte tugs on her coat and buttons it around her. As the kettle boils for tea, she shoves open the back door and heads to the shed where she stuffed the wedding dress just days ago. It's bitterly cold this morning, and a spider lazily coils itself around the handle of the lawnmower. Charlotte shoos it away and then peels back the tarpaulin. She half-expects the dress to have disappeared like Cinderella's gown at midnight. But it's still there.

The skirt is filthy from the miles Maggie trooped along in it. The bodice smells of sweat and the train is slashed and tattered. It feels wrong to chuck it away; it doesn't belong to her. And at one time, Maggie had invested her last shred of hope in this gown as well as what little money she had. That counted for something.

Oh, Maggie. How to square that childlike optimism with the apparently brutal way Anne had died? So far the specifics of the death had not been reported, and Rob had struggled to give details, but when Charlotte tries to picture Maggie, her small hand driving a letter opener into Anne's chest, she instead sees her haunted moonlit face that night on the bridge. She sees her thin fingers worrying at the borrowed jumper. The way she desperately checked her phone in case her fiancé had messaged.

And if that fiancé has let her back in to his life, if there is a fresh start for Maggie, wouldn't it be wrong to have got rid of the dress? Wouldn't her fiancé have a lot of questions if it's gone? No, she'll get it cleaned and bring it with her on Friday. Give Maggie the option. If she really doesn't want it, she can sell it and use the money for her future.

When she's ready to leave for work, she loads the dress onto the backseat of the car, lying it down as if it's in a faint. When she catches sight of it in the rear-view mirror, it's almost as if Maggie has come back. She has so much to tell her, so much she wants to ask.

She heads out towards Bristol, knowing there are a few dry cleaners on the edge of the city that offer a fast service, places she's never been a customer and isn't known. She pulls up near one called Green Street Cleaners, parks outside the newsagent next door. As she climbs out, the local newspaper board outside makes her catch her breath.

BUSINESSWOMAN MURDER
'MOST BRUTAL' IN BATH'S HISTORY

She looks through the doorway and is immediately confronted by a wall of headlines. Not from national newspapers; it doesn't seem to have reached that level of interest. But Anne smiles out from the front pages of the *Bristol Post*, the *Bath Chronicle*, the *Echo*, the *Western Daily Press*, even some Gloucestershire papers that have made their way into the mix.

Most of them carry the same photo of Anne – shiny smile, shiny hair – but a couple of them also have photos of the police tape around her house, of the serious officers in boiler suits. What are they looking for? A long red hair that will send them in the right direction? The mustard fibres of Charlotte's jumper?

KILLED IN BROAD DAYLIGHT one headline says. Another, **ANNE'S FAMILY: SOMEONE MUST KNOW**

She stumbles back outside.

Charlotte

'Do you clean wedding dresses?' she asks, the door chime still sounding behind her, the image of all those newspapers still buzzing in her head.

The dry cleaners' shop is as neat as a pin but old-fashioned. Posters hang on the walls at perfect right angles, advertising cleaning products she's not seen since she was a child. Framed photographs of freshly cleaned, old-fashioned clothes hang behind the counter and a neatly pressed kipper tie is pinned to the wall like a prized catch.

'Certainly do,' says the serious man behind the counter, peering through half-moon glasses, zoning in on the state of the fabric lying across her outstretched arms. He frowns. 'What on earth did you do to it?'

'Oh, it's not mine,' she says quickly. 'A friend of mine got married outside, bit of mini-festival type thing. It was muddy.' *Don't overdo it.*

'Pop it up here,' he says, patting the counter like it's a triage stretcher so she lays the dress down. Frowning with concentration, he peels back the satin and looks at the taffeta underneath, then turns the dress over and gently runs his fingers along the hidden zip and onto the bodice. As he brushes the beading with his fingertips, a few loose beads scatter on to the floor. He looks up at her and frowns. 'She's done a real number on this, when did she get married?'

'A few weeks ago,' Charlotte says. 'I'm sorry but I'm in a bit of a hurry. How quickly could you clean it?'

'It's a big job, love.'

She sighs. Of course. 'I need to collect it on Friday morning,' she says. 'I don't mind paying extra.'

'It'd normally be a week, give or take, but for a hundred pounds I'll try to do it for Friday. I can't guarantee we'll get all of this out, though. It looks like years' worth of grime.'

'That's OK,' she says, her leg starting to jiggle with the urge to run. 'That's fine.'

'Paying with PIN?'

'Cash,' she says, pulling the notes from her purse.

'We'll give you a call when it's ready. What's the best number to catch you on?'

She doesn't want to give out her number, doesn't want to be linked to this dress that closely but she can hardly give a false one. And it's not like he's going to add it to some police database. Even as she's thinking this, a small part of her is watching the scene from above, a sense of déjà vu, of regret.

He notes the number down carefully, each digit precise.

'Name?'

She swallows. 'Pamela,' she says, her mother's name.

'Don't get many Pamelas your age,' he says, as he slowly forms the letters in block capitals then passes her a neatly folded carbon copy of the receipt.

She can see the police car outside the office as she pulls onto the trading estate. She considers turning around, driving away, but they know where she lives and what's she going to do? Go on the lam?

She crawls forward and parks next to it, sitting for a moment to catch her breath and try to slow her heart, to not seem wild and guilty. She opens her door and they follow suit.

Charlotte walks across the car park carefully like she's doing a roadside sobriety test. Her knees catch each other and adrenaline prickles all over her skin. She wants to run, wants to jump in her car, drive as far away as she can. But no. She must walk, she must maintain the illusion that she is a normal person. A normal *innocent* person.

She unlocks the door and turns on the lights. She shivers, even though the temperature is kept ambient for the antiques. 'Sorry to keep you waiting,' she says.

'That's no problem, you didn't know we were coming.'

She resists the urge to explain her late opening, layering up with unnecessary and false detail. Instead, she offers them a drink but they demure.

'I know you're busy so we won't keep you long,' Kashani says. 'We've been speaking to Miss Wilkins' neighbours again this morning. Some of them weren't available when we first called and sometimes people remember things a little later on.'

'Did any of them see anything?' she asks, unable to stop herself. *Just rip the plaster off.*

Hall and Kashani share a look and she shrinks a little.

'Several different households report seeing a regular visitor to Miss Wilkins—'

'Can you call her Anne? Sorry, it's just . . . I knew her as Anne.'

Kashani nods and continues. 'Someone, a man, used to visit Anne frequently when she first moved into her house in Bath.'

'I don't . . . I didn't see Anne when she first moved back. I was living in London at the time.'

'Understood,' says Hall, his voice tighter than Kashani's. 'But when you did *reconnect* with Anne, did she mention anyone? Maybe someone she'd been seeing and broke up with or—'

'She didn't mention anyone at all, not to me directly. Rob said she was seeing someone for a while but I didn't know about it.'

Please go and ask him and just leave me alone. They seem to be waiting for more so she carries on. 'The whole time I've known Anne, I've never known her with a boyfriend. That's weird, isn't it? I'd not thought of it before but even at school . . .' she trails off. This is irrelevant. 'I guess I didn't see her for a long time.'

'Anne was briefly married,' Hall says, a little spikily.

'She was?'

Hall nods. 'In her twenties. She lived in New York with him, did she not tell you about that?'

Charlotte shakes her head.

'Interesting,' says Hall.

'Well, is her husband a suspect? Didn't you say an ex, that's the kind of—'

'Miss Wilderwood,' Kashani says softly. 'He hasn't seen her in years and he was in Connecticut with his second wife at the time of Anne's death. We know this is a harrowing time for you, and we really are looking at every avenue. That's why it's so important we identify this man seen visiting Anne. Some of the neighbours said he had a dark car, which, given what you told us yesterday about a visitor . . .'

'You think it's the man who was here last week?'

'We're looking at every angle,' Kashani says.

'As you know,' Hall interrupts, 'the houses are mostly detached on Anne's road and there's quite a bit of space between the buildings so no one has given a very clear idea of what he looked like but they mostly agreed he was average height or taller, probably white with very short hair, either grey or fair.'

'That doesn't sound like anyone I know,' she says with a mixture of relief and disappointment.

'The man that visited Anne here—'

'He was definitely dark,' she says. 'Not grey or fair.'

'Bearing in mind people can dye grey hair, we really need to consider if this was the same man.'

'The neighbours said he was a boyfriend?'

'Some of them thought so, yes. Based on seeing them kiss goodbye, that kind of thing.'

'I—' she hesitates. What is most useful, to make them chase two men or one? *Two, definitely*. 'I'm sure this man the other day was just a business contact. There was no body language, you know? No affection or even . . .' *Stop laying it on so thick.* 'It just didn't seem that way.'

'Any chilliness? The way it might be with an ex?'

She shrugs. 'I mean, I'm not an expert but that wasn't the impression I got.'

All the way home she churns it over in her head. She still has the business card, which could send the police off the track even more, but only until they rule out Harry Sedgemoor. This way, they're still searching two bogeymen, and not her and Maggie. No, she decides, she'll keep this card for now and if she feels them getting too close, then she can send them in a new direction.

Traffic slows through Chew Barton, a quaint little village between Bath and Bristol with thatched cottages and an old-fashioned telephone box. She pulls over, thinking, then snatches a pile of coins from the little compartment in the car.

So much has happened since she said goodbye to Maggie: Rob finding Anne; the police talking to them, talking to Dorian. The business card; the red herring that Harry Sedgemoor offers. If Maggie is worrying, and surely she is worrying, Charlotte can ease that worry a bit. And this way, she thinks, as she pushes a pound coin in and copies Maggie's number from her mobile phone contacts and onto the cold buttons of the phone box, she won't leave a link between their phones.

As it starts to ring, she imagines Maggie curled up at her mum's house, phone in hand. She imagines her smiling with relief, pressing to answer, happy to hear Charlotte's voice. It feels wrong, somehow, that she's not heard Maggie's voice since they parted. But the phone is still ringing; she's not picking up. It rings four more times and as a group of women laugh manically, bursting out of the thatched pubs nearby, the voicemail cuts in. A generic recorded message, so she doesn't get to hear the reassurance of Maggie's voice. Charlotte puts the receiver down gently, sadly, and climbs back into the car. Until Friday then.

Rob is sitting in his truck on her drive when she arrives home.

'I'm so sorry,' she says, knocking on the door but he smiles weakly and hops down next to her. 'I know I said I'd cook but I've got no food in,' she says. 'And I've had a really shit day.'

He climbs out of the car then retrieves a bag from the passenger seat. The contents clink reassuringly. 'Let's just get drunk then,' he says.

'I don't deserve you.'

Maggie
Tuesday

She woke up this morning thinking about the blood. Or maybe she was dreaming, and the blood seeped through from her subconscious. She washed her hands, scrubbing them with the nail brush, two rounds of soap. It wasn't there anyway, and there's no getting it off. She can't tell him about this, so she swallows it back and lets it swirl in her chest.

'I'm the one who should be in a mood,' he says this afternoon, when she tunes out something he's saying and drifts back to the weekend. 'I'm the victim here.'

Anne is the victim, she thinks. Anne and Charlotte. But she can't say that, those names cannot become embroidered into her life here, into her future. Or maybe, deep down, she doesn't want this life here to embroider Charlotte. To tattoo her with fine and permanent threads. But it's too late for that.

'Fuck this, I'm going out.'

She eats dinner alone, looking at the microwave clock tick slowly on. He was supposed to be working later but he'll be drunk at the pub, she's certain. If he goes to work in that condition, he'll make a mistake. That'll be her fault too. But how many ways can she apologise? How many times can she explain? He'll never fully understand. There is only one person who shares the same shorthand, only one person who knows but doesn't blame her – or didn't. Maybe she feels differently now. Maggie imagines Charlotte pacing the cottage, reconsidering everything . . . Maybe she won't even show up on Friday. Maybe the police will instead. She starts to breathe fast.

Her phone is charging in the bedroom and she eagerly pulls it free from the cable. Could it really hurt to call Charlotte? She could withhold her number, does that still leave a record?

The screen says one missed call. Hardly anyone has this number. Her boyfriend left his phone here when he stormed out and so she hopes for a moment that it's Charlotte, that she's cracked first and called to say she's thinking of Maggie just as much as Maggie is thinking of her.

But it's not Charlotte's number, it's a Bristol landline. Oh god, Bristol Police? Could they know somehow? Could her phone have been traced to Anne's house at the time of the . . . shit. Shit. She drops her phone back down and tries to think. It was over an hour ago that they called and nothing else has happened. If they thought she was involved, and they knew where her phone was, the local police would be here, surely? Please let that be the case. Let it be a random cold caller or a wrong number. But she doesn't want to take any chances.

What can she do? She definitely can't call Charlotte now, not if there's a chance they're tracing her phone. And she can't tell him; he's still not forgiven her for everything that's happened, and this is . . . it's definitely too much. She rushes into the kitchen, fumbles to remove the SIM and then snips it roughly into pieces with the rusty old scissors they keep meaning to replace. From the 'stuff drawer', she pulls out a spare SIM, one of several he keeps and then, as an afterthought, she chooses a different phone too. An old one, unused for ages, that they'd been meaning to sell for a bit of cash. She'll tell him she broke hers.

Just then the front door to the flat opens with a bang. She rushes back to the living room and, with clumsy fingers, shoves her old phone under a sofa cushion.

'I'm taking tonight off,' he says, rushing over and scooping her up off the sofa, twirling her around while the downstairs neighbour bangs on his ceiling.

'I'm sorry for earlier,' she says. 'I didn't mean to upset you.'

He presses a finger to her lips, a silly smile on his. His skin tastes of salt. 'All is forgiven,' he slurs.

'For real?'

'For real. Because I've worked it out.'

'You have?' Her heart races. What has he worked out?

He nods and puts a finger to his own mouth now, pulls it across like he's zipping his lips.

They fall on the bed, his heavy arm lying across her and his hot beer breath in her ear. She thinks for a moment. 'Tell me the story of how we met instead then. Please?'

At first he says nothing and she shakes his side gently. 'Please,' she says again. His eyes are closed but he smiles as he says, 'you were like a lonely princess in a tower.'

'I was,' she says, closing her own eyes.

'Like something from a fairy tale. And I saw you watching me,' he says languidly, as if that summer sun was still beating down on his back. Slowing him down, slowing everything down. 'I looked up at your little face through the bathroom window and you just looked so sad.'

'I was sad until I met you,' she says.

'You were being kept prisoner by an old dragon. And when the dragon sent you out to the garden and I saw the body that went with that face, I thought I'd die on the spot.'

He'd been nut brown from the sun, his skin beaded with sweat. His T-shirt was draped over a wheelbarrow stuffed with pulled weeds, their roots already rotting in the heat. She could smell him as she'd approached, the richness of him, catching in her throat. She'd never smelt a man before, smelt the honesty of raw male work. She'd felt drunk.

Her mother had sent her out with the tray – a glass of water with ice in and some Rich Tea biscuits – to avoid dealing with him herself. Men made her nervous. A lot of things made her mother nervous.

He'd asked Maggie so many things while she'd stood awkwardly next to him, holding out the glass and trying to keep up with the flurry of queries and guesses and requests. She'd tried to gather them all up, hold them in the crook of her arm like a bouquet, but she couldn't.

It was like he knew her already, like he'd traced around her in pencil years before and now that he'd finally met her, he wanted to colour everything in. 'When's your birthday? What's your star sign?'

'My mum says star signs are—'

'You could be a ballerina. *Are* you a ballerina?'

She'd lingered too long and was called back inside and chastised. 'He was just making conversation,' she'd protested, just once, catching her mother's expression and shrinking.

Behind the garden, a place she was not normally allowed to go, a meadow lay laced with tiny purple flowers. And now, as he tells their story for the hundredth, thousandth or millionth time, she is there in that soft meadow. And it's a week on from when they first met, or maybe two. He's no longer working at her mum's. As far as anyone knows, he's left the town entirely. Her mum thinks Maggie is still in her bedroom.

Her knees bear the blood-rust streaks from the old drainpipe she carefully climbed down and she can feel the tickle of the grass on her skin and the sting of her sunburned shoulders.

He lies next to her, his eyes closed then as they are now. His nose not yet broken, his skin not yet weathered. A tiny clutch of scars bearing witness to an adulthood that he'd beaten her to, that for her lay ready to unfurl.

'Thank you for rescuing me,' she says now.

As he falls asleep, she creeps out of bed and into the living room, pulling the phone out from the sofa and shoving it deep into the bin.

Charlotte

1999

Anne's house looked like a little ink bottle. Squat, with a flat roof like a lid and a window either side of the blue front door. Identical to its neighbours except for the deep, ragged groove running down the door, which told a story Anne didn't want to share.

'Are you sure you want to stay the night?' Charlotte's mum asked, looking up and down the road.

'Yes,' Charlotte snapped, irritation and defensiveness bristling. It wasn't Anne's fault. And how bad could it be?

'Come on then, let's get this lot inside,' her dad said, grabbing her sleeping bag from the boot and pulling her rucksack onto his thick shoulder.

'You don't have to walk me in, Dad. I can manage,' Charlotte huffed, but he seemed determined.

Anne opened the door at first knock, a mixture of excitement and anxiety on her face. 'I need to tell you something,' she said, pulling Charlotte inside and shunting her towards the living room.

'I'll just say thanks to your mum,' Charlotte's dad said to their backs, both girls ignoring him.

'What is it?' Charlotte asked Anne inside the living room, readying herself.

'I promise I did tell my mum that you're vegetarian but she's made meatballs.'

'Oh.' Charlotte laughed. 'Don't worry about it. I was getting bored of veg anyway.' She didn't mention that she'd actually forgotten her declaration of vegetarianism almost immediately, eating a Wimpy the next day.

Anne deflated with relief.

'Mum's obsessed with that Naked Chef.' Anne's cheeks glowed red. 'Keeps saying everything's pukka.' They both laughed, Anne covering her mouth to stop her mum hearing. 'Apparently these are the Naked Chef's balls.' They laughed openly then.

In the neat kitchen, Anne's mum – Janine – was stirring a tomato sauce, chatting to Charlotte's dad and glancing cautiously at the casserole dish full of browning meatballs and the bubbling pan of pasta.

Charlotte's dad was sitting at the small table, watching Janine and smiling. He could – and would – talk to anyone. Market stall training coupled with natural charm. As he realised the girls were there, he stood up, patted his pockets for keys and then reached over to give Charlotte a kiss goodbye. She struggled to get away, mostly for laughs, and then he kissed Anne's mum on the cheek, followed by Anne, who blushed immediately beetroot.

'Nice to see you, Janine,' he called out, as he left.

'You too, Charles,' she called after him, smiling to herself as she stirred.

Anne spun to face Charlotte. 'Charles? Is that why you're called Charlotte?'

'No,' Charlotte said, blushing. 'It's just a coincidence.'

'Sure it is,' smirked Anne.

The table was set for three with a little bowl of parmesan in the middle and a big bottle of cola to share.

'I hope you like meatballs?' Janine said, smiling and turning briefly then tending the food again.

'I love meatballs,' Charlotte lied. It was clear, even at her age, that all the stops were being put out. She wondered who pushed for the effort, Anne or her mum.

'They're Jamie Oliver,' Janine added, blushing the same way Anne did when talking about boys she fancied but never got anywhere with. 'And they've got about seventeen fucking ingredients in them so they'd better be nice.'

Charlotte was asleep when everything changed. Stuffed in her sleeping bag like a cocoon, lying on the floor next to Anne's bed. The Travis CD had long clicked off, and the chat they'd exhausted themselves with had dried up hours ago. It was late enough to be totally dark, the street lights switching off around midnight. She didn't know why she was awake until she heard a series of thuds.

'It's Dad,' Anne whispered.

'What is?'

A bang on the front door shook the whole front of the house. A rattle of locks, chains. Then the scurry of Anne's mum's feet coming out of her bedroom and into theirs.

'Don't worry,' she said, sounding extremely worried. 'Fred's just come over for a visit.'

'Oh god,' Anne murmured as her mum left again, skipping down the stairs. 'She promised this time.'

Downstairs, the door was unlocked and a cacophony of shrieks, shouts and shushes took over the house. Next to Charlotte, Anne drew her knees up and rested her forehead on them, sobbing. 'She promised he'd not come back.'

Charlotte wriggled free of the sleeping bag and put her arm around Anne, who shrugged it off. 'Go to sleep,' she said sharply. 'This is none of your business.'

Charlotte lay staring up at the ceiling, listening to adult noises she'd never heard before. Shouts and pleading. Anne had a pillow over her head, tuning it all out. Charlotte crept out into the hall and down the stairs. She could hear Janine placating Fred in the kitchen, telling him to come back in daylight when he was sober. That she wanted to talk too, 'but not like this'.

Behind the shut door of the living room, she called her own house from the phone.

166

Her dad arrived in ten minutes, goodness knows how. She let him in and then went upstairs to gather her things, rolling her sleeping bag and stuffing it in its sleeve. Anne lay either asleep or faking it, curled like a prawn in the middle of her bed. By the time Charlotte got downstairs, Fred had left and Janine was sobbing onto Charlotte's dad's jumper, apparently pulled hastily over his pyjamas.

'You go back upstairs, love,' he said to Charlotte. 'There's nothing to worry about now. I'm going to stay for a bit just in case and then I'll come back for you in the morning.' She nodded, the adrenaline slipping and tiredness taking over as she trudged back up the stairs with her stuff.

'And darling?' her dad called out, Janine still sobbing onto his chest, rings of tears darkening the thin wool.

'Yeah?'

'Let's not worry Mum, though, eh? We'll just say you got a bit homesick and called me, no need for her to know about Anne's dad.'

Wednesday Morning

Dorian calls just as Charlotte is pulling up on a street she's not seen in years.

'Charlotte,' she says. Over the phone her voice sounds the same as it ever did, back when Charlotte would call to speak to her dad at work – to complain about her mum or ask for money. They would have the standard small talk – school, boys, hobbies – and not speak again for a few weeks. In her head, she pictures Dorian as she was then. The neat cardigan and shift dress, the long hair in a bun, the neat little brooches. Not as she is, edging into elderly life with an efficient short crop and sensible shoes. And now Charlotte is the one in charge, the one answering the phone, the one making decisions. Just like she always wanted.

'I'm sorry, love,' Dorian says. 'But I can't come in.'

'That's OK, I don't mind at all. It's been a horrible time and—'

'I mean, sorry to interrupt, but I can't come in *again*. I'm ready to go, Charlotte. I didn't realise it until now but with everything that's . . . I want to spend some time with the boys and their kids, I need to get this garden sorted out and . . .' She takes a deep breath and when she speaks again, her voice is slightly wobbly. 'It's time to let go.'

'I understand,' Charlotte says quietly, feeling surprisingly alone at this news. Dorian had made it clear multiple times that she'd rather be carried out of there in a coffin than retire and become 'an old lady'. But people change.

'Well, thank you for everything,' Charlotte says and then sets a reminder in her phone calendar to send a retirement gift. Then, before she can talk herself out of it, she climbs out of the car.

The ink pot house has a new door, painted in bright-red gloss paint. The tiny front lawn is mown carefully, with stripes like a tennis court. Her stomach churns.

Whatever lies in there, whatever aftermath, whatever pain, she put it there. Her and Maggie. She wants to run, wants to go back to her cottage. Wants her dad. She could always call her dad; everyone could. But he's dead and she's thirty-five. So she lifts her fist and raps quietly on the door.

It's still early. But Fred, Anne's father, opens up, fully dressed, as if he's been waiting. He is almost unrecognisable. That live charge of terrifying electricity he used to bring to the house fully snuffed out. He looks healthy – drug-free, booze-free, smoke-free – and somehow dead for it.

'Charlotte,' he says in surprise, his thick grey eyebrows rising. 'It's been a long time.'

In the living room, Anne's mum Janine sits slumped on an armchair. She doesn't look up at first but says, 'Thank you for the flowers.' The words are painfully slow. Charlotte looks around but doesn't see the bouquet in a vase anywhere.

They sit for a while in silence, Charlotte taking in the changes – the flat-screen TV instead of a box on wheels. The walls a bright clean lemon, where they used to be headachy red, slashed by a dado rail. But the school photos of Anne, the old seventies wedding photo of Fred and Janine, wild eyed and hopeful, they're the same. Charlotte looks away.

'If you'd like any help with the funeral,' she says and Janine's eyes shoot up.

'We can't have one yet,' she says, bitterly. Her mouth, which was always talking, always laughing, shouting, swearing, singing, close-lipped as if stitched half shut.

Fred puts a hand on his wife's knee and she sags even further. 'They can't bury her yet,' he explains softly. 'Because of the police investigation.'

'I'm so sorry,' Charlotte says.

'It's not your fault, love,' he replies with eyes that mean it.

The sofas are different. These look new, not a speck on them, no sag. The sofa that was here before was a hand-me-down from Anne's granny, the middle seat had no springs and her dad would prank visitors by gesturing them to sit and watching them fall through. She almost smiles at the memory, even though she was mortified when he did it to her. She pictures him that day, a tin of lager in his hand, handsome and wild. How angry her own dad had been when he'd heard Fred was back in the house, and that she'd spent time with him.

Now he wears a neat sleeveless jumper over an ironed shirt and this breaks her heart.

'I could . . . I could pay towards the funeral, if you—'

'We don't need your money,' Janine says, her face anguished.

'I'm sorry, I didn't mean to upset you.'

'Anne had money,' Janine snaps. 'Plenty of money, not that it did her any good. Your family . . . you think you can fix everything with money. Lure people into your web, make them rely on you and—'

'Janine,' Fred says, with a brittleness that Anne inherited.

'She went all the way to America and made a success of herself. America with all its guns and murders. And then she comes back here, to this sleepy little shithole, and gets killed.'

'I—' Charlotte struggles to breathe. All those times she stayed here, Janine treated her with nothing but kindness. And now she's so angry. So angry it's like she knows. *Could she know?*

'Love,' Fred says to his wife, his voice soft again. Janine turns to face them, tears pooling along her jaw and wetting her jumper. 'It's not Charlotte's fault.'

'I'm so sorry,' Charlotte says, addressing her, Fred, the TV, anything. 'I'm just so sorry. It was stupid to offer, I just feel useless.'

Janine's head turns, jolting like a marionette. She climbs to a stand as if exhausted, and wearily shuffles across the carpet, sitting heavily next to Charlotte. Charlotte holds her breath until her lungs scream. *She knows, she knows, she knows.* But then she's being held, she's being surrounded, her mouth and nose fill with air fragranced by an unknown detergent.

'I'm sorry. I'm so sorry. It's not your fault,' Janine says, holding her tightly. 'You lost your mum and dad too. And now you've lost Annie as well.'

Charlotte grips Janine's arms, crushes her chest against her and cries. And thank god that guilty tears sound the same as grief, and that the two can be so easily buried in each other.

Pamela

2003

Charles must think I'm stupid. A year of random fishing trips and the closest he's come to bringing a fish home is a tuna sandwich from the Spar.

And I can smell her on him. Her cheap washing powder, her cheap sweat, her cheap sheets. He engineers an argument, leaves in a hail of tuts and eye rolls, then glides back hours later like a cat whose had a fish supper at someone else's house.

Do I mind though? That's the question that gives me pause.

I don't mind the sex, is the answer I've reached, but I sure as hell mind that he thinks I'm stupid enough not to know about the sex. I don't have to follow him to Chew Valley Lake to know he's not going anywhere near Chew Valley Lake. He glows bright red every time he lies. But I'd have liked him to at least try to cover his tracks. A kind of foreplay to the lie, a bit of an effort.

Charlotte comes home from Rob's house and her first question is 'where's dad?' It's an accusing question, like I've locked him away in a cupboard. She's still sour that Rob can't come here, which was a decision Charles laid down. Somehow it's my fault though, it always is. My face is searched for signs of deceit. And my sadness is surely written all over my face. I would love a moment of understanding, a hug, but she screws her face up and stomps upstairs. She wouldn't believe me even if I told her.

Charlotte

Thursday Morning

'Do you think they'll ever find out who killed Anne?' she asks Rob, knowing from his movements that he's awake next to her and has been for some time. The rain outside is a curtain of sound, cutting them off from the world.

He breathes in sharply. He hates to discuss it. And she kneads at it constantly, worried that if she stops, it will sneak up on her and eat her alive. It's not just Anne, of course; it's David too. Has he been found? Do the police think it was an accident? Do they know, somehow, that it was her? But she can't possibly say any of that to Rob. She would prefer to talk it all over with Maggie, of course, the one person she could talk to in real words rather than proxy words, half-truths. But she didn't answer the call and that's probably for the best.

Tomorrow, she tells herself. *Tomorrow I can fully exhale.* 'No one seems to suspect us,' Charlotte will whisper. And that's the truth, isn't it? Her belly stirs at the thought. Just two women, strangers bumping into each other in a shop and having a chat. What could be more innocent? She can't wait.

But in the interim she needs to hear from Rob that the police are stumped. As if he is a divining rod to the man on the street, to the rest of a society of which she's not a full member.

'Rob?'

He sits up and rubs his hair, greased with bad sleep. 'No, probably not.'

'Really? They said something again about that man she was seeing.' She looks over but he's not looking at her. He's out of bed, pyjama bottoms pulled back on from where they'd been lost to distraction sex last night.

'If they knew anything, they'd have him already, Charlie. Trust me, this guy's a red herring. He didn't do it.'

'How can you be so sure?' she asks.

He exhales. ''Cos it's been days and there's no CCTV, no leads, no DNA matches, nothing.'

'They're trying to find some man that came to see her at the business too,' she says, hopeful that he'll agree this is promising. Even though it isn't really.

'Oh, really?' he asks but he sounds unconvinced. Knackered. 'Sounds like they're clutching at straws all round.'

'You're not worried they'll come after you?'

He looks at her, frowning. 'Of course not. You've said this before but I don't get why?'

'I just . . .'

'Do you think I did something to her?'

'No! Oh god, no. No, Rob. I don't. I'm just worried about you, I don't have a lot of faith in them and I couldn't live with myself . . . I mean I couldn't cope, if you got caught up in what happened to Anne.'

He sits back down on the bed heavily, stares out of the window. His back bends like a little kid watching cartoons. Her mother would have corrected that posture with a sharp prod.

'They know I was with you and they have receipts and CCTV from the shop where I bought wine on the way so they know I wasn't near her when . . .'

'You bought wine?' It's out before she can help it.

'I was planning a difficult conversation with an old friend,' he says and stands again, walking out of the bedroom but then coming back in with a bang.

'Look, what's going on here, Charlie?'

'What?'

'You say you don't think I'm involved but I feel like I'm being accused of something and it's not fair. If you do think I did something to her then I don't know how you can let me in your bed. And frankly, I can't be with you if you think for a second I'm capable of—'

'I don't! I've already said that! My god, where is all this coming from?'

'I found the fucking body . . . I found her. Have you any idea what that was like? And I'm trying to forget it, to move on, but you keep churning it over, questioning me . . . I just never thought you'd doubt me. I would never doubt you.'

He sits heavily on the bed next to her.

'Oh god, Rob, I'm so sorry. I don't think you're involved. I *know* you're not involved. I know with a hundred per cent certainty it wasn't you.'

He turns to look at her. 'Then why do you keep asking these questions? Why do you keep reacting like . . .' he trails off. 'We're going round and round in circles. You say you

173

don't think I'm involved and then you start asking things again. I get that you're trying to piece it together. And that she was your friend, even with what happened with the business, but you're not going to solve this. And trust me, this other man is a dead end.'

'How can you be so sure?' she asks.

'Just please trust me. You said you believed me one hundred per cent, so believe me on this. OK? Please.'

'OK.' She shrugs, hoping that the police don't give up so easily, that they keep digging in this wrong direction for as long as possible. And when they stop, she'll lob in Harry Sedgemoor's business card and send them off down another rabbit hole.

How far can they be sent in the wrong direction before the police turn sharply and head back? How long do they need to wait until Maggie and Charlotte can start their friendship afresh, and no one suspect a shared past? She imagines Maggie downstairs on the sofa, legs tucked under her, and stifles a surprised smile. But the last thing she wants is for the police to think Rob's to blame. That's not a wrong direction she's willing for them to start down.

'I just want to move on,' he says, as she pulls his head to her chest, kissing his crown.

'I want to move on too,' she says into his hair.

She swallows, replays what he just said. No leads, no CCTV, no DNA matches. And whether they disregard this old boyfriend or not, they're still looking for the wrong kind of person. They're not considering a woman. And why would they? Maggie was a perfect stranger. And Charlotte was a perfect stranger to David. She'd never even been near that bridge before last Friday, has no connection to the area. Two random deaths and two random strangers. If she tells herself this enough times, maybe she'll really believe it.

They sit in silence for a while. If they're not talking about their past, and if Charlotte is not needling for answers on the present, silence seems to swell for longer and longer.

She used to dream of this. Of waking up with him, free adults. But sometimes, if she's really truly honest, she feels like she's treading water. Like she's play-acting, going through the motions set down in her dreams decades ago. But if she doesn't have Rob, who does she have? A flash of Maggie's red hair, piled on her head, an interlace of understanding fingers. She shakes her head sadly. Not yet. And maybe not ever.

Charlotte Wilderwood and Rob Parsons. Rob, who she first fell for in maths class, aged fifteen. Whose knee she would watch jiggling with boredom under the table and think stupid things like 'I wish I was his trousers'. Whose house she once called fifteen times in one night waiting for him to answer instead of his parents or siblings, so the family thought they were victims of a prank caller.

Rob, whose body was the first one she touched outside of her own, as if they were moulded to each other and could never truly fit with anyone else. Rob, who let himself be led into fool's errands and bad ideas because he didn't want to say no to her. Rob, who dropped everything and enveloped her into his life as soon as she came back.

'I was waiting for you for so long,' she says, folding into him.

'I was waiting for *you*,' he says, his voice muffled by her hair.

She sits with this a moment. 'But you were the one who broke up with me,' she says, finally. 'If you changed your mind, you could have got in touch.'

'I didn't have your number,' he says. 'You went to university and didn't look back.'

'Didn't look back?' she says, pulling away from him and staring in shock.

'What?' he says, as she climbs out of bed and reaches for a dressing gown.

'You could have got my number from my parents, they didn't go anywhere.'

'They hated me.'

'Friends Reunited? *Facebook*?'

He looks down at the covers and then back up at her as she ties the tendrils of the dressing gown too tight and winces.

'You managed to do just fine by yourself,' she snaps. 'You moved on and got married, had Ruby . . . you really want to talk about not looking back?'

'OK, I'm sorry, you're right.' His voice is chastened and that makes her more annoyed. *At least fight me!* As she stares at his guileless face, she allows herself to wonder if she would have chosen him now. If she'd bumped into him on the street as a stranger, would she have given him a second look? *Is* he her type? Her type of adult, not her type of teenage boyfriend? She is still swallowing these uncomfortable questions when he says, 'let's move in together.'

'Move in with you?'

He looks her in the eyes. The same marble bright-blues now lined from smiling into the sun all these years. 'Or I could move in here, I mean that would make even more sense, wouldn't it? Life is short and precious. I wasted enough of it without you.'

'But what about Ruby?' she says, swallowing. 'I've not even met her.'

'Well, I think you should.'

She takes a breath, lets her shoulders drop as she thinks. He's not the boy he was, and she's not the girl she was but he's all she has left now.

'Yeah,' she says eventually. 'Yeah, OK, I think I should meet her too. You have her this weekend, right?'

He nods. 'Let me talk to her when I pick her up tomorrow. She knows I'm seeing you, but not how serious it is.'

'Does she?'

'Of course. I told her as soon as you came back, told her you were my first love.'

She can't imagine having that kind of conversation with her own dad. The very thought of it.

'Well, OK, whenever she's ready, I'd love to meet her.'

'How about you come over for dinner tomorrow?'

'Tomorrow?' She thinks about Maggie, about Cribbs Causeway. The focal point that's been getting her through these days. But that's at lunchtime, and they'll be pretending to be strangers making small talk . . . how long can they really drag that out?

'I'd love to have dinner tomorrow.'

Maggie

Thursday Afternoon

She makes them cheese on toast under the grill, staining the bread with drops of Worcestershire sauce. Outside, the rain spits listlessly at the windows and splutters across the roof. It's more wind than anything, the wheezy gusts toying with the water in the air. It feels, right now, like sunshine is just a myth, summer a mass delusion.

The police haven't shown up, maybe it was just a random call. And anyway, he's since taken the binbag down to the big wheelie bin on the street so the phone is gone. So far so good. But tomorrow she'll tell Charlotte about the call. Try not to scare her but make sure she's alert. Maybe she's had calls too. That would be a big worry.

She takes a bite and swallows without tasting it. 'So I'm going to get the train to Bristol tomorrow,' she says, more to herself than him; she's told him her plans already. 'There's an express at ten thirty, and then I'll get the bus out to Cribbs Causeway.'

'Nah,' he says. 'I'm driving you.'

'What?'

'Yeah,' he says, looking at the window as the rain frantically pelts the glass. It's the kind of weather people make conversation about, but that's not his style. His shoulders rise, the thick slabby muscles around his neck stiffening. She holds her breath as he releases the tension and says nothing. He's trying. He's really trying now. Her belly feels warm with gratitude.

'You don't have to do that,' she says, smiling.

'I do,' he says, an edge to his voice. And it hits her then. He doesn't trust her. Doesn't trust her to do what she says she's doing, go where she says she's going.

'OK,' she says and puts the rest of her cheese on toast back on the plate, unable to stomach it.

Pamela

2003

I've sat outside this council house so many times, talking myself into – and then out of – confronting them. And now Charles is here again, the second time this week. Fishing, my arse. He doesn't even look around before he lets himself in, the key swinging from his set like some talisman of virility. It takes enormous effort not to pull it from the keyring, where it touches and taints our house keys, and stick it in his eye some days. But how would that help our daughter?

Dignity, always. That was my mother's greatest lesson to me, and one I hope to share.

Today, though, I've had enough. I've had enough of him barely caring enough to lie adequately. Enough of calling him at work and being lied to even less adequately by Dorian. Enough of his big hands pawing at me on the nights when his fancy piece Janine hasn't been available. And I've had enough of the stupid glint in his eye, the charge it obviously gives him to think he's pulled off the swindle of the century. And Charlotte is due to go to university soon. It's been a struggle to drag that particular horse to water – she's not exactly a self-starter – but she's almost over the line. Almost.

And the safety net I knitted for her has held well for all these years but now, today, I'm done.

Janine's door has a deep slash in it, some lover's mark from her husband Fred or another suitor perhaps. Or maybe the end result of one of Fred's various crimes, none of which he appears very good at as he's constantly being caught and thrown back in prison. Much to Charles's delight, no doubt.

I have dressed in my best clothes and feel queenly, which is a must. I glide down the path, chin up, chest out. My make-up is perfect. I am above what I'm about to do.

And I knock politely, no slashing the door for me. I adjust my rings, my necklace, my handbag while I wait. But when the door opens, it's Anne standing there and my resolve folds in on itself. How could they? With Anne in the house?

There's a new poise to her; I noticed it recently when she was in our home. Even though they're technically adults, Charlotte is still pudgy with teenage hormones, grunting with adolescence. Anne is upright and tall, almost elegant. And she's old for the school year – we celebrated her eighteenth birthday last September so she's approaching nineteen – but she's still a child in my eyes and should be in the eyes of Janine. What kind of mother does this with their child in earshot?

'Anne,' I say, trying to suffuse my voice with all the warmth she'd usually find in it.

'Are you OK, Mrs Wilderwood?' she says, tucking her hair back behind her ear. She's cut it into a bob recently, showing her slim neck, and it suits her. She is learning how to make the best of herself and I hope it rubs off on my daughter.

'I just wanted a word with your mum,' I say, although I don't anymore. Not in front of her.

Anne hesitates. She has likely been given instructions for this very circumstance, a verbal cyanide pill in her teeth in case of capture. And here it comes. She flicks her eyes just once towards the stairs, the ceiling, the bedrooms above and then lies to me. 'She's not in, sorry.'

'That's OK,' I say, glad of the reprieve, but all the more disgusted that they've involved her in their treachery. 'Tell her I'll come back another time.' I reach over and kiss her on the cheek, squeezing her thin arms.

'Actually,' I say, trying not to run away from this crunch point, my knees trembling at the missed opportunity wrapped around a dodged bullet. 'Don't tell her I came, I'll catch up with her another time.'

'OK,' she says.

'Good luck for your A-level results tomorrow,' I call, my voice sounding sing-song as I try to make it back to the car without crying.

Dignity, always.

Charlotte

Friday Morning

She must have slept because she always does in the end, but it was an agitated sleep, drenched in bittersweet anticipation. Dreams that gave way to verbatim re-enactments, so she bubbled to the surface numerous times with incriminating words on her lips. Over and over last night, she pushed at David's chest, and again he hit the water with that sharp shriek. The guilt, the relief and the shame at that relief all pulsing through her dreams. She said goodbye to Maggie all over again. Over and over she woke up, calming herself with thoughts of being reunited, of talking to the only person who truly understands.

Charlotte makes tea and sits at her kitchen table, planning her day. She doesn't want to go in to work and deal with the paperwork she's been putting off. The 'irregularities' that started this whole mess. But she needs to get it done this morning, stop it hanging over her so she can meet Maggie with a clearer head. Then, after that, as if that's not a big enough headline of the day, she's going to Rob's for tea to meet Ruby.

The grand unveiling of girlfriend to daughter. She looks across at the reflection in the kitchen window. Against the grey gloop sky outside, she sees a ghoul staring back. Poor kid'll be terrified.

Charlotte feels and looks more human for a shower and several layers of make-up, but she's still in her dressing gown, standing uselessly in front of her groaning wardrobe. In her parents' room, the walk-in wardrobe is almost the size of another room, but it's still filled with their stuff and she's not ready. Sorting out their clothes and switching rooms would be like pulling out the grenade pin. Everything would follow whether she wanted it to or not.

She yanks open her overstuffed chest of drawers. An eighteenth-century walnut. Not her style at all. Charlotte took her degree in history of decorative arts so she could prove herself useful to her dad. Which seems . . . absurd now. But she soon found that her own tastes were decidedly twentieth century. Give her a sleek Eames lounger, a Danish mid-century teak chest any day. But she has to honour what's here.

So she stares at the useless patchwork of fabrics and wools, trying to choose an outfit. What might Maggie wear? They need to blend in to the background, two normal women making small talk in a shopping centre. She can't imagine beautiful Maggie blending into the background, but Charlotte's been doing it all her life.

She tugs a flattering grey jumper from the drawer, pulls on a selection of rings, slips into her usual black jeans and sighs. Remembering her mum's old mantra 'dignity, always', she stands up taller, pulls back her shoulders and holds her head high.

Maggie

Friday

'Time to go.'

His voice is curt but his eyes are dancing. In his hand, keys twirl like wind chimes, their stems catching the light. It's still raining, great sheets of water scything down. She's spent half an hour getting ready, all while pretending she hasn't. Her pool of clothes isn't exactly vast, but she still felt overwhelmed, eventually pulling on an oversized grey jumper and black jeans. A cheap imitation of the kind Charlotte wears.

She's carefully applied make-up to make it look like she's not really wearing make-up, and brushed her hair into submission, wearing it loose down her back. They need to blend in and disappear, something at which she's an expert. Charlotte, on the other hand, with her beautiful clothes and expensive boots, she surely turns heads everywhere.

'I'll warm the car up,' he shouts, and she's touched by the thoughtfulness. 'Thank you!' she calls as the door slams shut.

She checks the flat quickly before she goes, folds the tea towel, closes the cupboard, runs her eye along the window locks. A tic she learned from her mum, which has never left her. As if everything needs to be right or everything will go wrong. A fire, flood or burglary. Though no one in their right mind would break in here.

He's fiddling with the radio when she gets into the passenger seat, drenched from the run between front door and car. It was only a few seconds but her coat is dripping so she tosses it in the back.

She wants to remind him about the driving lessons that he'd started giving her, until she was almost ready to take a test, then stopped because, 'you shouldn't be filling in DVLA forms with your name on'. But that's a conversation for another day. She buckles up – he never does – and pulls the cuffs of her jumper over her hands, sliding her knees towards him as he accelerates down their road.

When they'd been meeting in secret for a few weeks, she'd slid into a car much like this. She'd smiled nervously at him then, his hands on the borrowed wheel, a map in his lap. 'It's Luke's car,' he'd said of a one-time friend when asked. But it wasn't. She knew that soon enough. They'd only been driving for ten minutes when he'd heard a distant siren and pulled quickly into a winding lane, cutting the engine.

'I've just borrowed it from someone,' he'd said. 'But they didn't exactly give me permission. So if you want me to take you back home, I understand.' She wonders sometimes how different life would have been if she'd said yes, take me back home. But no one had ever liked her enough to steal a car for her, so she'd stayed, and here they are. At least this really is his car, bought for cash from the proceeds of a few really good night's work on a clutch of holiday homes.

They pull out onto the M4, feeling like a micromachine compared to the great monstrous lorries that power along next to them, wheels spraying water up to their windscreen.

He puts a heavy hand on her knee and squeezes. And now she's back there, fifteen with his hand newly on her knee, his chipped hard-working nails catching on the fabric of a summer dress handsewn for her by her mum. That new aching feeling inside her, the one that had grown like a peach pit, the day they met.

And that peach pit was her undoing, and her becoming. From the very start, the flesh around it became soft for him. She would have let him take his teeth to her. To bite out her core and leave her hollow.

She would do anything for him, even on that first day and ever since. Even today, when her head is full of Charlotte. Still she slides forward a little as his hand moves up her leg.

His hands are so different now. His thin fingers now thick and bent. Still marked from work but different work. These are dangerous hands, she thinks, as she unbuttons her jeans for him and moves her own hand to his.

He grips the wheel with his right hand, still staring ahead at the surging traffic and the wild rain. She closes her eyes. And she's here, and she's there, back where it all began.

She would never have told him to take her back.

Pamela

2003

I get back in the car, feeling less like royalty and more like a court jester. Anne is bound to tell her mother that I came round, and Janine will tell Charles and he will double down and then my moment, my chance to strike, has gone. But what else can I do? Storm back into the house, barge up the stairs and drag him out by his bare bollocks? In front of Anne?

I turn the ignition key, pull out slowly and roll away. Not two cars down I see Charles's car badly parked, as bold as brass. He must have swung in with such glee, driven by the rush of blood between his legs, and doesn't even care if he's left his back-end hanging out ready to be clipped. I shake my head and press the accelerator of my tired Volvo. I need to be inside the cool quiet of my cottage. I want to lose myself in the make-believe of home decoration and magazines, of re-arranging the fucking cushions twelve times only for Charlotte to rise mid-afternoon and flop lazily onto them, complaining that I've bought the wrong cheese or that she needs new jeans.

As I pull away from the estate and join the main road, I immediately have to brake. An old bus fills the carriageway, shaking and panting while its cargo dismounts and spills all over the bus stop. And there, standing amongst them, four shopping bags hanging awkwardly from her thin fingers, is Anne's mother.

Charlotte

Friday Morning

It's gone nine when she turns into the trading estate, not that anyone's counting. She doesn't even have to think about Dorian now. Charlotte is her own boss with the keys to the castle, just like she always dreamed. Only it's all happened in nightmare circumstances.

She noses around the corner and is about to pull into the car park when she sees it. A big shiny BMW parked in the same place as last week. She turns away abruptly and carries on through the estate, picking up speed, heart racing.

She turns at the end of the cul-de-sac and waits, engine whooshing patiently, while trying to catch her breath. Plenty of people drive BMWs, she tells herself. She's not checked the diary for appointments and Dorian or, god, even Anne, could have made this one. And it's not beyond the realms of reality that someone random could just be waiting to browse. It is an antiques showroom, after all, and she's been improving their website and even put up a few Facebook ads targeted at local decor enthusiasts. Maybe her work is paying off?

The right thing to do is go and deal with whoever is there. And if it *is* Harry Sedgemoor, so what? He's just going to ask her if she's interested in selling a stake of the business to him as an investment and she's just going to say no and everyone will move on. Just like they did when he came to see her dad, and then Anne.

If she goes and has a conversation with this man, he'll no longer be a mystery investor who she can use as a red herring with the police. She wouldn't be able to do that to someone she's spoken to since, to someone whose eyes she's looked into. That's what's holding her back, but maybe it's a sign that that's a bad idea anyway.

It is odd, though, she thinks, creeping forward, why someone that slick would be so determined to get an interest in a small antiques company. Maybe he knows something about this estate and the property is worth more than she thinks. It was valued as part of the wills and probate process but maybe he knows something below the radar. Some new development plans or something. Something she could find out and then discuss with Maggie later.

She carries on back towards Wilderwood Antiques but, as she nears the showroom, she realises the BMW has gone.

It's now gone ten, she's jittery with coffee and she's still got so much to go through. She's made the classic mistake of getting everything out, like pulling everything out of cupboard you need to tidy, and it's stacked around her like a paper city.

Her dad was old school. Everything in a handshake, paper rather than digital. He'd only got a website in the last few years and she despaired when he told her he wouldn't use it for online sales. 'Don't trust what you can't touch,' he'd say, and when she'd tried to explain that the world wasn't really like that anymore, he'd changed the subject.

The new online shop she'd set up wasn't exactly Amazon, but she'd been proved right with the trickle of steady sales.

Everything is here, dating back years. Charlotte decides to set some kind of parameter or she'll be here for months so she focusses on the last year alone. Six months with her dad at the helm, six months with her. And Anne.

Charlotte makes another coffee, her hands shaking as she sloops in a drop of milk, then puts things into teetering piles. Invoices, bills, statements. She remembers her own pile of paperwork, missing from her cottage after David's impromptu visit, and shivers. Then a sudden thought: if the police find them in his property, it'll be a link to her. Fuck. But why would they search his premises? He had an accident and drowned, she tells herself. Still, though, fuck. How many other connections has she missed?

★

The sun shifts outside and two people drop in, one looking for directions and another wanting to buy a mirror. None of them are driving BMWs. She tries to look happy to help them, but mostly she wants everyone to just piss off so she can think. By the time she's gone through everything, her back aches and she can feel a headache brewing.

There are indeed duplicate invoices, like Anne said, and quite a lot of them, but when she tallies it all up, the right amount of money for them went into the accounts, cash, just like the invoices said. More confusing are the purchase orders for products her dad bought that are no longer here. He must have sold them off-book, cash in hand. To avoid tax maybe?

The overheads here are small, just her and Anne drawing a proper salary, and part-time for Dorian, albeit on overly generous wages. The company owns the building outright now, so it's just the running costs of heat and light, Wi-Fi and business tax.

Since she took over, despite the online improvements, she's not brought a lot in. Nothing like the amount her dad did per month. There's less in the kitty than when she took over but still a decent buffer.

Her dad had probably just created new invoices by copying an old invoice, changing the details and saving it under a new number. And he's obviously not paid attention and has kept the same product details on there by accident. Put the wrong date a few times. Quite a lot of times. Some for months in the future when her dad was long dead, even, but certainly drawn up when he was alive – she can see when each document was created. God, maybe he was going doolally? He wasn't young . . .

He'd printed them all out as well because he was old school, but the invoices saved on the computer match up when she checks a few at random.

Despite what Anne suggested, none of the duplicates were created by Charlotte and she can prove it. There was no great conspiracy, not enough for Anne to go to the police with anyway. It was all a bluff.

If she'd just held her nerve, sacked her friend . . . Anne would still be alive and so would David. Fuck. She wonders if telling Maggie this would make her feel better or worse. David would still be out there, troubling her, but she'd not have Anne's death on her conscience. An almost impossible weight to carry, as Charlotte knows.

She gets into the car, checks her make-up in the mirror and then starts towards Bristol, still thinking about whether to tell Maggie what she'd found in the paperwork. As she joins the main road, her phone starts to ring: a Bristol number she's not seen before.

Maggie

Big things get decided on little journeys. A chance to talk, just the two of them without the distractions of TV, without the ability to drift into different rooms. Forced to follow a conversation all the way through to its conclusion, no slip road to bail out onto, no excuses to grasp. So it was when he first floated his idea for getting her away from her family home, from her mum, over ten years ago. And so it is today, as he talks of future plans for the two of them. So am I really forgiven, she wants to ask, but doesn't dare.

The rain has slunk back to a drizzle and the grey sky shows glimpses of a pale-blue underskirt. The car is warm now, condensation trickling from the windows and the radio a low hypnotic hum.

They are relaxed and loose in the afterglow of heavy petting, the kind she should probably have grown out of by now. She finds herself nodding and murmuring to everything he says. If not assent then . . . not refusal either.

They're approaching Bristol, ahead of schedule. Cribbs Causeway is to the north of the city and they skim its edge, the little car chuntering along. The last time she came here was with her mum and auntie, when it had just opened. A long fractious drive during which the two women had argued non-stop and Maggie had held her hands over her ears. She'd been allowed to choose some clothes, a first, but everything she'd picked was put back until she'd finally gone along with a pinafore dress her mum found. She'd hated it.

'What will you do when you drop me off?' she asks. 'I don't know how long I'll be.'

'I'm coming in with you,' he says, amused. 'I'm not coming all this way just to act as a bloody chauffeur.' She tries to slow her breathing, not to let on that this is the last thing she wants.

'Is that a problem?' he asks, putting his hand back on her knee. She shakes her head quickly.

'Don't worry, I won't cramp your style, I've got other things to do.'

She stares out the window and wonders if she should call this off.

Charlotte

She answers the call uneasily, trying to keep her voice level. Is it the police? Do they know something?

'Pamela?'

For a moment she's struck dumb, her foot pulling back from the accelerator to the chagrin of the driver too close behind her. Who could be trying to reach her mum, and on this number?

'Is that Pamela? It's Green Street dry cleaners here, about your dress.'

'Oh, yes,' she exhales. 'Yes, it is.'

'It's ready to collect as promised.'

'Oh, thank you. I'm on my way to you now.'

The door chimes and the man with the half-moon glasses emerges from the back room, pulling the door closed behind him as if to preserve the modesty of all the mismatched garments hanging in their see-through sheathes.

'Pamela,' he says and she nods. 'I've got bad news.'

She swallows. Bad news that the police want to swab it?

'I'm afraid we couldn't get every stain out and there are quite a few marks that are just too old and deep to stand a chance.'

She says nothing, staring back like an imbecile, so he adds, with the careful manner of an oncologist, 'I'm very sorry we couldn't do more.'

She snaps to. 'Oh god, it's fine. Honestly. My friend absolutely trashed it so she knew it might not . . . how old? You said some of the stains were old but her wedding was only, um, a couple of weeks ago.'

The man shakes his head, his half-moon glasses rattling slightly on the bridge of his thin noise. 'No, these were much older than a couple of weeks. Was it second-hand to her?'

Was it? Maybe. She didn't ask. Her main priority that night was getting Maggie safely off the bridge. What a simple challenge that now seems, compared to every horror that had followed.

But it seems odd that a wedding dress she walked down the aisle wearing just last week would have lots of old stains on it. The man coughs politely.

'Sorry, I mean, I don't know if it was second-hand.'

'Let me get the dress for you and I'll show you where the damage is.'

'It's fine, don't worry, I'll take your word for it.'

He opens the door behind the counter just a crack, slips between it sideways and emerges with the dress zipped up like a body bag, lying across his arms. She takes it gingerly, as if she can't really be trusted to keep it safe, thanking him.

Charlotte lays the dress in its neat bag on the back seat where it had slumped, tattered and smelly, last week. She wonders if this was a mistake, if Maggie will be pleased to see it or traumatised by the memory. But then, Maggie herself is a reminder of everything that happened last week, and Charlotte is still desperate to see her. More desperate than she'd admitted until now, as she smiles and accelerates towards Cribbs Causeway.

Maggie

H&M at 1 p.m., that's what they'd agreed. She'd prefer to have some time alone to prepare, to walk around and think about what she'll say. But he insisted on getting an early lunch together first and now he's ransacking a Pizza Hut buffet like a medieval king while she picks nervously at a bowl of salad. 'No point paying for "all you can eat" unless you get your money's worth,' he says through a mouthful of crust. You've eaten enough for both of us, she thinks but doesn't say.

It's nearly half past twelve when he finally leaves, joking that she mustn't spend too much. She forces herself to smile and watches his back as he goes, then walks as calmly as she can along the huge corridor at the heart of the mall. It's not hugely busy but there are enough people mooching along that she doesn't stand out. She looks into a discount shoe shop, sliding her feet into some high heels and walking up and down like a newborn calf. She buys some lip balm in Boots and does a full circuit of the mall before coming back to the strip containing the familiar white and red sign of H&M. Ten minutes to go.

There's a New Look next door and she drifts in as if browsing aimlessly, lifting up a thin cotton T-shirt and holding it to her body. It's way too big. She usually shops from the children's range at supermarkets or in charity shops. She trails through the shop, trying not to rush but feeling her pulse dancing across the surface of her skin.

Five minutes to go. Her palms are sweaty and she wipes them discreetly on her jeans and wishes she'd chosen something more lightweight to wear. There's an unhealthy dry heat being pumped through the mall and it's enough to make someone dizzy. How people shop in places like this for pleasure she'll never understand, but perhaps it just takes practise.

For the last minute, she's been carrying a reduced-price maxi dress that would trail a foot behind her if she tried it on, and as a bored shop assistant looks her up and down, she slides it back onto a nearby rack. That's not where it came from and the assistant rolls her eyes but Maggie is already out the door.

She takes a deep breath and then peers through the window of H&M. She can't see Charlotte inside. Well, OK, there's still a minute to go and maybe she's the late sort. Unbelievable really that Maggie doesn't know this kind of thing about her. She feels like she knows Charlotte under her very skin, so realising she doesn't know such a pedestrian detail feels like an assault.

She heads inside, picking up items and putting them back as she walks around, still unable to spot Charlotte. She looks at the list of departments as casually as she can, realising there's another floor. She bounds up the escalator quicker than she intended, stomach churning. It's now two past one and if she's not here then—

Maggie stops dead just in front of the escalator's metal jaws and sighs with relief. There is Charlotte, a basket crooked over her arm with a small stack of monochrome clothes inside. She wears a nonchalant expression that almost hides her nerves as she looks at a rack of black jumpers.

Maggie turns to quickly check behind herself but why would he follow? He said he's going and he's gone. She takes a step closer and smiles.

Charlotte

'That would suit you.'

She spins around. Maggie. Oh, thank god, Maggie.

She smiles and puts the basket down but they can't touch so for a moment they just smile awkwardly. 'I'm so glad you're here,' she whispers eventually.

'Are you OK?' Maggie whispers back. Charlotte nods in relief.

Maggie coughs and looks around then picks up Charlotte's basket and hands it to her. 'You should try those on,' she says, nodding towards the unmanned changing rooms. Charlotte walks towards them, hearing the scrape of a hanger as Maggie picks something off the rail behind her.

The changing rooms are empty, and Charlotte can only spot one camera trained on the entrance so she walks to the furthest cubicle and waits with the curtain open, breathing hard. A minute later she hears the soft pat of Maggie's light feet, stop-starting her way along, probably checking the cubicles in turn. Eventually her bright hair appears and her pale face and she's suddenly inside and the curtain is pulled and the clothes they picked up are on the floor as they cling to one another in a desperate hug.

'I'm so glad you're here,' Charlotte says into Maggie's hair.

'Me too,' Maggie whispers, pulling back from the hug and seeming to take a long look.

'Oh my god, we're matching,' Charlotte says, looking at their uniform of grey jumper and black jeans.

Maggie laughs quietly and then covers her mouth. 'We need to be really quiet but please tell me everything.'

Charlotte slides slowly down to sit on the floor with her back to the mirror and Maggie copies. There's barely enough room so they're scrunched together but it feels good, it feels . . . it feels like not being alone anymore.

'Rob found Anne,' she whispers.

'What?'

Charlotte nods and closes her eyes, any trace of a smile now gone. 'He went to argue with her about what she was doing and—'

'Did he call the police?'

'Of course. They took a video statement from him and then checked his alibi the next day.'

'His alibi?'

'Me, I was his alibi.'

'Of course,' Maggie says, her voice barely audible. 'Just like we . . . but the other way round.' Charlotte hears her swallow, their throats side by side.

'Is Rob OK?'

Charlotte shrugs. 'As OK as he can be.'

Maggie opens her mouth then closes it, the smack of her lips loud in the tiny room.

'The police don't seem to have got very far,' Charlotte adds. 'They're looking for an old boyfriend, some guy the neighbours saw visiting when she first moved back.'

'That's good.'

'Not for him,' Charlotte says. 'But yeah. I mean, he didn't do it but the longer they keep looking, the longer . . .'

'Yeah.' Maggie closes her eyes and Charlotte reaches for her hand and squeezes it. 'And there's another red herring too. A guy who came to see Anne at the showroom. It's a total dead end but it keeps the sniffer dogs away from us.'

'Sniffer dogs?' Maggie's eyes spring open.

'No, no,' Charlotte whispers hard. 'Not actual dogs. It's just a saying!' And they can't help it, they both start to laugh, covering their mouths with each other's hands, shoulders shaking.

'We shouldn't stay in here too long,' Charlotte says then, bringing the guilty laughter to a halt. 'But I don't want to say goodbye again.'

'Same. There's no one else who understands,' Maggie says, and reaches for Charlotte's hand again, letting their shared knot of fingers fall onto her lap.

'Are you back with Mike?' Charlotte asks and Maggie pauses and then nods. 'Oh, that's good,' Charlotte says, unsure if it really is good given his behaviour at the church and the way he blamed Maggie. But now is not the time and there's a more pressing question. 'And has anyone . . . has *he* been found?' Maggie shakes her head. Charlotte breathes out a long whoosh of air she didn't realise she'd been holding in.

'Nothing, and no one is missing him. No posters in the town or . . . anything. It's like he never even existed,' Maggie says. Charlotte leans her head against Maggie's shoulder just briefly. 'Thank fuck.'

Maggie does another loud swallow and then, 'Yeah, thank fuck.'

A few metres away there's a sound of metal on metal. 'Someone's here,' Maggie says, her eyes wild. 'It's OK,' whispers Charlotte. 'Just hang on, don't panic.' They stay silent and still. From a couple of cubicles comes the noise of belt buckles and zips, a grunt as someone struggles out of or into some clothes, and eventually the slow thud of receding feet.

'We should go,' Charlotte says, standing up and offering a hand to pull Maggie to her feet. Maggie keeps a tight hold of it even when she's standing, and then pulls Charlotte into a hug as forceful and meaningful as any she's ever felt before. 'I'll miss you so much,' Maggie says, choking back what sounds like a sob. And then she kisses Charlotte's cheek, stoops to pick up the clothes she'd brought in, and rushes out.

Maggie

The rain stopped while she was still hermetically sealed in the shopping mall and everything in the car park glistens. He's not here at the pick-up point but she dare not wander around in case she bumps into Charlotte climbing into her Tesla. It would negate the efforts to organise a random conversation in H&M if she then had a broad daylight follow-up, but more than that, if she's really honest, she doesn't trust herself not to climb inside, lock the door and beg Charlotte to step on the accelerator.

She can still feel the weight of Charlotte's hand in hers, the faintest trace of her make-up on her lips from where she kissed her and ran. Judas, she thinks. *I'm Judas Iscariot. Except instead of the garden of Gethsemane, my betrayal took place in the temple of trade.*

What has she done? Oh god, poor Charlotte. Maggie could still call and warn her though; he's not here yet and there's still time. She could tell Charlotte everything. How scared she is when she closes her eyes and remembers Anne's face, the disbelief turning her pretty face into a gargoyle. She could even tell Charlotte how scared she is of *him*, something she's barely able to admit to herself. They could bunker up in the cottage while they work out what to do. Doors locked, lights off, under a blanket like two children. She forgot to tell her about the Bristol phone call, that's reason enough. Maggie pulls out her phone, fingers trembling as she navigates to the contacts. *Just do it, now before you never get another chance.*

She hears the car before she sees it, the exhaust coughing as it pulls up a few metres away. It's too late. It's all too late. He watches from the driving seat as she slides her phone back into her pocket. Her original sin smiling back at her like a serpent. And as she starts to walk towards the little red car with the grey patch, she sighs a little. No going back.

For a moment, they share no words. Then he puts his meaty hand on her leg and squeezes so hard that his fingers seem to burrow under her kneecap. The glovebox is still open; inside is an empty Tupperware box that until today had contained the jewellery he'd taken from Anne's house and the little piece of charred paper.

'Tommy, that hurts,' she says but smiles to keep things nice.

'Call me David,' he jokes and she shrinks away.

He's excited, childlike, and she tries to swallow away the sadness of saying goodbye to Charlotte again. Of lying to her again and again, letting her believe she's a murderer. Instead, she tries to focus on the future. On what this is leading to. On the life they're building. She spent two days with Charlotte but she's spent ten years with Tommy, and that's what's important. She's been telling herself that, but it's not really sticking.

'She doesn't suspect anything?' Tommy asks, serious now.

'Not a thing,' she says, and tries to look happy.

Charlotte

Charlotte is in a daze as she enters the toy shop, the feeling of Maggie's lips on her cheek, the memory of their conversation playing across her mind like breaking news. They met up and nothing happened. No sirens and flashing lights. No one is looking for David – 'it's as if he never existed' – and the police this end are certainly not looking for a little red-headed woman.

She should be relieved, but her body hasn't caught up and her stomach is still churning. She leans on the nearby shelf and puts a hand on her belly, realising with dismay that she still feels this way because nothing fundamental has changed. No one is missing David, but that doesn't undo her killing him. It just makes it sadder. He was a nasty man, but he was still a living, breathing person. And once he'd been a child, playing with toys like these.

A concerned shop assistant starts to drift towards Charlotte so she turns abruptly and heads decisively towards the LEGO, unable to face conversation.

Is this what getting away with murder feels like? If she'd ever thought about it before, she probably would have imagined it to feel more exhilarating, more like relief. Mostly she feels like she's behind glass, separate to the rest of the world.

She wonders again how long they can tread water before they trust that it's really over. That they can find a new path to friendship, to a kind of fraternity. And if she will have stopped feeling sick by then.

But could it ever really be over? She thinks of Janine, slumped in her armchair. The other day, she seemed like she'd given up, disinterested in the why or how, just dealing with what happened. But shocks wear off, Charlotte knows that. Will Janine pressure the police for answers? What about David's family, when they finally realise he's gone?

Charlotte closes her eyes and tries to do yoga breathing that she can barely remember from a long abandoned health kick. She needs to focus on the present, not the gruesome recent past or the worst-case scenarios. Some bastardisation of mindfulness.

She wants to take something for Ruby but is utterly boggled by all the brightly coloured options. In the end, she buys an art set, remembering how proud Rob was of Ruby's drawings on his fridge. They gift wrap it for her, and she immediately worries it's too much and considers unwrapping it all when she gets back to the car. Instead, she touches up her make-up, flinching at the black shadows that have crept under her eyes.

'And what's your teacher's name?' she asks Ruby, the latest in a long line of awkward questions, but the little girl doesn't seem to mind. She answers them all cheerfully – 'Mrs Howard' – and eats with very good manners.

'How old was Daddy when you met him?' Ruby asks, putting her fork and knife down, just so. And having seen how Rob eats, this can only be from her mother's side. Charlotte looks at Rob, guiltily, as if caught out. But he just laughs. He seems lighter in his daughter's presence, less haunted by his experience last weekend. She hopes it's catching, but she still feels jumpy as all hell. And even grubbier amidst a wholesome family unit.

'We were both eleven,' Charlotte says, and Ruby's eyes widen. 'That's only two years older than me!'

'Yes, but we were only friends then,' Rob adds, quickly. 'Too young for boyfriend and girlfriend stuff.'

'We didn't start going out until we were a few years older,' Charlotte says.

'Did you ever kiss?' Ruby asks and Charlotte laughs and leaves it for Rob to answer.

'That's enough questions, Paxman,' he says.

'Who?'

They make coffee while Ruby watches TV in the lounge. This cottage, which Charlotte has slept in, woken in, eaten in so many times, has never felt so warm or full. 'Fatherhood suits you,' she says. 'You're . . .'

'She makes me whole.' He shrugs.

'I'll leave you two to it,' she says after finishing her coffee. The strain of acting normally has exhausted her and she pulls him towards her for a parting kiss.

'Woo,' calls Ruby, paying full attention all of a sudden.

'Eyes on the TV, you,' Rob jokes, and Charlotte pats his chest and steps away.

'See you soon, Ruby!' she calls and Ruby waves and calls, 'Thank you for my artist things.'

'You're so welcome. See *you* soon?' she whispers and Rob nods.

'Tomorrow night?'

'Yeah, perfect.'

'I'll come after I drop Ruby home to her mum.'

Instead of heading for her empty cottage, Charlotte drives out to a garden centre just outside Rob's village that also sells paint and a few bits of furniture. She grabs a slippery pile of colour charts and tucks them in her handbag, determined to put her own stamp on the cottage at last. If nothing else, it'll be a distraction. She also buys a few potted herbs that will die just like all the others. Her repeated purchase of basil is how she knows that, despite everything, she's an optimist.

When she gets back to the cottage, she'll decide on a new colour scheme. Try to force in the new era, the bit where she really has got away with all this. Where, perhaps, she could even see Maggie and it not be clandestine. It could just be . . . lovely. Could they ever deserve that?

She pulls up to the front door, plugs her car in to the charger and then grabs her handbag from the passenger seat. It's getting dark now and she shivers in the gloom as she pops the boot open and leans in to lift the box of herb pots. All it would take is someone to come out of the shadows and pull the boot door down hard and that would be it. She straightens up and stares that idea dead in the face. But who would do that? Why? And not for the first time she reminds herself that she is the only person around here who has proven capable of that.

He deserved it, she tells herself. But her chest still feels heavy like she's trying to breathe underwater.

Charlotte walks unmolested to the front door and unlocks it, balancing the box awkwardly on a raised knee as the security light clicks on overhead. The yellow light leaks into the dark hallway but when she kicks the door closed behind her, everything is dim again.

And then she feels it.

Is it a power exclusive to women? The tiny lift of the hairs along the neck. The sudden awareness of blood in the ears, the acutely focused hearing. She's felt it so many times in so many alleyways and car parks that she can't pluck any specific example from the soup. But she knows it when she feels it and she feels it now.

The atmosphere is not as still as it should be. As she flicks on the hallway light, she can almost see the broken air. The extra warmth from someone else's breath. A trace of it so scant, she chases it away by trying to find it. But it was there. And someone was here. Maybe they still are. It's the same feeling she had when she realised the statements were gone. But David is dead, so it can't be him.

She places the box of herbs and paint charts onto the floor as quietly as possible, and pulls her phone from her pocket, moving it to her left hand. In her right, the stronger, she flays her house keys between her fingers like claws. She takes a step, stops to listen. Nothing. She walks first into the lounge, turns on the light to an empty room. No surprises. It's dark outside, and she feels exposed by the large picture window but too rattled to pull the curtain and let her guard down.

Next the dining room, barely ever used, ornate as hell and empty too. Pewter candlesticks crown each end of the oak table, an antique salt cellar sits on a decorative trunk to the side. This room is like an extension of the showroom, almost oppressively so. The only difference is the framed family photographs dotted along the wall. Her mother thought it was uncouth to have family photos 'strewn through the house', so this was the only room in which any sat. Her parents smile out from gold frames, as does a photograph of her and Rob as teenagers, recently added. This is a treasure trove to burglars, surely, but nothing has been touched.

Don't let your guard down.

The kitchen is empty and dimly lit but for the lights running along the underside of the cupboards. It's empty, but the sense of intrusion is just as strong. She feels it in her tailbone, an acute ache pushing her to run out. She grips the keys tighter, slips her shoes off and mounts the stairs, dodging the creaking steps, using the muscle memory developed when she was a teenager creeping in after curfew. She checks every room, every wardrobe and cupboard, even tiptoeing over to peer into the bath tub expecting god knows what to be lying in there.

But no one is hiding. Nothing has been taken. Nowhere are there signs of forced entry.

The feeling does not diminish, but her willingness to believe in it does. She can either leave – go to a hotel, intrude on Rob and Ruby? She doesn't have enough electricity in her car to drive all the way to London, even if one of those old friends would take her in. Or she can stay. Of course she will stay.

She tells herself that she's a grown-up. Telling herself she's safe. But she has never felt more vulnerable.

Maggie

Friday Evening

Tommy's taking a really long, unpredictable route back, stopping to fill the car up and paying in cash. Like all those years ago on their first road trip, she's content to go along for the ride. Unlike their rented flat, the car is all theirs, the only place on earth that truly belongs to them. More than a vehicle, it's a slice of home, a much-loved snail shell that has taken them far.

He bought it from an elderly widow who had never learned to drive and didn't plan to after her husband died. The little Fiesta was already old then, but had barely been used, less than a thousand miles on the clock.

They keep it clean. He washes the outside once a week while she vacuums and polishes the interior. The only problem they've ever had was when someone skidded into it on a motorbike and dented one of the doors. Their car is uninsured, unregistered, hidden off the road when it's not being used. 'I can't have my name on the paperwork, can I?' he'd said, when she'd asked if they weren't pushing their luck. But it meant they'd had to replace the door out of pocket and found a spare from a wrecker's yard. It doesn't match the colour but she's always found it endearing, like a dog with a patch of different coloured fur.

It's started to kick out smoke and no doubt the engine will give up soon and she will grieve. But for now, she strokes the fake leather of the door, wipes a speck of dust from the wrinkled skin of the gear stick casing, and smiles.

She remembers how scruffy Charlotte let her luxurious car get, wonders if she could ever relax into money enough not to look after things. She wished she'd got to sit in the Tesla with her one more time, get whisked to the safety of the cottage before it was out of bounds again.

The rain has given way to biblical shards of late-afternoon sunlight, surging between clouds from on high like laser beams. They are the only car on this stretch of A road and she feels herself pull away from her body as if seeing the car from above. In her mind, she floats higher and higher as the world around gets larger, emptier, and the car becomes a pencil prick.

'You in there?' he says, and from his tone it's obvious he's been speaking to her as she floats away.

'Sorry?' she says, back in her seat, the car a normal size again.

'I said let's go in for old times' sake,' he says, pointing down the road to a Harvester.

'Oh yes, let's.'

That first day out, paid for with notes thumbed from a little brown wage envelope, back when he was still labouring, they'd had their first meal together at a Harvester. She'd never been to one before, and he'd had to talk her through it. 'You order your main and then you go over there to the salad bar . . .'

They pull in now, one of only five cars, and he pats his jeans pocket for cash. The last of Charlotte's cash, she thinks, guiltily, handed over so kindly on parting the first time. Inside, they sit in the window, watching over their little car like anxious parents. They've not seen mention of it anywhere, but it is distinctive thanks to its door and its age, and they've got by this far by being careful. The waitress comes over and slides a menu to each of them but they already know what they're having.

'Ribeye with chips and peppercorn sauce and a glass of Coke,' he says. And then catching Maggie's look. '*Please*.'

She orders Coke plus gammon steak with a pineapple *and* an egg. Starving, suddenly. But even if she wasn't, that's what she would have because that's what she *had*. Ten years ago and change.

And it was at a table like this, drinking bottomless Coke, that they had come up with their very first plan. The kind that starts as a joke but hardens and crystallises. Becomes, through dint of no one blinking first, definite. Then life-changing.

That first plan worked, albeit not in the way she'd expected or signed up to. But she was out of that house and living with him within the month, that part was true. And so, somehow, this plan should work too. Yeah, she thinks, it has to. Too many people have been chewed up already for it not to work. To not even win after playing such high stakes, that would be worse than anything.

'Are you listening?'

She snaps back to the present and looks at him then gasps. In his hand is an open box with a sparkling ring poking out. She covers her mouth and smiles.

'Well?' he says. 'Do you want to be my wife or what?'

Charlotte

Charlotte turns on all the lights in the kitchen. The window becomes a black mirror, reflecting her own face and making her jump.

She lowers the blind quickly and opens the fridge to get out a bottle of wine. She needs something to slow her brain down. To try to short-circuit this endless churn of guilt, fear and loneliness. God, she feels alone. If only she could have invited Maggie back to share this bottle. Two accidental killers, unable to talk to anyone else about what they'd done.

She slips off her shoes, pours a glass and drains it in one. Then she goes to change and wash off her make-up.

She looks in at the spare room again, checks under the bed one more time. There is no one there. The last time someone slept in here was Maggie. No wait, she never actually slept in here. Was she really only here that one night, passed out on the sofa?

She imagines Ruby settling down for the night in here some time and smiles. Maybe the things she always wanted are still in reach. Maybe she still wants them just as much, even if more pressing worries have taken all her headspace.

She closes the door. In the pocket of her dressing gown, her phone vibrates. She pulls it out but it's caller withheld. She rejects the call.

Pamela

2003

She's standing at my front door. The girl I've made packed lunches for, worried over, even defended to my own daughter when she started to tire of the friendship and wriggle loose. Anne, once so knock-kneed and skinny, so awkward in her own shoes and desperate to please. Now willowy and wry, her bobbed hair shining like a knife. She is a woman now, a duplicitous woman. And it had happened on my watch.

I can see her through the living room window, from tucked behind the lace curtain, but I can't move. I can't let her in and pretend nothing has happened, but how the hell can I tear the strips off her that I want to – that she deserves – with Charlotte here?

So I stand doing nothing until the knock comes again and Charlotte stomps downstairs, her body growing ever plumper, and flings open the door.

'What did you get?' asks Anne.

'Two Bs and a C,' Charlotte says proudly and I bristle. It's not bad but it's not exactly going to set the world alight. I worked two part-time jobs through school and got up at five in the morning to work on my art portfolio, getting three As at A-level that mystified rather than delighted my parents. We have supported Charlotte, helped her with homework, given her pocket money so she never had to have a distracting part-time job, and what's happened? It's made her soft. She says she wants to work for Charles, which further underlines her lack of imagination and drive. I blame us both. Trying to make sure your kids don't have the same uphill battle you did is a sure-fire way to ensure they seek out the downhill route every time.

'What about you?'

Anne pauses and I hear Charlotte shut the door; Anne is now fully swallowed up by our home. 'I got three As.'

'Oh my god,' screams Charlotte, as shrill and fake as I've ever heard. So she *does* care that she limped over the line. That's something, at least.

'Mum, Anne's here,' Charlotte calls out.

I run my tongue over my teeth, straighten my face and glide like a tiger into the hall. 'Hello, darling,' I say. 'I hear congratulations are in order?'

Anne blushes and thanks me.

'So where are you off to for university then?' *Somewhere far away, I hope.*

'I'm taking a year out,' she says. 'I've really enjoyed working at the company and—'

'The company?'

She looks at me with pity, as if dealing with a doddery pensioner. '*Your* company, in the holidays and that. And Charlotte's dad said he'd give me a full-time job so I can earn some money and get some proper experience.'

'Isn't he a treasure,' I say, my guts flipping over one another like decked fish.

Charlotte grunts something about making them both milk-shakes – her latest obsession – and I let her get on with it. I grab Anne's elbow, tugging her gently into the lounge. She feels like she's constructed from knotted rope. 'A word?' I say quietly and she colours pink but follows anyway.

'Be a dear and shut the door.' As she turns to close it, I push her against it slowly, one hand on her throat.

'You will not be getting a job with my husband; do you understand me?'

'He just wants to help me,' she gurgles, her eyes as wide as a cartoon cat's.

I smile and shake my head. 'You will not be seeing my husband again, or my daughter. Is that clear?'

Anne stares back, trying to look bewildered. But she knows that I know.

'She will be going up to Manchester University with her subpar grades, and she will be leaving you far behind her.' Anne starts to squeak, about to say something, to argue. I cover that thin little mouth with my other hand.

'And I don't care what you say or how you say it, I don't care what reason you come up with to stop seeing her, but you will stop seeing my daughter and you will sure as hell stop seeing my husband. Or I will tell *every*one about you and Charles. Your mother . . . your *father* . . . tell me, is drink the problem with him at the moment or is it drugs? They can really make a man violent, I believe?'

Anne swallows and two tiny tears squeeze from her eyes. I notice that she's wearing a necklace she couldn't possibly have bought for herself. It's probably auction stock. My husband is such a cliché.

'Charlotte doesn't want to go to Manchester,' she says, the words muffled by my hand. I loosen it, slick with her breath, and wipe it on my dress.

'What?'

'She wants to stay here, with Rob. She's planning to refuse the place.' Her voice is quiet, but there's a steel to it that I've not heard before. 'So if you're worried about me getting in the way of your daughter's bright future, you might want to look at him instead.'

I let her go, unable to find a suitable retort, and listen as she rejoins my daughter in the kitchen.

I allow myself a few deep breaths and then steal out into the hall, one ear to the kitchen door.

I hear the murmur of chatter and the clatter of a spoon in a glass. Charlotte drinks so many of those lurid milkshakes it's amazing she's not turned bright pink.

I miss what Anne says but the clattering stops followed by Charlotte's astonished, 'what are you on about?'

'I said I'm glad you're going away to university,' Anne says now, loud enough for me to hear.

'What? Why are you being such a cow?'

Anne pauses, her voice wobbles a little as she says: 'I've been in your shadow for far too long and honestly—' her voice is clearer now '—I'm just so bored of it.'

The voices lower to angry hisses and I creep back into the lounge and wait another few minutes until a succession of doors slam and I watch through the window as Anne marches down the lane without looking back.

'What's wrong?' I ask, finding Charlotte standing stony-faced in the hallway, a milkshake still in each hand.

'She does my head in,' Charlotte says, clearly holding back tears. 'I'm going to Rob's.'

One door closes, another flies open.

Maggie

Saturday Evening

She uncorks some wine for herself that she'll mete out over the next few evenings, then opens a bottle of beer for him. He takes it, wipes it on his sleeve in a way she's always found endearing, and takes a long pull. She sips her wine and tucks in next to him on the sofa, then unfurls her legs and lies across his lap, holding her hand up to the light and smiling at the ring. It's a little large, and the stone slips under her finger but he's said they can get it altered, they just to have to wait a little bit. She dares not think where it came from.

Maggie takes a deep sip and feels her head prickle. She's never been a big drinker, even the few glasses she'd sipped at Fox Cottage while Charlotte drank the lion's share had fogged her head. She'd fallen asleep without checking her phone was safe, without checking it had recorded properly, ready to send to Tommy. She half wishes it hadn't captured anything; it would have been safer for everyone. She looks guiltily at Tommy, as if he can hear her thoughts, but he's not looking. He just swigs as she flips the channels for something to take her mind off Charlotte. And of her mother, who always looms large and demanding at this time of year.

Alcohol also makes her think of her mum because of her belief in total abstinence – 'temperance' she called it – and intense worry that if she ever had so much as a sip, she'd have her knickers round her ankles and be knocked up within the hour. Her mother's faith in her appeal to local boys was wildly off-kilter. Drunk or sober, she was invisible. But not to Tommy.

Tommy looked at her like she was made just for him. And for her, he was Cinderella's glass slipper. The stories her mother once read to her, made flesh.

With his empty left hand, he rubs her knee half-heartedly.

'Can't wait to be your wife,' she says and he smiles in profile, his dimple emerging. He takes another gulp. Swallows.

'Finally gonna make an honest woman of you,' he says, deadpan.

She pictures her mum in the congregation, sombre, grey, and puts the glass down. 'I should visit my mum on Monday,' she says. 'It's her birthday.'

'Already?' he says. 'That goes fast.'

'Is that OK though?'

''Course it is.'

He doesn't have a mother to visit but he's never stopped her visiting hers. As soon as it was safe anyway. Birthdays, Christmas and anniversaries. It's not that he wants to go, of course he doesn't, who would? But he takes her anyway and then sits in the car for the allotted time to pass, head down, waiting like a sentry.

Never mind that it's him who pays for the flowers that she always takes. Him who pays for the petrol to get them there. Him who gives up his day for someone that never liked him, never trusted him. People don't see this side of him, but it's right there if you look. If only her mum had looked. But her mother didn't believe in happy ever afters, and her own prince had turned out to be such a frog that she saw frogs everywhere she looked.

Charlotte

Saturday Night

Rob pulls up in his battered work truck, which looks improbably bulky next to her sleek low Tesla. Her *mother's* sleek low

Tesla. He needs to replace it, but he's barely making enough to pay his rent as it is. She almost offered to buy him one but he's old-fashioned and he'd never accept a handout.

She feels safer now he's here. Tonight he will lie, as he always does, between her and the bedroom door. Protective by nature from even before he was a father. Every time she lied and told her parents she was staying at Anne's house and then sneaked into Rob's, he would lie nearest the door, one arm protectively across her chest.

Her phone starts to vibrate, another call withheld, which she rejects as she opens the door to let Rob in. He looks tired and she kisses him softly. 'Are you OK?' she asks.

'Not sleeping so well,' he says. 'Lots of, y'know, flashbacks.'

She wants to ask him what Anne looked like when he saw her. She wants to ask if he sat with her, if he cried, closed the skin of her eyes, thought about pulling the letter opener back out. *God no, don't ask that. You don't know about that!*

Did Rob scream when he realised Anne was dead? It's not a noise she could imagine him making but then David had shrieked, hadn't he? People surprise you.

She doesn't ask any of those things. She buries her head firmly in the sand as she always has and always will and, instead, she leads him upstairs to distract them both.

When he goes to the toilet afterwards, she checks her phone. There's an answerphone message from the latest withheld call and she listens, phone pressed to her cheek, other hand tugging the duvet off to let some of the heat out.

'Miss Wilderwood, it's DCI Kashani here.' Charlotte sits up as she listens. Is this it? Is this how it all unravels?

'We've recently discovered that Miss . . . that Anne's contents insurance included some high-value items that were photographed for the policy, and some of these items appear to be missing from her home. Can you call me back to discuss? The number is . . .'

Missing items? Maggie didn't take anything so . . . she rubs her hand over her face. David must have taken them after

Maggie ran out. Did he have them with him when he went into the river? Or when someone finally realises he's missing, will they search his home and find them there. Will that lead to her somehow? Those, plus the missing letters and statements? She tries to make sense of it, but it's all such a tangled mess. She needs to talk it through with Maggie again but they've been so good with their phones, calling is a bad idea.

'Shall we get a takeaway?' Rob says, strolling back in but then looking at her in alarm. 'What's wrong?'

She swallows. She could lie but he's in touch with the police too, they could ask him the same things they ask her and how would that look?

'DCI Kashani left a message for me, something about Anne's insurance and missing things. I, er, I think I should call him back.'

Rob frowns and nods. 'Yeah, 'course.' He sits down lightly next to her. 'Do you want me to stay or shall I leave you to it and go and pick up a Chinese or something?'

'Takeaway would be good,' she says, not caring. 'Thanks.'

DCI Kashani has already left, but she's put through to someone else in the department who tells her quite breezily that she's been sent an email with some photographs; could she take a look and see if she recognises any of the items?

Charlotte opens her personal email account on her phone. She checks the company email inbox constantly but forgets to check her own. It's cluttered with sale announcements and order confirmations. And, from yesterday, an email from DCI Kashani.

It feels oddly informal, flinging an email over. Although it looks legit, with Kashani's badge number – she presumes – in the signature, a link to the victim's code and the address of the investigation centre in the footer.

Dear Miss Wilderwood,
    As mentioned on my answerphone message, the attached items were not found at Anne Wilkins' address and we're trying to establish if they were stolen at the

time of the attack. As you worked closely with Anne and
were good friends, we were hoping you could let us know
if she may have left them at the office, perhaps, or lent
them to somebody. Perhaps even yourself?
Kind regards,
DCI Farzad Kashani

She scrolls down, the attached jpegs automatically opening on
the screen. She immediately recognises one of the necklaces.
She remembers Anne wearing it as far back as sixth form so
she's surprised it's worth enough to insure. Maybe Anne's dad
stole it for her.

She scrolls down to a familiar-looking bracelet. She doesn't
recognise everything and if she was appraising all this for work
she'd have valued the collection at over five grand. There's a
diamond ring here that's worth over a thousand, easily. And a
pair of ruby earrings that she remembers admiring when Anne
wore them to the office.

She replies carefully.

Dear DCI Kashani,
Thank you for your email and all your efforts to find out
what happened to my friend. Some of these items look
familiar but none of them are at the office and I definitely
haven't borrowed any. I'm sorry if that doesn't help much.
Please let me know if there's anything else I can help with.
Best wishes,
Charlotte Wilderwood

She re-reads her reply, then reads DCI Kashani's email again.
Nothing about its tone suggests they're looking at Charlotte
as anything but a grieving friend. She clicks send, but she
feels no relief.

This missing jewellery has blindsided her. *Could* Maggie
have taken it? She feels guilty even considering it, but she's
only got Maggie's word for what happened, and she was short

of money, she said so herself. Maybe she swiped something before Anne confronted her? Or maybe David took it, and then what? She imagines him creeping through Anne's house, planning to do god knows what to Maggie. Could Anne's jewellery have caught his eye? Is that what distracted him so Maggie was able to run out? When Charlotte pictures him like this, David is still monstrous. But whenever she thinks about what happened later that night, about his body and his little cry, he shrinks down until he is simply someone's child. Someone's child whose chance to become good again was snuffed out. And it's almost more than she can bear.

Shaking away tears, she scrolls through the photos again but can't make sense of this by herself. A thought occurs. The wedding dress in her boot, she totally forgot to tell Maggie about it. She could drive to Maggie's mum's house and drop it off there, leave a note for Maggie and ask to meet her at Cribb's Causeway again. No phones, no names, nothing incriminating. Just a quick tête-à-tête about this new development. Yes, she thinks, this is perfect.

Maggie
Monday

They left before dawn, feeling special as you do when you're the only ones on the road. Like you're getting ahead of the world, winning some game.

They surged along the motorway as fast as their little car could rattle. 'I don't know how much longer she's got,' he said after one particularly tortured gear change and she nodded sadly. Everything runs out of time in the end.

Her mum had driven a similar car once upon a time, but it

was newish then. She never took it over forty miles an hour, never left their little town in it. 'A ladies run-around', she'd called it. Like everything else in the house, she'd protected the keys like precious eggs in a nest.

Her paranoid magpie mum.

Growing up, one of the few books of which her mum approved was a beautiful old copy of *Grimms' Fairy Tales*. Maggie would curl up on the bed to be read to each night until she was old enough to read it herself, whereupon she feasted on its romances and tragedies the way her classmates followed bands or talked about soap operas. The one time she dared to question her mother was inspired by the compendium of fairy tales. 'Why do you lock me in the tower like the wicked sorceress from "Rapunzel"?'

And that was the last of the beloved book.

On trips like this Maggie often wants to talk about her mother. Her quirks. Her tight grasp. Her paranoia. How she always thought someone was out to get her, coming for her jewellery, her car, her daughter. She called the police so many times about double-glazing salesman or travellers or the new neighbours or just imagined shadows that they must have put her on some kind of list, slowly rolling up in their car, after she'd waited for hours at the window.

'Something's not right about that lot,' she'd say to the ever-patient police, gesturing through the net curtain to a new family on the street. 'I can feel it in my water.'

'We'll make a note of it,' they would say, their notepads and pens staying in their pockets.

Charlotte

Monday Morning

The road in Newport is busier than last time. A scattering of teenagers dash about, laughing in dishevelled uniforms that were probably neat when they left their homes. Men and women file out of their houses in uniforms and smart-casual work clothes. A young mum pushes a buggy, the child sucking contentedly on a biscuit. It looks like a nice place to grow up.

Maggie's mum's house looks as clean as a new pin. The same blue car is under the car port and she wonders if her mum still works; maybe she's about to leave, or has already left. She wonders how old Maggie's mother is, she could even be in her forties – Maggie is only mid-twenties, after all. Maggie could even be here still, she didn't say she's moved back in with Mike yet, only that they were back together. The thought warms her.

Charlotte heaves the dress out of the boot and starts down the path. She can feel her phone buzzing but it'll have to wait. Before she reaches the front step, the shiny red door has opened a crack, held in place by a chain lock. A woman of around sixty peers out with alert brown eyes, flushed pink skin and a crown of yellow hair. 'What do you want?' she says, a slight tremble in her voice. 'I've seen you hanging around here before.'

Charlotte stops, stays a few feet from the door and awkwardly holds her palms up in surrender, the dress sliding around on her outstretched arms. 'I'm here to return Maggie's dress, is she still here?'

'No,' the woman says, closing the door. Stunned, Charlotte waits a moment and then knocks. 'What?' comes the muffled answer.

'I'm really sorry to bother you but I'm a . . . a friend Maggie's and I've got her wedding dress here. Is she with Mike? Could you maybe give me the address?'

The door opens fully this time, a man of the same age is standing next to the woman now. His face is kind but his words are firm.

'There's been some mistake, love. There's no one here by that name and never has been. I think someone's sent you on a wild goose chase.'

She drives aimlessly, trying to think, trying to make sense of it. She saw Maggie go into that house, she's not imagining things. But did she actually see her go inside or just head towards the door? The jacketed wedding dress is slumped on the backseat like an angry adolescent and Charlotte appeals to it for answers in the rear-view mirror. No answers come.

She *could* just call her. She could just phone Maggie and ask her what the fuck is going on. She shakes her head involuntarily. They've been so good with their phones, she doesn't want to blow it now and link their mobile numbers all over again. She looks at her phone again now, wondering who rang from a withheld number earlier. The police? Or maybe Maggie herself. She has to speak to her somehow. If Maggie has been lying about her mum's house, what else has she might have been lying about? Anne's jewellery? Oh god, *what David did to her*? She feels suddenly dizzy at the thought. No, not that. Never that. Because if . . . no. She stops herself, shuttering the thought behind iron gates.

A garage appears on the horizon and Charlotte puts her foot down harder on the accelerator to reach it. She pulls in a little before it, tucks her car on the street kerb to avoid any forecourt CCTV and then walks towards the garage shop, spotting a payphone. Keeping her eyes down to avoid cameras as she approaches, she then dials carefully by copying each digit from her phone onto the cold metal number pad. Unlike last time, it rings just once then the mechanical voice starts.

'This number is not in use'.

Shit, shit, shit. What the fuck is going on? She rushes back to the car and slides into the driver's seat, sets the satnav for home and drives off at speed, feeling suddenly like she's been stranded behind enemy lines.

Maggie

The butterscotch town is half-lit, warm with dawn sun and glistening from last night's rain. It looks like a theatrical stage. Old timey names on the butcher and baker shop, a greengrocer, a thatched roof on the library. It looks, to fresh eyes, like a lovely place to grow up.

They drive down her old road and turn into the church car park where the Fiesta can tuck into the corner of the plot and no one can see it from the road.

'Love you,' she says as she gets out.

'Don't be too long, eh?'

She leans in to pull her coat from the back seat for the short walk to her mum.

The place is neat and tidy, probably from her auntie's help but maybe her mother has friends. She wouldn't know. She stands back for a moment, wishing now that she hadn't come, but she is made of elastic and will always return eventually.

'Happy birthday, Mum,' she says, offering the birthday flowers, which are not taken. She places them down.

'I have some news.' She pauses. 'We're getting married.'

Silence is the stern reply.

In the corner of the graveyard, she sees the stooped figure of the same old vicar who christened her, confirmed her and comforted her – briefly – when her mother died. She tucks in tighter to the gravestone, not wanting to be seen. She's recognisable, always was. She's often wondered if she got her red hair from her father. Her mother was dark and wouldn't be drawn on 'him'.

The flowers she brought with her have slowly slid to the floor like little drunks and she pulls out the drooping lilies from the vase that's built into the grave, replaces them with her own. Her auntie must have brought those lilies, there are often flowers here when Maggie comes. A small stipend considering her Aunt Vanessa – Van – and her kids got a whole house out of the deal.

Van was supposed to inherit Maggie as well. But she'd turned sixteen a couple of days before it happened and no one much cared where she'd gone. Certainly not Van, who always found Maggie 'odd' and openly said so.

The vicar slips into the church, unaware of her, and she exhales in relief.

'We might go abroad to get married,' she says to the grave, although Tommy has snuffed that idea out already. 'We're just waiting on a payout for some work we did.' She wonders if Charlotte crouches down and talks to her parents' graves like this. If she has confided in them about Anne, about the man she thought was called David, whose body she thought had stayed in that perilous water. It's something else they have in common of course, dead parents, but Maggie couldn't have said that. She had to deny both of them that mutual understanding. If they could have one more conversation, just one night in the cottage, suspended outside of reality, and really *talk*, she would want to talk about that. About loss and grief and guilt. About living up to expectations, sticking to promises, and what millstones those promises can be. And about the soothing stories we tell ourselves, when the truth is too jagged.

Although of course Charlotte lost both of her parents in one fell swoop, whereas Maggie never knew her dad. He was a black hole from the get-go. The most she ever got out of her mum was that his name was Mike and that he had been in town to work on the new housing estate that everyone in the village had hated. She liked to imagine what he was like sometimes. Strong and calm, a protector. Like Tommy but . . . not exactly. But for all she knows he's dead too.

'Happy birthday, Mum,' she says as she unfolds her legs and stretches to a stand. 'We'll save you some wedding cake.'

She slides into the passenger seat. Tommy glares at her. 'How was your mum?'

'Still dead,' she says, buckling her seatbelt.

She looks at the phone propped next to the gearstick. This latest one was plucked last month from a second home in Penarth that he'd been watching for weeks, doing his due diligence. You can't actually get much for phones if they're not the latest model, but he couldn't resist scooping it up alongside the watches and the jewellery, the cameras and a pot of cash.

The guy who owned the Penarth holiday home must have shoved this older iPhone in a drawer whenever he'd upgraded, immediately forgotten. But Tommy will look after it, keep it clean and treasure it. This way it doesn't go to waste.

'I tried to call her again but she's still not fucking answering.'

Maggie swallows, trying not to show any relief. A shadow passes over his face. 'I've been thinking, though. Little Miss Inheritance is much more likely to answer if you call her.'

'I've changed my number though,' she says, trying to sound panicked. 'Remember? I told you my phone broke and—'

'If she doesn't answer, you can just leave a message and she's bound to call *you* back.' He smiles then. 'Special bond, you said. Time to cash in on it.' She swallows, desperately thinking of ways out of this. 'No time like the present, mate.'

She stares at her phone, desperately trying to think of a way out.

'You know what to say, don't you?'

She thinks about shaking her head and feigning ignorance, but the script has been in place for days and she knows it by rote. Every horrible word of it. 'What are you fucking waiting for then?' he says, jabbing her in the arm.

Charlotte

Charlotte's heartbeat fills her ears as she skates along the speed limit all the way to the Severn Bridge. Cars stream in both directions. The sun glinting off bonnets and windscreens, the tall metal structure holding them all like some kind of miracle.

As she lands back on Somerset soil, her phone starts to ring, the noise filling the car. Withheld number again. It could be DCI Kashani with a follow-up to her email. Or maybe it could be Maggie. Maybe she's paranoid about the police, or someone looking for David, and has told her parents to say she doesn't live there. Are they in on these lies?

Fuck it, only one way to find out. She presses to accept the call. 'Hello?'

She hears whispering and tries to make it out. 'Hello?' There's a hiss and then finally, a voice. 'Charlotte?'

'Maggie! Oh, thank god. Where are you, I've been trying to—'

'Charlotte, I'm sorry but, um . . .' her voice trails away to nothing and the silence is thick.

'Maggie, are you OK? I tried to see you, I have your dress and, no that's not really why. The police called me, someone took jewellery from . . .' she stops. Something is not right. Maggie is not joining in, she's not reassuring, she's not denying anything. She's waiting for Charlotte to finish.

'Maggie,' Charlotte says, a leaden feeling growing in her chest. 'What's going on?'

There's a pause and then the sound of a drawn breath. 'I'm sorry, Charlotte, but you see . . . you need to do exactly what I tell you or I'm going to tell the police that you killed David and Anne.'

'What? Is this a joke?'

'No,' Maggie says, sounding pained at the idea. 'I wouldn't . . . this is serious. I'm sorry but I have no choice and neither do you.'

Ahead of her, shimmering waves of brake lights roll up the road. Her teeth have started to chatter, her jaw and shoulders aching with tension. How can this be happening? Maggie, saying these things now, when they've worked so hard to avoid getting caught?

'But I didn't kill Anne,' she says, her voice small.

'You did kill David though,' Maggie says softly. 'And, um . . . well, there's evidence that you killed Anne too.'

'What?! What evidence? Why are you saying all this?'

'What evidence?' Maggie seems to be asking herself the same question. There's a pause and then she carries on in a stronger voice. 'You looked up her address on your phone, for one. And there's evidence all over your house, Charlotte. Some of Anne's jewellery and a, a piece of paper with her blood and your fingerprints on it.'

'But we burned all of that! Did you . . . did you keep some of it?' Charlotte gasps, trying to picture when it could have happened. A betrayal right in front of her. 'How could you?'

'I'm really sorry,' Maggie says. 'I'm really, really sorry.'

'Then why are you doing this?!'

Maggie pauses, there's a hiss in the background that Charlotte can't make out and then she carries on, her voice almost robotic now, scripted. 'The murder weapon is in your house,' she says.

'But . . . what, that was left . . . wasn't it?'

'And other things too.'

'What? What things? The jewellery, do you mean the jewellery?'

'You'll never find it all so there's no point looking.'

'No point looking?! What are you saying? Why are doing this to me?!'

'Your Tesla,' Maggie continues, her voice shaky. 'It records everywhere you go and it will show you near Anne's house just before . . .'

'It'll show me driving away again!'

'After you ran inside and killed her.'

'But I didn't!'

'And it'll show you driving to the bridge when David . . .'

Charlotte starts to cry. This girl, this woman she took into her car, her home, her life . . . she's one step ahead in every way. 'How could you, Maggie?'

'You need to do exactly what we tell you—'

'We?' Charlotte sobs.

'I, exactly what I tell you, or I'm going to go to the police. Please, Charlotte, just do this and then it'll all be over. I promise.'

She almost doesn't dare ask, and the question comes out barely above a whisper. 'Do what?'

'I want a hundred thousand pounds.'

'What?! A hundred grand! That's impossible!'

'Please don't lie to me, I know you have it.'

Charlotte thinks about the bank statements, what else Maggie might have unearthed that Charlotte's not even realised.

'It's not that simple though,' she says, head spinning and heart breaking. 'Most of that money belongs to the business and there are procedures, tax implications, I don't have lots of cash lying around, I really don't.'

'Who would you rather have after you, the tax man or the police?'

Charlotte says nothing, mind whirling.

'Bring the money to the bridge at midnight tomorrow.'

She doesn't need to say which bridge.

Maggie

He's talked about finding an opportunity like this for years. They've been biding their time, treading water. She didn't expect their golden ticket to be a woman, didn't expect her to be so kind. To feel like, though she can hardly admit it now, a friend. An older sister, even.

223

They'd done the bride thing to death and, actually, it just wasn't that lucrative. And sometimes she'd try it on the wrong Samaritan and they'd turn out not to be so good. Tommy would be listening under the bridge and scramble out if it went too far, but sometimes people had seemed nice until she'd got into their cars. Then she'd had to send an SOS text to Tommy, following at a distance, when the driver wasn't looking. There were times she'd be given pity cash for a hotel room, for the mark to then try to follow her inside. Times she came away with bruised wrists, a trampled train. On the worst nights she had begged Tommy to let her stop. To hang up that dress for good. Her pleas winding him up so tightly that his rage would suck up all the oxygen in the car and leave her gasping for breath.

But it wasn't all bad. Once she was out there, she did like the challenge of choosing the right backstory, building up a character, navigating ad libs. *Improv*. And when Charlotte shared her conundrum about Anne, Maggie realised that with the right plan, this could be the chance they'd been looking for. And her chance to finally stop. Then she texted Tommy her original idea and any second thoughts became irrelevant.

'You think I like this life?' he often said, as she wriggled and moaned while he zipped her into the dirty dress, ready to drive her out to a new bridge he'd found. 'You get to play dress-up and make-believe. You're not the one crawling through fucking windows and dodging guard dogs.'

But, actually, she does think he likes this life. He thrives on it. That's why, for all their talk, he's let so many other possible pay days pass them by. Always looking for Baby Bear's bowl of porridge, while they get skinter and skinter, running out of places to target, and places to hide.

They'd probably not be working towards the 'end game' now if she hadn't started it, unsanctioned. He'd already started talking about her doing a new turn as 'a battered wife'. A phrase and idea that made her sick. But by the time she'd got a proper message and the recording to Tommy that Saturday morning, crouching on Charlotte's toilet in borrowed pyjamas, she'd already laid the foundations. And when he'd wanted to end it simply by burgling the cottage, she'd upped the ante with a bigger plan: Take the paperwork from Anne's house and sell it back to Charlotte at a price.

But then he took things too far with Anne. And even worse, the handover of the cash to buy 'David's' silence was a complete mess and Tommy ended up nearly drowning in the river and didn't even get the money. So this is all on her. He's right.

'Maggie?' he says and she turns.

'You in there?' He taps her forehead like a coconut and she blinks. She hates it when he does this but never says so.

'Sorry, what did you say?'

'I said you need to stop apologising to her so much.'

'But she doesn't deserve this.'

For a moment, there's silence. The whistle of a bomb falling, and then, the explosion. 'She tried to fucking kill me!'

'I'm sorry, Tommy.'

'She pushed me off that bridge and then walked away! She wanted me to fucking drown! She got us to kill someone for her, risking our necks!'

'She didn't . . . I didn't . . .'

'And she's sitting on a pile of cash she didn't do anything to earn. But *she's* the victim? She's the fucking victim here?' He lifts both of his heavy arms and smashes them down on the little steering wheel so the car judders for a moment.

She covers her ears and cries. 'I'm sorry, Tommy, you're right.'

'And don't you fucking forget it,' he growls.

Charlotte

Charlotte drives all the way to work, eyes raw with tears. Even as she's doing so, she's aware it's absurd. To just keep going, as if she hasn't just had that call, as if she isn't coated in sweat, as if her world isn't on fire.

A hundred thousand pounds? Where did Maggie pluck that figure from? Shit, of course. The stolen bank statements . . . David didn't take them, Maggie did. It's so obvious now. This must have been her plan all along.

From the moment she picked Maggie up, Charlotte was fucked, she just didn't know it. And this is not the kind of fucked where she can talk her way out of it or buy some time or plead ignorance. This is not the kind of fucked her dad could solve even if he was here. This is the kind of fucked where someone poured a ring of petrol around her feet and Charlotte struck the match. *Oh Maggie, how could you?*

She pulls into the car park but there are no customers waiting. The phone call is still echoing around her head, snow-balling and distorting into a town crier slur of the same phrases.

'But I didn't kill Anne.'

'You did kill David though.'

And she did.

'Please, Charlotte, just do this and then it'll all be over.'

She stoops to collect the post and then turns the lights on with her elbow. Surely she's missing something about this situation. She can't just hand over that much cash on the say-so of a con woman? Charlotte is riddled with guilt; her head is wrecked and her heart is broken by betrayal. She might never move past what she did, but Maggie is no better. She killed Anne *brutally*. So brutally it made the news, and now she gets to claim some kind of reward for that? No. No fucking way.

She looks at the stacks of paper on the table, adds to it with the small pile of post. As she does, a familiar business card slips out from under the envelopes in her hand. It must have been posted through her door and she snatched it up from the floor with the rest. She frowns as she looks at it.

Harry Sedgemoor
Tel. 07815 163718

She flips it over. Unlike the other one, this has something written on the back in slanting black writing. 'Call me, we have business to discuss'. *Oh fuck off, you absolute ghoul.* He must have heard about Anne and decided it was a good time to strike again. She slides the card into her back pocket; she doesn't have time for this now.

'You'll never find all of the evidence so there's no point looking.'

Is she really going to take Maggie's word for that? She scoops her bag back up, leaves the post and the paperwork where it lies and heads back out.

She still remembers the feeling of sneaking up on this cottage during the day as a teenager. As if the creamy yellow bricks themselves were watching her through narrowed eyes. She bunked off with Anne once, forging sick notes for themselves the next day. But Anne had spent the whole time wracked with fear about Charlotte's parents coming home. They'd ended up having a big bust up and not speaking for weeks. Or maybe it was hours; everything felt epic at that age.

By year eleven, Charlotte had become so adept at forging parental sick notes that she'd do it once a month or so, when fumbling around in bushes and behind classrooms got rained off and they wanted to spend an afternoon in a real bed. She got caught eventually, when a teacher noticed she and Rob were often off on the same days. The school called Rob's house and when there was no answer – because they ignored it – the woman in the office called Charlotte's home. Her mother answered. Unlike her dad, her mother didn't cover for her.

Pamela told the school her daughter was lying, then drove round to Rob's and rapped tightly on the door.

'Considering your dad spends his life trying to protect you, you still manage to comprehensively mess up,' she said, as Charlotte slunk out to the car. 'We've given you the world on a plate but you'd rather eat junk food out of a box.'

She'd forgotten all that until today. But now the cottage still wears that look, that quiet judgement bordering on disappointment as she arrives home at noon and bursts in through the door.

And she clearly hadn't been imagining anything on Friday. Someone *had* been in the house. It must have been Maggie, after they'd parted. Did Charlotte tell her she wasn't going straight home? Maybe, it's all a blur. She'd been so relieved to see her, it had felt like coming home.

This isn't the time to get upset. Be strategic.

She puts her bag down carefully, opens the email from DCI Kashani and the photos of Anne's missing jewellery and starts to search.

Maggie

Monday Afternoon

They re-enter the fringes of Cardiff. They've lived in at least thirty cities across the UK since they first fled Devon, choosing them at random on a map based on three criteria only:

1. Somewhere neither of them has been before.
2. Somewhere they don't have any friends or relatives – not difficult.
3. At least 100 miles from the mid-Devon town where they first met.

They've lived in mobile homes (a holiday in summer, a cryogenic freezing chamber in winter), bedsits, squats and occasionally, most happily, bargain flats available cash only for short lettings. They've criss-crossed from Scotland to East Anglia, Northern Ireland to Wales. They travel light, only with as much as they can take in their car in a rush.

She thinks of the sheer number of *things* in Charlotte's house. The big pieces of furniture, the sets. Glasses for every type of drink, *dessert forks,* for goodness sake. An accumulation of proof that Charlotte gets to stay put. People like her take it for granted that they can tie weights to their life. They will never have to move so quickly that they can't wrap the Emma Bridgewater teapot in newspaper and place it in a packing box, snug to its swaddled sugar bowl.

Their time at this poky flat in Cardiff is the longest they've ever stayed anywhere, but this place has never felt like home. Not that anywhere really has. Not Devon, certainly, where she was always monitored and questioned. Where behind every curtain was a pair of eyes with nothing to do but watch the strange girl with her red head in the clouds.

The watching continued right through her mother's funeral, the flashbulbs of the press behind her making it impossible to hear the well-meaning and inaccurate eulogy. A pillar of the community? Only in the sense that her mother was immovable and never left the town. A traditionalist with good Christian values? That was one way to look at it, she supposed.

As well-wishers she barely recognised pushed egg sandwiches into their mouths at the funeral reception, she told her glassy-eyed aunt that she needed to stay with a friend to clear her head. That was ten years ago.

She wonders sometimes what they all thought when she just upped and left. They would have blamed her grief, of course. She was certainly under no suspicion. She'd been at school the evening her mother had died, relishing a bit part in a performance of *Cat on a Hot Tin Roof* that her mother had helpfully declared unseemly and refused to watch.

The teachers had no one to call when she stopped showing up; she didn't give them her aunt's details. She would have just slipped away in total silence and been instantly forgotten if it wasn't for the local news coverage of her mother's death.

It was a home robbery gone wrong, police said. Jewellery taken from an address in Church Street, a middle-aged mother of one battered to death. In a town where the largest marrow at the summer fete would normally constitute headline news, it was like finding themselves at the centre of a Hollywood movie. She imagines they feasted on it for weeks.

She left that day carrying only her rucksack. It contained a few handmade clothes and what little birthday money she'd saved over the years. She'd looked everywhere for the *Grimms' Fairy Tales* book, hoping her mother hadn't really thrown it away and had instead slid it somewhere for safekeeping, but it had truly gone. There was nothing else she wanted.

Tommy was waiting at the bus stop, a hood down over his face, standing in shadow. He'd been selling the generic bits of jewellery miles away and had ridden the train back to come and get her, hiding in the toilet to avoid the fare. The identifiable pieces of jewellery had been thrown in the village pond the very same night they were taken.

'You OK?' he asked, as she approached. She wasn't OK. But she was free, of sorts, so she nodded. As the bus pulled up and they mounted for Plymouth, where they would take a train to wherever, she reached for his hand.

'You're all I have now,' she said. 'Don't ever let me go.'

'I will *never* let you go,' he replied.

As a girl she'd been christened Meredith – a family name – but that day at the bus stop she picked a new name: Maggie, the 'cat' from *Cat on a Hot Tin Roof*, the part she'd coveted but would never have been given.

Tommy loves Maggie and Maggie loves Tommy. An instant and forever love, even as everything around them waxed and waned. It couldn't be anything less than a forever love, the price they'd paid for it was too high. He had kissed the sleeping princess, so they would live happy ever after.

But while their love is forever, this life can't be. No matter how careful they are, how strategically they plan, luck will always play a part and theirs will eventually run out. He'll get caught for house breaking, her for creaming cash from bleeding hearts. And even though his eyes still blaze with adrenaline when he gets back with a haul, when that seeps away, it takes longer for him to recover each time. They're exhausted, old before their time. And it's in tiredness that mistakes will happen.

They just needed one jackpot, that's what he said. Then they could become real people. They could pick somewhere to stay, find jobs and a nice little house to fill with dessert forks and matching things.

Maybe she could even use her real name again. Retire the name 'Maggie'. She wonders what Tommy would think of that.

It's not like anyone was likely to be looking for them still, not for what happened to her mum. The investigation fizzled out years ago and it was in no one's interests to start it up. The jewellery was a dead end, her aunt was quite settled in the house and the local paper had been shut down. Even the police that investigated the case had been lost to retirement and redundancy. But they'd been careful not to be spotted back in the town, just in case; there was still no need to jog anyone's memory, give them a two and two to put together.

She thinks of Charlotte and Fox Cottage. The home that was so warm and comfortable, the one she opened up so willingly. She wonders, just briefly, if Charlotte plans to raise her own family there. So many life-and-death topics they talked about, but not that. She wishes she could go back somehow, slip in between the days and snuggle back on the sofa, settle in for a good chat. It was all over so soon.

When Charlotte pulled over that night, it was meant to be. The stars aligning over their pot of gold. So why does the thought of taking her money and setting light to her life to build their own, feel a lot like the grief she was supposed to feel ten years ago?

Charlotte

The hallway is fairly clean. It's not her mum's level of clean, but it's pretty dust-free at least. Charlotte runs her fingertips carefully along the top of the console table, checks behind the diffuser then picks it up. Nothing. She's looking for a piece of paper of whose size she has no idea, knowing only that it is marked with blood. When did Maggie take it? It must have been after they'd got back here if it has Charlotte's fingerprints on it. She couldn't have slipped it in her pocket in the car, it would have been too obvious. But then, she's clearly a professional, three steps ahead at all times. A fucking mastermind.

A scrap of paper could be slid anywhere, in the pages of a book, under a mat, behind . . . anything . . . But somewhere that the police would find it. Somewhere they wouldn't question why she'd kept a damning piece of evidence – somewhere it could have fluttered unknown, perhaps.

Charlotte peels up the welcome mat, a cloud of dust and grit puffs up her nose, but no paper. She checks down the sofa cushions, inside the antique trunk that's full of board games she doesn't remember ever playing, checks piles of magazines, most of which were bought by her mum. *Good Housekeeping, Country Living*. Only a handful of *Grazias*, which are hers.

The whole house seems to swell in size; how can she ever hope to search it all? And it's not just the piece of paper, even if she finds that there's all the jewellery and, most importantly, a letter opener. Although, actually, she can't be sure that's what it was. The police haven't released that information to the public and if it was missing from the scene, no one would know for sure. So, *the weapon*. Maggie said it was a letter opener but who could know if that's true. Maybe a letter opener, maybe just some random sharp metal thing, presumably marked with blood.

She sits in the middle of her parents' bed. The afternoon has been swallowed by frenzy, she's not eaten since this morning and she's wired on coffee. She's checked every other room, this one is all that's left. She has pulled the sheets and duvets off the beds, shaken them so vigorously her arms ache. She has checked every drawer of every antique chest, every cupboard, and polished trinket box. Nothing. She's checked corners and cubbyholes a second time, not trusting that she really looked before, believing she may have entered some kind of dream-like state and imagined it. And now she's in the final room. If they're not here, they're not anywhere.

The bedding in here is the same White Company set that her mum last put on, probably the day they left for their holiday. Her mother always made sure the house was as polished as a pin when they went away, thinking ahead to when they returned. Charlotte hasn't touched it since, not even slapped the pillows to chase away the dust, and it still feels naughty, disrespectful, to have plonked herself down where she was never allowed. But Maggie won't have known this. They covered a lot of topics during their cosy fireside chat, she thinks bitterly, but not that.

She hops down and crouches next to the bed, turning on her phone torch. There is a vacuum-sealed bag containing the winter duvet that would normally have been switched by now and a few neat lidded wooden boxes that she recognises from childhood, nothing else.

The dust under here sits in silent judgement, at first glance six months' worth undisturbed. But when she looks again, there is a slight sweeping away leading from one of the boxes.

Maggie

'Tommy,' she starts. He's on the sofa, tired from the drive. He looks up, jaw thrusting forward, mug resting in his meaty hand.

'What is it, mate? Feeling out of sorts from seeing your mum?'

She shakes her head. That never makes her feel out of sorts. She always comes away sharper, her world more precise when she's reiterated the evidence of it. Touched the gravestone, laid the flowers, traced her mother's name with a finger. Every time she goes to Devon, whether at night or dawn, skulking in the nether times when people are looking the other way, she is reminded of the two key facts of her life. Her mother is definitely dead, and Tommy loves her enough to kill for her; about who else could she say that? *Charlotte still thinks she killed for me.* She swallows back a sob and turns slightly so he doesn't see her tears.

'No, it's not that.'

The afternoon sun picks up the grey in his stubble. I've done this to him, she thinks. I've aged him. He barely knew her back then, and he chose to offer her his life on a plate, lock, stock and barrel.

'What is it, then? It's not about little Miss Silver Spoon, is it?'

Of course it is. But her tongue can't find the right sounds, the right shapes. What does she even want to say?

He sits up straighter, lowers the mug. 'If you're having second thoughts now, I'll bloody swing for you.'

She looks down. 'It's not that. I just don't want to . . . I don't want to hurt her any more than we have to, that's all. She was really good to me.'

'We're a bit late for that,' he says. 'And let's not forget that it was your idea, bowling into that bloody Anne's house instead of waiting. If you'd just distracted her properly, I could have snatched that paperwork and sold it back to that Charlotte for a song, not as much as we're planning now admittedly, but—'

Charlotte's not long lost her mum and dad, and her friend double-crossed her and—'

'This was your bloody idea, Meredith!' As he rises, the mug hits the floor, spraying soup and tiny croutons everywhere. His body becomes cartoon huge and his roar fills the room.

He only ever uses her birth name when he's furious. 'I didn't start this!'

She crouches down, gathering up the bits and righting the mug. He softens immediately, collapses down next to her, the knees of his jogging bottoms staining.

'You can't have the prize without entering the competition,' he says, softer now. 'Remember what we're doing this for. A chance, mate. A place we can call home, a wedding dress that you didn't buy from a charity shop, no more running. And this Charlotte character has all of that in spades, way more than that, and it was just handed to her. Yeah, her parents died, but so did your mum.'

'And even after we're done, she'll still have so much. She told you she inherited everything, she's swimming in money.'

'How much does she have, Tommy? Are you sure she can put her hands on a hundred thousand?'

'I don't know, numb nuts, but that cottage is worth a bob or two and—'

'I mean in her bank. You took the statements, didn't you?'

'What statements?'

'From her house. After Bath, we got back and you'd taken her post.'

He wrinkles his nose. 'No, I hadn't.'

She thinks back. Charlotte was so sure someone had taken the post and she'd assumed . . . She shrugs, what does it matter now? Maybe Charlotte was imagining it, too hopped up on the adrenaline and fear.

'She can afford to lose a bit,' he says. 'And then we'll finally have *something*. That's all.'

A hundred thousand pounds is more than a bit.

'She was so nice to me.'

'Not as nice to you as I am. And,' he says, walking out to the kitchen to get a dishcloth for the mess, 'she doesn't just lose in this, she gains too. Don't forget she wanted rid of that Anne.'

She nods.

'And she gets a little life lesson into the bargain,' he says, back with the cloth, pressing it onto the tomato Cup a Soup like he's trying to stem bleeding.

'What's that then, Tommy?'

'Never trust strangers.'

Charlotte

The box is only two by one foot in old money, as her dad would have said, but it contains whole lives. A knitted pink bonnet she's seen in her baby photos. A tiny wristband with 'Baby Wilderwood, girl' written by a nurse's efficient pen. Her first school report, handmade cards, little handmade books, toddler drawings, photos of her with bunches, with purple teenage hair, in fancy dress, red-eyed and fuzzy.

And underneath that, neatly stacked well-filled envelopes addressed to her dad. She lifts them out, prepared to open them up and rifle, but then she sees the distinctive ruby earrings wrapped in a carefully folded piece of paper dotted with blood. They were tucked underneath the envelopes. But where is the rest of the jewellery? The necklace, bracelet and ring? And more importantly, the weapon?

She drinks tea. Medicinal. Her lips cracked from a dehydrating day surrounded by dust. She hasn't found a letter opener and still doesn't know for sure what was actually used. Maybe there never was a letter opener. Perhaps Maggie took something from Charlotte's house without her knowing, killed Anne with it and then slid it back in situ? A knife from that set? The pizza slice she used just the other day? Or is something sitting in the drawer that was brought back from Anne's place, something she can't tell apart from the rest?

She burns the piece of bloody paper with a match over the

sink, let the black ash rain gently onto the white ceramic. She washes it briskly away then fills the sink with scalding water, adding bleach and Fairy Liquid, unsure if that will help get rid of traces of blood but too scared to google and plant that red flag. It's a huge Belfast sink, installed in the penultimate round of renovations. Practically a bath. Into it she slides every knife she can find and any utensil with an even slightly sharp edge or point until she's facing a boiling hot torture chamber. She snaps on rubber gloves and grabs the scratchiest thing she can find under the sink – an old Brillo pad that predates her return – and starts to scrub.

By the time she's finished – a metal mountain drying on the side – her hands are stiff and aching, the tips of the gloves worn away. And still she doesn't know if she's found it, if this is all there is.

When the phone rings, she can't face answering. She places the phone down on the kitchen table and watches as it vibrates uselessly, eventually ringing off. In the middle of the table, Anne's earrings sit like a strange centrepiece, and she nudges them gently with her finger, thinking. They have a delicate Art Deco design, ruby studs encased in white gold. If someone brought these into the shop, she'd offer £500 and sell them for three hundred more.

She wonders, just briefly, if there's a way to throw the police off the scent with them. Hide them somewhere strategic and incriminating. But incriminate who? She's not prepared to drag anyone else into this. Perhaps she should tell Kashani she found them at the office. She tucks them in her handbag and thinks about other loose ends.

The dress. She hasn't used the barbecue since Maggie was here, but it's the obvious solution. Charlotte changes into her old scruffs, empties a small heap of rubble from the belly of the barbecue into a bin liner, which she carries down the lane and dumps in Joan's wheelie bin. It will be collected tomorrow.

Back at the cottage, she retrieves the dry cleaning bag from the front seat, feeling guilty about all the time that fastidious man had spent working on it.

She wads the bottom of the barbecue with the last of the briquettes and gets the fire going, then goes inside to get the paper, grabbing her phone at the same time.

One voicemail.

At first, Charlotte doesn't understand. There are muffled sounds, a cough, something that sounds like glasses clinking. When the voice starts, it's her own.

'I need to get Anne off my back too, for good.'

The message ends and Charlotte can barely breathe. Maggie must have recorded their conversations. *Fuck.* This really was her plan right from the start. She's a stone-cold mastermind. And not a fragment of their connection was real.

Maggie

Unable to stand it at home, she said she'd go and get some shopping and he quietly peeled some notes from the curl of money in his pocket. Possibly some of the very same notes that Charlotte had handed over, never imagining it would be dutifully passed to him, a man whose life she thought she'd ended. Or maybe this is the proceeds of the necklace that she took on that first night, when she still saw Charlotte purely as a mark and not a human. He claims he sold it for a tenner, but she knows he's not that stupid.

She wonders if Charlotte has noticed it missing. There were so many pieces of jewellery in that room, none of them seeming like Charlotte's style . . . Even though Charlotte must already hate her, Maggie hopes it wasn't missed.

How has Charlotte slept since they met? Is she having flash-backs over pushing the man she thought was called David into the water? She should have asked when she had the chance. Maggie has managed to sleep most nights, as long as she stops herself thinking of Anne. It would have been far worse if she'd been there for her final moments rather than stepped aside for Tommy as he appeared in the office doorway. As with her mother, she was able to snip the optical cord between her eyes and her imagination, stopping herself picturing those final moments. Focusing instead on the kindness that he'd showed by protecting her from it, taking one for the team as he always does. As he always will. Whether she likes it or not.

It's grey out here. The clouds swelling low, the pavement still painted black from an earlier downpour. She draws her coat tighter around her. In her right pocket, the cash sits loose and she fingers the individual notes nervously, checking they're all still there. And a coin, one she has secreted there and touches from time to time, one she took from Charlotte's car when she wasn't looking. When they go straight, she'll get a purse. A nice one, with a shiny buckle and a space for all the loyalty cards she'll sign up to. In her real name. Her *married* name. And she'll keep the special coin in a tiny little zipped section in the middle, like a heart.

Realistically, they probably could have eased off these measures years ago. She's sure no one is actively looking for them for what happened with her mother. But they've not exactly led an honourable life. Everything cash, everything fluid. So it's not like they could have registered their true selves anywhere, paid their earnings into a high street bank, notified the tax man. Those are the lives of people like Charlotte.

She grabs a basket and bundles through the doors of the supermarket. They don't do 'big shops', as her mum used to call them. Never knowing when life will turn on a penny and they'll need to move, steal away in the night with only what they can fit in the car. No point buying food only to waste it.

She still cringes over the ham incident, back when they were in Glasgow, or maybe it was Fife. She'd been watching a lot of travel shows at the time, dreaming of lying on the sand just the two of them, of bobbing on a boat surrounded by azure seas, squinting into the sun and drinking cheap wine.

When she saw a leg of Spanish ham on special in Lidl, she'd grabbed it, along with olives, a great hunk of Manchego and a bottle of almost-Rioja.

'What the fuck is this pig's leg doing here?' he'd shouted, barging in through the door at 3 a.m., telling her to wrap up and get in the car, they needed to shift it out of the city. Something had gone wrong. She'd tried to bring it, to prove a point maybe, to rescue that sniff of holiday feeling, but he'd pulled it out of the footwell and chucked it in the gutter to make way for a bag of tools that were obviously more important.

The whole drive down to Newcastle they'd talked about nothing but how much the leg had cost, her lying early on about it only being four pounds and him not believing her. A long impasse down a dead motorway. He'd even smoked with the windows closed, something he knows she hates. The kind of precise punishment only long-term love can foster.

But he'd got a lot better at his job. And she'd become accomplished at her part too, taking the pressure off him a little. Things rarely went wrong now and the midnight flits were more or less a thing of the past. So she buys a few items on special offer these days, a few BOGOFs. She slots two large cartons of orange juice into her basket, smiling beatifically like a woman in an advert. She imagines a camera trained on her as she walks down the aisle. 'My husband and I live busy lives,' she would say in a friendly tone, using non-regional dialect. 'So for me, it's important that I can get quality goods in a jiffy.'

Of course, the closest she came to an acting career was that final speaking part as a plucky servant in *Cat on a Hot Tin Roof*. She did a memorable turn and even the drama teacher who had never liked her had to admit her Southern accent was flawless. Maybe he regretted not giving her the lead; she liked to believe so. It was an extra feat given that she had a rich and burbling Devon dialect back then, something she's since worked hard to flatten.

But soon, they will re-enter the atmosphere, give up their anonymity, go straight. She can't quite believe Tommy is really going to do it. He'll only do it for her, he says. Because she's so persuasive. She doesn't remember persuading him to do anything, but she must have. A tiny thrill charges through her, a little bolt of power.

And like spies, they will need to build their legends when they rejoin civilisation. Job history, address history, financial history. No hope of a mortgage, no chance of a decent landlord taking them on. But with the money they're going to get, they can buy a tiny place in Cumbria, one bedroom, maybe a box room too if they're really lucky. A doer-upper.

Just the thought of Cumbria slows her heart rate and unclenches her muscles. A safe word, one she's clung to for years since they first drove through it. The drama of the landscape cocooning them on all sides, with an awe-striking hugeness like nowhere else they'd ever been. They'd originally intended to set up there for a bit but, once they fell in love, on that very first drive, they chose to leave it unspoiled. Somewhere they could return to when they were ready to be real.

So the place was decided but not how to fill their time in it. What will they do for jobs? With acting off the table, perhaps she could work in a shop. Maybe a little village shop selling Kendal Mint Cake and jams, where she'll know everyone's names and they'll know hers. A village where Tommy might play skittles at the pub, get some labouring work again, maybe learn to be a thatcher or something. Honest work. Maybe she could join a local amateur dramatics club, be the star of the local pantomime.

Maybe that's more than she could have a right to hope for, but she allows herself to anyway.

When she gets home, Tommy takes the bags from her and hands her back her phone. He's keeping it safe in case she bottles it and calls Charlotte to tell her the truth. He's protecting her from herself. 'We need to keep the pressure on,' he says. 'Make sure she doesn't do anything stupid.'

Charlotte

She tears the veil and train from the carefully cleaned wedding dress, ripping through the stitching in seconds and stuffing it into the barbecue where it splutters and pops. With the garden shears, she hacks the rest of the dress to pieces and dumps them next to the barbecue ready to burn.

Charlotte is as fucked as this dress. She cannot go to the police about the blackmail because part of what Maggie is saying is true. It doesn't matter that David was a bad person. It doesn't matter that he was goading her or that all she did was push him. He's dead, because of Charlotte.

Whichever way you slice it, Charlotte Wilderwood is a killer. And she didn't touch a hair on Anne's head, but she covered up her death. She has literal and figurative blood all over her hands, and she is cursed to live with that for the rest of her life. She can't begin to ask someone for help, because she'd be passing the curse on to them. And she wouldn't wish that on anyone.

She places a chunk of skirt on the flame, black choking smoke billowing out as she closes the lid.

And she definitely can't tell Rob. Rob whose calm and level life she's already upended with her return, demanding his time, his body, and then chucking a corpse in his path for him to find.

The phone rings again, and this time she accepts the call but says nothing. The fizzle and spit of the burning dress is the only sound until Maggie finally speaks. 'I hope you've not wasted too much time looking for evidence when you should be gathering my money,' she says. It sounds hollow, like she's play-acting. Like a stupid little girl.

'You recorded me,' she says, more hurt than intended.

'I'm s . . . well, I hope this underlines that there's no way out of this.' A pause. 'Make sure you bring the money in cash, and no funny business.'

Charlotte's legs go cold and the line goes dead.

Every individual hair follicle and its stubble stands to attention as if going to war.

One hundred thousand pounds.

When did Maggie decide to do this to her? Did she watch Charlotte driving down the road that Friday night and pick her at random? Decided she was the ideal stooge to get rid of David for her, and the rest? If Charlotte had driven a different way that night, would the next car that passed by have become embroiled in a two-way murder scam? Does *everyone* have the kind of secret strings that people like Maggie can pull on at any time?

She finds that hard to believe.

Because this isn't even the first time someone has run rings around her. Anne was just shunted out of the way by a more serious opponent. So no, most drivers wouldn't have stopped. And even if they did, most people wouldn't have believed the bride's story. And no one else would have allowed this to turn into murder. It's blackmail, but it's also just deserts.

But all of this is academic. There's no way out, there's no answer and every time she tries to escape, she just tightens the noose. Maggie is far slyer than she ever would have thought. And more fool Charlotte for her trust.

She has to pay.

Maggie

Monday Evening

'You should wear a life vest this time,' she says to him as he sits on the side of the bath and runs his fingers through her bubbles, turning them to cream. The Molton Brown bubble

243

bath was a treat he'd brought back for her from a house a few weeks ago when she was having one of her down days. He'd appeared in the bedroom with a huge bottle of the stuff, almost full. She'd cried when she'd seen it, knowing he'd weighed his backpack down and further risked his freedom just to cheer her up.

'She's not going to push me in again,' he says with an affectionate laugh. 'But I love it when you worry about me.'

'But what if—'

He shushes her.

Tommy has never learnt to swim and he's cagey about it. She's offered to teach him, thought they could find some warm and private stretch of river somewhere in summer, thought it might be romantic even. He was unmoved by the idea. When she suggested the local council pool in a quiet time instead, he got angry. She's not mentioned it since.

Growing up in Devon, in a town riddled with rivers and streams, swimming lessons were one of the earliest reasons Maggie's mother let her leave the house. For safety, it was essential she learn. She was picked up by her Aunt Van and her kids, sitting between them in the back of the car – the seat with the broken lap belt. Her younger cousins would ask her about her favourite TV shows or pop songs, knowing she wasn't allowed to enjoy either, and Maggie would catch her Aunt's smirk in the rear-view mirror. But once she got in the water, it was worth it. A mermaid freedom, where just briefly she was in full command of every dimension: height, width and depth. A flick of her legs, a swipe of her arms, was all it took. It was a joy Tommy had never experienced and she felt for him.

And that river outside Usk was furious. As 'David', he'd hit the freezing water with such force that Maggie had let out a shriek. Luckily Charlotte didn't seem to notice.

His body had rushed past her so fast that Maggie nearly fell in after him while reaching from her dark slippery shelf under the bridge. Even as she tugged at his arms, his head was bobbing under more than it was staying out. Afterwards, they'd sat huddled and shivering, both soaked to the skin with dank river water, skin stinging in pain from the cold, but daring not move until they were sure Charlotte had left. Impossible to tell from sound alone with that silent electric car and the roar of the river.

And then, of course, they'd had to scramble back to the car that was tucked away down a lane. Heating on full, peeling the wet things off and pulling on fresh clothes from home, then flooring it to get back to Newport for the meeting, overtaking the Tesla with their heads bowed. The little car coughing and spluttering in protest. Tommy raging about the money he'd missed out on, and the gall of Charlotte to push him in. But it opened the door to greater possibilities and, without those extra steps, they couldn't have paid for Cumbria.

Maggie shivers despite the hot bath water and tucks her knees up to her chest as he starts to wash her, his fingers clumsy but gentle.

'Don't worry, princess,' he says.

But how can she not?

Charlotte

Now

The fire in the barbecue has formed into mountains of ash, just a hint of orange along their tips. She throws the last few pieces of the dress on top, but they just damp it out even more. As she scatters a few dried leaves on top and reaches for the matches to get it all going again, Charlotte hears a car pull up. She's not expecting anyone and this lane leads to nowhere. This isn't good.

She looks at the burning dress in the barbecue. How will she explain this if it's the police who have turned up? She couldn't look more like she was concealing evidence if she tried, even if they don't know anything about the bride.

As a knock rings out from the front of the house, she closes the barbecue lid with a squeak. Her hands are black, thick chunks of ash and dirt lying under her nails, fingerprints all over her jeans.

She stays still. Her car is here; they'll know she's inside, but she could be bathing for all they know. Could be on the phone, listening to music, asleep. Maybe it's a delivery driver, though it is getting a bit late for that. Besides, it was the sound of a car, not a delivery van. So not Rob's truck either.

She remembers being here as a teenager, when her parents first reluctantly trusted her to stay alone if they went out to see friends or for dinner. She would beg them for the freedom but as soon as their car lights disappeared down the lane, her brain would be awash with urban myths and horror films. One time they came home to find she'd booby trapped the hallway with string and was sitting on the sofa with a knife in her trembling hand.

But nothing ever happened.

She stands stock-still in the cold dark, breath streaming visibly. Can whoever it is see that? Can they see the smoke? She listens for the sound of the engine starting again, the smell of burning turning to old smoke, to decay. It's a plump white moon tonight but it's tangled in the tall trees that mark out the upper boundary of the garden and she can see very little.

Please just leave.

It's a standoff. Whoever is out there is not leaving. They're no longer knocking though, and when she concentrates really hard, she can make out the chilling sound of metal on metal. She creeps back towards the house and peers over the fence. She can make out a dark car, black or navy.

She hears the catch on the side gate squeaking, a huff as

246

someone shoves it open. She pats down her pocket for her phone. If it's a choice between getting murdered and taking her chances explaining all this to the police . . . But as she feels for it, she remembers putting her phone down in the kitchen. She turns and waits, holding her breath as a shape comes out of the darkness towards her.

'What are you doing out here?' Rob asks.

Rob's perching on the table looking at the beer she just poured him and the sooty fingerprints that cloud the glass. Charlotte is furiously scrubbing her hands at the sink, dirt, ash and dust turning the water in the sink grey, the great heap of utensils and knives on the draining board splashed in filth.

'I thought I'd have a barbecue for dinner,' she says. 'But I didn't have enough briquettes and—'

'I was calling for ages,' he says, taking a thick sip of beer. 'I was getting worried.'

'My phone was in the kitchen.' She shrugs, smiling in what she hopes is a normal way but catching sight of herself in the mirror and flinching at the great black streaks on her face like Adam Fucking Ant.

'What are you doing here anyway?' she asks and for a moment he looks embarrassed.

'I just . . . I wanted to talk something through with you. I just came from Cole's place and he had some stupid idea that I need you to talk me out of but . . .' he trails off, looking around the kitchen again. 'Look, what's going on, Charlie?' he says, putting the untouched beer down and reaching for her. She steps forward. Where to start? What to say? How to even put words to this?

'Honestly?' she says as he pulls her into him. She feels him nodding, his chin on the top of her head. 'I just wanted a distraction,' she manages, then tears overwhelm her. 'First my parents and then Anne.' The words are staccato and strangled. 'Now . . . the business is in trouble. Some back payments I didn't know about need to be paid and I have to find the money.'

'Oh,' his voice is muffled by her hair. 'Can you not delay the payments?'

'No, I can't. They're not the kind of people who will be reasonable and . . . fuck. My dad never trusted me to take over the business and I was so determined to prove him wrong but he was right, wasn't he?'

'He had decades to learn how to run a business,' Rob says. 'It landed on you in the night. Go easy on yourself.'

'That's easy for you to say. You don't understand what it's like, you don't know how high stakes this all is.' *And you've never had to live with this kind of guilt, burning you from the inside.*

He stiffens but doesn't let go. 'I understand very well. There are some months that I only barely scrape through. Look, I started a business *way* too young, because I thought it was what I wanted, and . . . I was kind of backed into a corner, but I've nearly gone under twice, and came very close a few more times than that. I've made more mistakes than you can even imagine but I have learned some along the way.'

She loosens her shoulders.

'I'm not claiming I'm a businessman like your dad was, I doubt he ever struggled to make rent, but I've managed to stay afloat and maybe if we talk it through, we can find a way through your stuff?'

But I'm in the frame for two murders unless I pay a hundred grand to a con woman I thought I cared for deeply, I'm haunted day and night by the blood on my hands and this is nothing like the trials and tribulations of a village gardening business!

'And I don't want to eat whatever the hell is in that barbecue so how about you go and get changed and washed.' He laughs a little bit and she can't help but laugh too. 'It's pie night at The Bell and I reckon we can scrape together enough for that. Alright?'

'Rob, I really have to try to sort this.' She looks at her wrist even though she has no watch on. 'I can't—'

'What can you possibly do tonight that you can't do first thing tomorrow?' He looks at her, his blue eyes wide and hopeful. And she has no argument. She imagines grains of sand slipping through the slim neck of an egg timer but there's nothing she can do tonight.

'Alright.'

'Where's the truck?' she asks, as they leave the house, her freshly washed and dressed.

The lights on the black car flash as he opens it remotely. 'This has been shut up in the garage for ages and I'm going to have to sell it but I reckoned it would be nice to give it a final spin.'

Her heart seems to stop and she grinds to a halt on the driveway. 'Rob?'

'Yeah?' He opens the door for her, as if she was waiting for that, but she doesn't thank him. 'How long have you had this car? Did you have it before I came back?'

'Yeah, why?'

'Did you ever go to see Anne in it?'

'Once or twice perhaps, why?'

He slides inside and she does the same, thinking hard about the police and their ex-boyfriend theory. Could they be looking for Rob?

'Was there really nothing between you and Anne? Before I came back, I mean?'

He stares at her in dismay. 'How many times do I have to say this?'

'I wouldn't mind, it wouldn't be any of my business even, I just—'

'Nothing ever happened between me and Anne,' he says, irritation creeping into his voice. 'She was completely obsessed with someone else, a real dickhead who strung her along and made her think he was going to share his life with her.' He looks away. 'It didn't work out and she was heartbroken. But none of that is relevant now, is it? Let's just get some dinner.'

'Yeah,' she says, trying to fit all the pieces together and not seeing the big picture no matter how hard she tries. 'Sorry. Let's.'

Pamela

2003

'Hello, Robert.'

He smiles, the guileless smile of a boy with absolutely no idea what is about to happen.

'Charlotte's not here, Mrs Wilderwood,' he says. He's just wearing shorts, a fact of which he seems painfully aware.

Oh don't blush, I want to say, you're just a child. But he's the same age Charles was when I met him, and I know what children can do.

'It was you I wanted to speak to actually. Can I come in?' He peers nervously behind me then opens the door widely and invites me in. He's been banned from our house by Charles, and probably thinks it's about that. He's in for a surprise.

'Can I put a top on?' he asks, sounding worried.

We sit in the little kitchen, one that clearly belongs to an all-male household. I vaguely remember Charlotte mentioning a divorce. He crashes about trying to make a cup of tea that I've already determined will not be drinkable. The spoon he pulls from the drawer has a stain as big as my thumb.

'What do you want from life, Robert?' I ask.

'Um.'

'You've got your results now, haven't you?'

'Yeah, did Charlotte tell you? I didn't do so well but—'

'I don't think it matters,' I say. 'Exams aren't for everyone.'

He smiles gratefully.

'So now you're looking for a job?'

'Yeah, well, I think so. I want to be a gardener. That's why we . . .' He stops, his ears glowing red, and drops the wet teabags in the bin. 'Anyway, I'm signed up for a course but it's hard, 'cos, well, I mean it's not hard, I could get an apprenticeship and work for someone else but—' He slides the tea towards me in a Tetley tea folk mug and I nod my thanks, and wait for him to gather himself and stop rambling.

'I want to work for myself, Mrs Wilderwood.' I could tell him to call me Pamela, but I don't. 'I want to work for myself like, you know, like Charlotte's dad.'

'And what's stopping you?'

'Well, I need to do this course like I said but then I'll need a second-hand truck, proper tools, money for adverts in the paper an' that . . .'

'And how much will all that cost, do you think?'

He starts to tell me, the enthusiasm rising off him like steam but then he tilts his head. 'Sorry, I shouldn't be boring you with this. What did you want to talk about?'

'But this is exactly what I want to talk about,' I tell him. 'Because, as you know, Charlotte is bound for university. And you are not.' His eyes flash briefly but he says nothing.

'We'll still see each other in the holidays,' he mutters. 'And I'll drive up when I can.'

'That's just the thing.' I smile. 'You won't. My silly little girl is not as bright as she thinks she is and she's planning to do something very dim indeed. She's planning to turn down her place at university and stay here. With you.'

'She is?' His face lights up but he catches my expression and his smile fades.

'So I'm going to pay for your truck.' I tell him. 'And your tools. And your adverts, and your first month's pay. I think five thousand pounds should do it.'

The upside to Charles's self-obsession and sloppy paperwork is that he's barely aware of how I'm spending his money. And, I suppose, as long as I'm tied up decorating and shopping, he thinks I'm too busy to look closely at his behaviour.

'Really? Oh my god, thank you so much! I mean, I'll pay you back, as soon as I can.' I shake my head.

'No. You're not going to give me the money back. You're going to keep that money and you're going to be a success and you're going to be a businessman, just like Mr Wilderwood.'

He looks stunned, his yokel mouth dropping open.

'And the way you'll pay me back, Robert, is by releasing my daughter. You let her go to uni—'

'I'd never stop her going to uni!' His wide eyes are totally genuine. At his age, Charles was running his own stall. In Charles's case, he seemed so much older. I can picture him back then on his stall, eighteen and full of piss and vinegar, his gift of the gab already finely honed. Flogging old brass trinkets as if they were the crown jewels, tacky old melamine vases like Mings. He wasn't classically handsome but he was manly already, striking. Those big generous features, a personality that filled a room.

Back then, women would collapse in girlish giggle fits around him. But not me. I was there with purpose, I needed trinkets and old objects for setting up still-life ensembles to paint and he sold that type of bric-a-brac cheap. The irony being, of course, that he got me for cheap in the end. Wearing me down with words and special discounts and pleas until I gave in and dated him. He said he'd never stop me following my dreams either. Boys say lots of things. But then of course I got stuck in the age-old way, a shotgun wedding to avoid a fiasco. I'm damned if I'll let the same thing happen to Charlotte.

Unlike Charles, Rob *is* classically handsome, almost pretty. I can understand precisely what Charlotte sees in him but it's not enough to ruin a future over.

'So,' I say briskly, because my resolve is wobbling in the face of his confused puppy eyes, 'you'll set her free and she'll go merrily off to university. She can spread her wings and do all those things it's essential a young woman does if she doesn't want to end up used and bitter.' I smile. 'And you'll be able to concentrate on your business and becoming the man you want to be. And then,' I say, my voice softening into bedtime story tones, 'if it's really meant to be, it'll still be meant to be in three years' time. And you'll both be all the happier for having had that—' I search for the right words '—space to grow.'

I see him ready himself for protest. Puffing that narrow chest out, standing up taller.

'You get the money,' I say softly, handing back my untouched tea, 'when you say goodbye. And if you don't say goodbye, not only will you not get that money, but I'll be speaking to the police about how you and your cousins have been handling stolen goods and trying to sell them to local businesses.'

I see myself out.

Maggie

Tuesday Morning

'I found this little place on Rightmove,' she says, showing Tommy the iPad screen. To try to shake the thought of returning to the river, and of pulling the rug from under Charlotte, Maggie has focused on the future to an apparently 'psychotic' degree. And even though Tommy was the one to describe her this way, the one to hold up his palms in surrender when she started to tell him all about the month-by-month climate in Cumbria, and the local dishes they'd learn to love, she can't tell anyone else anything so she still tells him. It's always him.

The back of the iPad is engraved 'To our lovely Georgia' and she feels a pang of guilt every time she sees it, even though Tommy reminds her that it was bound to be insured by 'those silver spoon fuckers' he took it from.

'Yeah, looks nice,' he says, his voice non-committal, passing it back with his eyes on the TV.

'There's loads more places like this too,' she adds, but this is the one she's been living inside in her mind since she found it last night. This is the one whose tiny open fire she's loaded up with logs that Tommy has carefully chopped in the courtyard garden, whose bathroom she's painted cream and filled with fruity shower gels and shampoos like at Charlotte's.

'It'd be most of the money gone, though,' he says. 'And we don't *have* the money yet, don't forget.'

He has his feet up on the sofa and she's scrunched in the other corner. She won't miss this manky piece of furniture, left here by whoever rented this place before them. Nor the bed whose mattress springs have been dampened down by old towels under the sheets, but still tap her on the shoulder and scratch her bum when she's trying to sleep.

'I'm really looking forward to furnishing our own place,' she says. 'I've never had my own furniture before, not stuff that I picked.'

'I've done my best,' he says, and she blanches. 'No, god, that's not what I meant. I'm sorry.'

He keeps his eyes on the half of the screen showing some morning show, panellists in pan stick make-up pretending to drink coffee from empty mugs.

'There's a college near that little house in Cumbria,' she says, keen to change the subject but grasping a dangerous topic in her haste.

'Yeah?' he says, eyes still on the working bit of the telly but eyebrows twitching.

'I was thinking I could maybe finish my exams. It might make getting a job a bit easier.'

'Right. And you'd make a lot of new friends too, eh? People more your type?'

'No, not that.'

'I don't think I like that house,' he says, easing himself up and padding out to the kitchen on socked feet. 'Let's just wait until we've got the money, eh? See what's what.'

Charlotte

It's no good, she's got no hope of sleeping. She'd had a few glasses of wine with her dinner, hoping that might help her relax but this isn't executive stress, it's existential panic laced with killer's remorse, and Malbec wasn't going to cut through. She'd slid her peas around the plate and half-listened until Rob said, 'you could just get a loan'.

She hadn't told him how much she needed to raise, and he was probably imagining a much smaller number but the principle was the same. And an unsecured loan, unlike one borrowed against the house, could be almost instant. She told herself she could apply first thing and came up to bed a few hours ago but it's no use. Rob is flat out next to her, mouth slack, radiating heat like a hot water bottle, and all she can picture is that egg timer, and Maggie waiting on the bridge, police on speed dial if Charlotte didn't show. Only yesterday the thought of seeing Maggie would have filled her with warmth; now it sends a chill across her scalp.

Making Charlotte return to that bridge, to the scene of the crime, is such a vicious touch. Its sweeping arch is permanently tattooed on Charlotte's brain already. The smell of that river curdling everything she tastes. She already sees David's face whenever she closes her eyes and feels the bounce of his chest muscles when she reaches across Rob. How can Maggie be so cruel?

She slides out of bed carefully, three decades of muscle memory helping her to avoid the squeaky floorboards, and creeps downstairs. She flicks on the lights and makes a herbal tea then opens her laptop.

*

255

Until her parents died and she inherited the house, Charlotte had always limped over the line at pay day, never quite making it all stretch, frequently bouncing cheques or leaving tills red-faced when none of her cards went through. Working in temp jobs and then the heritage sector was never well-paid and the idea of being able to borrow, of having good credit and equity, is so new to her she didn't consider it for a moment. But it's true, it says here on the screen that she can borrow up to £10,000 right now.

It takes three minutes and the money will be in her account today. She takes a sip of the tea but it tastes chalky, everything tastes off at the moment, as if she has mud in her mouth. Or river water.

Maybe Maggie plans to kill her once she's got the money anyway. She killed Anne, after all. Those fine narrow fingers, those slender shoulders, mustering a strength Charlotte can barely imagine. She's almost too exhausted to care – at least that would be an end, eh.

Charlotte has forty thousand more or less sitting in the company accounts, another ten in the safe. With no salaries to pay except her own – which she'll have to wait for – she only needs to hold a bit back to keep the lights on. She winces when she remembers why she has no other salaries to pay. But including the loan, that's sixty grand already.

She pours the tea away and goes upstairs to try to sleep, mentally pricing up everything she passes in the dim light along the way. Did Maggie do this when she was trusted in the house? Or perhaps when she broke back in, running her greedy eyes along everything as she booby-trapped it with evidence.

Even if she put absolutely everything here on sale in the showroom at half its value, it's not like she's inundated with customers. It could take weeks, and she has a matter of hours.

She twists her parents' rings on her fingers as she climbs back into bed, thinking about that cash for gold place that advertises on the radio but she can't. She really can't. Perhaps some of the more meaningless bits of her mother's jewellery though? It's all sitting there upstairs in their room. A room that her blackmailer could have ransacked but didn't. She's forcing Charlotte to do it instead. Yet more cruelty.

Why do you hate me, Maggie? I really, really liked you.

She's back on her computer when Rob leaves for work, a small pile of her mother's jewellery next to her on a weighing scales. She's not been able to find everything, so maybe Maggie did help herself. But she doesn't have time to think about that now. She's too busy looking on the cash for gold shop website and despairing. This lot doesn't scratch the surface, and even though she knows very well how much it is really worth, it's academic due to the deadline.

And if she did somehow sell it all for its true value, that's still only another £5,000 for the pot. Alongside around £1,000 that was in her current account and £10,000 in her savings, that's . . . fuck . . . nearly thirty grand short. No amount of jewellery will hit that figure. She sighs, looking at the Tesla key card on the worktop where she left it last night. The one thing she can sell that will fill the gap.

Maggie

Tuesday Lunchtime

'Nearly there, mate,' he says, stirring his noodles. 'Maybe tomorrow we'll eat caviar.'

'Yuck,' she says, wrinkling her nose.

'We need to do something to celebrate though.'

'Now who's counting the cash before we have it?'

He teases out a noodle with his fork, slurps it. 'Ow, too hot. Yeah but—' he fixes her with his eyes. Those same intense eyes she first locked onto in the heat of her mother's garden, eyes that told the kind of stories she'd been warned not to read, even darker than her Grimms' compendium.

'But what?'

He takes another mouthful and fans his open mouth. Swallows with a grimace. 'But she is going to pay. I know she is.'

'How can you be so sure?'

''Cos I heard it in her voice when you were talking. She wasn't fighting it, wasn't even questioning it. It was like . . . it was like she'd already paid the money.'

She swallows drily.

'You did a good job,' he adds, borderline paternally in a way she hates but has learned not to react to. 'I know you fluffed it a bit at first and you went rogue a couple of times, but it came good. And, yeah, she could technically take her chances. She could tell the police everything, about the weird bride—'

'Hey!'

'You know what I mean. And I guess she could tell them that she just innocently dropped this random untraceable woman off to collect a bit of paperwork from a woman who ended up dying but really, who would believe that? She'd be sticking her head in the lion's mouth and hoping it could see her side. And she thinks she killed David, don't forget. Stupid bitch.'

'I just want it to be over,' she says, aiming for finality but sounding petulant.

'Want, want, want,' he jokes. He's so fired up he's practically singing.

'I just can't wait to leave this stuff behind,' she says. 'To be able to buy our way into normality and be good people. Properly good people.'

He smiles but says nothing.

Charlotte
Tuesday Lunchtime

Charlotte realises just after handing over the paperwork and key cards that she has no way of getting around now. 'What's the cheapest car you've got on the lot?' she asks the dealer, as he transfers the money into her account on the computer, cautious big red fingers tapping.

'One tick, I've got just the thing.'

They're walking around the corner, away from the shiny impressive motors, when a lad of no more than seventeen jogs over. 'Just been cleaning your old car, madam,' he says.

'That was fast work,' she says, trying not to think about how much less she'd sold it for than her parents paid for it. How keen they are to flip it. She's probably accepted a rubbish price.

'They're popular motors,' the salesman says, smiling. 'What do you want, Dean?'

'Just found this under the seat,' the lad says. 'Thought you might want it, madam.'

He hands over a folded piece of glossy paper. She unfolds it, realising it's a photograph, and nearly drops it in surprise. 'It's my dad,' she says quietly. 'My mum must have had this for some reason. That's . . . they weren't really like that so . . . it's nice to see.'

The men stand awkwardly, waiting for her to explain.

'They both died,' she says. 'The Tesla was my mum's before it was mine.'

'She was the previous owner on the paperwork,' the salesman nods sagely. 'I wondered.'

'Not sure how it was missed for so long, I've had it valeted a few times since.'

'Where do you get it done?' the boy asks, keenly.

'The place out on Warminster Hill,' she says, not really

caring. 'The old garage, you know?'

'Yeah, we're more thorough than them for sure,' he says proudly, before the older man dismisses him.

'I'm sorry about your parents,' he says, as he takes her elbow and guides her towards an old Renault Clio with an 'Ideal First Car!' ribbon across it.

Now in the bank, the same branch she'd opened her very first account, excitedly receiving a china pig, she tells them she needs to draw everything out. The ten grand loan that just went in today, the money transferred by the second-hand car dealer, the fifty grand moved over from the company account, the dregs of her last paycheck. Everything. She's exhausted, has barely slept, and the account manager looks at her with concern from under her blonde fringe.

'Please,' Charlotte says, 'I'm in a bit of a hurry.'

'It really would be better to have this as a banker's draft, there's a ten pound fee but it makes it a lot safer than carrying this much cash.'

'But it's a cash sale,' Charlotte says again. 'I'm buying an old property.'

'You've said that but . . . I mean, it's not normally that literal,' the account manager says.

'Sometimes things *are* literal,' Charlotte answers. 'And I need it in cash. Today.'

Pamela

Eight Months Ago

It all makes sense, of course. The diet and the new close-cropped haircut to better disguise the grey, the absurd leather jacket and the shiny black Tesla lying on the drive. I wonder if the smaller, ladies' version he bought me is a guilt present, or a distraction to throw me off the scent. He seems to be awash with cash at the moment.

And this afternoon, when Charles showered, changed and said he was going out – no longer pretending to fish, at least – I nosed my car carefully after him and hung one or two vehicles back.

Now I've followed him all the way to Bath. He's as bad and unobservant a driver as he is an arrogant, lazy husband, so he hasn't so much as looked this way. I don't think he's used his mirrors once through the whole journey. It's a miracle he's never had a serious crash.

I've followed him past Alice Park, where we used to go as a family when we still had Bingo the dog and some semblance of a future. When I once looked at my little daughter playing and thought, maybe if I just care you enough, you'll be OK, you'll have a bigger life. As if that's all it took.

And now I'm slowing to a stop, waiting and watching as he parks (badly) outside a smart Bath stone villa and practically skips out.

I pull in neatly, silently, switching off the engine and watching as he opens the little gate and strides down the path to the front door. He has a key in his hand, a sense of ownership, a spring in his step. I see him externally, as if I haven't been married to him for nearly forty years, as if I don't know where he creases and cracks. And I get the appeal. He still exudes that same market trader confidence. His purposeful ownership of every situation. The way he seems somehow bigger, better, *more* than anyone around him. It's astonishingly effective. A girl can easily get sucked into the vortex, and it takes a long time to find out that he's no bigger or better than any other man. And in that time, an awful lot of damage can be done.

The door opens before he has a chance to use the key. A bobbed head looks out, a smile slashing the face in two, hair reflecting the sunlight. She is a every inch a woman now, well-dressed, tall and slim instead of skinny, perfectly made up. But as she coils herself around my husband like a snake, pressing her lips to his, she is every bit the teenage girl of whom I thought I'd seen the last. Anne.

I get back in the car, pull neatly out of the space, and drive away. The new knowledge sitting in my lap like a Molotov cocktail.

Charlotte

Tuesday Afternoon

She's shaking as she transfers the money from the bank envelope into the antique briefcase in front of her. It's frightening how small ninety grand actually is. A final ten is still in her handbag in an envelope, drawn from her not-long-opened savings account.

Until her parents died, she'd never even had savings. Had lived in her overdraft since she was at university. She tucks the small stacks neatly into the case, the musky mothball smell swirling into a montage of memories. Her dad, always her dad, and her desperation to be in his orbit aged two, five, ten, fifteen . . . Even more than that, that need to *embody* his orbit, his essence. To play him at his own game or to become him? She's never sure so she doesn't dwell on it too long.

She hears a car pull up and rushes to the window to look out. It's a black BMW and her heart thuds but when the door opens, it's not Harry Sedgemoor.

A neat Fair Isle jumper peeks through the unzipped anorak. He is skinny, a little stooped, sandy-grey haircut in a timeless, fashionless way. Probably around sixty-five, the type to retire and then take up collecting of some kind. Hopefully she can make a sale and put some money back into the empty accounts.

'Can I help you?' she asks, a little too eagerly.

'Charlotte Wilderwood?' he asks in a brisk Welsh accent, rubbing his hands together after the windy walk from the car. She stares at him, unable to speak. A Welsh detective? Do they know? Or – oh god – could he be one of David's relatives? Could someone know? *Could they fucking know?*

'Do we have an appointment?' she stammers. 'It's not a problem if not but . . . can I take your name?'

'It's Harry,' he says, smiling now. 'Harry Sedgemoor.'

'Harry Sedgemoor?' she repeats, mind wheeling. What are the chances of two visitors sharing the same name? And does this mean he's not here about David? It must do, mustn't it?

'It's funny,' she says, trying to look calm, buying time while she gathers her thoughts. 'I met another Harry Sedgemoor a few weeks ago. What's . . . are you here to browse or . . .?'

He's still in the doorway and maintains his smile as he locks the door slowly then slides his hand down to close the shutters.

'I'm here for the money, love.'

'What?'

He's still smiling as he comes closer. Meek, almost apologetic. Charlotte shuts the lid of the briefcase but it's too late, he's seen.

'How much is in there?' he asks.

'Why?' she manages to say, her mouth dry. She thinks about the only other living person she knows from Wales. 'Are you with Maggie? Is she your—'

'I don't know any Maggie, love. But your father owes, oh I'm sorry, *owed* us seventy-five thousand pounds. He'd just had delivery of another hundred in total so seventy five of that should have been transferred to our organisation. Only,' and at this he winces and almost whispers, 'he sadly died before the transaction could be completed.'

Charlotte grasps one of the Rosewood dining chairs and sits heavily in it, trying to make sense of what she's being told. 'But why did my dad owe you seventy-five thousand pounds?'

'I'm sorry, Charlotte,' he says, 'I really am, but I don't have time for this.' He crosses to the table and opens the briefcase so quickly she jumps. This little man isn't much bigger than her but there's something in his energy and his wiry frame that suggests she'd stand no chance against him.

'This looks about eighty, eighty-five,' he says, looking at the money and then back at her. 'Going somewhere with it?'

'Auction,' she manages to say and he laughs at the obvious lie.

'Go on, I love this. Am I warm?'

'What?'

'The money. How much? Eighty-five, am I right?'

'Ninety,' she manages to croak. 'Ninety thousand pounds.'

'Oh, that's wonderful,' he says. 'Really, what are the chances? Quite wonderful.' He snaps the case shut and it's as loud as a gun. 'You know, I was worried I was going to have to take drastic action.' He looks bereft at the thought. 'And god knows you've been through enough, your parents and your friend . . . No one deserves that.' Her eyes fill with tears and she cuffs them on her jumper as he slides the case off the table and makes to leave.

'You said he owed you seventy-five,' she says, trying to keep her voice level.

He smiles sympathetically and nods. 'You're quite right,' he says. 'But you were very late with the payment and we do need to charge interest. Fifteen thousand is a nice level sum, isn't it?'

'But he died, I didn't know about this. Do you have paperwork? Proof?'

'Angel,' he says, squatting down in front of her and placing one narrow hand on her knee paternally, the other still holding the case, 'it's not that kind of arrangement.'

'Please, I need this money! How can you take it when I didn't even know anything about this?'

'This has been a long-term arrangement with your dad and he's had plenty of deliveries over the last few years.' He slides his hand off her and stands back up.

'Long term? But my dad didn't . . . I mean, where was the money from? Where did it go?'

'What your dad did with it was his business,' the man says, gently. 'But I certainly noticed a couple of nice cars over the years. I think one of them is outside now.'

'I don't understand. I'm sorry, I can't . . . please, I can't make sense of it but that money, it's not for you.'

'We told your little sidekick all about it, Charlotte. So as far as notification goes, we did our bit.'

'My sidekick? Do you mean—' she frowns, surely not? 'Dorian?'

He laughs heartily then, a surprising boom from his pigeon chest as he stands up again. 'No, darling, Dorian already knew all about it. No, we told Anne Wilkins everything. She was very happy to resume the relationship, she said. Just needed to tie up a few loose ends. Anyway, I'm sorry but I'll have to love you and leave you. You've got our card if you want to pick up where the others left off.'

Maggie

Tuesday Afternoon

'Will you call me as soon as you have it?' Maggie says, knees tucked under her chin, nesting in the corner of the sofa. He glugs a glass of water. 'Have what?'

'The money,' she whispers, although no one is listening to them.

'What are you talking about? You need to do this.'

'What?'

'Of course you do. I'll be there as back-up but it's you's got the arrangement.'

'No, I . . .' What can she say? That she can't bear to see Charlotte's face again, that kind face contorted in hurt and mistrust. This money is supposed to be for a fresh start for *them*, but it's a rotten end for Charlotte. And seeing that for herself would taint everything.

'I'm worried I'll make it worse if I'm there. I don't want to screw it up for us, you know how I get.'

'You started this thing in the first place,' he says firmly, that hated paternal seam running through his voice. 'And you'll bloody well see it out.'

'She was nice to me,' she says quietly. 'I'll find it hard to be mean to her when I'm looking her in the eye.'

'Tonight isn't about being mean to her, it's the opposite. It's putting her out of her misery,' he says and she gasps. 'No, not like that, get a grip, I mean she's buying her way off the hook. Tonight she gets her life back.'

'Minus a hundred grand.'

'Trust me, it's a small price to pay. And she has deep pockets, you said so yourself.' Before she can answer, he puts the glass down with a bang. 'And what the fuck are you talking about anyway? It's a bit fucking late to start putting spanners in our plans.'

'I'm sorry, Tommy, I didn't—'

'I can't believe you sometimes, Maggie. You want out of this life, you complain about the best I've been able to do for you.'

'No, no, it's not that. I don't mean it like that!'

'You want your little place in the country, you want to be married, you want me to hang up my tools, and now—' He's shouting now and the hermit below starts banging on the ceiling.

'Fuck off!' he shouts and stamps one heavy foot hard as a warning. 'And now you're getting cold feet about the final fucking puzzle piece. What the fuck do you want from me, girl?'

'I'm sorry, Tommy, you're right, I'm just getting antsy.'

'Anyway, don't you want to be there to make sure she stays in one piece?' His voice is low now and his face suddenly dark. She nods in a hurry.

Charlotte

Now

It doesn't feel like a cause for celebration that she still has the ten thousand from the building society in her handbag. It doesn't feel like a cause for anything but panic. She can barely digest what she's just been told, what's just happened. Is it even true? That man called himself Harry Sedgemoor, but the other man was Harry Sedgemoor. There's no record in the paperwork about any of this. And Dorian knew all about it? But then, her dad trusted her completely so is this really such a surprise. She probably didn't really know the extent of it, probably didn't understand it but that does explain why she didn't want Charlotte to tell the police about the 'investor' coming here. Protecting her dad's name even in death. But Anne knew . . . and she was planning to resume the deal. She just needed me out of the way, she thinks bitterly.

But did he say he *was* Harry Sedgemoor or that he worked for a Harry Sedgemoor? Maybe that's a company name? Maybe she can appeal to that man's boss, explain the situation, get that money back. She can't turn up with just ten per cent of the agreed sum tonight. She can't.

Charlotte pulls out the identical business cards, one with 'Call me, we have business to discuss' written on the back. She dials the number and waits.

'Harry Sedgemoor,' booms the voice. It's not the same man who just left, that's for sure. He was clearly, frighteningly, Welsh, whereas this man sounds northern and she doesn't think the first man had either of those accents.

'Harry Sedgemoor,' she repeats. 'Is that er, is that the name of your company?'

The man pauses. 'You could say that, yeah. Who's this?'

'What, um—' she tries to slow her breathing, to sound normal and calm. 'What is the nature of your business?'

'If you have to ask, sweetheart, then consider this a wrong number.'

The line goes dead. *What the fuck?*

She locks the front door and leaves the shutter down. In the back at her desk, she wiggles the mouse to bring her computer to life and then types 'Harry Sedgemoor' into Google.

Pages and pages of news stories about small businesses becoming embroiled with a money laundering organisation where all members use the same false name 'Harry Sedgemoor' and wrap their endeavours up in swirling umbrella companies and properties registered on obscure islands. Police have been unable to identify the real people behind what one source called a 'trading name for a criminal enterprise'.

MONEY LAUNDERING: SMALL BUSINESSES TARGETED

Small businesses are urged to be vigilant about overseas or unsolicited investors showing an interest in their companies, says Action Against Fraud. The scam will often start with an email or phone call from fraudsters offering to invest in small or start-up businesses, especially those dealing in cash transactions.

Over time, a relationship is established that at first seems mutually beneficial. Money is often transferred into the business's bank accounts in small amounts to avoid bank systems flagging them as suspicious. In some cases, large cash advances will be paid to businesses

to pay into their own bank accounts in small and innoc-
uous-seeming amounts.

This money is 'dirty money', often the proceeds of
drugs gangs, prostitution or the gun trade. The money is
effectively 'cleaned' by going through the small company's
books and paid back to the organisation minus a 'kick
back' for the business owner. Businesses will then create
false invoices and purchase orders to explain the arrival
and release of the money, which will sit side by side with
real paperwork.

It is believed that fraud of this kind costs the UK
purse millions each year, and when discrepancies are
discovered, it is the small business owner who takes the
fall. Often, such as the recent case of SGB Engineering
and their mystery 'investor' Harry Sedgemoor, the
owners do not realise they're breaking the law until the
police intervene.

'This man turned up one day and he made it all sound
so convincing,' SGB's owner said, on release after an
18-month prison sentence. 'Then another man arrived
calling himself the same name, and that was when I got
cold feet. But it was too late.'

Oh, Dad, what were you thinking?

Nausea rolls through her stomach as a new possibility
emerges. Maybe Anne really wasn't trying to steal Charlotte's
family business from her; she could have been trying to save
Charlotte and preserve her dad's legacy. And now she's dead.

Oh god. How could she have thought the worst of her
friend like that? Her oldest friend? And why the hell didn't
Anne just tell her the truth? No, she shakes her head, don't
put this on her.

She looks around the showroom. All this junk. To think she
wanted to join her dad in business, to follow his example, well,
she did that with bells on. Fraudsters, cash payments, lies . . .
it's straight out of his playbook.

Fuck this. When all this is over, she's out. She'll sell the business, maybe even sell the cottage, have a proper think about what she wants to do. Not who she wants to mimic. But that's for the future. Right now, she's swinging on Maggie's hook and ninety grand short.

She opens the locked jewellery cabinet where the most expensive gems lie. Slides them into her handbag with the final envelope of money, the little boxes rattling as she moves. Maybe she can convince her to accept these instead, at least as a holding payment. Maybe it'll be enough.

She locks up and rushes to her new car, crunching the unfamiliar gears as she heads for home. That man said that her dad had been given one hundred thousand but there wasn't that much in the account when she took over the company. Those articles on small business fraud and money laundering, they all said money had to be drip-fed in. Maybe her dad hadn't finished paying it in when he died. She thinks of the envelopes that lined that little box under the bed.

Just one quick stop off first, with her family solicitor. Just in case.

Maggie

Tuesday Evening

She watches him carefully loading his work bag. A torch, a change of clothes, his tools. 'Just in case,' he says gruffly, cutting off her questions. She stands reverently to the side, the cuffs of her jumper pulled down over her hands in that way her mother always despaired about, but Tommy seems to find endearing.

'Worried?' he says gently, when he sees her doing it.

She nods. 'I just want it to be over.'

'Make yourself useful and get us a flask of tea to take.'

An onlooker would see this as gruff and dismissive. Such is the shorthand of a ten-year love. But she snaps to attention gratefully, boiling the kettle and making a brew in their fancy teapot – another magpie gift he brought home for her, its spout trimmed in gold – before pouring it carefully into the flask. The action calms her, channelling her energy as he knew it would. Sometimes he knows what's best for her better than she does.

Charlotte

Tuesday Evening

She locks the door carefully and runs upstairs in her boots, mucking up the cream carpet. She scrabbles under the bed where she'd replaced the box and tugs it out, yanking off the lid as she does.

It will be horribly ironic if in hiding those earrings in here, Maggie had inadvertently led her to more cash. How much simpler it would have been if she'd just robbed her. *God, what a thing to wish for.*

She pulls the envelopes out and then tears into the first one. No cash, it's just letters. She pulls them all out and shakes them just in case, but there's no money. She moves on to the rest, a horrible pain growing in her gut as she shakes the last of them. No cash, no hope. Instead, a small photograph slips out from one of the letters and slides to the floor. She turns it over and lets out a laugh. Not in humour, in shock. Why the fuck did her dad have a picture of Anne?

She picks up the top letter from the pile and turns it over. It's Anne's handwriting, she'd know it anywhere. As she reads, the last drop of admiration she had for her father dries up.

After the rush of chasing around to scrabble together a huge sum of money, then the shock of her discovery, now she just feels flat, like she's watching herself from behind glass. You can get used to anything, she figures, no matter how bad. Grief, heartbreak, bankruptcy, shame. You can wear it all if you wait long enough. Maybe even guilt. Yes, you can get used to that. But can you ever get over it?

She's in the frame for multiple murders and the only thing standing in the way of arrest is the say-so of a con woman. And there's no way to deny it, Charlotte *is* guilty. She will live with what happened for the rest of her life, regardless of what happens tonight. She wishes she was brave enough to own up. To walk into the police station, tell them everything and take the punishment. To stand in a court room across from whoever cared for David and look them in the eye. And, she realises, do the same with the ruins of Anne's family.

But she is not brave. She is not strong. So all Charlotte can do is hand over ten grand in cash and a load of jewellery, and hope that some small part of Maggie will be willing to play fair. And if this isn't enough for Maggie then fuck it, she's out of ideas. But she has to try, she's too weak for the alternative.

She's one car down and has a bank loan to pay off and no savings, but that's nothing compared to a prison sentence. And she has very few outgoings now, the opposite to her life in London, which was a constant waterfall of cost. If she can sell the business, she can pay off that loan and still have money to live on. She's OK. She's limping out of this more or less intact. At least on the outside. Unlike Anne. Anne who lied and cheated, slept with her dad, but then, maybe, tried to take the bullet.

She drinks a glass of water, has a pee and picks up her handbag. It's still earlier than she needs to leave, but she can't stay here a minute longer treading water, waiting to drown.

Maggie

Tuesday Night

They drive in silence, just shy of the speed limit, indicating at every junction, doing nothing to risk getting pulled over and derailed. 'We're so close, I can taste it,' he says, his voice low and rumbling, the voice he uses when he tells her what he wants in bed. He puts his hand on her knee and starts to work it up towards her zip but she pushes it away as gently as she can. The promise of tonight is not having the same effect on her as him, clearly.

'We need to stay out of sight at first,' he says, slipping back into work mode as they approach Usk. 'Need to be alert. 'Cos if she's done something stupid, we might need to revise the plan.'

'Stupid like what?' she says, twisting her engagement ring. 'Police?'

He shakes his head, changes gear smoothly. 'No, she wouldn't take that risk. We've got too much on her.' He pauses, staring intently through the windscreen, freshly washed at the weekend. She loves him so much for that, the way he takes care of their shitty stuff.

'Stupid like, I don't know, bringing fake cash or roping someone in to come with. You listening?'

She nods but he doesn't see.

'I said are you listening?' he snaps.

'I am.'

'Don't fucking flake on me now, girl.'

'I won't. I promise.'

When they first arrive, this visit to the bridge echoes every other time they came. When he would drop her off in her stinking gown to stand up there and wait for Good Samaritans.

273

Then, as now, they'd tuck the car out of sight down a nearby lane and Tommy would wait below the bridge, in that handy little cut out, listening, keeping her safe.

They have so many of these places dotted around the country – spots identified from research and planning – with just enough footfall and passing cars at kicking-out time to catch some soft hearts. But none make her shudder like this. The place she found Charlotte, and nearly lost Tommy.

They climb down the bank and ease into place under the bridge, snug together, well used to waiting, listening for opportunities. Tonight, Tommy is not still. He vibrates with excitement. A flammable intensity, ready to go up at any time.

She squats just above the damp ground, coat around her like a duvet, and listens for the whoosh of the Tesla. The ghost car that had snuck up on her that first night. They hear a car drive slowly over the bridge but she shakes her head. 'That was a petrol engine, wasn't it?' she whispers and Tommy nods. There's still ten minutes until Charlotte is due.

'When she gets here, you go up first,' he says. 'And then while you're talking—'

'You'll come up to count the money,' she says.

'And keep an eye on you,' he adds. 'Where would you be without me, eh?'

Charlotte

Ten Minutes Earlier

It took longer to reach the Severn Bridge in this wheezy little car. Passing over it, she was more aware than ever of the great churning beneath. As she drove, her hands stayed on the wheel, her feet on the pedals, but she seemed to float higher and higher away until she was watching her car as a tiny iron filing, tugged along by a giant magnet.

This is the soil that David grew from, she thought, as her car landed in Wales. There's no built-in satnav, but this route is etched in her brain.

Now she is nearing the end of it. The bridge. A pivot point from which her old life and her new swings in the balance just like David had, his body swaying back and forth until it plummeted. *Until I pushed him.*

Her new car is dark blue, the colour of the sky overhead. Inside it, she's wearing black jeans, a black jumper, black boots and the thick new layers of grief she uncovered today. How *could* her dad? How could Anne, for that matter?

But then, how could Charlotte do all the things she's done? Neither Anne or Charlotte's father ever killed anyone.

Charlotte approaches the bridge from the same direction she did that first night. It is barely illuminated tonight. Just a dark, dirty shape against a lacklustre sky. She drives past slowly but Maggie isn't here yet, so she drives on a little and turns into a lane a few hundred metres away. She tucks into the entrance of a field, the little Clio easily snuggling up to the gate out of the way of what scant traffic could come along.

She cuts the engine, dizzy from the sudden silence.

This countryside felt swollen with ghosts when she first drove through it, checking her locks and imagining the worst. Now it feels dead. The fields stink with rot, the sky is damp and the road is potholed and gritty. She closes her eyes and listens, expecting to hear echoes of David's voice, accusing and taunting her from beyond the grave. But there's no trace of him.

Maggie *could* kill her like she killed Anne. Especially when Charlotte admits she's not got all the money. On paper, she should be terrified. She was frightened when Maggie told her what had happened to Anne, frightened of getting in trouble. She was terrified when she came face-to-face with

David. But she is not scared of dying, not now. She's tried to pick apart why, to test it from different angles. Is she just so tired of being scared that she's run out of fear? Is she deep down *hoping* Maggie'll kill her, some kind guilty suicide by proxy? An eye for an eye, even if David's eye was in a rotten head.

Just in case, Charlotte has changed her will. Her friends in London, fair weather as they have turned out to be, will get a smattering of jewellery and the pick of her clothes. The business goes to Dorian, what's left of it. Let her and her sons make a go of it, god knows she's earned it through her loyalty. Everything else goes to Rob, and, by extension, Ruby.

'Are you sure?' the solicitor had asked, eyebrows raised. 'This is a new relationship from what you've told me. You're not married or even cohabiting, and if something were to happen—'

'Yes, it's technically new but, in another way, it's been decades.'

'Charlotte, if the relationship were to break down, you'd need to amend this will immediately or—'

'Look,' she said, 'I'll deal with that if it happens but there's no one else. There's literally,' she said, trying to keep her voice crisp and business-like, 'no one else.'

She walks slowly to the bridge, handbag heavy with the jewellery boxes and not enough cash. There's no one on the bridge as she reaches it, and she touches the handrail gingerly. It feels brutally solid, but it was not enough to stop David falling. She takes a moment to close her eyes and breathe deeply. The river water rushes underneath and, in her mind, she hears that terrible splash and that fragile shriek again.

She swallows, and waits, the bag still on her shoulder. And then she hears the voices, rising from below her feet. She crouches carefully and she listens.

Maggie

Now

Where would they be without each other? When they met, he was an odd-job man, bobbing around the south west because it was sunnier than Lancashire where he grew up. He had no specific ambitions but he was brighter than the work. His prison record held him back, a miscarriage of justice he's stopped talking about now but that she runs her tongue over occasionally, considers looking up online but doesn't dare. She has no one else, whoever he turned out to be.

She dredges up a smile and says. 'I'm so excited for Cumbria.'

He kisses her on the nose. 'Me too, mate,' he says. 'Somewhere new, anyway.'

'But what do you mean *somewhere*? It'll be Cumbria, right? We always said so.'

'Well, *you* always said so. And you know me, I just want you to be happy. But I do wonder if we should be so far away from our cash cow. It might be handy to stay closer.'

'What do you mean?'

He tilts his head and she can just about make out his expression in the dark now her eyes have adjusted. It's amusement.

'What cash cow, Tommy?'

'Charlotte Wilderwood, dummy.' He laughs.

'But—' she sags. It's all so obvious what he means. 'But we had a plan.'

'Listen,' he says, his voice paternal and sharp, 'we're getting a nice little sum to set us up but it'll run out fast. And you don't know what it's like 'cos you don't pay the bills. You've never managed our money, I protect you from all of that, but once we've bought the house like you've demanded, there won't be much left. And this bitch is dangling on our hook, why wouldn't we make the most of that? Why should we keep struggling?'

She swallows. This is not what they agreed, not what he promised. Not to her and not to Charlotte.

'Tommy,' she says, louder, sharper than intended. Even in the darkness she can see his face harden. 'You promised. You crossed your heart.'

'What are you, *five*? It's not like I can just get a job, is it?' he growls. 'I've spent the last ten years on the fucking run thanks to you and your mum. It's not like I have a nicely printed fucking CV, is it, girl? '"Thomas Addison, master fucking criminal".'

She shakes her head. 'But Tommy, you promised. We'll have everything we need, and we have each other, we just need some cash-in-hand jobs and we'll be fine. Better than fine, 'cos we won't have to watch our backs and run in the night and—'

'Shut up,' he hisses. 'Someone's up there!' He crawls out of the hiding space and starts to make his way up the bank towards the road, scrambling like a bug.

Charlotte

Now

That man's voice, she'd know it anywhere. She hears it when she's lying awake in bed, its cruelty threaded through every word. It pins her in limbo, exhausted by guilt but unable to fall asleep. It whispers to her, whenever she dares to think of the future, 'but you're a murderer, you don't deserve a future'.

It is the voice of a man that she believed attacked Maggie. It is the voice of a man who goaded, pushed, and sneered at her on this very bridge. It is the voice of a man she truly believed was dead. And dead by her own hand. But David is not dead. He's not dead!

And he's not called David. His name is Thomas Addison and he and Maggie are in this together. He's not her attacker, he's her fucking boyfriend. And he's intending to keep pumping Charlotte for cash. She gulps the air, as if she has come back to life at the same time. As if it was her that had drowned, when in fact no one had. No one had! Her knees give way with relief and her legs collapse under her like a felled tower block. As she hits the Tarmac of the road, grit slashes her palms.

David is alive!

I'm not a murder!

She is not a murderer, and she owes these people *nothing*. She scrabbles back to her feet, legs still trembling, palms stinging, but now desperate to get away. She needs to get to the police now, she needs to tell them everything, enough is enough.

Oh god, I'm not a murderer!

She gasps the air hungrily as she dusts herself down, coming back to life with every breath. She was set up from the very beginning. A victim, like Anne was a victim. And she was acting under duress, a marionette at the end of these bastards' strings. And these bastards have names. They can be caught. Stopped.

She starts to jog away from the bridge, holding her bag to her chest to stop its contents rattling.

In the dark, she collides suddenly with Tommy's barrel chest. She cries out on impact, her shock and desperation echoing back to her from the emptiness surrounding them.

'No you don't,' he says, a thick arm grabbing her. With the other, he pulls her bag onto the ground.

'Please,' she says, 'I was just—'

'You were just legging it,' he says, rifling through her bag and pulling out the envelope. He flips it open and holds it up. 'And what the fuck is this?'

She reaches a shaking arm for the bag but he slaps her hand away.

'I thought you were dead,' she says. 'I don't owe you anything.'

'You don't owe me?' He recoils as if he's been shot. 'You don't fucking owe me?'

'I don't—' She winces as he grabs her by the hair with one hand and twists her neck sharply to the side. 'You bet your fucking life you owe me.'

'I'm sorry, I—'

'There's hardly anything in here,' he spits, tiny globules landing on her face. His left hand is still yanking at her scalp, his right holding the envelope as if it's covered in excrement. 'This is an insult.'

'I couldn't . . . I tried but this was all I could get. I sold my car, I got a loan, and they just took it. You know how much was in the accounts so I know you think I'm lying but that wasn't my money and—'

'What the fuck are you talking about?'

'Please, that's ten thousand in that envelope and there's another twenty grand's worth of jewellery in there, it's the most I could do.'

'Jewellery?' he says. 'Do you know how easy it is to get caught for nicking jewellery?'

She thinks of Rob all those years ago. 'It's not stolen,' she says, grimacing as he disentangles his hand from her hair but stays inches from her. 'I'm giving it to you.'

'Guilt money for trying to kill me?' His voice loses the sneer and takes on a more serious, chilling tone. 'Creeping around up here like a little earwig and then trying to make off without paying.'

'No.' She shakes her head. 'No, I was just—'

'You broke the conditions,' he says, his face so close to hers she can smell the cigarettes on his teeth.

'No,' she pleads. 'I promise. This is the best I could do!'

She can feel her bladder prickling, fear is threatening to take over her body.

'Maggie!' he calls, grabbing Charlotte with a vice-tight

grip, clamping both arms to her sides. 'Come up here, darling, we've had a change of plan.'

The more Charlotte fights and wriggles, the more he smiles and the tighter he grips. To the left, from beneath the bridge, Charlotte hears footsteps. Light, careful, timid. She can make out red hair tied in a bun, followed by that pretty face, the one her mum would call striking. Then that little body emerges, hugging itself and holding a thin torch.

Charlotte swallows but Maggie doesn't look at her.

'Maggie, this little bitch has come here with a tall tale about someone taking her money. I'm sorry,' he growls, 'I mean *our* money.'

'I,' she hears Maggie start, her voice gentle, nervous. 'I think she might be telling the truth, Tommy.'

'Oh, Jesus Christ, girl, get your head out of the clouds.'

Charlotte starts to shake so violently that she can feel his hands rattling on her. He raises one hand and slaps her, hard. An outrageous pain spreads through her cheek and across the bridge of her nose. Her eyes water, she might be crying, she's too scared to really know. Maggie winces at the slap but keeps talking.

'I'm . . . I'm serious, Tommy. Someone took bank statements from her house while I was there and we thought it was you but—'

'We thought . . . we thought. You two are a real pair, aren't you?' he snaps, and Maggie shakes her head fast. She is cowering a little, her shoulders stooped. Charlotte stares at her but she is studiously avoiding Charlotte's eye. For a brief moment Charlotte imagines, hopes, that it's guilt.

'Maggie,' she says. 'Please help me. *Please.*'

'She heard you talking,' he says as Maggie takes the handbag Tommy is offering and looks inside with a torch. As she moves her hand, Charlotte notices a familiar-looking diamond ring. The one from the police photographs. 'And the deal's off,' Tommy adds. 'We're moving to plan B.'

Maggie's neck snaps up quickly. 'What's plan B, Tommy?'

she asks, her voice quivering and eyes finally darting briefly to Charlotte's face.

'She knows our names. You know very well what plan B is.'

Charlotte feels her bladder empty, her own body betraying her just like everyone else has.

Maggie

Now

She has never, not in ten years, ever contradicted him. Each step towards him is newborn wobbly, cuffs over hands, torch light bobbing. 'Isn't there something else we can do? Please, Tommy?'

'No, Maggie, no, there isn't,' he says, and it's that damn paternal voice again. 'She's exactly the kind of pathetic do-gooder to confess everything to the police. Especially now she knows my name—'

'I don't know your name,' Charlotte cries. 'I mean, I know it's Tommy but I don't even know if that's your real name or not.'

'You stink of piss and you're a liar,' he hisses and Charlotte shrinks, her arm still clasped in his strong hands.

Maggie stands dumb, trying to think of a new tactic in a game she's never played before. Charlotte is twisting from his grasp and he clamps tighter, making her cry out. Still she begs. 'If you let me go, I promise I won't tell anyone. Not anyone! I can't, you know too much about me. Please. *Please.*'

'She's right,' Maggie says, stepping forward to catch his eye. 'Tommy, she's right. Please, can't we just—'

'Don't be so fucking naive, girl,' he says, his jaw working angrily. 'She'll spill her guts the second we leave her, so we need to make sure she can't say another word.' He smirks, just slightly.

Last week, in the frantic moments immediately after, Tommy had insisted that what had happened to Anne had been quick and painless. 'Like putting an injured animal out of its misery,' he'd said. But there'd been that smirk then too. The same smirk he'd tried to hide at that bus stop ten years ago, where she'd ran to meet him after her mother's funeral.

Maggie had been in the bedroom when Anne had died, carefully picking up the framed photograph of Charlotte's dad. Afterwards, she'd realised she'd left the file in the office and had gone back to grab it while Tommy had stalked through the house. She hadn't wanted to look at Anne, but that had felt disrespectful somehow. How she wishes she hadn't seen her. The blood. The look etched onto her face. And then Maggie had fled. 'Without so much as a goodbye,' as he'd bitterly complained afterwards.

'I'm sorry, Charlotte,' Maggie whispers.

'I know you don't want this either, Maggie, I know deep down you feel something for me too!' Charlotte cries, her voice ragged and tearful. 'You're my friend, I know you are. And I forgive you! I forgive you, please just help me.'

'I'm sorry,' she says again, finally locking eyes with Charlotte in the moonlight. 'I'm sorry for all of it.' A look passes between them, a look that Maggie optimistically hopes is understanding. Maybe even forgiveness.

'Maggie wants what I want,' Tommy says, pulling Charlotte's chin so she faces him and breaks the connection. Maggie sags.

Tommy pulls Charlotte to standing and starts to tug her when she suddenly kicks her leg out and catches him in the knee. He yells and slackens his hold in surprise so Charlotte slips away and starts to run across the bridge. Maggie stares in horror as Tommy sprints up behind Charlotte, gaining on her easily, and tries to grab her again. He pins her to the steelwork of the bridge as she thrashes, grunting and crying as she struggles. Suddenly she slips sideways, out of his grasp, and manages to pull herself up onto the handrail.

'What the fuck are you doing?' he says, that laughter in his voice again. He's thriving on this, revelling in it. He stands back and stares at Charlotte as she inches towards the upright beam and grips hold of it.

'You'll have to come up and get me,' she says.

'God, could you be any more dramatic?' he says, looking at Maggie as if she'll find this funny too.

'Tommy, please,' she starts.

'Women,' he spits. 'Irrational, the lot of you.'

'I'll jump if you come near me,' Charlotte says and Maggie's stomach flips. She looks at Tommy and can almost see the calculations in his head.

'He wants you to jump!' The words are out before Maggie even realises she's speaking.

'Oh, Jesus Christ, what's got into you, Maggie?'

'I just don't want anyone to get hurt,' she says.

'Oh!' he cries. 'Oh, I see! Queen Maggie doesn't want anyone to get hurt!' He's almost *jolly* right now. Like a jester. But his eyes are blazing. 'You want the spoils though, don't you? You just don't want to see how the sausage gets made.'

Above them both, Charlotte is gripping the steel strut so hard her arms are trembling. Her hair hangs in damp ribbons. Maggie hadn't noticed the rain until now, but she feels it suddenly. Cold water drips down her neck.

'You don't know what I want,' she says quietly.

'I know you want some cottage in Cumbria where you can pretend to be a good person. I know you want me to do all your dirty work while you don't lift a finger.'

'My dirty work?' she says. 'None of this is my work, this is *you*. I've been doing what you tell me since I was fifteen years old.'

'You were sixteen and now's not the time for a fucking tantrum. We need to get this bitch down one way or another and end this before someone drives along and then we've got another body to deal with.'

'No,' she says, standing upright. 'No. I won't, Tommy. If I help you do this, it will stain everything. It'll ruin Cumbria. It'll ruin . . . me. Us. I can't do it to her, she was *nice* to me! She won't tell anyway. You won't tell, will you, Charlotte?'

'No,' pants Charlotte, her eyes wild with fear. The rain is coming down harder now and Maggie can't help but notice how Charlotte's boots slide around on the metal of the bridge.

'No! I promise, I won't. I won't. We can just go our separate ways. I'll never tell. *Please.*'

'You were happy enough for me to do this to your own mum, princess, so who's this bitch to you?'

'Happy? You think I was happy about what you did to my mum?'

'More than happy. You couldn't get enough of me once I told you I'd go along with your plan to get rid of your own mother. What kind of person does that anyway?' He's smiling, running his tongue over his teeth. This is sport to him. She's seen him like this with other people but not her. Never her.

'I wasn't happy, Tommy. And it wasn't my plan, it was yours.'

He sat there in that Harvester, her teenage hand in his, and told her she deserved more. That he would get her mum off her back, that he would talk to the woman, explain they were in love. That was the plan she bought into. And she'd melted at the romance of it all. A knight in shining armour, jousting for his princess.

And then afterwards, he said it had gone wrong. Her mother, a woman scared of her own shadow, had turned on him. The dragon attacked the knight. It was lucky, he said back then as he held Meredith's body – not yet Maggie – juddering with sobs and still dressed in her Tennessee Williams costume. Lucky that he was able to think straight at all while he was being attacked. While he was defending himself, protecting their future.

He had the forethought, he explained, wiping her tears so tenderly she could hardly breathe, to take some jewellery and make it look like a robbery gone wrong. Just like he later did at Anne's house. And Tommy did all that for her, he said. And no one had ever loved her like that.

But this isn't love. What's happening right now in front of her, this is the opposite of love.

'Please, Tommy, please let her go.'

'Grow up, Maggie,' he sneers. 'And keep your fucking voice down.'

Rain runs into her eyes and she wipes it away. 'Grow up? Grow up?! God, I'm still that fifteen year old in the window to you, aren't I, Tommy? So fucking sad and so desperate for love and just ripe for someone like you. And I think that's all I'll ever be to you, isn't it?'

'I rescued you, you ungrateful little—'

'You took away any chance of me rescuing myself!'

Oh my god, she thinks. *We were never going to go to Cumbria.*

She thinks back to that first night on the bridge. How Charlotte had climbed up to join her, to talk her down. How she risked everything for a stranger. Maggie grabs the handrail and starts to climb.

Charlotte
Now

She has never been so cold, or so frightened. Though neither of those words cover this; she's used them too many times in her life.

Her teeth rattle and her neck and spine ache. Her scalp is screaming in pain from where his hand pulled her hair. The rain is coming down hard now and she can feel herself sliding underfoot. *If he pushes me, I'm fucked. But if he pulls me back down, I'm just as fucked.*

But then Maggie starts to clamber up. She is clearly a deft

climber, used to this bridge, of course. And if she managed it in a dress, jeans and trainers must be a doddle.

'I'm coming up with you,' she whispers to Charlotte, smiling with reassurance. 'I won't let him—'

But as she nearly makes it up to the handrail, Tommy suddenly yanks her back down.

Maggie hits the floor hard and cries out but Tommy is already climbing up in her place.

'Fuck this,' he says, as he moves from a crouch to a stand. 'I'm getting too wet for this shit.'

Charlotte shakes her head and clings on tighter. 'No, please, *please*,' but Tommy is reaching for her. He stands one side of the beam, she stands the other, but she can see what he's going to do. She can picture it so clearly, it might as well have happened already. With one hand still holding on to the beam, one foot still firmly in place, he lets go with the other half of his body and swings around so he's right next to her, sharing the same space on the handrail, his breath mingling with hers.

He tastes stale.

He's going to push me in. Everyone will think it was suicide and he'll get away with it.

She feels the pressure release as he pulls back to gain momentum, but, as he's about to strike, she sees Maggie scrambling to her feet, trying to stop him. Maggie manages to connect with his chest, but it's too late, he's already grabbed Charlotte. For a moment nothing happens, even the rain seems to hold its breath. But then they're falling.

They plummet together, Tommy and Charlotte. Tangled, arms flapping, wordless. She just has time to hear Maggie scream. Then they hit the surface with a huge, excruciating slap.

For a moment, Charlotte thinks she's dead. Everything is still and black, there's no sound. She opens her eyes and the river water stings them. She gasps for air but sucks in the freezing water and coughs and sucks in more water. She thrashes in the dark, unsure which way is up, kicking for all she's worth.

But then she sees a glimpse of light, just a tiny shard and she follows it, kicking her aching legs towards it. The torch, it must be Maggie's torch. She almost reaches it, when she feels a hand on her ankle and a sudden tug back down.

Maggie

Now

She thinks about diving in after them but that would be madness. Instead, she grabs the torch from the floor and runs back down the bridge and half falls, half runs down the river bank.

'Tommy!' she shouts. 'Charlotte!'

She can hear nothing over the roar of the water.

She shines the light over the surface but they're not there and the river is flowing fast and deadly. She runs under the bridge, still shining the light on the water in the hope she'll see an arm waving, a head bobbing. She thinks she sees something break the surface but then it's gone.

After what feels like hours, she sees Tommy. His head pops up above the water and then down under again, as he's thrown around the river like a marionette, someone invisible yanking his strings.

'Maggie!' he shouts, his voice gurgling as he goes back under, dashed away, out of the torchlight. He's much further away than the last time, and the river is faster, angrier.

'Swim to me!' she calls out. But he can't swim and she knows he can't. The torchlight picks him out once more, just briefly, his head bobbing along in the current for just a few seconds. But then he slips, silently, beneath the surface.

She waves the torch all around but there is still no sign of Charlotte. The water has swallowed them both up and now their names are leaking out of her, *Tommy, Tommy, Tommy, Charlotte, Charlotte, Charlotte*, over and over.

It's like she's watching herself in a play, somewhere up in the nosebleeds, but these are not lines she's ever rehearsed and this is not a scene for which she's ever prepared. Ad libs were always her strength but not now. All she can say is his name. Tommy. The director of her show for ten years now, the star around which she's orbited since she was still a child. And hers. Charlotte. The woman who changed everything.

Charlotte's handbag is still lying on the bridge, propped against the handrail where she left it. Maggie picks it up and hugs it to her. Then she holds it reverently in front of her like a wedding bouquet.

They're gone. She is on her own. Completely on her own.

She tries to think. What is the right thing to do here? What *can* she do?

She opens the handbag carefully and sees Charlotte's phone is inside. She could call for help. She could call for help and say she's just a bystander and saw some people fall in but . . . all those questions. Her name. Her real name. And to what end? It's too late. It's all too late.

She can't unlock Charlotte's phone when she tries, it needs a code or a thumbprint. And all those questions it might raise if it's examined . . . Perhaps it's better if . . . yes. She puts it on the ground carefully and then, with one firm stamp, smashes it. She crosses to the other side of the bridge and throws it as far as she can into the river, catching into the current so it's whisked away.

She dips back into the bag, pulling out Charlotte's keys. She can see the thick brass key for the front door to Fox Cottage, and a Renault fob dangling from the same keyring. She heard Charlotte say something about selling her car, and the thought makes her even sadder. She swallows, stepping further and further from the bridge. Stepping further and further from Charlotte and Tommy. And her mother. And the bride. And everything that has happened.

As she walks, wiping her wet hair out of her eyes and ears, she presses the key fob, listening hard. Nothing. She checks behind her, suddenly spooked, but she's not been followed. The only other people out here are gone for good.

She walks on, stops and presses the fob again. In the distance, she hears the clunk of locks releasing. She follows the sound, pressing and pressing until finally she sees the lights of a car flashing on and off down a nearby lane, and finds a little Clio in a gateway.

She climbs inside and straps the handbag with its envelope of cash and handful of jewellery into the passenger seat. It sits patiently, waiting for her to decide what to do.

She thinks of Tommy's mouth sucking in water and sludge as he sinks, his strong heart lying dormant like useless meat. It barely seems possible that he's dead. But death is always possible, she should know that by now.

There is a pair of ruby earrings in here and she imagines Charlotte appraising them, turning them over carefully in her hands. She slips one, then the other, into her ears and squeezes her eyes closed for a moment.

It's years since Tommy last took her for a lesson in an old car park, and when she first turns the ignition and pulls away, she stalls so badly she worries she's broken the engine. It takes another three goes to even get into second gear and find the headlights.

She still hasn't cried. And she worries for a moment that she might not have even blinked, so she shuts her eyes just briefly and then edges out onto the A road away from Usk. There is no satnav in here, but she knows that Cumbria is north and Devon is south and those two poles – future and past – are the only guiding stars she can summon. She needs to lie low while she decides what she wants from life now she is alone.

From her pocket she pulls her lucky coin, the one she took from Charlotte's car, and tosses it. Heads for north, tails for south. It lands on her knee, and she slaps one hand over it, the other still holding the wheel. Then she lifts it carefully and follows the road.

Pamela

Six Months Ago

It's the black hour. Even though the road is strung with lights and the plane bellies blink as they pass over, it's still the black hour.

We sit in silence. Spent. Nothing left to say, nowhere left to turn. The myths made in our marriage have thinned like wet paper now the spotlight is on them. The vows are long broken, as if they were never said at all. And there's no hope for improvement, no matter how many wishbones I snap.

I have been with this man for nearly forty years. I have given him the best years of my body and he has used his body to batter my brain. And I'm sure as hell not going to be dropped now, to waste away.

'I was thinking,' he says, in a faux casual way that hasn't duped me in decades.

'Yes, Charles?' I say.

'Maybe . . .'

'Spit it out.'

'Maybe it's time for me to retire.'

We sit in silence a little more. He blinks and rubs his face. He's not been sleeping, I know, because neither have I. And now a 3 a.m. start to catch a plane is catching up with him fast.

'You want to retire?'

This is not what I was expecting from this last hurrah holiday for which I have packed and planned so carefully. I have thought of nothing else for the last two months. How to ensure that Charles cannot pull the rug from under me, under our daughter. Sliding all his poker chips over to Anne and playing out the final years of the game having his tummy tickled by his lap dog. I have collated evidence across decades, a whole archive of letters she sent him from America, in case

291

he tries to cite irreconcilable differences, and stiff me from what I'm owed. This is adultery, pure and simple, and this girl has really played the long con. I'm almost impressed.

'I've got the ideal person to take over. I mean, it's practically keeping it in the family.' He pauses and smiles, a fake, gormless smile I can't believe he thinks I'll fall for. 'Charlotte'll be happy, she must've worried I'd expect her to take over.'

I stare at him. 'If that's really want you think,' I say, 'you really don't know your daughter at all. She's always been desperate to work there.'

He sighs and I straighten my jacket on my lap. 'Well, I don't think she's right for it anyway. She's too . . . head in the clouds, doesn't understand what it takes to make difficult decisions.'

'So who,' I affect ignorance, 'do you see taking over the business?'

'Do you remember Anne Wilkins?' he says.

'Vaguely.' Unlike Charles, I am very good at faux casual.

'Charlotte's friend.'

'Mmm. What of her?'

'She's back in town and I've had her doing some consultancy work for me.' He can't help but smile, just a fraction. 'She's a real little firecracker,' he says. 'In business, I mean.'

'And have you told Anne your plans?'

He pauses then shakes his head, which is a lie. 'I wanted to talk it over with you first.'

'How kind of you. And what will you spend your time doing, while this little firecracker is running the show?'

He looks across at me, just briefly, just enough. 'I'd like to spend a lot more time fishing,' he says. It takes a second, less than. A splinter of a moment to touch the wheel. The car, doing ninety, one hundred, some middle of the night motorway speed, is up on one side now. My husband, that big, brash, bold, liar to whom I've pointlessly dedicated my life, flails his arms. I sit still. Ground to the chair in pure defiance.

I think of that box sitting under the bed. Of Charlotte finding it. Realising, finally, who her father is. And in doing so, I hope upon hope, realising that she backed the wrong parental horse. And I hope, more than anything, that she never sets aside her own ambitions for a man. Especially one like this. It's too late for me, but she has her whole life in front of her.

Charles is above me now, the car diagonal, wrong, tilted and spinning. His eyes wide, apologetic even. I look away. As we finally flip, the car he bought to impress his protégé proving as vulnerable as any other when flung onto its roof, I let out a lifelong sigh. And everything goes black.

I guess I've won, in the end.

Rob

Two Months Later

It's his night to have Ruby and he's made fajitas, her favourite. They're a little burned in places, the chicken slightly browner than anticipated, but she doesn't say anything. He's still learning to use the Aga, still adjusting to life in a cottage, all these idiosyncrasies.

They eat in silence, the sky outside far quieter than it was in his old place. He wouldn't have been there for much longer anyway. Would have had to rent somewhere even smaller, try to make the money go further. That's if he hadn't ended up in prison. Fuck, he can't believe he nearly went along with his cousin Cole's dumbass plan. Rob's clients trust him, they let him into their homes, they bring him out cups of tea while he works. Recommend him to their friends and neighbours. He remembers Cole scoffing and rolling his eyes. 'You're just the hired help, man. And anyway, they've all got

293

insurance.' And he nearly did it. Rob really nearly agreed to tell Cole about the places without security cameras, the days and nights when he knew people were away. For a cut. For rent. For Ruby.

He'd hoped for a while that Charlotte would ask him to move in. But when he'd broached the subject, she'd seemed taken aback. So it was even more of a shock when the solicitor told him the cottage was his, that although he'd lost the person he'd hoped was part of his future, she'd helped him secure the rest of it. He won't have to worry about rent ever again. There was a note too, written by hand and sealed in an envelope. Handed over by the solicitor as Rob sat in stunned silence.

Be the dad she deserves, no matter what.

When Cole offered his sympathies after the funeral, Rob told him to fuck right off.

At first, Rob couldn't understand what Charlotte was doing out there in Wales. When the police rang, he drove out immediately. He would always come whenever Charlotte clicked her fingers, no matter what. In life and in death. He wasn't ashamed of that, it was a choice. If you care for someone, if you can do what they ask of you, you should. It drove his ex-wife to distraction; Deb thought he did things for the wrong people. But she was wrong. Except about Cole, anyway.

'What's this?' Ruby asks, picking up the local newspaper that Rob had meant to hide. The headline declaring: **DEAD BURGLAR LINKED TO MURDER**

'Not for little eyes, is what it is,' Rob says and slides it back under the pile.

'Actually,' he says, 'I'm going to take it upstairs. Back in a sec.'

Charlotte's room is now Ruby's for when she stays and the spare room has become a holding pen for Rob's stuff that doesn't yet have a home and things that used to be in the master bedroom.

The boxes from under Pamela and Charles's bed have been neatly stacked in here, on top of the wardrobe. He slides down the box that he wants and teases the lid off. He only found this the other day and hasn't told anyone, although none of it was much of a surprise. From the paper, he rips out the article about Thomas 'Tommy' Addison, the violent burglar blamed – posthumously – for what happened to both Anne and Charlotte.

Rob folds the newspaper carefully, and lifts the top layer of baby photos, handmade cards and letters to Father Christmas. Below this, the newspaper article joins the other artefacts that make Rob's stomach turn.

Photographs of Anne as a seventeen or eighteen year old, taken on a Polaroid camera – unfit to be developed in a chemist. Letters sent from America, Anne's careful handwriting on the envelope, addressed to Charles at Wilderwood Antiques. This box of secrets he had collated and hidden, presumably right under his wife's nose. In the last letter, she defiantly declared she was moving on and getting married. Well, he knew how that worked out.

Rob shouldn't have read them, but both parties are dead now and who was going to complain? And besides, Anne had told him most of it, when they'd first got friendly again after she'd moved back. Despite her big talk about moving on, she and Charles had been emailing the whole time she was in the states too, unable to leave it alone. After her divorce, she'd moved back at Charles's request.

'He's going to let me run the business and he's put me up in Bath,' she'd said, smirking over drinks when she'd first come back. 'He's just got a big cash injection from some investors and he wants to put it towards our future.' Rob had tried not to grimace at how tawdry it was, how utterly beneath her. 'He bought me the Mercedes, do you like it? And he's going to take Pamela away soon and break it to her gently and then when he gets back, we'll finally make a proper go of it. He even wants to put the business in my name.' She'd gone on about something to do with paperwork and moving money around and he'd tuned out entirely. The whole thing had revolted him, though he hadn't felt particularly sorry for Pamela.

When Charles died before any of this could happen, Anne had refused to talk about it with Rob, except to make him promise never to tell Charlotte. 'What good would it do now?'

He'd agreed.

Rob's glad Charlotte didn't leave him the business as well. It really was a complete mess, Charlotte wasn't exaggerating. Dorian inherited it and immediately sold it on to a relative, some guy called Harry Sedgemoor. Apparently she'd introduced him to Charles a few years before he died and he was the investor Anne had mentioned. It all came full circle and Rob was glad to stay out of it. One struggling business is enough.

He hears tyres pull up outside and puts the lid back on quickly, slides the box back into place and jogs downstairs.

'Daddy!' he hears Ruby call. 'There's a lady here!'

Rob stops for a moment and takes a few breaths. He thought everyone knew by now. The hardest phone calls done, the news delivered, Charlotte's funeral suffered through. The inquest was worst of all. Hearing about her final moments. Charlotte must have worked out who hurt Anne, somehow, and tracked Tommy Addison down. If only Charlotte had told him, Rob could have urged her to go to the police instead, or at least gone with her. One of Anne's neighbours had finally come forward to say someone matching Addison's description had been hanging around that day; they'd dithered over reporting him. But by then it was too late.

At the inquest, it was called 'death by misadventure'. Most likely Charlotte argued with this Tommy and it ended in a struggle. An attack. But they'll never know for sure as there were no witnesses.

He swallows and starts down the stairs. Perhaps it's one of Charlotte's friends who was travelling, there were one or two ex-colleagues from the museum he didn't reach and he was so exhausted from it, so sick with grief, that he drew a line under them and stopped trying. Instead, he put a memorial notice in the local news, the *Evening Standard* and online. Covering all bases. Hopefully anyone who was looking for news of her would find out eventually.

In the hall, Ruby is standing by the open door even though he's told her repeatedly never to unlock it by herself, that you never know who you could be letting in. In the hallway stands a beautiful, tiny woman with long red hair, sparkling red earrings and the saddest face he's ever seen. She's wearing a ripped dress, the skin revealed is slashed and bleeding. She's nervously twisting a sparkling ring.

'I'm so sorry to trouble you,' she says. 'I had to get away from, from . . .' she collapses in sobs and he catches her, bewildered, as she stumbles.

'It's OK,' he says, patting her shoulder. 'It's OK, don't worry, you're safe. You're safe here. What happened?'

'You won't throw me out, will you?'

'No, of course not,' he says. Ruby watches, eyes widening.

'You're so very kind,' says Maggie, gazing around the hallway as she drops the needle at the start of a new story.

Acknowledgements

Firstly, I have to thank the brilliant team at Orion, in particular Sam Eades and Zoe Yang, whose energy, drive and insight elevated *The Woman on the Bridge* to become, I hope, my best book yet.

The gratitude, affection and respect I have for my agent Sophie Lambert grows with every book. Having Sophie in my corner has been genuinely life-changing.

I have to thank my ever-patient, rallying (and handsome) husband. We are each other's champions, a team of two, and that's the foundation on which everything is built. I am beyond lucky to have created a family with him. And, of course, I have to thank my children. Trying to make them proud, proving to them that it's always worth following your dreams, is what pushes me every day.

This is my fifth book, a sentence I feel very privileged to say. And the more books I write, the more I realise that almost all of them are about friendship. From the unique friendship between Amy and Alex in *Try Not to Breathe* to Robin and Callum in *Don't Close Your Eyes* and Kate and Paul in *Love Will Tear Us Apart*.

The Hit List was not, I admit, about friendship, but it was through my friendship with Gillian McAllister that the story developed. She had my back the whole time I was writing it. Even when I wanted to quit. Especially when I wanted to quit. Friendship is in the spine of that book as much as any other.

The Woman on the Bridge is undeniably about friendship. Fast and dangerous friendship that is every bit as intoxicating as love at first sight, but friendship nonetheless.

It seems only right that it should be dedicated to Carole, my oldest friend. Next to whom I was told to sit on my first day of secondary school. A thirty-year friendship that blossomed from the seed of our surnames being next to each other on the register.

Ours was not a dangerous friendship – although we have led each other astray quite a few times – but it was immediate and unbreakable. Living in different countries, we can go months without speaking, then talk over each other for four hours straight as if we only saw each other the day before.

So this book is dedicated to Carole, but really it's for all my friends. I'm so incredibly lucky to have them.

About the Author

Holly Seddon is the international bestselling author of four novels. Alongside fellow author Gillian McAllister, Holly co-hosts the popular *Honest Authors* podcast. After growing up in the English countryside obsessed with music and books, Holly worked in London as a journalist and editor. She now lives in Amsterdam with her family and writes full time.

You can find Holly on:

@hollyseddon

@hollyseddonauthor

@hollyseddonauthor

Credits

Orion Fiction would like to thank everyone at Orion who worked on the publication of *The Woman on the Bridge*.

Agent
Sophie Lambert

Editors
Sam Eades
Zoe Yang

Copy-editor
Laura Gerrard

Proofreader
Donna Hillyer

Editorial Management
Rosie Pearce
Charlie Panayiotou
Jane Hughes
Claire Boyle

Audio
Paul Stark

Contracts
Anne Goddard
Jake Alderson

Design
Joanna Ridley
Nick May
Clare Sivell
Helen Ewing

Finance
Jasdip Nandra
Rabale Mustafa
Elizabeth Beaumont
Sue Baker
Tom Costello

Marketing
Brittany Sankey

Production
Claire Keep
Fiona McIntosh

Sales
Jennifer Wilson
Victoria Laws
Esther Waters
Frances Doyle
Ben Goddard

Georgina Cutler
Jack Hallam
Ellie Kyrke-Smith
Inês Figuiera
Barbara Ronan
Andrew Hally
Dominic Smith
Deborah Deyong
Lauren Buck
Maggy Park
Linda McGregor
Sinead White
Jemimah James
Rachel Jones
Jack Dennison
Nigel Andrews
Ian Williamson

Julia Benson
Declan Kyle
Robert Mackenzie
Imogen Clarke
Megan Smith
Charlotte Clay
Rebecca Cobbold

Operations
Jo Jacobs
Sharon Willis

Rights
Susan Howe
Krystyna Kujawinska
Jessica Purdue
Louise Henderson

Help us make the next generation of readers

We – both author and publisher – hope you enjoyed this book. We believe that you can become a reader at any time in your life, but we'd love your help to give the next generation a head start.

Did you know that 9 per cent of children don't have a book of their own in their home, rising to 13 per cent in disadvantaged families*? We'd like to try to change that by asking you to consider the role you could play in helping to build readers of the future.

We'd love you to think of sharing, borrowing, reading, buying or talking about a book with a child in your life and spreading the love of reading. We want to make sure the next generation continue to have access to books, wherever they come from.

And if you would like to consider donating to charities that help fund literacy projects, find out more at **www.literacytrust.org.uk** and **www.booktrust.org.uk**.

THANK YOU

*As reported by the National Literacy Trust